THE LONG GAME

Inspired by True Events
by Ben Rose

Published By
Breaking Rules Publishing

Soft Cover – 0791
Published by Breaking Rules Publishing
St Petersburg, Florida
www.breakingrulespublishing.com

Authors Note:

This story is inspired by true events. In my travels I met a few young men who fit the profile and activities of the main character. I have, likewise, met others upon whom I based the secondary characters. In every case I was granted permission to turn the stories into a novel, with the proviso that I never disclose the identities of the people. The names have been changed. Any similarities in name to persons living or dead is coincidental.

Ben Rose

"Give 'em the old razzle-dazzle"
Billy Flynn

Dedication

For Bonnie and Clyde, my Missouri pals

Chapter One

Harvest Junction, a hamlet of provincial rusticity, is a speck in northern New England. If a cat were to attempt location on a map, he would meet with failure. I called the place home for three years of my adolescent angst. The western side isn't *Better Homes and Gardens*, but it has its charms. The east side of the tracks runs south of the slots.

On the west side, one finds the soothing sounds of loving voices drifting out upon the crisp night air, a family together, and the warm glow of a fireplace casting light in the window. I dug the ambiance. Redolent of gemütlichkeit, the highlight of the year is the annual family reunions. Relatives arrive from everywhere and spend the weekend reminiscing, hugging, feasting, catching up on the gossip, getting acquainted with new babies that have been born, or an in-law that has been added since kinfolk were last together. There are tears for those loved and lost, and one of the cats might go heavy on the corn juice. Endgame, everybody ventures home happy, proud, and enriched for the time well spent.

There's a chicken in every pot, and three pies cooling on every window sill. One pie is for the family, one is for a neighbor, and the third is for a passing stranger. Always has been. Always will be.

Those residing east-side are hard-scrabble and less tolerant of strangers. The roads are dirt and gravel, lots filled with ramshackle trailers, and rows of domiciles that have seen better days clutter the landscape. Both sides share a school district, but even in school the division in social status is clear. The entire area is defined by the endless horizons that stretch beyond it into infinity.

Each season in Harvest Junction has a kind of Rockwellian specialness to it. Springtime is full of promise and the excitement of brand-new beginnings. Summers are long and hot. Everyone is moist, if not dripping wet. The young go shoeless, at a minimum, and run through the freshly mown grass. Summer is the time almost no one wants to see end. I was partial to autumn. Autumn in New England is melancholy, a smoky time of turning leaves and chilly nights. The atmosphere is soulful with a bluesy vibe. Folks go to bed early as the younger cats and kitties think toward Halloween, and the elder set prepare for Thanksgiving and Christmas. Winter in Harvest Junction is the most magical time of all. There's a radiance to everything, and a warm glow surrounds everyone. Perhaps it's a glimmer of the same light that issued forth for eight days from the miraculous menorah, or the luminescence that guided the magi to the manger in Bethlehem. Words barely suffice. It's the last gasping of the authentic American Dream.

***

Life had been blowing a discordant riff for several years, but my tensions eased with every breath of rustic air. My parents had both gone through a long bout of bleakness, but moving north had a miraculous transformation on their mental circuitry. My two older sisters dug the ambiance as well.

Within days of our arrival, my father and I went shopping for a mahogany swing which we set up on the front porch. We prepared a garden in our back yard, re-painted our back porch and did other minor repairs. My mother and sisters baked, decorated the inside of the house, and entertained neighbors; family life at its finest.

Neighbors appeared with covered dishes, breads, pies, and assorted jars of homemade preserves. They would sit and visit, or tell us about places to see and events in the town. For being a rustic town, the neighbors were multi-cultural. There was a fair blend of Latino, Asian, and Caucasian; a veritable melting pot.

Every Saturday my father would play a jazz CD, bake brioche, and cook enormous brunches. The rest of the week found him ensconced in his office from early bright until dusk. Three months in, my oldest sister Gina left for college. My mother took on the role of traditional house-wife, leaving my other sister Tori and I to fend for our-selves.

This sounds gravy and groovy, no? The life that everyone should aspire to in these hectic days of political malfeasance and chicanery? Well, let me clue you to a universal truth. Even in the prettiest garden one can find a hornet's nest.

The day I first fell in love was the middle of that summer. The yards were full of young boys tossing their balls, rolling around with each other, and playing tag. Young girls played with their boxes, pretending to be in a house or castle, had tea parties, and swung on tire swings. Older boys stood around flexing their muscles, and ogling the older girls. Older girls gossiped, and pretended not to notice the boys. On the porches, under the watchful eye of parents, the babies sat in playpens playing with each other and themselves.

I was sitting on the porch, reading the last chapter of *The Prince* by Machiavelli, and drinking lemonade when I first saw Stephanie Ann Baker. She was twelve, with one of those faces that remain forever youthful. The cut of her jib had my guts doing the flips. She was doe eyed, with a small dainty nose, full pouty lips, and a dark red mullet. She had pale, freckled skin that revved my motor. I took one look at her chassis and reacted priapically. She was a solid sender from go to stop.

When I first cast my eyes on her she was in her

front yard raking up grass cuttings. I waved, and she waved back. I walked toward her house, fixing my grey porkpie hat, straightening my stone washed jeans, and tucking in my designer shirt. I shined my loafers on the backs of my pants legs, and was about to introduce myself, when a guy stepped onto their porch. He was muscular, with sunburned, freckled skin, a red brush-cut, and rabid eyes. The Clyde was dressed in scuffed work boots, cheap jeans, and a stained, white undershirt. He saw me approaching, gripped his daughter by the shoulder, shoved her toward the house, grabbed the rake, and went inside. I stopped in my tracks, unsure about ringing the doorbell.

The next day I was performing kata in the back yard, watching until brush-cut climbed into a truck and drove away. I meandered inside, showered, changed into chinos and a polo shirt, exchanged my sneakers for loafers, dabbed on some Aramis, grabbed my porkpie, approached the chick's house, and knocked. The lady who answered was dressed in blue gingham, and was younger than my mother by several years. She had the same looks as Steph, but with a smaller mouth and a much fuller bust.

"May I help you?"

"How do, ma'am? Name's Vinnie Il-Cazzo. We moved in down the block a couple weeks back. Saw your daughter in the yard yesterday, and thought I might introduce myself." I gave the lady my best smile.

"Which daughter? Stephanie Ann is your age, and Caroline June is a couple years younger. My name is Heather Baker, by the way." She spoke with a Midwestern drawl, seemed anxious, and kept scanning the street behind me.

"Pleased to meet you, Mrs. Baker." I shook her hand. "I'm thinking it has to be Stephanie Ann. She has long, red hair and is a bit shorter than me."

"That would be Stephanie Ann, alright." Heather

looked me over. "Well, I suppose you could introduce yourself. We don't socialize with our neighbors much, though. Myron prefers that we tend to our own. He's my husband."

"I might have seen him. He pulled Stephanie Ann inside before I could come over."

Two chicks came to the door. "Hi. I'm Steph. This is my sister Caroline." Steph looked at me with a slight blush. "Sorry about yesterday. I saw you coming over but…"

"It was time to eat. Myron likes us all at the table." Heather interrupted. Her voice was strained.

Caroline nodded, twisting the toes of her kicks into the floor. She walked back into the house. Heather follow-ed her. Steph stepped out onto the porch dressed in tight Levi shorts, a pink t-shirt, and red Converse sneakers with no socks.

"How do?" I tipped my hat. "Vincenzo Cassiel Michelangelo Il-Cazzo is what they tagged me with, but cats call me Vinnie. Some call me Il-Cazzo," I winked. I had never, to that date, had the urge to swap chews with a chick, or to cop a feel, but the urge was powerful.

"Hi. Nice to meet you, Vinnie. I'm sorry about yesterday but – yeah -- we were having lunch. Ummm, meatloaf and potatoes." The last words were forced.

"Savvy. I wanted to introduce myself. You're definitely all that, and I was hoping we could get acquaint-ed." I blushed and had a case of the nerves.

"Thank you. Most boys don't notice me. I'm not that popular." Steph blushed harder. "I'd like to be friends, but Caroline and I don't get to play much. When I'm doing yard chores Pa expects me to focus on them. By the way, I better get back to the breakfast dishes."

When Steph turned to go back inside, I noticed a grayish-green bruise on her right thigh below her shorts. I returned home, poured myself another lemonade, and sat on the porch swing. I had finished *The Prince*, and next on my hit parade was *Son of a Grifter,* by Kent Walker.

For several weeks following my initial foray, Steph came outside to do yard work while I read. I never approached her, although she filled my thoughts. Myron would come home each afternoon around five looking angry, and often staggering a bit as he climbed out of his truck. I had to make my move. I couldn't stop obsessing about this total knockout.

I was sitting on the porch swing late one morning, reading *Ponzi's Scheme* by Mitchell Zuckhoff, when I decided that I needed expert advice. My father was in the yard next door discussing business with our neighbor, Chuck Bianchi. My mother was inside with Tori making lunch. I saw my father returning, so I closed my book.

"Papa? I need to bend your ear. I've got a problem." I moved to one side on the porch swing, and he sat beside me.

"Sure, son. What's the pitch? Hey, great book by the way. That man was a legend." My father looked at me, waiting.

"There's this hot dish a few doors down." I looked away, blushing. "I noticed her a few weeks ago – and, I got...I mean...I..."

My father chuckled. "I'm with you, Vinnie. It's normal to react that way."

"So, I went to her place to ask her over for a soda pop or something. She's a real doll, but it seems hopeless trying to make a move. I'm not totally shut out here. I mean she seems interested, but aloof. I don't mean she's unfriendly, but she's got the nerves. Her papa doesn't want people coming around. He makes that clear with his glare. This chick and her mama confirmed the fact. Thing of it is, I can't get her off my brain. Her name's Steph Baker. Isn't that name the most?"

"To say the least. Trust me, I dig the riff. First love can be quixotic and awkward, more so when you've got a rocket in your pocket. As to your assessment of the Baker family; I've been making the rounds in the community, staking out places to turn a buck or get food, clothes, and supplies. Not much in this town, but there's a small metropolis about fifteen miles southwest ripe for plundering. I was talking to Carlos Sanchez from down the block. He says that Myron Baker is a tough one. It was unspoken, but the vibe I got was that he leads his family with an iron first. I'm given to understand that the Baker's don't even attend the holiday block parties, or let their children play with the neighbors. No one around this area meddles with the lives of others unless asked. That's a major draw for me and your mother, but it has setbacks in playing this hand you've been dealt. You might be out of luck." My father ruffled my hair.

I looked toward the street and shrugged. "I guess. Thanks for letting me pick your brains. It's cool." My chest tightened as if I might cry, but I wasn't sure the reason.

My father reached over and side-hugged me. "There are a few ideas that occur to me, however. First of all, in Sweetbriar, which is the city I mentioned, there are some major steak chains. We can make some calls and try to hit up some of them. We might already have some gift cards for one of them. If we have enough credit, we might could invite the Baker's to join us." He rubbed his chin. "The next thing is that Myron works at a scrapyard compacting metal. Those places hire on the regular. You might ask him if there's any weekend work for you around there. I know you're twelve, but, if necessary, we can adjust that figure to match your intelligence. It's an opening sally anyway." He paused for air. "The final idea is that I'm told that the Baker's are church-goers. That's not my bag, but perhaps you might have a shot that way." I smiled, and he grinned at me.

"Thank you, Papa. I knew you'd have some ideas." I hugged him.

He stood, dusted off his designer slacks, and fixed the collar on his blue silk shirt. "Vinnie, being a pirate isn't solely about plundering stuff. It's about understanding people and knowing how they think, knowing their needs and wants, using that knowledge to get what you want in return.

That advice summed up the essence of the relationship I had with my parents.

Chapter Two

It occurs to me that some of this might be confusing. I can already hear the questions from the peanut gallery: *"Piracy? Like Hook, Frederic, and Ed Teach?" "Plundering?" "Hitting up steakhouses?"* Allow me to move the needle back a few grooves, it won't take long.

My introduction into the world of urban piracy came at a tender age. It was a spring day in the year two thousand. I was four years old. My father, Francesco "Frank" Il-Cazzo, took me for a ride in his shiny, black Town Car. He purchased the car from a colleague named Giuseppe Ladro. I knew him as Uncle Joe or Joey Wheels.

At the time I knew nothing about the purchase, but later research indicated that a car lot several states to the south had been robbed of thirty vehicles. The manager of the lot had closed the business for ten days in order to have some maintenance and extermination done on the main building. Upon returning he noticed the missing cars. After filling out the proper police reports and paperwork, the owner was compensated by his insurance company. The manager received forty percent from the resale of each car by the "thieves." The cars were retagged and one of them was purchased by my father for a low price. The insurance companies, run by the wealthy at the expense of the poor, took a small beating. The rich car manufacturing companyies took a hit by not getting a cut on thirty cars and trucks. Everyone else either got paid or saved a fortune on purchasing prices. Such were the efforts of urban pirates.

That sunny spring day my father and I drove to a warehouse a few miles outside of the city. As we neared the noisy and dark building, my father looked over. "I'm going to introduce you to a cat with whom I conduct certain affairs. Call him Uncle Sal. He's not a blood relative, more like a colleague." I was absorbed in watching the big trucks. I didn't pay much attention when my father introduced me to Salvatore Testa.

"How you doing, Vinnie?" Sal asked as he bent down to shake my hand. He had black, slicked-back hair, a face that was all points and angles, a toothpick in his mouth, and was dressed in a blue one-piece uniform with his name embroidered on the left breast. A working stiff's working stiff. Sal and my father stepped back into the cargo area to discuss business. I couldn't hear a word they said over the roar of the engines. I explored the dusty cargo area, saw some open wooden boxes with silk dress shirts in them wrapped in plastic, crates full of laptops, and one crate full of New Balance sneakers. Sal was talking in earnest, waving his arms around. My father was shaking his head, pointing at the boxes. After a few minutes they shook hands.

My father and I were leaving when Sal stopped us. He reached into the crate of shoes and pulled out a pair. "Try these kicks, Vinnie. A gift from your Uncle Sal." They fit perfectly. I was thrilled.

It wasn't long until I saw Uncle Sal again. The following Saturday, in the early bright, he pulled up in an SUV filled with crates of fresh fruit. There was regular fruit like bananas, apples and oranges, but also exotic fruits as well, like kiwis, star fruit, guava and pineapples. My sisters and I stood and watched as Sal unloaded the crates and brought them into the house.

My mother, Antoinette, shook her head as she sorted through the crates, "Have mercy, there must be enough citrus here to cure the Navy of scurvy!" She looked bemused.

"Just a little gift from my family to yours," Sal murmured. The following Sunday he showed up with cases of expensive red wine and boxes of imported chocolates. My father gave me a sip of wine one night. It was dry, and quite strong to my taste. I pulled a face and asked for another sip.

The next weekend Sal brought a box full of motorcycle jackets in various sizes. Trailing behind him I asked where he got all this cool stuff. "It's F-O-T, Vinnie." I looked confused. "You know, it fell off a truck." Sal chuckled.

I was shocked. How could a driver be so careless? This was a lot of stuff. It was worth major bread. After a few more weeks of receiving "gifts" I began to wonder why the drivers didn't pick the stuff up and put it back inside the truck.

There were enough leather jackets that my father was able to outfit six neighboring families. We had a giant block party one weekend, and my father handed out the jackets as well as hiking boots, designer jeans, and mirrored sunglasses. Neighbors brought pot luck for the party. Scotty McGregor, who lived three houses down, brought thirty pounds of boneless ribeye steaks. Other neighbors provided salads, hors d'oeuvres and desserts. My family sent large quantities of leftovers home with neighbors after the party. That was par for the course.

That night, as my father tucked me in, I asked, "Papa, where does Uncle Sal get all that swag he brings us? I asked him and he said it fell off a truck. But none of it looks damaged to me."

My father laughed a moment and then his eyes lit up. "You're no slouch, Vinnie. F-O-T is an expression. The breadbox has been full for a while now, but the stock market's been playing teeter totter. With the recent election of George-the-Second, the prosperity is set to take a dive. People have to improvise if they plan to stay afloat. No matter what it takes, we can't let the corporate defenders roll us. So, sometimes, urban pirates like Sal plunder the cargo from the ships hauling freight; or rather the trucks."

I yawned, digging little to nothing. He tucked me in. "I'll explain more tomorrow. You're coming with me to work." I smiled at that, and fell asleep dreaming of pirates, plunder, and things falling off of trucks.

The next morning, I came to in the early bright smelling fresh coffee, waffles, and frying bacon. I made my way downstairs with my mind fogged over. My mother was still asleep, as usual. My father was awake and cooking. A recording of *Aida* filled the kitchen as he poured batter onto the hot waffle iron. After eating waffles, and drinking half-coffee-half-milk until my belly hurt, I was shooed upstairs to get bathed and dressed. "Jeans, long sleeved shirt, bandana, and boots, Vinnie. Oh, and don't forget your backpack, you'll be wanting it." My father winked at me. I was confused that he wanted me to bring my school knapsack, but I figured that he would explain later.

After scrubbing myself to a glowing pink in the tub, and dressing, I tied a black and red checked bandana over my long, sandy hair, grabbed my sack, and headed downstairs. My father was already dressed in a long, white, cotton coat with deep pockets, worn over cargo-jeans, a black hoodie, boots, and a black baseball cap. I knew he worked unloading boxes at the grocery store, but I'd never joined him.

"Son," my father patted me on the head as we pulled out of the drive way, "today I'm going to let you in on some secrets. You have to promise not to tell anyone."

I nodded at him, proud to be included in his confidence. "What kind of secrets?" I inquired.

A half hour later we entered the parking lot of a supermarket. The place was like a series of mammoth, neon-lighted streets of food. As I followed my father toward the back of the store, he stopped at a bulk food section and filled a bag with cashews, almonds, granola, yoghurt covered raisins and chocolate chips. He wrote a number on a sticker from a bin of flax-seeds and put it on the bag.

As we walked, he handed me the bag. "Here's a nosh for you, Vinnie. We can pay on the way out. Did you catch that the flax seeds are eighty-five cents a pound? The cashews are six bucks a pound. The almonds are four bucks a pound. So, what you do is write the number code for the cheap flax seeds, and then load up on the quality food. Later, you pay for a couple pounds of the cheaper item."

I looked up at him in awe. "Isn't that like stealing? And, fibbing?" I wasn't sure how to process the information. I was hungry, and ate a handful of the trail mix he had created.

"Son, urban pirates have been plundering supermarkets on the regular without raising the slightest suspicion, ever since the supermarkets began. It's a crime not to plunder them. The fact that so much of this occurs and the supermarkets still bring in huge profits indicates how much overcharging occurs in the first place. They're the swagmeisters. We pirates are on the right side. Like Robin Hood." My father stopped at a rack of all beef summer sausages and hard salamis. He picked up two salamis, and, before I could blink, they disappeared up the sleeves of his sweatshirt. Three summer sausages went inside the big front pockets of his coat.

"I thought Robin Hood took stuff to give to the poor." I looked up, my eyes wide, my forehead wrinkling. I knew my father was a good man who took care of our neighbors whenever they needed anything. Therefore, what he was saying had to be true.

"He certainly did, Vinnie. But we aren't rich anymore. Never really were. None of our neighbors are minting the green, either. Your mother and I barely make enough to pay the bills. Besides, supermarkets, like other businesses, refer to plundering as 'inventory shrink.' It's as if we pirates are helping fat businesses to diet. So, I view our efforts as a method designed to trim the economy, and I plunder with a positive attitude." My father winked and removed a couple of cans of Coke for us from a case. He popped them open and handed me one.

We walked through several aisles that were full of mid-morning shoppers. I didn't see anyone else trying to help the grocery store lose weight, but I wasn't sure what to look for. As we passed through an aisle of candy and chips, my father checked the prices on some bags of chips. I lifted four family sized bags of Reese's Pieces, sliding them into the pockets of my sweatshirt. As we made our way toward the back of the store, I opened my bag of trail mix and poured in two bags of the candy. My father grinned.

"You catch on fast. You're quick." He chuckled. "I have to work now, but sit on the loading dock and watch how the job's done." My father showed me a chair. I sat and sipped Coke in between handfuls of trail mix.

For the next three hours I watched with interest as my father, and three other men I knew from our neighborhood, loaded and unloaded trucks in the rear of the store. Every half hour or so a car would pull in and someone would talk to my father. After a brief conversation the other three men would unload a few cases of food, beverages, and various non-food items. They would transfer the cases from one of the trucks into the trunk of the car. The driver of the car would hand my father cash. The men would continue bringing merchandise from the trucks and loading it into the warehouse.

After three hours I drifted into slumber. An hour later my father woke me up and said he was done working. We re-entered the grocery store and found a cart. I rode the back as my father filled the cart with meat, seafood, cereal, and other items. After he scanned an employee card to get a ten percent discount, I helped him unload items at a self-checkout. He moved so fast that it was impossible to tell which items he had scanned and which he had not. He placed his scanned items back in the cart with the rest of the unscanned groceries. Some items got packed into my knapsack. After a few minutes, he swiped a visa gift card and bagged everything. Instead of leaving through the main entrance, we pushed the cart into the gardening section and left through an area that sold plants and seeds.

"Vinnie," my father looked over at me once we were in the car, "we never cut out from the front entrance. There are sensors that might beep if you have unpaid items. The gardening section doesn't have those sensors on their exits, I'm not certain why, but since they don't it's easier to leave that way. We paid a C-note and change for almost $300.00 worth of groceries. That's why you always use self-checkout. No one can keep track of what you scanned and didn't scan. If you do get fingered, feign confusion and start over."

I nodded. My guts did the flips, but I noticed how his motor revved when he took it to the system. I was sure that Papa knew best.

"That credit card I used, I got it from a lady your mother knows, Agnes McGillicuddy. She works at another store. Agnes adds funds to a dozen cards every week. After doing so, she slips the cards to your mother and some other friends. The cash register will read short unless she pays for the cards, but there are ways around that." My father drove toward home. "The stuff uncle Sal brings us is his way of paying me back for getting him some visa cards, and helping him finance a motorcycle. A bit of quid pro quo, if you will."

"Those boxes that the guys were loading into cars, were those F-O-T?"

My father chuckled. "Bingo! Very good, Vincenzo,

my lad."

I thought for a moment. "So, things don't fall off a truck. They're removed and put in another place. Pirates take the swag and share it around like Mama and you do at our parties. Right?"

"Exactly so, my boy. You're sharp as a tack." My father beamed at me. "Stores are covered by insurance. It isn't a huge deal to them if they lose some stock."

"I kited two bags of M&Ms for Gina and Tori. I grabbed a coloring book too." I pulled the coloring book of wild animals from the front of my pants where I had half stuffed it using my sweatshirt to cover it. "I hope that's cool."

"You have a knack. I'm proud of you, son. Just remember, don't take more than you need, don't operate without someone to cover you, and never take cheap items. You should always plunder high end goods. After all, it's free." My father turned on a CD and the voice of Babs Gonzales filled the car as I watched the other rides whizzing by.

Chapter Three

By the end of my fifth year, I understood the varied methods by which my parents and their friends operated. My mother was a homebody, introverted by nature. Our home was always tastefully decorated and clean, she was aces in the kitchen, but she wasn't a social butterfly. She did, however, venture out of the house to go shopping. I never saw her shopping without a large handbag. My sisters, who were eight and eleven, would each carry one as well. In those crowded aisles all sorts of goodies would be shoved into her purse. Small bottles and jars would often have the same size cap as the larger expensive sizes. If they had the price stamped on the cap, my mother or father would switch caps, getting the larger size for the cheaper price. In the produce department of an organic food store near us there were brown paper sacks for the potatoes. My mother would slip a few packages of steaks or some pork chops into the bottom of a bag, and pile some potatoes on top. She would have a cat in a white coat weigh the bag, staple it, and mark the price. Some grocery stores even carried packages of socks and underclothes. My mother always stocked up.

Our job as kids was to act as look-out, and shield our parents from the eyes of nosy staff. In extreme cases, where the risk of capture was great, I would feign clumsiness and knock over a display tower of cans. I might fake a temper tantrum in front of an approaching store manager. Sometimes, in stores where we weren't known, I would act lost and distract the manager long enough so that my mother could escape with the plundered items.

During the week I journeyed to the local park and the community center. There were free classes offered in a variety of subjects from cooking and knitting, to swimming and martial arts. My parents encouraged me and my sisters to take advantage of these classes. I began studying both Judo and Zui Quan. I also joined a ballroom dance class, and learned to swim. These activities cost next to a heap of bread if taught for profit, but there were places that believe-ed in passing on one's skills to others free of charge.

On weekends I would join my father at his job. He would leave one gig and get another every so often. When-ever I went to work with him, I would be sure to snag a few items from the shelves. I might lift a bag of cherries or grapes and eat them. I made sure to pack a spoon in my pocket and open some yogurt. The Greek kind was the best. A quarter pound of deli meat and cheese went well with a few bagels removed from a package. I always carried some cellophane packets of mayonnaise and mustard from local dives to add flavor. Life was happy, and my internal con-flicts about piracy abated. I enjoyed the ends, so why sweat the means?

Then came a fall day that changed the course of our nation. The 9/11 attacks are a historical happening now, but for us young people the pain is lasting. I imagine it must be for everyone. The bastards who hijacked those planes sent three thousand cats to their maker. Those cats left behind three thousand kittens under the age of eighteen.

Over time the events of 9/11 changed my entire perspective on life. Certain peripheral matters were set in motion that day, matters that would affect my views on piracy, and my whole life up until now. At the moment I was more concerned with the why of the situation.

I watched news reports on TV every day for a few weeks with my parents and sisters. The angry voices of the reporters, the violence I was seeing, was something I didn't dig. On top of that, my father was no longer employed. My parents spent most of their time with friends, drinking cof-fee and having long discussions about protests and politics.

Gina invited her school friends, Dalir, Reyhan and Soraya Pahlavi over almost every night. Their parents, Amir and Nasrin joined them. They weren't urban pirates, and seemed square, but they were friendly toward me. Dalir would bring math books with him and tutor me. The food Nasrin cooked for our family was out of sight. The spicy stews, hearty meat and rice dishes, and various kinds of bread were like nothing I had ever tasted. I would eat to the point of surfeit.

One evening, I asked my father to clue me. I had only met this one family, but if all Muslims were like them then I couldn't reconcile why Muslims would hate Americans. I couldn't dig the rabid mania it would take to crash airplanes into buildings.

The next morning my father took me to a chain name diner for breakfast. He ordered coffee and bought me a glass of orange juice. A man with an enormous beard sat next to us draped in a red checkered sports coat and black slacks. He was eating an extensive breakfast that included steak, eggs, toast and hash-browns, anchored by a carafe of coffee.

"Can I order some pancakes, Papa?" I asked while sipping juice.

"In a short-short, son. I want to hep you to some information about what you've been seeing on TV the past couple of weeks." My father got a refill on his coffee. "Vinnie, a couple of weeks ago, as you saw, terrorists attacked the United States. They hijacked four airplanes in mid-flight. That means that they threatened to kill people or hurt them unless the pilot did as they said and flew where they said. The bastards flew into the twin towers. You've seen the towers before, but you might not remember it. You were three. A lot of people died." My father sipped coffee. "Another plane destroyed part of the Pentagon. That's the nation's military center in Arlington, Virginia. The fourth plane crashed in Shanksville, Pennsylvania. No one knows for sure, but like as not the terrorists on that plane intended to destroy either the White House or the Capitol Building. Passengers on that fourth plane fought the scumbags and prevented them from reaching their goal. In all, close to three thousand people were killed."

I listened, digging the action, but confused about the why of it.

"These people weren't pirates. Not like we are. They belonged to a fanatical group of cowards. Theirs was an act of pure hatred, and I'm not even sure I can do justice to where that hatred stems from. All of the dirtbags were from nations in the Middle East. They belonged to a Muslim sect called Al Qaeda led by a real son of a bitch named Osama bin Laden. Al Qaeda practices an extreme version of the religion of Islam. They're Muslims, but not like the Pahlavis." The man next to us stood up, grabbed a check, and went to pay.

"Al Qaeda is opposed to the United States and democracy. They're opposed to our military presence in Arab nations. Since the group's creation by Bin Laden in the eighties, Al Qaeda has engaged in bombings world-wide. That's it, soup to nuts, son. They hate us because we're in their country. A lot of people in their region seek refuge in our country." My father picked up our check and did a double take.

"Well, if it's their country, and they don't want us there, then why don't we leave? Then they wouldn't hate us." I looked up at my father.

"Hold that thought, Vinnie. Excuse me, miss?" My father summoned our waitress. "There seems to be a mix-up. We had coffee and juice. But this check is for a pretty big meal. I think the guy sitting next to us took our check by mistake."

"Oh, my goodness!" She exclaimed "I apologize,

sir." She wrote a new check. My father paid and left a twenty-dollar tip.

We left and drove about two miles, before pulling into the parking lot of a family-style restaurant. "Vinnie, you can order anything you like here. If you recognize any-one, please keep it quiet. Pretend that you never saw the cat." My father winked at me as we entered.

We sat at the counter, and sure enough I recognized the man in the red sports coat. I started to say something, and stopped myself. The man was drinking coffee, but not eating. We ordered a couple of lumberjack breakfasts with extra biscuits, and apple pie. As I ate, my father kept talk-ing to me.

"You asked a good question before, Vinnie. Why don't we clear out of these countries Al Qaeda owns? The answer is two-fold. First of all, we need to have a military presence there in order to protect our nation and our nation al allies. If we're not there then certain other countries will put their own military there and threaten us." He cleared his throat. "Furthermore, most of the regular cats in these countries want us around. Al Qaeda are bullies, and they abuse women and children. Our presence in those countries helps stop that behavior. There's no easy way to explain these matters, but that's the gist of it."

I nodded and we ate while watching sports on TV. After we ate, he left a ten-dollar bill on the counter, grab-bed a receipt, and paid at the cash register.

"Vinnie, that cat in the sports coat is a friend of mine. His name is Mike Horowitz," my father backed out of the parking lot. "We have that system down to a science. He orders breakfast in one restaurant, and grabs my receipt for coffee. Then we switch it up at the next restaurant. We never hit the same joint inside of three months. It has yet to fail. If you plunder in that manner, never hit mom and pops. Hit big chains, or pricey diners that are ripping people off on the costs. The most important thing is to leave a heavy tip for the server. Servers don't even get paid minimum wage. They live on tips and ought never be screwed alongside their greedy employers." My father ruffled my head and turned on the radio. Coltrane's riffs filled the car as I contemplated all I had learned.

Chapter Four

By 2004, I fit in the skin of a junior pirate. The cards dealt the average cat weren't a total bust, and, while some bluffing was still required, the worst fears of my parents hadn't been realized. There were hate attacks upon Muslims, but there were also hate attacks on Blacks, Jews, and Hispanics. Ours is a nation of hatred and bigotry, has been since Cotton and Increase first knocked on Plymouth Rock. Certain news stations thrived on such bigotry, and delighted in shouting theater at crowded fires. The war fronts of Afghanistan and Iraq were featured daily, as I watched the evening news with my father. He drank beer, I sipped San Peligrino. Afterward, we discussed current events over dinner. Sometimes he let me sip his beer. I liked it from the start, and tried for a larger sip each time.

At school, I wasn't a great student. I wasn't a behavior problem; I was bored. Math presented enough difficulty to leave me challenged at moments. I was already reading at a high school level, and I absorbed and applied much of what I read. I found more practical learning came from books, and discussions with adults, than ever came from the cold, sterile facts teachers droned at me.

By the time I was nine, the riffs at my house turned melancholy. My father was depressed and aloof. My mother, low key by nature, stared into the abyss as the abyss stared into her. There were moments where my father still appeared normal, but despondency undercut everything. I maintained my practice of watching the news with my parents and my sisters, we still went out plundering together on the weekends, but there was a definite change. Whereas my father had been an early riser, both he and my mother remained in bed until after I left for school. Sometimes I would catch one of them staring out a window at nothing in particular. The longer that went on, the more my sisters and I began fending for ourselves. I had already developed a daily routine which allowed me a sense of stability. I would rise at six, practice my katas, shower and dress, start the coffee maker for my parents, draw one on the dark for myself, and head to school. On the way, I would stop at a fast-food chain and complain about a meal I had ordered, or not, the day before. Sometimes the counter people asked for a receipt, but more often they agreed to replace my "messed up order" with a breakfast sandwich and a Coke.

I had a few friends from the neighborhood who were also junior pirates. We would enter mega-chain convenience stores, and while two of us caused a distraction, the other three would plunder lunchmeat, cheese, bread, and soda. There were several cafés on the way, and we would take the free packets of mustard and mayonnaise from the counters. Every Friday I would bring a couple of large Ziplock bags to a grocery store, and empty plastic containers of cold fried chicken into them. The bags would be placed in my knapsack under my school books. We never lacked for a good lunch, and, in fact, provided lunch for several other students who were strapped for bread. There was a surge through my body when I saw one of the impoverished students light up with a smile as I made her a sandwich, and offered around chips and soda.

The best part of the day, however, was after school. My friends walked home, or looked for somewhere to play sports. I would head to the library or the park. I had received my first library card when I was six. By the time I was nine, I was a known patron. I rarely checked out books in the children's section, either. I preferred the adult section, and my reading choices were eclectic. Once a year the library gave away books that they no longer wanted, and I started building a formidable library of my own.

As I mentioned, we didn't live in the epicenter of New York City. My home since birth had been in proximity to those five boroughs, each more deliciously squalid and insalubrious than the rest. Not that our neighborhood was great shakes. About a half mile from our house was a huge park. I hung out there when I wasn't in school. The park was always full of interesting characters, like these three old men who would sit on the same bench every day. They had a hungry look about them, as well as a look of boredom. I began bringing them day old donuts on my way back from school. I would spy my sisters gossiping with their friends, or doing homework. I loved that park. It was there I would read until dusk.

The park was located in the northern section of town. The area was in the midst of gentrification. Some called it squeezing out minorities, but I didn't buy that. The park gravitated to an extreme after dark. It held the honor of a savage, and well-deserved, reputation -- especially in the later hours.

The park covered thirty acres, and by the seventies, long before my entry into the world, the area where I would sit and read had already developed a sordid reputation. The reputation was compounded by years of neglect. There's an urban legend that if an outsider walked through that park, he or she would never survive. The first event, in a short chain, was park denizens mugging the tourist. The second event involved a second mugging. In that the first mugging had already divested the Clyde of all possessions, the second mugging ended in demise. For female victims there was another possibility, but that was considered a fate almost worse than death. For the record, the urban myth is correct. Also, for the record, I had no problem with fighting. After the first few fights those cats with a bent toward bullying sought out easier prey.

One Friday, after school, in the early evening, I awoke from napping on a bench. I was catching cold, and yet I knew that if I told my mother, she would limit my activities until I felt better. Most of my reading indicated that time was all I needed. Time, good food, and maybe a beer or two.

I didn't drink heavily at that time. Sometimes I hung out with an older crowd, however, and they did drink. Once in a while we'd plunder six packs of cheap beer or a bottle of inexpensive wine. The beer was never the same quality my father drank. His was rich and nutty in flavor, ours was soapy and sour. Those cats and I would split the contents of the plunder amongst ourselves and get dizzy. I found that I could drink more than my colleagues, and I didn't get sick like the other cats and chicks. In fact, I grew bold and powerful. I also knew that drinking was frowned upon for minors, even by my parents. So, it remained a closeted activity.

The air after my nap was crisp, unseasonably chilled, and deliciously fetid. I reached for my sack to make sure it was still there, got erect, and had a good stretch. Holding my sack, I turned to walk through the park, picking at my teeth with a library card. By the age of nine I was muscular, of medium height, with a square face and chin. I kept my sandy colored hair cut short so that nobody could get a grip on it in a fight. I had contacts amongst my father's friends, and dressed in designer jeans, Bugatchi shirts, and Doc Martins. I walked with my thumbs tucked into a belt, and sharply clicked my heels on the concrete. My threads were either F-O-T, or traded-in at thrift stores. The trade-in was a technique my father taught me. I would enter an establishment, peruse the racks, and find an outfit I liked. In the changing room I'd remove all price tags from the clothing, leave my worn-out threads in the room, and walk out wearing my new outfit. Since people donated the clothing to the thrift shops, the prices they charged were obscene. I registered no guilt over taking for free what they received for free. They received my old clothes in exchange.

Approaching a vendor's cart, I held up two fingers. "Two with everything, heavy onions, and a sprite." I paid the vendor, took my Nathan's hot dogs, and found an empty bench. I ate and read my latest book, *P.T. Barnum: America's Greatest Showman,* by Phil Kunhardt Jr.

A month prior I had given a report at school about Barnum and Willie Hammerstein, another great showman from the vaudeville days. Barnum was a childhood hero of mine. After the second hot dog was devoured, I grabbed my sack and headed home. That was my existence. I grew accustomed to the pacing and the routine.

Excitement in my old neighborhood was rare. Outside of school, life for my peers was spent seeking distraction and playing games. Love games, street games, card games, video games, pool, bowling, and games like basketball, stickball and handball. Then, when the young cats grew tired of playing with their balls, they delved into capture the flag, truth or dare, and hand grenade, a game played with water balloons.

Sometimes I played, most of time I remained disengaged. I was too young for some of the games, and in many ways, I preferred finding new hustles. I was my father's son, and was already drifting toward a life of dedicated piracy.

On my way home each day I stopped in the produce section of a grocery store. Large chain-stores often threw away day-old vegetables, the outer leaves of lettuce, stalks of celery, and the like. This stuff was sometimes found in crates outside the back of the building. I got to know a few people in a store and told them that I raised rabbits. They saved the produce cast-offs for me. The free produce was washed, and put into the stewpot my mother always had on the back burner. The stew she made was out of this world, and she would freeze plastic containers so that anyone in need of food could always have some. To me that was more important than tossing balls on the street corner.

That evening, after the news, and reports of a recession brewing, I chatted with my father. "Papa? I had a notion. I've noticed that on the back of most food packages, like cookies, chips, soda pop, that kind of stuff, there's a statement about writing in if the customer is dissatisfied."

My father cocked his head and looked at me. "True. So, what's your idea, son?"

"Well, I was thinking that if I created an email account, and wrote to these places, we could get some free stuff. Even if I didn't buy the stuff, I can still write down the barcode numbers, expiration dates, proof of purchase codes, or whatever I need. That way we still get free stuff, but without buying anything"

"You're a chip off the old block. Urban pirates have been doing that very thing for years. Through the mail instead of email. Your idea of writing down the codes and dates while in the store is a nice twist. Send the companies all the email letters you can. Complain about how the last box of cereal was half full, or you found a dead fly in the can of peaches. Tell them your ice cream bars were crushed, or tasted grainy like they'd been melted and refrozen. Depending on the item, they'll send you a supply of replacements to keep you from complaining to your friends, or worse, filing a class action. More often, yes, they'll send you coupons to get free products as a replacement. You can sometimes get stuff sent to you by telling them how good their product is compared to the crap you see nowadays. You dig the riff? *Rice Krispies have had a fantastic effect on my sexual prowess,* or, *your frozen succotash has given a whole new meaning to my life.* In general, though, terse letters get the best results."

I laughed "Rice Krispies get you hard?" My father joined my laughter. "What about dropping email on restaurant corporate offices. We could score free meals at nicer places than fast food that way."

"That's a Jim Dandy notion, son. If you write a libretto, I can help with the score." My father smiled at me. "You do me proud!"

That night I went to sleep dreaming about sailing on the oceans, and plundering cargo. The region between crooked and straight had become blurred. I felt righteous down to my jockeys. My parents did nothing to dissuade me.

Chapter Five

In every major city there are bars that cater to the yuppie riff-raff trying to hustle their way up the escalator of big business. Many of these bars have a hot buffet, or several warming containers of hors-d'oeuvres, served free as a come-on to drink overpriced booze. My mother and father would take me, Tori, and Gina to the bars on the weekends. My father and mother would take half-empty glasses from a table and use them as props to ward off the wait staff. My sisters and I ordered Cokes. The bars even offered free refills. We would walk around sampling the free food until we had eaten our fill. If the food was easy to transport, like pigs in a blanket or chicken strips, my sisters would cover me as I dumped large quantities into plastic Ziplock bags. I would stuff the swag in my sack, or inside my mother's purse.

Furthermore, these bars were good places to cop things like condiments, shakers of salt or sugar, toilet paper, silverware, and cups for home. We'd each carry a knapsack, or an empty purse, and load up after we'd cased the joint. I'd make sure to pack soft clothes like t-shirts and socks to buffer glass items from breaking.

Sometimes, if no one was looking, I would take a partially consumed glass of whiskey or vodka and dump it into my Coke. It eased the butterflies my guts. It wasn't that I saw anything wrong with plundering silverware and dish-es. It wasn't that I thought there was anything wrong with taking advantage of free appetizers. The action wasn't quite copacetic, however. My stomach did the jumps when I en-gaged in these acts of piracy. A couple shots of bourbon in my Cokes, though, and I was cool like the arctic.

On my tenth birthday we hit a full buffet at a bar. Being a few days prior to Thanksgiving, there was dinner with the trimmings. They even had three kinds of pie. After dinner, I received some outstanding presents.

Gina was sixteen, and a junior in high school. She gave me a book by Frank Abagnale called *Catch Me If You Can*. I developed an admiration for the man, even if he did sell out in the end. She also bought me a life changing book by Edward Thorp titled *Beat the Dealer*. I later learned that the book covers only the most rudimentary techniques for card counting.

Tori gave me a birthday card, and inside was a piece of grey plastic, rounded on one end, and rectangular on the other, with several grooves. I had never seen an item like it before. Tori explained that custodians at certain restaurants used a key of that sort to open the toilet paper dispensers. She had found one on a sink in a restroom and decided to clean it up and give it to me. She also gave me a used computer scanner that she had rescued from an apartment dumpster. The scanner still worked. But I had no computer.

That is, I had no computer until I opened the present from my parents. They had purchased a laptop computer complete with the most up-to-date programs. I had no idea if the computer had fallen off a truck or not, nor did I care.

The next day we had a party at our house. There was the usual cake and ice cream, Dr Brown's for the kids, and Cristal for the adults. Our neighbors and friends showed up with some sharp new threads for me. They also brought books, and DVDs.

Three weeks after my tenth birthday, I came into my own as a junior pirate. I spent the night at the home of my friend Moses Feingold. He was a year older and had seen some rough going over the years. His father was in recovery from the dope. His brother, Herman, was eighteen and lived in a world of rackets and grifting. Herman used a high-tech computer scanner and special rag paper to create reasonable facsimiles of ten and twenty dollar bills. Nothing spectacular, but passable. That was one of his nicer activities.

That evening, Mo and I attended a twelve-step meeting with Mo's father. Afterward, we planned to get pizza and watch Christmas movies. The meeting was dullsville. The participants shared full-on blues numbers, and I found it hard to understand how they could be such dimwits. I drank, but I could stop. Right? I thought it weak of them to let the juice ruin their lives.

It was during the halfway point of the meeting that I had a proverbial lightbulb moment. The lead person, who referred to himself as the chairman of the meeting, read some bulletins and mentioned something about a seventh tradition. A basket was passed and everyone put in some scratch. I noticed that some even put in ten or twenty dollars and took out change. A thought occurred to me. If I had some of Herman Feingold's funny paper, and if I attended several meetings, why couldn't I drop a phony twenty and collect nineteen real dollars in change? As a matter of fact, I could collect twenty- eight dollars in change if I slipped a ten in with the stack of ones. This idea was a germ. I wasn't certain if the people in these meetings were square-johns, or if the organization itself was an acceptable target. I would need large meetings and meetings attended by the well to do. I now had a scanner, and a computer. I could mint my own green.

The next afternoon I asked my father and his friend Vasily Mogilevich if we could get lunch together. Just us guys. "I need to rap -- to pick your brains. I have a complicated situation going." My stomach was tight.

My father gave me a knowing look and agreed. Vasily was large from every angle. He was six and a half feet tall, with hands like slabs of stone, a shaved head and a sloping brow. He was a computer programmer, and my father and he worked together with several other people on something called the dark web. I had no idea how that operation worked. However, the fact that he understood computers made me consider him as a potential resource in discussing my money-making scheme.

We drove to a Chinese buffet in midtown. I made sure to bring several Ziplock bags inside my knapsack. After we loaded our plates, we sat in a back corner.

"I may have stumbled onto a chance at big money, but I need help with it, Papa. It involves using computers as well, Uncle V. I need to know something, though. Last night I was at this recovery meeting with my friend Mo and his papa. You know how his papa was hooked and is recovering? I saw how much money those cats collected. There was seventy dollars at least. What I need to know first, are they regular folk? Are they square-johns?" I asked.

"Moses and his family? Of course they are, son. If you mean the other Harveys at those meetings, they are too. The meetings as an entity, not so much. What's your idea?" My father sipped tea, and bit into a spring roll.

I lowered my voice. "I know that Mo's brother, Herman, makes fake twenty-dollar bills. I'm not certain how real they look to an expert. I have a scanner and a computer now, which that is what he uses. If I could make passable looking bills, couldn't I put them in the money basket? Put in a fake twenty, take out a real nineteen? Maybe a real twenty-eight if a ten got mixed in with the one-dollar bills?" I saw a light in Vasily's eyes.

My father pointed a finger at me. "You have something there. Let's kick it around, see what we stub our toe on. That has to be the safest method I ever heard of for passing counterfeit bills. It's all but foolproof. That sort of action would require finesse. Can't hit the same meetings every time. You'd need a reason for you to be there." My father ate food and pondered.

"Perhaps he is doing a report for health class? The open meetings surely attract a larger crowd, no?" Vasily sipped some tea.

"Yes, that might work. Son, you need to have the right clothes for this. You want to blend in. You need to research the meetings and make a schedule. I can help you with that." My father gave me a broad smile. He was always engaged when the topic turned to con-artistry.

"As you might suspect, I know people who can get you real looking twenty dollars bills. They will cost you five dollars apiece. So, if you bring me the money, I can purchase a stack of them. You are still making fourteen dollars profit or more." Vasily rose and filled another plate with food.

"But, understand, young Il-Cazzo," he said after returning, "making bills on a scanner is the act of an imbecile. The process is far more complicated and labor intensive. It is an art form." Vasily chewed on a clam. "To be good, not just scanner or photocopier adequate, one must make negatives. One must precisely carve masking materials and burn metal plates. The lining up of plates must be exact to the last nanometer. The mixing of the inks alone is a grueling task. So, please, do not try making your own prints, and do not deal with this rank amateur you are discussing." He gave me an icy glare while shaking his head.

I nodded solemnly, and stood. I loaded a plate with peel and eat shrimp, before dumping the shrimp into a Ziplock bag. I filled another bag with fifteen egg rolls, and yet another with fried dumplings and crab Rangoon. I filled a plate with desserts, and sat eating as my father and Vasily discussed business. I didn't dig everything they discussed but it involved pharmaceuticals, overseas banks, and helping people to escape foreign countries.

"Vinnie? Do you recall some years ago when I

taught you about shopping with pre-paid cards?" My father looked at me and then Vasily. I nodded. "Well," my father continued "Agnes McGillicuddy gets fifty-dollar bills from a partner of mine and Uncle Vasily. She loads the cards with cash on her register. Then, later, on her lunch break, she puts the fake fifties into various money pouches stored in the manager's office. She removes real ten and twenty dollar bills, and returns them to her drawer. That way she never comes up short. After a while the store realizes that they've been passed fake money, but it's never associated with her."

I chuckled. "Sweet. If a store that's set up to spot fakes can't stop the action, no way is anyone stopping me."

My moral qualms were growing blurrier and more distant by the day. I still wondered if innocent people got axed in the process.

We left the server a fifteen dollar tip and drove home. Vasily exited my father's car and climbed into a SUV. After Vasily drove away, I turned to look for my father. He had already gone inside. My mother sat in a chair staring through the TV set. My father put the food we had smuggled out of the restaurant into the refrigerator, and sat next to my mother while pulling a mental fade. I was worried, but all I could do was head upstairs to read my latest book *Dead End* by Jeanne King.

Over the next several months I would come home to find strangers talking with my parents on the porch. The visitors were always draped in dime-store threads and cheap kicks. I would overhear words such as depression, suicidal, psychiatrist, disabled. A lawyer's card lay on the kitchen counter one afternoon. I didn't understand the need for lawyers, but I knew that my parents moods were growing bleak, and that my father was tuning out further with each passing day. While never a ding-dong-daddy, my father always had a certain cut and drape that showed him some class. Now he sat in the house with his shirt untucked, his pants wrinkled, and wearing slippers. Instead of Aaron Copeland filling the kitchen, he gravitated toward Samuel Barber's *Adagio for Strings*.

A dark period consumed my life. I was ten, although I passed for fourteen. I had little in the way of rules and structure. My sisters had their own friends and often spent the night with them. I began spending time with a rougher crowd. I was a voracious reader and I never got into serious trouble, but I found myself at parties with kids several years older. It was easy to fade into the shadows and drink cheap beer. Sometimes, if the party was at a more upscale pad, there would be liquor as well. I never got drunk, or out of control, although others appeared to be. One beer could last me for half an hour. There was plenty of lip locking, kids buffing each other's back pockets with their hands, activities that held no interest for me.

At one party I moseyed into a room where a cat I knew was slung on a wrap-around sofa with several other cats and chicks. His name was Gerry Trice. He patted the empty seat beside him. "Hey, dude, plant it here and talk at me. Glad you made the scene, Il-Cazzo my man. Here, have a toke." He passed me a short, hand-crafted, glass pipe of marijuana. I had never smoked before. "Suck in when I light it up, and swallow the smoke before letting it out."

I did as Gerry said. There was little effect at first. The smoke made my throat raw was all. Four pipes were being passed around, and I was taking hits off of each one in turn. After a few tokes, the action turned foggy and faded. I was enveloped in a warm cocoon of numb pleasure. My slacks seemed to melt into the couch and my purple satin shirt felt amazing on my skin. I had no desire to move as Pimp C crackled through speakers in the background. I was digging the vibe, whereas on the regular I considered rap to be compost city.

Thirty minutes later I realized that Gerry was talking to me. "Il-Cazzo! Hey, you with me, man? She-it this white boy is baked like Betty Crocker. Ground control to Il-Cazzo." Gerry laughed.

I cracked up at that line. "Houston, we have a problem. I need a martini, shaken not stirred. Make it a double." My words sounded spaced and slow.

One of the chicks sat beside me, wrapping an arm around my waist. She had light brown skin, long black hair, deep brown eyes, and was going for the minimalist look in her red leather mini-skirt, and a blouse opened to expose a matching lace bra. "How about a beer instead? She handed me a bottle of beer. I sat sipping as my mind floated. The girl had her head on my shoulder, and was cooing incoherently. A real gone chick. Long gone.

Several hours later Gerry gave me a lift home. We smoked a bowl before I got out of his Cadillac. My parents were already in bed and I went up to my room. I sat in my boxers reading *American Roulette* by Richard Marcus. The man was a genius. I dozed off and woke up at ten the next morning. My first thought was how to get more weed. I loved the sensation.

Along with fending for myself while my parents tuned out the world, I attended recovery meetings. I didn't think of myself as needing what they offered, but I looked the part. I managed to find a pair of designer jeans with the tag still on them at a thrift store, exchanged several old t-shirts for polo shirts in pastel colors, and picked up three pairs of F-O-T Italian loafers from a family friend.

At each meeting I would sit in the back, my fedora strategically dipped below one eye, and trade in a fake bill for real cash. Uncle Vasily had provided me with a stack of counterfeit twenties as promised, and over several weeks I had paid for them out of my profits. Fifteen minutes after the basket was passed, I would slip out the door, either finding another meeting or heading home. During the meetings I finished my homework instead of listing to the members sharing their stories. I was bringing home almost $150.00 a week profit. It wasn't a massive haul, but it beat the allowances most kids received. No one at the meetings noticed a shy kid in the back sipping a cup of coffee. I even managed to score free pizza, cake, or donuts at some of the meetings.

By the time I turned eleven my parents fog started lifting. It was noticeable, if not extreme. My mother remained low key, and my father continued to stay home more than he went out. Both of my parents also began attending long sessions at a local hospital with doctors of psychiatry and psychology. On weekends, or school holidays, our family would drive north to other towns. On those rides, my parents were their old selves. My father would tune in NPR or an easy listening station. We would hit up pizza buffets, or use vouchers to get lunch at one steakhouse or another.

When we went out of town, we would often attend open houses at properties that were for sale. My father was always razor sharp, wearing designer slacks, and a red power tie with a cat's eye tie-tack over a black silk shirt; his shoes buffed to a high mirror shine. My mother would sport a designer dress and a tasteful amount of jewelry. My sisters and I were instructed to wear our nicest school clothes. We looked like nothing so much as an upper class yuppie family.

My parents were, in fact, looking for a new house. They planned to move us north, for reasons as yet unknown to me. I was content in our old neighborhood. On one trip I recall my mother talking to us from the front seat.

"Kids? There's something you should be aware of. In many areas, when people are selling houses, they have what's called a realtor's day. Anyone can attend the open house, of course, but it's a special day to entice real estate agents who have interested clients. On these realtor's days the sellers often put out hors d'ouvres, finger sandwiches, sweets, and drinks. Enjoy the free lunch."

We visited numerous houses on each trip. Some were well beyond anything we needed or could afford. However, the pricier the neighborhood the better the snacks. I would sneak at least one small glass of wine. I didn't care for the taste of wine, but the warmth in my belly was sensational. I had a feeling that if my parents saw me drinking, the warmth would transfer behind me. The risk was worth it.

Over spring break, the year after I turned twelve, we travelled well into northern New England. The towns were antiquated and charming. The cats we met seemed more welcoming than those back home. There were less places that would lend themselves to plundering, of course, and yet the open space and beauty of the region more than made up for that. It was in one such town that they settled on a house.

Chapter Six

Late May, when I was twelve and a half, we moved. It had been a blustery day in April when I found out that my parents had been denied twice for disability. That was the reason for the lawyers and the doctor's visits. They claimed that they were clinically depressed which prevented them from working. They also claimed to have severe social anxiety. My father had always seemed social enough to me before the onset of his depression. My mother was never antisocial, she was introverted. Social Security was not impressed by the claims, and refused to put my parents on disability payments. In response, my parents hired a lawyer and sued. After going before a judge, and putting on an act to make John Barrymore proud, they had been granted disability. They each received several years of retroactive paychecks from social security, and, with the fifty-eight thousand dollars between them, they put a down payment on a small, three bedroom house. The basement was turned into a master suite. After selling our previous house, they finished paying for the new one with enough left over money to give me and my sisters each ten thousand dollar savings accounts for college.

It was in this town where I encountered that solid sender known as Steph Baker. Myron Baker was outside working on his truck one morning, so, as suggested by my father, I put on an old t-shirt and a pair of faded jeans.

"Mr. Baker? Sir?" I tried to sound confident but polite. "We moved in down the block about a month and a half ago. I haven't had a chance to meet you. My name's Vincenzo, and I was hoping maybe you knew if there was any part-time work at the recycling center."

Myron Baker looked up from his truck and then stood. He looked me over with a wary eye, grunted, and put out his hand. I shook, giving as good as I got. "I've seen you over there eying my daughter, boy."

"I don't mean to be rude, sir. I think she's pretty is all." I tried to look like an adult instead of a scared boy.

"Yeah, both my girls are. They take after their mother. So, you want a job? I think I might be able to find you one. We need people to clean the area some. It's dirty work. Kind of surprised a white boy would want it." He looked me over some more. "Anything else you want? I've got things to do, boy."

"Well, I was wondering about the churches in the area. My parents don't attend often, but, I was thinking I might start. I have some interest anyway." I tried for nonchalant.

"Sure, boy. There's a church a few miles down the road, we attend every Sunday, and on Wednesdays. If you need a ride, I guess we have room. But, boy, stay away from my girls. I don't like people meddling in my affairs." Myron Baker returned to his truck and I walked home. I spent the rest of the afternoon weeding the garden, practicing kata, reading *The Republic of Pirates* by Colin Woodard, and napping in a hammock.

The following Sunday I awoke at dawn. My father and I had driven to Sweetbriar the day before. I had several coupons that were due to expire, and we used them to load up on groceries. We located a thrift shop, and I found a grey, tropical worsted, pinstripe suit, a black tuxedo shirt, and a white silk tie. I traded in a pair of old slacks and a shirt for the new outfit. When we returned home with pizzas that had been free with vouchers from a pizza chain, I put my new suit on my bed. After dinner, my mother ironed my clothes while I polished my loafers.

The next day I was getting dressed when my father knocked and entered. He smiled at how I looked, and sat on my bed. "Vinnie, you should keep that suit as long as it fits.

Piracy in these smaller towns is going to take finesse. Having a closet with the right costuming will help a lot. By the way, I got you a gift. The computer work I do with Uncle Vasily and our partners has been taking off." He handed me a white, leathery box. I opened it, and inside was a gold watch with a smooth band and diamonds surrounding the face and bezel.

"Oh my Lord, Papa! This is outrageous! This is like the coolest watch ever!" I hugged him and put it on.

"You're welcome." He grinned. "Don't wear it all the time, though. When you're draped in a suit, that's when you flash that watch. Your sports watch is for every day."

I nodded and beamed.

"I'm glad it didn't break when it fell off the truck." He winked at me.

After finishing dressing, I came downstairs. Tori giggled a little, and then snapped my picture with her cell phone. She brushed off my back before I walked down the block. I arrived as the Baker's were coming out.

"Hey, boy, didn't know if you were coming or not." Myron gave me a stern glare. "Next time don't cut it so close."

"Yes, sir." My chest tightened and a rivulet of sweat trickled down my spine.

Steph was dressed in a peach dress that came to her knees. She had on white tights and peach shoes. Her eyes looked red and puffy. I started to ask if she was OK, but bit my tongue. She gave me a weak smile as she climbed in the back seat with her mother and Caroline.

Caroline and her mother were dressed in matching violet dresses with black pumps. They were quiet except for a brief hello. Heather Baker looked tired, and Caroline winced as she sat and closed the door.

Myron pulled off in the truck. As we drove, he sipped a thermos of coffee. He looked at me. "Want a cup of joe, boy?"

Heather leaned forward. "Myron, honey, his parents might not like him drinking coffee."

Myron gave her a look through the rearview mirror and she shrunk back. "I wasn't asking you…dear." He pulled a Styrofoam cup from the glove compartment. "Pour yourself some, boy. It'll put hair on your ass."

I drew myself one on the dark, took a sip, and gasped. The coffee was laced with whiskey. I swallowed, and smiled at the familiar warmth. "Appreciate it, sir. Better than the stuff I make."

"I reckon. Must be my secret ingredient."

I sipped some more, and relaxed. After a half hour of listening to country music we pulled up in front of a brick and metal building. As we were climbing out of the truck, I noticed that Caroline had red marks on her thighs below the hem of her dress. My stomach knotted into a ball. Steph looked at me, her mouth turned up at the corners as her cheeks reddened, and she bit her lower lip.

We stopped at a counter, and I filled out a visitor's card. When Myron turned to get some coffee and a donut, I slid a pencil and paper into my pocket. I helped myself to a couple of donuts and a large coffee.

After we were seated, Caroline and Steph began shifting a bit. Myron glared and asked if they needed to go outside for a talk, or were they going to sit still. They looked down and sat still. My stomach tightened as I observed the action from the corner of my eye.

After the choir sang several numbers, Pastor Pehr Gaphals began preaching his sermon. It was on the dangers of drinking. His voice was at once oily and hypnotic. Myron shifted in his seat, fingers drumming on his thighs. His face turned as red as his hair when Heather tried holding his hands.

Fifteen minutes into the sermon Myron told Heather

to watch the girls so he could go use the men's room. I sat straight, looking ahead, as if I was paying attention. Instead, I removed the pencil and paper from my pocket. I wrote my cell phone number. Under that I wrote: *If you need help, or they do, call. Memorize this number. Then shred it. My family can help.*

I folded the paper. Still looking straight ahead, I slipped it to Steph. She looked at it, nodded, and put it in her pocket. Myron returned twenty minutes later.

"In conclusion, my brethren, The Bible warns us against drinking. Wine, beer and especially hard drink. If we want salvation, it is ours, but if we want to enjoy our time on earth then we need to forgo such worldly pleasures as alcohol." Pastor Gaphals finished.

A lady made some announcements, after which we were dismissed. We filed out and Myron drove us home. He drummed his fingers on the steering wheel, and his mouth was a thin hard line. Looking in the side mirror I saw that Heather and her daughters were staring straight ahead, expressionless.

Myron turned on the radio and Johnny Cash's "Sunday Morning Coming Down" filled the truck. After we arrived in Harvest Junction, I thanked Myron and headed home. Out of the corner of my eye I watched Heather, Steph, and Caroline scurry inside. I had the urge to vomit. I was a lot of things, but stupid had never been one of them.

Chapter Seven

The following morning, I woke up at dawn. After doing my kata, showering, and making some coffee and toast, I sat on the porch reading *If You Really Loved Me* by Ann Rule.

Two boys walked up to the porch and said hello. One was a short Hispanic with a baby face and black hair parted in the middle and greased back. The other was taller, older, with a buzz cut and a disarming smile. He was muscular and tanned.

The older boy spoke up. "Hey, man. My name's Billy Bob Fisher. I'm friends with Tori. This is Al Contreras. We live down the block. Thinking about getting up a baseball game or something. You interested in playing? Tori says you haven't made a lot of friends since you moved. We could introduce you around."

Al Contreras nodded in my direction, reserved, but friendly. I put a book mark in my book. "Sure. Give me a minute." I went inside and told my mother where I was heading. I put my book away and changed my shirt.

While I was leaving, Tori was in her room looking at a magazine. "Hey, thank you. Your boyfriend invited me to play baseball."

Tori smiled and gave me a thumbs up. "Sure thing. You haven't done much since we moved here, except garden, work out, read, and moon over that chick. I figured it was time you made some friends."

"I suppose."

I rejoined Billy Bob and Al. The three of us walked down the block and stopped at a few other houses. We were joined by some kids who were introduced as Joe Kurdy, Mike Casey, Ary Green, Natty Wolf, and her brother Vic. After being introduced I got the usual questions about what sports teams I liked, and what my parents did for a living.

Most of the kids were a grade ahead of me, and Billy Bob was the same grade as Tori. Mike and Al were my age.

We were joined by several older boys from Tori and Billy Bob's classes, and chose up teams. I wasn't much into team competition. I never understood the attraction of sports except boxing and the martial arts. Even so, I held my own, fielded a few ground balls, and managed one decent catch. It was a hot, sweaty day, but I got to know some neighbors. They seemed nothing like the cats from the old neighborhood. I wondered if they would understand urban piracy; if they had ever helped a store reduce itself.

After a couple of hours of playing baseball, everyone was ready to quit. "Hey, Il-Cazzo, you should come hang out more." Billy Bob reached into a backpack. He took out a bottle with a screw-on cap. Inside was clear liquid. He unscrewed the cap and took a swig before handing it to Ary. After Ary took a swig he handed it to me. I saw everyone looking at me. I was hot and thirsty, and while sharing a bottle of water seemed odd, I took a healthy swig -- and gasped. The water was warmish, and had a strange, thick, milky flavor.

"What the hell is that stuff?" My head was full of helium as a strange sensation filled my belly. The world was spinning.

"Best raisin mash in the county, Il-Cazzo." Billy Bob handed the bottle to Al. "I brew it myself." Al took a swig and passed it on.

"That...that's great. I dig that mellow taste. Yeah...that's great." I laughed and plunked down in the grass. "Hey, uh, do any of you cats ever smoke out? I don't even know where to score around here, but I used to smoke at parties. Back home." I was reeling and loose.

Natty looked at me. "You mean weed? There's a field two miles across the tracks where some dudes grow it. I wouldn't recommend going out there, though." A few other kids nodded in agreement.

"Yeah, man. We're all straight enough. Our parents demand it. You go east beyond the tracks, man, and that gets dangerous. Those dudes are serious bad news. Not just pot, but meth and shit. Bad place to go, you know what I'm saying?" Al looked at me with a serious expression.

"I can hold my own. I used to hang with a pretty tough crowd before my family moved." I was unsure how much to share about things. My stomach tightened again. I took another swig of mash, which helped.

"Hey, Il-Cazzo, if loco-bud is your thing, I can get you some. But it'll cost serious cash." Billy Bob chucked me on the shoulder.

"How much?" My head started pounding.

"Fifty bucks an eighth. But, it's good stuff. I have a friend whose brother gets it from a guy in Gainesville, Florida." Billy Bob smiled. "Most kids around here aren't into it that much. I am, sometimes. We all stay on the narrow path for the most part. Our parents would peel our hides if we got too far out of line."

"Fifty bucks? Deal. Can I have another swig?" I took another healthy gulp of the shine.

"Careful, dude. That stuff ain't water." Ary Green laughed.

The other kids and I lay around in the grass, talking and swapping stories. It was a nice afternoon. I didn't say much about piracy, but I sensed that I was a lot tougher than most of the others. It wasn't a pleasant feeling. My parents loved me, I was sure, but the other kids' parents sounded a damned sight more concerned and caring.

"So, you got a girlfriend?" Mike asked me.

"Not really. I mean I always like to keep my options open. There's this one chick, but I can't get close. Her father's a hard one. I get the feeling that he doesn't like me." I shrugged.

"Do tell! What girl is that?" Billy Bob asked.

"Her name's Steph. Stephanie Ann Baker. She lives down the block from me." I sighed.

Everyone started laughing. Not at me. Kind of in my proximity. "You better be careful there, Vinnie," Joe Kurdy laughed. "Myron Baker is not to be screwed with. His family is off limits. He's the last person you want to be involved with. Trust me on that. Al's old man works at the yard cleaning up. So do the Velasquez twins who were playing outfield. That's why they had to leave the game early."

I sighed again. "I can't tune my brain to another channel, Joe. Steph is the most, to say the least. I mean have you looked at her chassis? She's an A-1 knockout."

Billy Bob slugged me in the arm lightly. "You got it bad, Il-Cazzo. Be careful. Some of us have had run-ins with Myron. People around this side of town don't mind each other's business. We're all about live and let live. But we all know what's going on in that family. So be careful buddy. You might end up in a situation you can't handle."

Vic Wolf cleared his throat. "I was in Sweetbriar last winter with Nat and our mom. Saw the Bakers in the parking lot of a strip mall. Myron was screaming at those girls so loud I bet Canadian border guards heard him."

Natty shuddered. "Yeah, and he slapped Mrs. Baker so hard her head rocked sideways. I'd castrate any guy who ever did me that way."

After another hour everyone started toward home. My head was a bag of wet feathers, and I was a bit unsteady as I walked. I went inside, scurried to the bathroom and had a long, cold shower. It helped some. Dinner cleared my mind, and a quart of ice water improved my situation.

"Papa? Can we discourse on the back porch?" I looked over at him.

"Sure, son. I have work to finish, but I can spare a few." My father led the way. I sat beside him on the steps.

"I have a big problem. Well, I've had one a for a while but I thought I could figure it. I can't. You suggested some ideas about meeting Steph Baker. Your advice about attending church worked, and I have an offer for weekend work at the scrap yard. All good except that it might be all bad. I can't say I'm right and I can't say I'm wrong, but I know it's uncool to lay down a bum rap without proof."

"Vinnie, you're a good kid. All three of you kids are. Your mother and I are proud as peacocks about Gina starting at college. Tori and you have grown into caring, socially-minded kids. That brings a smile to my face. I dig you not talking outside of school, but sometimes a problem shared is a problem halved." My father ruffled my hair.

"I noticed a bruise on Steph's leg the first day we met. I didn't think much of it. On the way into church, I noticed some marks on Caroline, too. And, the way Mr. Baker talks to his wife and daughters gives me the shivers. It's like they're spooked, and he wants it that way. Another thing, on the way to church he poured me some coffee. It was spiked. He was driving." I looked across the yard at a squirrel. "Some neighbor kids were telling me that he has a temper like a tsunami, and a fuse set on mouse-fart."

My father sighed – paused -- shook his head, and closed his eyes a moment. "Shit! Son, that sort of riff requires dancing lightly. I grew up in a situation like that. Stay alert. Furthermore, I don't like being Mr. Bossy, but I forbid you to work for him. Your safety is more important."

"I wrote my cell number down and slipped it to Steph at church. I told her to memorize it and destroy the note. If you think I called the action right, I don't want to work for him, anyway." I watched the squirrel running.

"Smooth move, son. You think well. So that you know, I don't care if you sneak a few drinks. Kids do that.

It's part of the learning curve. Your mother would disagree, so deal her out. Myron offering you a drink and not asking us first, however, this upsets me a great deal. I don't want you in his car if he's going to drink and drive. Please, if you're ever in a situation where you can't get a ride except with someone who's been drinking, call me. Any hour of any day. I'll come get you." My father leaned over and hugged me. "I need to get some work done, but one Sunday maybe our family should attend church together. It's been a while."

Chapter Eight

Two weeks later, on a sunny and cool Sunday, I was decked out in my suit, sitting in the kitchen eating corn muffins, drinking coffee, listening to Vivaldi, and reading my latest book, *Disconnected* by Lynne Jeter. One of the few items I never plundered was books. I never paid full freight, however. I had a few apps on my cell phone that monitored activity. As payment for allowing the apps to survey my phone usage, I received codes for Amazon gift cards in email. The awards shaved money off the cost of my books and required me to do no work.

Tori walked into the kitchen dressed in a dark blue velvet, ankle length skirt and a powder blue top. She poured coffee and sat across from me. "Morning, Vinnie. I hear you've made friends with Fisher. He said you guys were conducting business the other day." She winked at me.

"Business? What are you talking? I hang out with him, and the other cats from the neighborhood. We play baseball or football."

"I don't care if you get mellow. I smoke out too. If Mama and Papa knew, you might be in the jam pot, but I don't care. Gina smokes. She told me in email." Tori lowered her voice. "But you have to share."

"After church let's take a walk. I found this great wooded area with a gnome fort formed by the trees. I go there to read and think."

My mother and father walked upstairs, poured coffee, and grabbed some muffins. He was draped in a blue serge suit, a black silk tie with a pearl stickpin, and polished loafers. She wore a chiffon number with white pumps, a choker of pearls, and matching earrings. Tori and I changed the subject and chatted about my current book instead.

After breakfast we headed to church. My father had traded his town car for a minivan. A family car fit the area better, he said. It had been a while since the family had made an outing together. Once in a while we would go to Sweetbriar and have dinner using some gift cards I received, but other than dinner each night, or weekend brunch, we rarely spent quality time together. When we had lived near New York City we went out pirating on the regular. There were always great places to get fantastic meals and make the scene.

Gina and Tori would look in the society pages of the paper and locate weddings, bar mitzvahs, social groups holding open houses, and the like. We would dress to fit the occasion, and schmooze our way in long enough to hit the buffets. I found that remarks such as, "I'm Louie's cousin," or "Gee, Dorothy looks simply marvy," worked great. Lines like "Betty doesn't look pregnant" tend to be frowned upon at weddings. Gina, Tori, and I could work this free-load like nobody's business. We would chatter back and forth while stuffing ourselves. My parents would be on the other side of the room holding their own.

It had been a while since we had enjoyed that sort of quality time. My father was consumed by his work. My mother spent her days cleaning the house, gardening, and cooking. The pantry was filled with jars of pickled vegetables and preserves. This particular Sunday, the church was having a potluck after services. It was a great opportunity to spend family time. We rolled into the church parking lot, and as we climbed out, I spotted the Bakers.

Caroline had a red mark below the side of her left eye. I looked up at my father who gave me a knowing nod. Tori squeezed my shoulder. I smiled at her. My father moved at an angle, and corralled Myron Baker. My mother turned and greeted Heather. While the parents were being kept busy, Tori and I approached Steph and Caroline.

"Hi, my name's Tori." She was all smiles and friendliness. "Vinnie tells me that you're Steph, and this is Caroline?"

Steph nodded and twisted the toe of her shoe into the ground. Out of the corner of my eye I watched Myron shifting from foot to foot, his face reddening. He couldn't get around my father, who was talking to him with the sort of smile I had seen on used car salesmen in commercials.

In a loud voice, Tori asked, "Caroline? What happened? You OK? Your eye's all red and puffy. Looks like some creep attacked you."

"I fell. Uh, I was getting up after dinner, and I tripped and bumped a chair." The answer was shallow and rehearsed.

"Really? That sucks!" I glared at Myron, just wishing he'd try me on for size. "Glad you. didn't fall too, Steph. I guess you must have a couple weeks ago when you had that nasty bruise on your thigh. Maybe I should teach you both some martial arts to improve your balance."

Myron pushed my father aside with a glare, and grabbed his daughters and wife. They scurried into church. My temples throbbed. My mother made a crude comment under her breath. We entered the sanctuary, and took seats in a pew two rows behind the Bakers.

The Bakers left before the potluck meal. My headache dissipated as Tori, my parents, and I filled ourselves on a plethora of homemade food. After we were stuffed, Tori pulled several plastic containers out of her purse. I brought fried chicken, corn dodgers, and other finger foods with which to fill them. I found a plastic bag and cleared off an entire platter of brownies. After we finished plundering food, my father drove us home. I relaxed while listening to a CD of Scott Joplin's *Treemonisha*.

I changed into black jeans and t-shirt, a black bandana, and donned mirrored sunglasses. After collecting my bag of cannabis and my pipe from behind my sock drawer, I walked downstairs and waited for Tori. She appeared, dressed in black boots, blue denim overall shorts, a red gingham shirt with the sleeves rolled up and a dark blue baseball cap. We packed a knapsack with cookies, brownies, and bottles of water. As we hiked toward the field where I had found the circle of trees, we passed Graeber's barber shop, Swenson's drug store, and Carlson's general store. Most of the businesses were closed on Sundays.

"You ever get the feeling that we climbed into a time machine and ended up in Hootersville?" Tori laughed.

"It doesn't much feel like home around here on Sunday. That's for damned sure." I laughed with her. "At least Mama and Papa are doing better these days. I was buggin' for a minute."

"To be honest, so was I. Gina too. The depression came on so fast. I figured that between the nation going cray-cray after the terrorist attacks, and the fact that they always have an ace up their sleeves, the situation would level, and it did." Tori and I walked across an area of high grass and entered the protective circle of trees.

"Do you ever feel guilty? I mean about the piracy? I enjoy the results, don't get me wrong. I'm pretty sharp at finding new ways to score, if I do say so. Sometimes, though, I wonder if it's kosher. I mean, somewhere there has to be a line between right and wrong." I grabbed my sack and unloaded.

"I dig the flip. I don't know where that line is, though. The rich don't care about us, so why should I give a rip about them? That's how I see it. I get it, though. There's a thin line between legal and criminal, and Mama and Papa use it as a jump rope." Tori pulled out a silver zippo lighter.

I loaded a bowl of pot and we smoked. In short order, I found myself enveloped in the warm, comforting cocoon that I sought. We smoked a second bowl and laid back with our heads resting on our hands.

"So, when did you start smoking out, bro?" Tori was mellow and subdued.

"Couple of years ago was my first time. Gerry Trice got me into it. I used to hit the parties with his crowd. I drank some too, but I never got hammered like the other kids. I mean, with everything so cray-cray at home, the parties seemed like a comfortable place to hang. I don't know why. You know I've always felt better flying solo than at shindigs." My brain flowed like thick molasses.

"Damn, bro. That's some hard dudes. I was hanging out with Ali Svinnef most of the time, or over at the Sourek's. Gina hung at the Sourek's, too. They always had plenty of extra food for dinner and they let us spend the night. I think they realized that our lives weren't all that happy. As you said, everything was so wigged out at home. I didn't know you were hanging with Fly's crowd. I might have stepped in. Glad you didn't get in too much trouble." She grabbed two bottles of water and handed me one.

"Those cats were cool. No one ever tried anything, or involved me in stuff. I sat and nursed a beer, or had a couple shots of whatever. After I smoked out the first time though, man it was awesome. I love this feeling." I laughed. "Have you tried some of that stuff Fisher brews? Outrageous!"

"Yeah. I have some now and then. I'm still not sure how I feel about Fly getting my baby brother stoned and serving him booze. I guess as long as you're not in trouble. I know parties and hanging out aren't your bag. You'd rather do your kata, or read a book. Fisher thinks you're a regular guy. I'm glad to see you try to make friends. So, what are we doing about your chick?" Tori smiled over at me.

"I can't even get near her. I'm worried. I know what's going on. It's obvious. Steph has my cell number in case she needs help. But, what the hell can I do? Nothing. Not a damned thing." I shook my head as a few tears fell. Tori hugged me.

"Once school starts you can see her every day. That's two more months. Make a move at lunch or something. I wish they could come over to hang out." Tori took out a bag of oatmeal raisin cookies we had grabbed at church. "Did you see Myron this morning? I don't think anyone's ever called him out like that."

"Pestilent douchebag!" I snarled. "I'd like to crush his knee and smash his face!"

We sat eating and relaxing. The silent void we occupied was pleasant. We smoked some more, and then wandered through the town sipping water. The supper smells coming from the various houses were enticing.

"It's weird, sis. I feel cool right here and now. And when I'm around Papa or his friends I feel like I belong. But, when I'm hanging with the cats from our neighborhood, I feel awkward. It's like I don't know how to react and a lot of their conversations seem sophomoric." I sipped my water.

"It makes sense. You've never been much of a kid. Since you were five you've always been a pirate first. You read far beyond your grade level and spend your time immersed in books. Plus, I think we've always had less structure than other cats. You compensated by growing up too fast." Tori shrugged. "I did too, and so did Gina."

We walked toward home feeling mellow. That evening I sat on the porch reading *Hetty* by Charles Slack. I was still relaxed, and yet the effects of my earlier activities were wearing off.

From the kitchen I could hear Miles Davis on CD. My father was deboning a ham he'd brought home a few days earlier. As I sat relaxing, Myron Baker flew down the road in his truck. People in their yards looked, and then looked away. Some children playing near the streets dove into their yards. At that same moment there was a vibration in my pocket. I reached into my shorts and whipped it out. Heather Baker was calling -- in hysterics. I ran inside and handed the phone to my mother.

Sensing something was wrong, I told my father. He put the ham in the refrigerator. Tori came into the kitchen. I informed her we might have a problem. We stood in the living room awaiting instructions. Ten minutes later my father walked to his office. He put on a lightweight jacket over his shoulder rig -- his Beretta M9 in place. He had packed heat maybe four times in my entire life. He handed me three empty rolling suitcases and I put them into the minivan. Tori returned to her room.

My father and I walked down the block, entering the Baker's house without knocking. The interior set-up was different than our house. My father had the pistol in his hand as he turned each direction checking the room. "We're clear, son! Move it. Help the girls pack, and load the van."

I stepped through the door, crabbed sideways with my hands in ready position, and mentally re-checked the sight-lines. Heather Baker was standing by the kitchen looking much like a deer in the headlights. I approached, and wordlessly hugged her. She tried to smile, and then pointed toward Steph and Caroline. I heard sobbing, turned, and saw the girls huddled against a wall holding each other. There was blood drying on the left side of Steph's mouth.

I let out a low growl, "You just sealed your fate, you bastard!" I took a deep breath and centered myself. There would be time enough later. "Hey, Steph. Caroline.

You're safe now. I brought my papa. We're going to help you. What happened?" I tried to sound comforting, but my voice quavered.

Steph hugged me around the chest, burying her face in my tank-top. "We got home from church. Pa was in a mood. He didn't like what you and your sister said at church." Her voice was raspy.

"He can bleed out!" I snarled.

We joined Caroline in their room and packed all the clothes, stuffed animals and books. Steph pulled out ten dollars from the bottom of her piggy bank. As we took the bags to the hall, I scooped Caroline off the floor and gave her a reassuring hug. "This ends here. You're safe now."

After setting Caroline down, I turned toward Steph. We hugged, and she buried her face in my chest. Something stirred deep inside. I tilted Steph's face up with a soft hand under her chin, and we locked lips. The oral action was hard, full mouthed, needful. We stopped sucking face as quickly as we had started, hauling the bags to the front door.

My father parked the mini-van on the side street, climbed out, and tossed me some threads. I backtracked to the girls' bedroom, and stripped. Steph stared at me in my socks and jockey shorts, her peepers round as banjos, casting her glimmers on the hard muscles I'd built up. I gave her a wink, replacing my shorts and tank top with black jeans and a grey t-shirt. I placed my wallet in the right pocket, house keys in my left, a collapsible baton in a pocket on my right thigh, and a thick money clip of cash into my shirt pocket. As I tied my ground-smashers, Steph knelt down and gave me a squeeze. "Thank you, Vinnie. Thank you."

We loaded the van with bags of clothes and personal items, and I placed three pillows on a seat for Steph. She gave one of them to Caroline, and sat on the other two. I climbed in the back of the van behind Steph and Caroline. My father and Heather sat in front.

As I repacked the garbage bags into suitcases, Heather filled in my father on what had gone down earlier. "When we got home from church, Myron went to the living room to watch a baseball game on TV and drink his beer. The girls and I got supper going, and tried to remain quiet. He was pissed that your daughter and Vinnie called him out for slapping Caroline. It seems like every day one of the girls manages to set him off -- or I do -- and he slaps us, or beats one of the girls. I can't break free. I've got nowhere to turn." Her voice was soft and strained. She held her head in her hands, groaning.

I finished the repacking, and climbed into the seat between Steph and Caroline. Steph leaned against my shoulder saying nothing. I held her close with my hand stroking her thighs. Caroline snuggled into my side and whimpered.

Heather rubbed her forehead. "Myron was finished with his first six pack. It's our life. Myron watches sports and gets drunk when he isn't at the lot running the compactor. I don't like his behavior but I'm scared. I mean, where the hell can I go? Who would want me?"

I scowled, and drew the chicks closer to my body. Caroline was looking over her shoulder repeatedly. She needed lessons in spotting a tail without letting on. I'd read enough Spillane and Robert Parker to keep my claws sharp in that arena. Steph closed her eyes, head on my shoulder, inhaling the smell of my aftershave.

Heather continued recounting the events, and my thoughts grew darker. I wasn't going to debate either way about laying hands on a kid, but there's a line where it moves into physical and sexual abuse. Myron left that line in the dust.

When Heather finished, my father patted her on the

shoulder. "It's going to be all right. This ends here and now." He sounded eerily calm. I'd experienced the vocal level only once, and it left me with the sense that my father could decapitate a man with his thoughts alone. He wasn't a violent man on the regular, but, when pushed, he could crank the levels full force. I was every inch his son in that regard.

Heather groaned. "I finally reached my breaking point. I tried to restrain Myron's arm. He turned and knocked me into the door jamb. Then he said he was going over to the Red Hen to have some whiskey and see the guys. He ordered us to clean the house and make dinner. After he left, Stephanie told me to call you." Heather held her forehead. "I'm having trouble seeing clearly. Everything wants to split in two. Where are you taking us?"

"A place I heard about. They can stash you for a few days until we handle this. Then you have to keep going. Believe me that this isn't going to end well. You can't go back." My father cruised down the street of a neighboring town.

The place was hardscrabble and decrepit. In the open terrain I could see the interstate a few miles before the car arrived there. Driving through an underpass my father made a right and floored the pedal hard up the sweeping on-ramp. We hit the four lane highway above at a good clip.

Steph leaned up and kissed me on the cheek. Her aim being off, I turned my head and kissed her full on the lips. She blushed. "Thank you for coming! Thank you, Vinnie!" Her voice was a frog croak. My father turned on the radio, pressed a button, and Pink Floyd's "Don't Leave Me Now" filled the car.

"I'll always come for you, babe. Just say the word." I stroked her cheek as she nestled closer and closed her eyes again.

Chapter Nine

Heather sat holding her head, looking pale. "Stand" by Poison crackled through the speakers. That was followed by "In My Time of Dying" by Led Zeppelin. An hour later my father pulled off at an exit, and drove past a sign that read "Welcome to Pardmest."

The town of Pardmest is nothing but a strip mall, a gas station, a hog feed store, and an adult video store. We stopped at the strip mall, and I dashed inside of a burger chain trading five gift cards for double cheeseburger meals. I paid out of pocket for milkshakes. I was in a hurry and had no time to dance with a manager in order to get the shakes for free. As my father drove toward the edge of town, we all ate in silence. "Crazy Diamond" by Pink Floyd accompanied our meal.

On the edge of Pardmest sat an old, three story, Victorian style house that had once been a motel. The motel had gone out of business instead of competing with the cluster of economy hives five miles to the south. An organization dedicated to assisting abused women and children purchased the hotel building for use as a shelter. There was an enormous garage below the building. My father pulled up to the front of the shelter at high speed and slammed on the brakes.

"Stay put, son. Watch the girls. I need to arrange for them to stay here. At least for tonight."

As my father climbed out of the van and approached the building Caroline leaned across me and whispered. "You OK Steph?"

"My butt and my legs are on fire, and it hurts to move. I'm scared. What are we going to do now?" Steph whispered back.

"I don't know. We have to take care of each other, I

guess. Like the time when Pa left for three days after he and Ma had that fight. Remember how Ma had to go to the hospital, and told us not to tell anyone? Remember she was in bed all day? We took care of each other. But now we have Vinnie and his pa." Caroline began to cry. I cuddled both of them.

"I'll take care of you like I always do. You have to be brave OK? You just have to be." Steph rasped, brushing the tears from Caroline's eyes with caressing fingers.

"Hey! If my father says you're going to be safe, then you can wrap your ass in a sling and bet it." I kissed Caroline on the forehead, and Steph on the lips. "If your dirtbag father comes looking around, I have a mind to take him jitterbugging at knuckle junction. He might be flushed out in the strength department, but if you take the tallest guy in the world, shatter his knee, that's a universal equalizer. Then it's a simple side kick to the face. End of story."

My father and Heather approached the house and knocked. A woman answered who was a few hairs south of six foot. She had short cropped auburn hair and the shoulders and chest of a wrestler I had seen on TV once. Dressed bottom to top in biker boots, jeans, and a sleeveless flannel shirt she looked intimidating. The lady eyeballed Heather, said something, and glanced beyond her at the van. My father was pointing at the van and motioning with his hands.

He and the lady were talking when, in a moment of inglorious agony, Heather blew her groceries on the floor of the porch, collapsing in a heap. I grabbed Caroline to keep her from jumping out of the van. "Both of you, grab some seat cushion. Please. We make like statues until Papa comes to get us." I looked out the window.

"Holy Hell! Roz! Come quick. Bring Becca with you." The burly woman shouted into the door of the shelter loud enough for us to hear her.

A woman, Steph's height, but built of solid muscle, came running. She had medium length, spiky blonde hair, a ruddy complexion, and intense eyes. On her heels was a chick barely out of high school. The barely-legal had straight, raven black hair to her shoulders and dark piercing eyes. Her skin was milky white in contrast to her hair. Seeing Heather collapsed in a pool of vomit and taking notice of the three of us in the van, the raven-locked girl ran to us, climbed into the driver's seat and spoke over her shoulder. "Hey guys, my name's Becca Dunwoody. Hold on tight, we're going in."

She turned the key and the motor roared to life. Pulling a remote from her pocket and pressing a button, she waited for the garage door to open, pulled forward, and parked sideways. We climbed out.

Up a flight of stairs, we entered a living room. Roz was setting Heather down on a couch. Checking vitals, she determined that Heather was breathing normally, but unresponsive. Roz did a bit more checking with a pen-light and stated that a concussion was likely.

"She needs medical attention, Pat." Roz said to the lady who had first appeared at the door. "I can call Otis. He's got corpsman training. If anything needs to happen beyond that he can call it in without involving us."

"I've had first aid training as well, and survival training as a young man," my father stated. "Why don't you get the kids settled somewhere, let me take a look at Heather."

Becca led Steph, Caroline, and me up a long staircase and into a bedroom with two double beds. The lady called Pat followed us, and Becca looked back at her. "Any chance of getting these kids some food, or ice cream, while we talk?" Steph's eyes lit up as did Caroline's. Not much bad can happen that ice cream won't excite a kid.

Pat headed downstairs and returned with three plates of roast beef sandwiches and chips. Placing the tray of plates on a side table with cans of Dr Pepper she told us, "you kids can eat as much as you like. If you want more let Becca know. I need to go tend to your mother but my friend here will keep you company."

Becca was talking to Steph and Caroline, when I heard someone knock a 1-3-2 pattern from downstairs. I assumed that Myron had shown up, or that he had sent someone else to bring back Heather and her daughters. On instinct I moved down the steps with the idea of protecting Steph and her family. A man entered the giant living room that had once been the hotel lobby.

I saw the moves I would need. A front kick to the right kneecap, and a single point punch to the manhood. Once he dropped, I would follow up with a kick to the ribs and a crushing stomp to the neck. I was moving in to make a preemptive strike, when the lady called Roz told my father that the man was Otis LeMar. Otis was six and a half feet tall, built like a brick wall, and had a rich, reddish-bronze skin tone inherited from his Creole mother and his Creek father. I learned his heritage later. His black hair hung down the back of his head in a braid. He wore tennis shoes, cargo pants and a combat vest over a bulging bare chest. His arms were built like two cannons and his hands like anvils.

"She's on the couch Otis." Pat pointed.

As Otis was checking on Heather, I moved over to my father's side. "Papa. What's the buzz? I mean, aside from the obvious. Mama and Tori are home alone. I know you left the gun, but even so. That scumbag comes back, and he finds his wife and daughters gone, he's for damned sure going to start looking. Our house is the first place he'll inquire." I remained calm and focused.

"Straight gospel. You do well under pressure. I

noticed you moving in on Otis. I appreciate that, but try to not act precipitously. Unless you know someone's a danger to us, please drop it into low gear." My father patted me on the shoulder to ease the rebuke, and then hugged me. "As to your sister and mother, Beth Stratton is picking them up. She's a friend of your mother's. In all likelihood they're on the way here. Carlos Sanchez and his sons are watching our house. They're armed. Uncle Vasily and some other men are driving to Harvest Junction. There's stuff you don't need to know, but trust me that there are procedures to handle this sort of problem."

I nodded. "What are my orders?" As I spoke, Becca stepped in and motioned me upstairs. My father nudged me toward the stairs so I went. "Son, please play it in a minor chord until I say otherwise."

I stepped into the bedroom upstairs. Steph lay on her belly on a bed. Tears wet her cheeks. Caroline was sitting far back on the other bed hugging her knees. They both looked petrified as the adrenaline wore off, and fear filled the voids.

I sat beside Steph, rubbing her shoulders. "It's copacetic, chicks. There's a regular bull of a guy down there. I could take him if needs be, but he looks to be friend not foe."

Steph looked up at me, her tears starting again. The adrenaline was wearing off faster now. She readjusted her position and put her head in my lap. I reacted in a way that didn't fit the situation. I tried breathing, and thinking about something else, but there was no hope for it. I had feelings for Steph.

Becca sat holding Caroline's hand. "I need to know what happened. I can't help unless I know."

Steph heaved an irritated sigh. "You can't help anyway. No one can. Pa told me to do something, and I didn't do it immediately. He had to give me a whipping.

Ma came in and told him to stop, and he pushed her away. She tripped on something, and fell in the doorway. It was an accident."

Becca gave us sympathetic eyes. "Do these accidents happen often? What could be so important for you to do that you deserve to be whipped for it?"

Steph glanced at Caroline who returned the look. "Ma's clumsy sometimes. We are too. I try to be good, but Pa told me to do a chore, and I didn't get right on it. Children have to obey their parents. It's in the Bible."

Becca shook her head. "It's important to tell us the truth about what happened. We need to know because your mother might get sicker if we don't treat her properly."

If looks could kill, Becca would have been six feet under and Steph would've been up on capital charges. "I'm not lying! I have to protect Ma and Caroline. I told you the truth. I'm not letting us get sent away to some home for bad kids. Not going to happen!"

It was time to cut the bluffing, and lay the cards on the table. "Steph? Caroline? Do you trust me? Do you trust my father?" I stroked Steph's hair. "I dig that you don't know us enough for full trust, but I've been playing every angle to spend time with you. I heard what your mother said went down. I swear I'll protect you both. With my life if it comes to that. You've seen me in my backyard this summer working out in the early bright. Have no doubts that I can keep you safe. Your father is only human, and humans rely on their knees to stand. Next time I see him, his knees won't work if you dig the riff. And, he's going to have problems his cranium can't tolerate. So please, tell her what she wants to know."

Steph and Caroline started crying and poured out the entire story. The more they spoke, the more I wanted to kill Myron Baker. For some reason, I also craved for some of Billy Bob Fisher's tonic. The anger welling up was making me thirsty, I figured.

Becca reached out and stroked the girls' heads one at a time. They flinched. She handed Steph and Caroline each a box of Kleenex. "I've lived through similar events. My mom was an alcoholic, and my dad too. I had to get help when I was fifteen because they were always beating on me. I never told anyone about them drinking. See, they said if I told I would be sent to juvenile hall, or a group home, and get nasty things done to me."

Steph looked up, shocked that someone understood. "Yeah. I know. I'm never going to those places, and neither is sissy. Anyone tries that and..." Steph slammed a fist on the side table, rattling the dishes.

I helped Steph sit up on a pillow, and held her in my arms with her face on my chest. On instinct I ran a hand over her back and behind, but stopped when she flinched. I could feel her against my body, and reacted to it. In the midst of the crisis, part of me wanted nothing so much as to make the beast. I never had, but I'd read books describing the process.

There was a knock on the door, and Tori walked in with Otis LeMar. Tori looked at me, and then surveyed the room, "He needs to talk to Steph and Caroline. Papa's downstairs with their mama. Mama's in the kitchen with two of the ladies who run this place. You and I need to talk, bro." Tori helped Steph move over to where Caroline was sitting. I stood and looked at Otis.

"Hey! What's your name?" Otis' voice had a snap to it.

"Vinnie. Be careful with them. They're real fragile. And, I'm real protective." I shot attitude right back.

"Vinnie. I'm Otis. I saw what you were starting to do down there. I don't know where you trained, but you have good moves and solid instincts. We should talk later." Otis put out a hand and we shook.

I walked over to Tori. Otis looked at the girls and squatted by the bed. "I have some herbs boiling on the stove downstairs. Mrs. Il-Cazzo is coming up in a few minutes with a poultice. Stephanie is it? You need to put it on your butt and thighs," Otis took a breath. "Your mother's going to be fine, given time. She needs help, and that over a long while. So do you both. She has a concussion. I can treat it, but I need to know what happened. No jive, no defense, straight."

Caroline looked confused. "We know she's sick. Why does everyone keep calling us liars?" Her voice turned defiant and almost irritated. "Fine. Pa drinks a lot. He gets angry a lot. We don't talk about that, see? We aren't supposed to ever talk about it. Not ever. Yes, Pa whipped sissy. He shoved Ma so hard she hit her head on the doorway. But, if you tell anyone I said so, I'll tell our friend Vinnie to bash your head in like Pa said he would do to me if I ever talked out of turn. You got that? I will tell him to kill you!"

I froze for a brief moment, and Tori stood staring at Caroline. Becca backed off several steps. Steph grabbed Caroline and pulled her away, scared, eyes focused on Otis.

Otis looked down at the girls. "Yes ma'am, I hear you. I don't need to tell anyone else. I got this. So, if anyone tries to hurt you, your sister, or your mother ever again I will personally cripple the motherfu…the dude. You best believe."

Steph looked up at him and nodded. She had an interesting firmness when she set her jaw. "Good. We understand each other. Sorry that my sister threatened you. I'll talk with her later about respect."

"No need. She's in defensive mode, and that's good." Otis left the room. Tori and I followed him.

"Vinnie. I talked to Mama. This whole situation's a train wreck. We're staying here tonight, and tomorrow morning, Papa, Mama, you, and me, our aunt downstairs, and our cousins are going on vacation. To see Gina, and then to The Spectacle Resorts. Someone at the resort will take over from us and move the ladies further." Tori looked a bit uncomfortable.

"Cool. I'm ready. Whenever we need to move, just give the word." I nodded.

"Papa wants you and me to teach our cousins in there some basic survival skills and basic piracy. That should be easy enough, maybe even fun. But I'm seeing another problem that they aren't. Vinnie, this whole situation is cray cray. As much as you're a giant ball of testosterone, you need to keep focused on helping out. Please don't try making a move on Steph. I'm serious. You need to chill with respect to her." Tori gave me a serious look.

"Savvy. I'll do my part, and try not to complicate matters. But I do like Steph, and if she obliges, I am damn sure going to let her know it by any means possible. Might not get another chance. You feel me?" I gave her a serious look of my own. We walked downstairs and I chatted with my parents about what was happening. Three cups of coffee and some cherry pie later, I knew enough to help out.

After talking to my parents, I spent a half hour with Otis. He told me about his background, and asked if I knew anything about the military. He suggested that I read about special forces, and that I keep training in the martial arts.

I returned upstairs with three bowls of vanilla ice cream. Caroline had changed into her nightgown, and Steph was in a long t-shirt on her belly, with a flannel poultice on her flanks. I served the ice cream, and climbed onto the bed next to Steph. We ate, and soon after we were holding each other in a warm, soft embrace. Steph relaxed as Becca turned on the radio in the background before leaving the room.

"What is this music? I've never heard it before." Steph rasped and yawned.

I kissed her on the cheek. "Mahler's Kindertotenlieder."

Chapter Ten

The next morning, I woke up moments before true dawn. Steph was asleep beside me under the covers minus her t-shirt. Caroline was in the other bed in her nightgown engaged in soft somniloquy. I had an issue to deal with. I needed a shower, and a change of underclothes. My t-shirt was good for another day, as were my jeans. I had removed my shirt and kicked the jeans off after Caroline was asleep. What remained clothing-wise needed to be either laundered or trashed. It had been pleasant, a lot of kissing and cuddling, nothing more than that, but it was enough.

I moved Steph's hand from my chest, and slid out of bed. I located the bathroom, turned on the shower, and shoved my jockey shorts under some trash in a can. After my shower I emerged in my clothes from the previous day. The girls were still asleep. A light knock on the door startled me.

I stepped back, and to the side, before flinging the door open. It was Tori. "Vinnie?" She whispered. "I heard the shower running from next door. I brought your knapsack last night with as many clothes as I could fit in it. I forgot to give it to you."

I smiled at her, and grabbed my sack. "Thank you. I was wondering what to do. I'm going to change."

The chicks were still asleep, so I laid out jockey shorts, chinos, a polo shirt, socks, and Nikes on a chair. I stripped and began changing, when Steph let a giggle escape. I turned and winked at her.

"I thought you were both asleep, else I would have changed in the bathroom."

Steph grinned like a Cheshire cat, and nodded. I chuckled and kissed her on the lips while stroking her face.

"You should go wash, and get dressed," I traced a

finger over her freckled belly and up to her chest.

Steph sat up gingerly, wincing, before walking to the bathroom with some clean clothes. Caroline came to, and a half hour later she emerged from her bath. The three of us crept downstairs. Two other families were sitting in their rooms. I waved, and several children waved back. I saw no men, but there was a black lady with an unkempt afro, and her arm in a sling. She had five children of various ages, in various stages of undress; three boys, two girls. In another room was a light-skinned Hispanic lady with black hair that had been shaved to accommodate bandages. Her eyes were swollen. She was in her room with two daughters, who likewise had swellings and cuts.

We entered the kitchen where my parents and the three ladies who ran the shelter were all enjoying coffee. Tori was in the living room with Heather and Otis LeMar. I gave my mother a kiss on the cheek, and hugged my father.

"Morning, gates, let's dissipate. I'd have come down sooner, but the ladies needed to freshen up first." I winked at my father who laughed.

Tori walked into the kitchen, and I hugged her. "What's cooking good looking?"

"Nothing but spaghetti, and that ain't ready." She hugged me back

Pat and Roz poured orange juice and started making bacon and scrambled eggs. "We usually bring breakfast to the rooms." Becca yawned. "Did you sleep all right?"

"It was very nice. The bed I mean." Steph blushed and hid her face in her hands.

Tori shot daggers at me with her eyes, and my father gave me a sideways look. "I'm glad you slept well, Steph."

"So, when do we light out?" I shrugged at Tori.

My father scowled at me a moment, shook his head, and chuckled under his breath. "First, you kids need to get your feed on. Then, I want you girls to sit with your mother while Vinnie helps carry food to the various rooms with Ms. Dunwoody." He motioned to Becca. "We'll leave after lunch."

Roz brought us each a plate piled with sliced melon, eggs, bacon, and toast. I drew one on the dark, sipped coffee, and looked at Tori. "Did you by chance grab my envelopes, and the stuff from my top dresser drawer?"

"I did. And your laptop and iPod. I wasn't sure what books to bring," Tori smiled. "Oh, and later on, I have a gift for you from Fisher, as well."

After we finished eating, Tori sat and made small talk with Steph and Caroline, while I carried trays of food upstairs. What I saw of the people made me angry. Why would anyone hurt someone that way if they professed to love them? It was clear that Steph, Caroline, and Heather were lucky relative to some. Externally, anyway. What they suffered was plenty bad. What I saw of the other families bordered on tragic. The anger welled up, and I found myself wanting a drink. I assumed that there would be beer or something in the kitchen. I was planning to look -- when I heard a commotion downstairs.

Otis, Tori, and my mother came upstairs leading Heather and the girls. Heather was propped on my mother's shoulder to steady her. Caroline was frantic, and Steph had a hand over her mouth as if to hold back vomit. They all slipped into a bedroom and shut the door. I walked downstairs, easy and loose. My father was nowhere to be seen nor were Pat or Roz. Becca was at the door talking to a police officer.

I gave a curt nod. "Thanks for letting me use the can, miss. Want me to get on weed whacking, or do I mow the lawn first?" Becca was quick on the uptake.

"Why don't you go get some water first? We have empty milk jugs, and hot as it is, you would waste less time if you put a gallon on the porch instead of running inside every fifteen minutes." Becca had some snap to her voice.

I entered the kitchen, and my father motioned to me from the door that led down to the garage. I tiptoed over to him, and on his signal slipped downstairs.

"The police showed up a few minutes ago. I suspect that Myron called them when he got home. This being the only women's shelter in the county, the cops must have made a beeline. They don't have a warrant, and Ms. Dunwoody insisted on one. We need to move, right now. Once we get the all clear help bring down the suitcases." My father was crisp.

As we waited on the signal, I helped my father unscrew license plates from the van and two cars. We switched up the plates in case anyone decided to run them. It was a simple trick, but one that would buy us an extra half hour or so to escape.

Becca opened the door upstairs and flashed the lights. Pat and Roz emerged from a closet. I hadn't heard them move inside their hiding spot, and my hearing was sharp. Roz climbed inside one vehicle, and Pat climbed behind the wheel of another. My father sat in the passenger seat of the van. He motioned me to move.

I gave the 1-3-2 knock, and Otis let me in. I helped load the suitcases into the back of the mini-van. Everyone got situated, with my mother driving. Steph, Caroline, and I snuggled together in the far back with the luggage surrounding us. I held my right hand just below Steph's belly, stroking her.

Pat took off heading east in a Ford pickup. She texted my father that she was being followed. Roz waited ten minutes and drove south in a Volkswagen. She texted that she was also being followed and that she'd picked up two more police cars. They were riding her bumper and, being the nice person she was, she led them through town for another ten miles before stopping at an adult video store. The police didn't follow her inside, for some odd reason. A half hour later, she led them back to the shelter. They departed without any further issues.

Pat, meanwhile, proceeded to drive thirty miles to a shopping mall. When she stepped out of her truck an officer asked permission to search the inside. She was agreeable, and, of course, he found nothing. She texted that he was irritated, but that she couldn't help how he felt.

While Pat and Roz were playing games, my mother pulled away in the van. My father handed Otis a cell phone to call to some friends. The van was presently surrounded by three slow moving farm vehicles. The cops behind us lost sight of the van as my mother pulled onto the freeway. A half hour later, Tori called out "Allez Allez Oxen Free!" The girls and I climbed into the rear-most seats and buckled up.

As my father explained to me later, constabulary presence is slim in the skidsville towns like Pardmest. Nothing like enough cops to properly tail anyone. So, it's easy to ditch them with some advanced planning. He and Otis had worked out the details for this contingency the previous night.

We drove west for an hour and then stopped to rearrange the seating and switch the license plates again. We turned onto a two lane road lined on both sides with establishments geared to the tastes and economic capabilities of lower income citizens. There were strips of pawn shops, off-brand fast food emporiums, used car dealerships, dollar stores, and no contract cell phone dealers. Bars and adult entertainment venues were crammed between the stores. A few miles ahead the businesses thinned out in favor of partially empty trailer courts and abandoned lots. Otis took the wheel and drove for another half mile until, to one side, I saw lights strung through the trees and a clearing in the woods.

The clearing had a hardscrabble shack in the center and tables and chairs set around it in the gravel and dirt. The shack had a chimney which was belching smoke and heat. The smell of slow-cooked meat wafted through the air.

"OK with everyone?" Otis inquired.

"Looks fine to me. Smells delicious." My mother sounded cheerful.

"Good for us, too" Heather murmured, holding an ice pack against her forehead.

Once Otis parked, I stepped out with my father and scouted the surroundings. After giving the all clear sign, we helped Heather and the girls out of the van. Tori, my mother, and Otis climbed out behind them. One happy family, we found a table.

The place had no name, and no menu. There was a choice of meat, slaw, either white bread or baked beans on the side, and three different kinds of canned soda-pop. Styrofoam plates, plastic forks, paper napkins, cash only. The place was as anonymous as one could ask for. Otis had been there before, and was planning to part company with us after lunch. He knew someone who would give him a ride back to Pardmest.

We each ordered a half rack of ribs. Tori and I chose the beans, as did my parents and Otis. The Bakers opted for bread. We all had Dr. Pepper. The air was warm, the food simple yet tasty. We ate with some leisure, but I kept an eye out for the police and other undesirables.

"Steph, what's your favorite subject in school?" Otis made an attempt at small talk.

"I like English and science." Steph's voice was improving, but still hoarse.

"I like reading and music class." Caroline took a large gulp of Dr. Pepper.

"Always liked reading, myself. Never much cared for science until later in life. I think it's good that you enjoy school. It helps later on." Otis looked everywhere and nowhere at once.

"You sound like you didn't like school." Heather frowned while sucking a bone.

"Didn't like it?" Otis cocked his head to the side, making a face. "I loathed it. To be fair it wasn't the education that bothered me. The teachers had big mouths, and they reported a lot of crap to my pops. I always felt like I was in his way, and then if they reported some imagined, or wholly fabricated wrong I'd committed, it caused more issues. He always believed the teachers, and after browbeating me, I would say that yeah, I had done whatever. Rarely had I done a damned thing. I suspect that my teachers looked for excuses to be jerks because they had unhappy lives. They knew my father would believe them, so I was a good target. I've always thought my father was irritated by life and used those reports as an excuse to get pissed at me."

Heather shuddered. "I've known people like that. One of the reasons I left home, and got involved with Myron, was to escape parents like that."

Caroline was shifting in her seat, so I escorted her to the facilities, no more than an old fashioned outhouse. We returned to hear Heather commenting that if Myron ever found the girls, he would kill them.

Inside my chest cavity a hot rage mixed with something stronger than sadness. I walked a short distance – stood by a tree -- and scanned the parking lot. Otis approached and gave me a chuck on the shoulder. "I'm out of here, Il-Cazzo. You're a real tough kid. I see it in your face. Take care of them. All of them. But, don't do anything hasty. Here, I want you to have this." He handed me a switchblade knife. "You know how to handle that?"

"Thank you. I know what to do if it comes to that. If you're ever in Harvest Junction..." I stared into space.

"Yeah. Take care." Otis walked away and climbed into a car.

Tori approached and put an arm around my shoulder. She had a twenty ounce pop bottle filled with Fisher's moonshine. "Here. Have a few slugs of this. Cool your jets."

I pulled at the bottle. The liquid numbed my sharp edges. I still wanted to hunt down Myron Baker, but the feeling was blunted. I took a third good suck off the bottle, capped it, and handed it back to Tori. We walked back and loaded up. I fell asleep in the car with Steph in my arms, and Caroline's face in my lap.

Two hours later we pulled into a hotel. It was a two story horseshoe with plenty of parking. Most of the slots were occupied which gave us some cover. The place was an off-chain establishment, plain looking, and built of stucco blocks with metal stairs and railings. Not a pay and lay, it was as anonymous as we could hope for. My father informed me and Tori that several support networks used the place while moving abused spouses across the nation. Pat had given him the location.

I entered the lobby with my father, and we secured a second story room with a view of the parking lot. After moving the ladies in for the night, my father set up a chair by the window to watch for police. Tori chatted with my mother, and then walked three blocks with me before we located a convenience store with supplies. I was uncomfortable with trying to plunder so we paid cash. Unsure what the girls would enjoy eating, we shot the works by food group.

On the way back, we stopped in an alley and smoked a joint. The effects were fast acting and caused the tension in my temples to ease. Returning to the room with two grocery bags, I unloaded large quantities of candy, chips, and snack cakes. Tori started the coffee, and we settled in as Steph and Caroline lay on a bed watching a cooking show on television. My mother was tending to Heather who said she felt better. After icing Heather's head my mother suggested she sleep.

The girls were drinking milk and eating Fritos and bean dip while they watched some Jacks and Jills making food for a panel of judges. I sat in a chair and caught a nap. The pot was having the desired effect. A few hours later, I woke up as Tori tucked in Caroline and read her a bedtime story about David and Goliath from the Gideon Bible. After Caroline fell asleep, Tori positioned herself by the door and was sawing logs in no time. I sat watch by the window with my father and drank coffee. Steph perched on two pillows on the floor beside me, resting against my legs, and dozed off. My mother had fallen asleep on the bed beside Heather.

At midnight I heard movement in the room. I looked over at the exact moment Steph sat bolt upright crying and screaming. I moved down to sit by her side as my father flipped on a light.

"Shhh. It's OK. You're safe. No one's going to hurt you now. Vinnie's here." I tried for soothing.

"I...I'm sorry. I should have fought back or behaved better or..." Steph rasped crying. Caroline climbed out of bed and walked over. Heather started getting up but my mother told her to lay still. Tori came over and sat holding a wet washcloth against Steph's face.

"It isn't your fault. You did nothing to be sorry for." Tori hugged Steph from behind and held her. "You let it out, ok.

A half hour later Tori tucked Caroline back into bed and sat down beside her. I fell asleep sitting against a wall with Steph's head on my lap. She tossed and turned several times but I stroked her and she settled down. At seven in the morning, I woke up. My father was sitting, watching out the window. He hadn't moved all night.

Chapter Eleven

The others woke and showered. We checked out, and I removed two gift cards for Pancake Shack from my envelope. They were each worth forty dollars. We raided the motel's donuts, juice, and coffee, before climbing into the mini-van. I saw a stout man in a John Deere hat filling a forty-eight ounce plastic cup with coffee. I made a mental note to procure a few similar mugs.

My father drove us to the state line before locating the restaurant. We parked in the rear of the lot, and my father left the keys in the front seat. I was about to say something, but he shot me a look. I put an arm around Heather's waist, and the other around Steph's shoulders. Tori and Caroline followed, and then my parents. We were greeted by a short, plump, African American lady who led us to a table in the back. I sat facing the entire restaurant with my father on one side and Steph on the other.

I poured a mug of coffee and patted Steph's hand. "Want some coffee, doll? Caroline?"

"I don't know if we're allowed. Pa never let us." Steph looked at Heather.

"You probably won't like the taste, but go right ahead. The rules have changed a bit." Heather smiled wanly.

I poured Tori a cup, and filled mugs for Steph and Caroline. Steph added cream and sugar. before sipping. She seemed to enjoy the taste. Caroline made a yucky face, pushing hers away.

"I guess coffee isn't your cup of tea. You'll develop a taste after a while. You seem to enjoy it though, babe." I looked at Caroline and then Steph. "By the way, if someone is ever bothering you, I mean in a threatening way, and you happen to have coffee in your cup, dump it in his lap." I chuckled. "Or, throw it in his eyes."

"Yeah. Then slam the mug across the side of his head. Or, if you have a paper cup instead of a mug, take your hands and clap them hard on his ears," Tori nodded.

"What are you teaching them?" Heather scowled.

"Some basic selfdefense. They could well use it. You too ma'am." I shrugged.

"Vincenzo! Torrence! Show a little respect for Mrs. Baker." My mother glared. "I should think you might ask before telling her daughters such things. That might not be her way."

We looked contrite. "Sorry Mama. Sorry Mrs. Baker." We both sat eating without speaking, until my father cleared his throat.

"Actually, honey, I might be to blame. I asked them to teach the girls some basics. Heather and they have a long road ahead. If anything happens it's for the best that they can survive on their own until help arrives." My father looked at Heather. "My dear Antoinette is correct about respect, however. You're their mother, and have full say so."

"I suppose it's fine. We need help, but I don't want my daughters becoming thugs. Young ladies, if you're in danger, fighting is acceptable. So help me, if you even think about hurting other people without a reason, I will peel your butts. Don't start down that path. Fighting is a last resort." Heather was sharp. She groaned and held her head.

Caroline nodded and ate her food. Steph set her coffee down. "Maybe if you knew how to fight we wouldn't be in this mess."

Heather began crying with her face in her hands. Steph started in crying as well. "I'm sorry. I should have done more. You girls deserve better." Heather took the napkin proffered by my mother, and blew her nose.

"I dig that you felt stuck in the situational morass, but that's over. Isn't it better that I teach them how to prevent a reoccurrence of the situation? I could teach you too, if you like." I put one arm around Steph, and one under the table in her lap. Her tears eased, and she dried her face.

"I appreciate that, young man. I grew up believing that girls only fight if there is no other option. Stephanie's words sting, but she is correct. So, yes, teach them what you can.

After everyone was finished, I paid with the gift cards, and instructed that the remaining balance be issued as a tip. I also left a twenty dollar bill. I noticed Heather looking at me with a wary eye.

"Yes ma'am?" I gave her innocent.

"I noticed earlier that you have a great number of cards and coupons and such. You were sorting them at the hotel. Seems odd for a child is all." Heather shrugged.

I looked at my mother who nodded at me. "It's something I do to help out. It saves us money, and you might try it when you get where you're heading. I send emails to restaurants and manufacturers. I tell them my complaints. They send me vouchers, gift cards, and coupons. It works out well."

We walked to the parking lot -- and I panicked. The van was gone. I looked at my father. He winked at me. When we got to the parking spot, all the luggage had been placed inside of a 1969 model Plymouth Satellite station wagon. It looked old but clean.

"Friend of mine swapped with us." My father reassured everyone. "Should hold nine people comfortably, plus a family dog and luggage."

"Guess that takes care of anyone tracking us." Tori said.

"Old trick, kiddo." My mother chuckled.

We all climbed in and got positioned. The adults sat

up front, Tori and Caroline sat in the back seat, Steph and I stretched out in the rear with the luggage. I lay there stroking her bruised butt and thighs through the cotton skirt she wore. My father tuned in an easy listening station and we drove away listening to Rex Smith sing "You Take My Breath Away." To all the world we appeared a family on vacation.

"What kind of tunes turn your crank?" I asked Steph, as I surreptitiously rubbed her inner thighs. She sighed with contentment and moved closer to me.

"Taylor Swift, Zach Brown, Sugarland, and Kenny Chesney. I don't get to listen to music too much. I like Jimmy Buffett too." Steph cuddled closer.

"Yeah, I dig Buffett. Country is cool. I can do without rap. Oldies, like Billy Joel and Elton John, are always a solid option. And I dig easy listening stuff like Mannilow or Zamfir. When I need to chill or want something in the background while I read, Zamfir is aces." I sat up with Steph, and we rested our heads on the back seat.

"Who's Zamfir?" Steph gave me curious.

"They call him master of the pan pipes. Gheorge Zamfir. He's an acquired taste, but I dig his stuff." I removed my iPod from my knapsack, and brought up a selection. "Here, tune your ears in."

Steph sat listening on my earbuds and smiling. In a few minutes her eyes closed, and she fell asleep with her head in my lap. I sat holding her as the miles blew by. Tori and Caroline were playing alphabet bingo while my mother filled in Heather about the plans. My father was driving and drumming on the steering wheel with his fingers.

Five hours later my father pulled off and drove down a smaller road. We stopped at a motel. "All right folks, we disembark here, spend the night and tomorrow visit my eldest daughter. After that it's a straight shot to

Spectacle." My father climbed out of the station wagon

After several hours with Steph's face in my lap, I was stiff. We got out, and I had a good stretch before reaching for my sack. Everyone followed my mother and Heather into the lobby.

My mother leaned over to Heather. "Watch and learn. You never pay full price at a motel like this. You'll be staying at many of these low-level places, too. It's safer, and far more anonymous. Plus, it's cheaper." My mother approached the front desk.

She pushed a bell on the counter and a lady in a crisp, black skirt suit came out of an office. She had olive skin, a tight bun in her jet black hair, and no visible makeup.

"Could I get a room for the night, or are you all booked?" My mother pulled a few bills from her purse.

"We have rooms available. You'll be wanting two of them? Adjoining? One hundred and twenty dollars for both."

"We need one room, and thirty dollars for the night. I doubt you get much business here, and I'm paying cash." My mother stared at the clerk."

"Too many for one room. I can do one hundred for both."

"I suppose we can go down the road. You aren't the only game in town." My mother turned toward us as if to leave.

"I really shouldn't do this, but I see your point. OK. Fifty dollars." The lady was annoyed, but semi-smiled when my mother handed her the cash. "Room 203. If you need anything, call the front desk. It's only me and my husband working here, and he handles the maintenance. You need anything, you call and ask for Phil Lazio." She pointed to a name plate on a door behind her.

Tori elbowed me when I started to laugh. It helped.

"What's that?" My father was standing back with the rest of us,

"Not suitable for children's ears." My mother muttered and took our key.

The room was sparse. There were two queen beds covered in white sheets and crimson comforters. The pillows on the beds were fluffy. A television was affixed to the dresser to discourage removal. There was a desk with an office chair.

"OK, everyone." My father smiled. "The plan is to leave our luggage here. I spotted a Walmart on the way over. If you ladies need anything, extra shorts, shirts, anything, I'm buying. Also, since we'll be traveling without many stops tomorrow, we might want some comestibles to pack out. Crackers, candy, stuff like that."

"You don't have to buy us clothes." Heather looked uncomfortable.

"No, I don't. I want to, however." My father gave Heather a side hug. "About time someone took care of you."

"If you insist, I won't refuse." Heather hugged back. "You did a real number on the lady downstairs. I doubt I could be so pushy."

"Sure, you can. It just takes practice." Tori giggled. "As Mama and Papa always say, never argue with a woman if you can dicker instead."

We left the room and walked three blocks to a Super-Walmart. Steph and I took point. We held hands, but I kept my left hand in my pocket holding the switchblade. Tori was behind us with Caroline and the adults brought up the rear. Nothing happened, but my temples throbbed and my chest hurt the entire way.

I let Heather and her girls lead the way inside. My parents, and Tori, brought up the rear. As we walked, I spotted a board full of posters. There were faces of missing children from across America, but none matching Steph or Caroline. It was far too soon in the game for that.

I caught up with everyone. Heather was buying underwear and socks. "Hey, if burgers and fries sound good for lunch, I have vouchers, and a whole mess of coupons for food."

"That sounds fine." Heather moved to a rack of shirts and shorts.

I turned to Steph. "Hey, while your mama picks out clothes, you and Caroline want a couple of board games or something?"

They both smiled big. Heather started to object, but gave in. Tori and I walked with Steph and Caroline to the toy aisle. The girls chose *Sorry* and *Scrabble*. I bought Steph a copy of a popular book about vampires, and Caroline a book about a kid who does magic. Not my taste, but opinions vary. I also bought Steph a copy of *In Broad Daylight* by Harry N. MacLean.

We found Heather talking with my parents. I pushed the loaded cart to the luggage aisle, where we picked out a rolling suitcase before wandering through the grocery section. I pulled out my envelope of coupons.

"Tell me again, Vinnie. Where did you get all of those?" Heather frowned, and her eyes narrowed.

"I can show you, rather than tell you. I've had my finger on the action for years now. Hey, Steph, grab a bag of chips. Whatever flavor you like. Caroline, grab a pack of cookies."

Tori winked at Heather, and my parents nodded in unison. Heather looked confused. The girls brought over a bag of Salt and Vinegar chips and a package of fudge stripe cookies. I took them and handed the chips to Caroline. I put the cookies in the cart.

"Read the back of that bag, please." I told Caroline. "There should be something on the bottom with a phone number." I winked at Heather.

Caroline studied the bag. "Oh, yeah, here. If you are not completely satisfied with this product, feel free to call our corporate office or email for a replacement." Caroline put the bag in the cart.

"All products have a variation on that. If you've got an address, they send you coupons that make purchases free or almost free." I laughed. "If you have several addresses you get more. A post office box, and several friends works well. You have the friends forward your mail.

Heather shook her head "Does the word scoundrel mean anything to you, young man?"

I shrugged. My parents roared in delight, and Tori looked at Heather "You ain't heard nothing yet, ma'am." Tori giggled. "Baby brother here is a genius at this."

We bought almost eighty dollars' worth of snack foods. With coupons, the cost of groceries was ten dollars. The clothes, toiletries, and other items brought the total to one hundred ninety three dollars. We used a gift card.

"There are ways to get clothes for free, but one step at a time." My father pushed the cart.

We walked to the fast food restaurant near the Walmart exit. As Heather and my parents packed the new suitcase at a table, Tori, the girls, and I ordered food. Using my vouchers, we paid nothing.

After returning to the table with seven large value meals, three family sized orders of chicken nuggets, and seven hot fudge sundaes, we all started eating. Steph stared into my eyes. She was starting to heal some, at least externally.

"You didn't even have to pay! How do you get restaurant coupons?" Steph's voice was improving. She dipped a chicken nugget in Polynesian sauce.

I gave her a wink and curled my upper lip like Elvis. "That takes a bit more creativity, babe. You have to look for restaurants that might make mistakes. Not exclusively in your city, but all over the country. I call and tell them I got an order to go. I asked for no onions, but they put the onions on my sandwich. Usually, the manager sends a few vouchers for free sandwiches, or free meals. All the major chains do it. Even steakhouses, and seafood restaurants, send vouchers to replace messed up orders." I finished my burger and moved to my fries and soda.

"Well, if they make a mistake, shouldn't they fix it?" Caroline chimed in.

I laughed. "Straight from the fridge, kid. Except that most of the time, you're telling them they did, even if they didn't. These places are corporations. They charge a lot of money, and don't pay their employees anything like enough. So, a few free vouchers help us, and doesn't hurt them." I drank soda. "It's the urban pirate way. It'd be a crime not to plunder them."

"You mean that you lie, and justify it to yourself?" Heather gave me a stern look.

My father rolled his eyes and shook his head. My mother and Tori grinned.

"Call it what you will. I'm Robin Hood. I'm also the poor. It gets trickier, too." I grinned. "One can also call directly to a restaurant, and often the manager asks you to come in for a meal on the house. In those cases, it's always the rule to duke the server at least fifty percent of the cost of the meal, and, if possible, closer to seventy-five percent. That way the server is getting the bread instead of the corporate office." I began eating my sundae. Steph belched and giggled.

"Excuse yourself, young lady!" Heather admonished.

"Excuse me. I think I ate too fast." Steph giggled more. Yeah, she was healing.

"So, you people are low level scam artists. But you

have a slight moral code." Heather shook her head at me. "Well, you couldn't have picked a better town to live in. No one ever reports anything, even if they should. And, if your scam works, and you need food..."

"That's my thinking." I interrupted. "By the way, I don't identify as a scam artist. I'm a pirate, but I operate on dry land for now."

My parents nodded, and Tori put an arm around my shoulders. "Pirates forever and always!" She raised a fist in the air.

We finished eating and cleaned the table. Since one should never leave without their free refill, we all topped off our cups before returning to the motel and settling in. Heather lay down for a nap with Caroline. Steph started reading *In Broad Daylight*. My parents were talking in hushed tones about things they said didn't concern me. I started thinking about what Heather had said at the fast food place.

I excused myself to go for a quick walk. My father told me to be cautious, and to check the neighborhood for any heavy police presence. I started walking. Tori walked behind me, and then was by my side. I didn't feel like talking though. For all my defensive bluster I was bothered. Was I a crook? Was piracy wrong? I didn't know. In the midst of the action, it seemed like a total gasser. Everything I read and heard on the news made me believe that my parents were right about corporations screwing the middle class. It was clear, however, that not everyone lived as my family chose to exist. For certain not everyone used prepaid credit cards that had been filled by using counterfeit money. And, what of the cashiers who were found to have accepted the fake bills. Did they lose their jobs? What happened when a recovery group deposited counterfeit money into the bank? Could their ignorance protect the treasurers from arrest?

As I thought about all of this, I realized that in the end, I didn't give a rip as long as I got what I wanted out of the deal. Sure, I helped other people as well, but when the chips were down it was more about helping me. That didn't sit well. I turned to Tori. "You bring the stuff?"

She nodded, and I took two healthy swigs. That stopped my self-analysis. "How much do we have? I can plunder some whiskey or rum if needs be. Might be hard, but it can be done."

"I brought a quart of Fisher's mash. That should be enough. It better be enough, bro. Don't ever let Mama and Papa know. I mean, Papa would understand, but Mama, she'd tear our asses apart." Tori took a swig and put the bottle away.

"Yeah. She's pretty strict for the fact that she abides stealing and scams." I shrugged.

"Scams? Is that what's eating you?" Tori shook her head. "You can't let some half-hipped goody-two-shoes mess you up that way, bro. We don't do a damned thing wrong. The world screws us big time. The rich keep getting richer, and doing so on the backs of the poor. You know that. Dammit, you know that! All we do is take back that which is rightfully ours. If you want to numb your brain, be my guest. But, not over that." Tori hugged me.

Chapter Twelve

Tori and I returned to the room. Caroline and Heather were asleep in one of the beds. My father was napping with my mother in the other bed. Tori sat by a window staring out at the parking lot, and I sat by a wall cuddling with Steph.

At seven everyone was awake. We piled into the station wagon, and headed east to a mom-and-pop diner. It was an honest to goodness, stick-to-your-ribs food, jukebox in the corner, kind of grease joint. I had forgotten that some people celebrated Christmas in July, but there in the corner was a statue of Santa dressed in boots and spurs. There was a Christmas tree decorated in a NASCAR motif, and presents were piled beneath. It was the exact sort of place that an urban pirate never plunders. My father didn't even use a prepaid card. He paid cash for the entire evening.

I was perusing the menu when Caroline asked if she could play the jukebox. There was a few other couples in the place, and some music was already playing. I took out my money clip and handed Caroline and Steph each five dollars to play some songs. Heather walked over with them as my father tracked their every move.

The burgers were juicy, the fries crisp, and the coffee strong. My father told a joke, and that led to everyone contributing jokes they'd heard. The atmosphere was relaxed, and my mind finally stopped debating with itself about the ethics of piracy.

As everyone was digesting, Kenny Rogers hit "She Believes in Me" started playing. I stood, and took Steph by the hand. We stepped away from the table and danced. Holding her close aroused feelings. I knew that she, Caroline, and Heather were in the jam pot, but good. I was equally sure that things were, in all likelihood, cruising toward crashville back home. Myron and the cops would be looking everywhere. At that time and place, though, my thoughts centered on holding Steph forever.

"All My Exes Live in Texas" was the next song. I dipped Steph and we slow danced to Bing Crosby crooning "I'll Be Home for Christmas." A series of faster paced rock and roll songs brought our entire group to their feet. My father was dancing with Heather, my mother with Caroline and Tori. I cut in, lifting Caroline off her feet, swinging her this way and that. She giggled and squealed in delight. To end the evening, Tori and I did the jitterbug to "Rockin' Robin."

At ten we returned to our room. My father sat watch by the window. I slept against a wall with Steph's head in my lap. The fear and confusion inside of me was dissipating. I was starting to believe that we were an extended family on vacation.

The next morning, after grabbing donuts, coffee and juice in the lobby, we packed the station wagon and drove across town. Tori and I were in the backseat with Steph and Caroline. I looked at Steph, feeling a jumble of emotions. I knew this relationship was on a minute timer, and that remaining in contact was going to be impossible. Heather and her daughters were escaping abuse, and, in fact, Heather was engaged in a parental kidnapping. My father and I had discussed the matter during a rest stop. I was afraid for Heather and her daughters, but I was in love with Steph. I wanted her to stay with me. A lot of people say that one can't fall in love at the age of twelve. Well, one can, and I did.

I also knew that being on the run could present serious dangers. The chances of someone taking advantage of the girls, or of Heather, were real. In that case, it was better to prepare them. "Steph? I wanted to give you something. You too, Caroline." I smiled at them. Tori looked at me as I whipped an adjustable club out of my pants.

"If you get separated from your mama keep this handy. If anyone gets cute you use it. Don't club with it. Taking a back swing is less effective. Leave it collapsed as it is now, and jam it as hard as you can into the crotch or the solar plexus. Then pop this side button and snap it open. I'll demonstrate later. Once open, swing it like you were delivering a slap to the face. Straight across the left side of the head. It may well bring about death, but better him than you." Steph shuddered and nodded. Caroline shrunk down, her face trembling.

I slipped Steph the baton, and looked at Caroline. "I think you'd be better with a whistle, and an airhorn. If you have problems, pull the strip from the airhorn and press the button, aiming it at the creeps ears. After that, blow this police whistle, and run at the same time. Get inside the nearest store and scream that you're being hurt. You'll involve the police, but that may be unavoidable." Caroline nodded at me. "I can buy you an airhorn later at a store." I ruffled Caroline's hair, and handed her a police whistle from my keychain.

Heather looked back at us. "I appreciate the need for this, I suppose, but you act like we're heading to war."

"You are." My father and I said simultaneously. My mother laughed. "You're engaged in kidnapping. There's a possibility that an Amber Alert might be out, although for several reasons I doubt it. The likelihood that the police are looking for you is high. Returning home isn't advisable. The only option is to move forward, alone. Knowing how to eat cheap or free, clothe and supply yourself, and how to defend yourself is not without reason. You are at war. Trust no one to be on your side." My father pulled into a parking lot and made a call on his cell phone.

Ten minutes later my sister Gina appeared from behind a building. She was dressed in a long, loose, patchwork skirt, and a light blue t-shirt over which she wore a denim vest. Her blonde hair was long and matted. It resembled clumped straw.

Tori and I ran over. "Gina! Hey, we've missed you!" I hugged her. She returned the hug with enough interest that my ribs liked to have cracked.

"Well, look what blows in when we leave the doors open." Gina hugged Tori. "It's great to see you guys! What's shaking? You were pretty cryptic on the phone, Papa. Who's this?" Gina motioned at Heather and the girls.

We walked along a path by brick and stone buildings. My mother filled in Gina as we approached the campus commons. We ventured inside a building, and Gina led everyone into a study room before locking the door. "It's soundproofed," she said.

Gina asked a series of questions, and Heather answered them. We sat around after that catching up. Listening to Gina provided an intermediate course in urban piracy. I filed the lessons away for future use.

"Life around here is aces," Gina told us. "On my first day I found two computer labs, and a small library that remains open day and night. There are study rooms attached. I keep a blanket and pillow at a friend's dorm room, and retrieve them at night. I study until midnight, and then crash on the floor of a study room. I can sleep until seven. The gym has showers, and the cafeterias have an all you can eat policy. I purchased the minimum food plan, and carry out fruit, miniature boxes of cereal, and sandwiches in my backpack. I use empty soda bottles to carry out juice as well. I even audit courses for free so that I can try testing out of them later." Gina blushed when my father ruffled her hair.

"You OK for clothes?" My mother looked concerned.

"Natch. You raised me, didn't you? There's a

couple of thrift stores in town, and also a warehouse where people drop off clothing to be given away free to the needy. I sign in, and can take two outfits a week. Plus, they have entire packages of new drawers and socks to give away." Gina laughed.

After a half hour we all walked toward a men's dorm. My father explained something to Gina in hushed tones, and slipped her a small fold of bills. She walked inside as we stood around. When she came out an hour later, she handed my father three plastic cards.

My father turned to Heather. He handed her the cards. "After we reach our final destination, you'll need new ID cards. Yours is a Wisconsin driver's license. You're Marion Arnaque. Your eldest is Laverne and her sister is Shirley. Nod and agree that you watch too many TV reruns if anyone asks."

"Where did you get these pictures of us?" Heather looked at the cards.

"I took them with my cell phone. It stays on silent so you never even knew." My mother shrugged. "That does present a potential danger. Even if someone texted your photo, as I did to Gina, you'd be gone before anyone could act on the information."

We left and went to a local Chinese buffet. While everyone was eating, Gina kept giving me looks. I asked her what was up.

"Let's go outside for a few minutes. I need some air," Gina excused us. "Vinnie, I was jawing with Tori on the phone the other day, and we text all the time. I know you don't want advice from your big sister, but tough. Tori tells me that you dig that chick, Steph. I want to be sure that you have protection. If not, I can get you some. I think you're too young to be knocking boots, myself. If you must, I know for damned sure you're too young to be a father."

"Hey, I know about the birds and the bees, OK? I know. Nothing we're doing could lead to pregnancy. I admit that I'm warm for her form. I wish we had time to hook up, but we don't. With fake names and fake ID's? They're running from the law as of two days ago. I'm not stupid, savvy? Don't worry about me." I was irate.

"I'm also not crazy about you drinking or smoking mojo, either. You're still a little kid"

"Little kid my ass! I haven't been a child since I was five. Neither have you or Tori. Don't worry about me. I don't have a problem. I need to relax sometimes. I'm cool. I'm good. I'm fine." I got testy.

"A'ight then. But, if you need anything, or ever aren't fine, text me." Gina hugged me hard, and we walked back inside and grabbed desserts. I filled up several carry out Ziplock bags for Gina.

That afternoon we said our farewells, and my mother took a bunch of photos of everyone. We piled into the station wagon, and my father started driving south. As evening hit, we stopped for a light dinner and restrooms. Afterward, Tori and Caroline laid down in the backseat to sleep. I slept with Steph amongst the luggage, our arms wrapped around each other.

"What was that with your sister earlier?" Steph whispered.

"Nothing. She worries too much. So does Tori. I can handle things. Been doing so since I. was eight. It's cool." I whispered back.

"Since you were eight? Where were your ma and pa?"

"They had some issues going on with dark thoughts, and too much mental pressure. It got handled. That was before we moved down the block from you. Things are copacetic now."

"I'm glad we're together. Can you teach me how to get vouchers and stuff?" Steph snuggled in closer.

"Sure, doll. I'll teach you everything."

Chapter Thirteen

I woke up at six in the morning with a kink in my back. We were parked at a rest-stop, and everyone was asleep except Tori and me. We slipped out of the car and headed to the vending machines for some coffee. My father woke up as we opened the doors, and then fell back asleep.

A half hour later I was in the middle of a strenuous workout from Zui Quan. I transitioned to Goshin Jutsu Kata. Tori worked with me through the forms. Steph climbed out of the car with Caroline, and Tori and I demonstrated some easy moves for them. I showed Steph how to release the collapsible steel baton, and demonstrated how to deliver a blow to the knees with it. The old saying is true; if you take the strongest, tallest man on earth and crush his knees, he'll fall. Then it's a lot easier to seal his fate.

After the self-defense lessons, we found some dirty, but serviceable, shower stalls. The water required a quarter for five minutes. Talk about a scam! I was going to invite Steph to join me in a shower stall, but I was sure that I wouldn't enjoy the response from my parents or her mother.

After breakfast at a hash house, we crossed into another state. My father said he needed to use the phone for a while, and asked my mother to drive. We stopped at a used book store just as the proprietor was hanging an open sign, and I asked to go inside. The place was outstanding. It smelled like dry oatmeal. I perused the true crime section. Steph wandered to the history section, and I followed her. My father joined us.

I wound up purchasing *And the Wolf Finally Came* by John Hoerr, and *Crisis in Bethlehem* by John Strohmeyer. My father recommended them. They were fascinating in their way, and educational. I also bought a copy of Richard Marcinko's *Rogue Warrior*. Otis Lamar had suggested the title to me. The book was an easy read and hipped my wig about Navy SEALs.

Steph picked out *Trials of The Earth* by Mary Hamilton. Caroline opted for *Pippi Longstocking* by Astrid Lindgrin. Heather picked out some romance novels. I paid for their books and also bought Steph a copy of *Catch Me If You Can* by Frank Abagnale.

"This is a great read, doll. Abagnale sold out on the cause, but understanding the way he operated will hip you to my lick, and to where my wig is at."

Steph giggled. "Thank you, Vinnie." She hugged me, and I snuck in a quick kiss.

Three hours later we were in the resort town of Spectacle. My father had been on his phone texting most of that time. We arrived at a resort that was built to look like a collection of antebellum plantation houses. The place was beyond anything I could have imagined. The room we were in had pictures that lit up with pulsating pinpoints when a button was pushed. Pictures of dolls draped in gowns and Victorian dresses adorned the walls. In a kitschy way the room was beautiful. Caroline was digging the portraits, and Steph had fun playing with the lighting effects.

Steph, Caroline, Tori, and I explored the resort while the adults rested. We discovered giant hammocks near one of the pools. Caroline and Tori climbed into one, while Steph and I lay in the other.

I let out a low whistle. "This is too cool for school, gate. This whole place is perfectly arranged so that, paying to stay or not, a cat could catch a nap, hit the pool, and be entertained for free."

"They'd need to have a card on a lanyard, wouldn't they?" Caroline looked over. Tori laughed and shook her head.

"This entire place is wide open with regards to security, doll," I laughed with Tori. "True, we have passcards that show we're paying guests, but did you notice that the same cards are for sale in the gift shop? Different colors and designs, like a souvenir.

"Yeah? So?" Steph snuggled closer.

"So, a card can be pocketed with ease. That means that any stranger willing to play it in a minor chord, and dress in a presentable fashion, can use any of the resort pools, and find places to nap free of charge. This is an urban pirate's wet dream."

"You mean stealing from the store?" Caroline was shocked. "I wouldn't sit for a month if I got caught shoplifting."

"It isn't shoplifting, doll. The corporations call it shrink. It's like I'm helping them to lose weight; I help grocery stores reduce a whole lot more. In this case, one could return the card and lanyard after they were done. You'd only need it to ward off nosy staff."

Steph giggled. "You're funny, Vinnie. You have answers for everything."

I cuddled her and sighed. "I wish we had more time together. I'm feeling it now. It took disaster, but it took what it took to get close to you."

Tori and Caroline stood up. "Let's go for a walk," Tori held Caroline's hand.

At one spot, on the north side, there was an entry through a wooded glen. This was not a purposeful architectural design, but rather an open space off of a main road. We cut through, and after walking along the roads, and stretching our legs, we discovered a major highway and several apartment complexes behind some fences.

"I'd bet plenty that employees jungle up in those complexes and hoof it to work, which would explain the unguarded opening to our resort." I rubbed my chin with a thumb.

"You have everything figured out, don't you?" Steph's eyes were wide.

"He's our parents' son. Especially Papa's. We've been raised to notice things like this." Tori smiled.

"Ma thinks you're scoundrels." Caroline giggled.

"Nuts to her. We have more going on than the average Clyde, and we can survive any trouble that comes our way. You two should learn how to observe, and how to use what you observe." Tori shook her head.

Steph pointed at a spot on the fence. "There's a big hole over there. If I was careful, and crawled through, I could get into those apartments, or out of them."

"Why for?" I grinned at the light dawning in Steph's eyes as she caught on to my ways.

"If I wanted to sneak away after Ma went to bed. You know, to make time with someone." She blushed.

"Make time?" Tori laughed.

"I read it in a book, once. I think it means something romantic."

Tori nodded, "it does." She looked concerned. "Steph, has your mama had the talk with you guys?"

Steph looked at Caroline and shrugged. "No, but I learned things in class at school. I explained it to sissy. She was grossed out, but I'm interested."

Caroline stuck out her tongue. "Yuck! I can't believe people do that."

I rubbed her head. "Believe it. If they didn't there'd be no Caroline or Steph."

Steph looked away. "Maybe that'd be better. Maybe then Pa wouldn't…"

Tori turned Steph toward her. "No. No, girl. You aren't to blame for his actions. Neither of you are. He's a creep from Creepsville, and he'll pay for it."

I hugged Steph close as we walked back to our

resort. As we crossed an area by the main lobby, she pointed to a sign.

"Hey, this resort has free movies and entertainment each night. Other resorts do, too; and the trollies to the other resorts are free. If you lived in those apartments, or anywhere, you could walk here and see free stuff every night."

Geronimo! I hugged Steph until she squeaked. "Hot damn, she might be a pirate yet. Yes, exactly. You could drive from anywhere, park in those apartments, and utilize the entertainment resources like gangbusters."

As we walked, I began having thoughts about who else might be able to utilize these unguarded entrances. I looked back toward where we had exited and entered.

That afternoon, I discussed the matter in the pool with my father and Steph. The others were swimming, and we were lounging in the shallow area. "Papa, you and Mama have always taught me to look a place over, to decide if the area is safe. This resort isn't, and the other accessible resorts aren't." I opened the conversation. Steph turned toward me; her eyebrows arched.

"In what way, son?" My father nodded at me to continue.

"Well, earlier, Tori, the girls, and I were walking. I saw several places where one could access this resort from an open road. It's a busy road, but no one even stops and looks at strangers appearing out of the woods. I would think that someone with evil intent could walk in as well."

"Evil intent? You mean like pirates?" Steph giggled.

"Hey, now. Pirates are the good guys in my book. But, anyway, no. I mean terrorists."

"Interesting. Walk me through it, son." My father encouraged me as he always did in such situations

"Well, I've read about these things from the eighties

called SADMs. Man-portable nuclear devices that fit in a backpack, and weigh sixty pounds at most. One can find the process to build them on the Internet. So, let's say I'm a super-rich foreigner, and I build ten. I have ten men walk onto the grounds separately, and ride the trollies to various resorts or restaurants on property. At a specified time, they set those off. Imagine that. Or, less dramatic than nuclear, a regular bomb with enough power to blow apart a room."

Steph gasped. My father looked thoughtful. "I see your point, son. Of course, the same situation holds true for any of the super-cinemas that exist in America, or for almost anywhere, except airports, bus terminals or train stations. I agree, however, that as a tourist draw for people from all over the world, these resorts are a prime target for starting a world war," my father smiled at me. "You have an exceptionally focused mind."

"That's kind of paranoid, isn't it?" Steph looked worried.

"I'm kind of paranoid most of the time." I gave Steph a wink, "Hey, let's go swim and forget about it."

We swam toward Caroline and Tori. The afternoon was a blast. We joined in the poolside activities set up by the staff members, and forgot our troubles.

After we'd checked in earlier, using two prepaid cards, my parents led us to the cafeteria. The fine folk in charge had a system in place that charged each guest for a refillable soda mug good for their entire stay. The price was excruciating, especially to those in the habit of paying rarely, if ever, for anything. My father, being the pirate king, purchased one mug. He then plundered six more from the cafeteria over the course of a half hour. By filling his mug, he could refill the others. The machines limited mug refills to one and a half cupsful before insisting on a three minute wait, but it was possible. The machines also had a sensor that indicated if a mug had been registered at purchase. And, wouldn't you know, one of the soda machines wasn't registering whether the mug had been set with a resort code. It also wasn't limiting refills. We filled the mugs to our hearts content. After swimming, we stopped in a cafeteria, and filled up. Steph pointed out that the coffee, and six varieties of iced tea, was free and had no mechanism to check mug registration. She was a quick study.

That evening, we took a bus to a swanky resort called The Spectacular where we could watch fireworks exploding for free across a lake. The men who greeted us as we departed the bus were dressed in top hats, spats and white gloves. The inside of the resort was breathtaking, with its crystal chandeliers and elegant architecture. The ambiance and decor were from the Edwardian time period, and the guests exuded more class than at our resort. There was a jazz quintet playing in the middle of the lobby, surrounded by settees, couches and well-crafted chairs. This was where I wanted to spend my life. This was worthy of my pirating talents.

The fireworks were, of course, spectacular, and we all oohed and wowed. Afterward, I was looking for a bathroom, and entered an elevator that required a card to access the top floors. A lady used hers, and I found myself in an even more elaborate setting. There was a coffee machine, with at least two dozen varieties of coffee, tables of desserts, as well as meats, cheeses and crudités. Best of all, there was a supply of top shelf liquor bottles accessible to the guests.

I had no idea what this area was, but, being a pirate, I helped myself to a cup of Sumatra. Since no one was watching I poured in two shots of whiskey as well. I walked downstairs, and out a door that led to the lobby.

"I don't know where I just was, Papa," I smiled at my father. "I was looking for the restroom sign, and this lady put a card into a slot in the elevator. When we arrived, there was a smorgasbord set up." I popped a chocolate covered strawberry in my mouth, and offered around pastry. I handed Tori half my cup of coffee, and winked at her. She sipped, and her eyes widened.

"Remember how you did that, son. You just happened upon free access to the VIP level. People pay plenty extra for that level, and honestly, except for the free nosh and being checked in a bit faster, the rooms aren't that much nicer. Even so, free nosh is not something one should pass up."

Tori giggled, loose and silly. "The coffee sure is grand. Strong too." She winked at me.

"Yeah, it said it was from Ireland, I think. Irish coffee."

We caught the trolley back to our suite and fell asleep. My father slept between my mother and Heather. Caroline shared a bed with Tori, while Steph and I shared a fold out couch. Steph snuggled into my side, and in minutes was deep in the grips of Morpheus. I lay there, my arms wrapped around her, and thought about how much I was going to miss her. With time, my mind stopped racing, and sleep came.

The next morning, I woke up early, knowing that my time with Steph had come to an end. We would be separated for years, and possibly forever. I asked if we could go for a walk together before breakfast. The adults said it was OK. Tori gave me a wary look, but said nothing. Steph and I walked out the door and around the property.

"I feel weird saying this, doll, but I love you. I mean forever love you. Head over heels, top of the ninth with bases loaded, love you." I realized how sappy it sounded, but I couldn't help myself. I nudged Steph inside of a single unit family bathroom and locked the door.

"I love you too, Vinnie. You saved my life. I'll

always love you. Umm…I don't need the potty." Steph looked at me confused.

"It's not the romantic place I would have preferred, doll, but it's as private as we can get." I tilted her chin up and kissed her.

In a matter of moments, she was in my arms, warm, soft, and fragile. My lips parted, as did hers, and our tongues explored each other. We stood there for a few minutes kissing and hugging. I rubbed a hand over her denim covered rear, and started to undo the button of her jeans.

"Vinnie, we can't. Not here. Not now. I want to, but I want to do it somewhere nice. Like in the movies. Can't you and I run away?"

"Would that we could, but no. Stephanie Ann Baker, I will never forget you. One day I promise I'm going to find you again. I wish we had more time right now. I'm going to find you, and light you up like a pinball machine. I swear it, baby." I gazed into her eyes, memorizing her features, as tears dripped down her face.

"Vincenzo Cassiel Michelangelo Il-Cazzo, you saved me. I would do anything for you. But Ma, Caroline, and I have to keep moving. You said so. Your family said so. I hope you come for me. I won't let another boy near me until you do." Steph squeezed my body in her arms for all she was worth.

We walked back to the suite, had showers, and changed our clothes before walking to the cafeteria area for breakfast. While we were devouring our platters of bacon and waffles the size of a plate, my father removed a stack of papers from my mother's purse.

"Heather, I need you to read these and sign them. They're legal documents allowing a realty company I know of to clean, repair, and sell your house. Don't worry about Myron, he won't interfere." My father looked as serious as

I ever saw him.

"But, how? How do you know that? And how will I get my share of the money?"

"The less you know the better. Please trust me that things are handled. You can't return, though. These papers will be faxed to Hawaii, then to Nova Scotia and finally to a lawyer in Nantucket. Your property and money will be delivered to a safe drop. You'll be informed of the location at another time. There's a process for that as well."

After Heather signed the papers and breakfast was consumed, we used the restrooms. When I stepped out of the men's room, Heather, Caroline, and Steph were gone. My father informed me that they had been transferred to a couple who would take them to the train. Their luggage had already been removed from the suite. I walked in silence back to our suite, packed my clothes and books, and carried my gear wordlessly toward the station wagon. It was gone. I returned to the suite to wait for my family to get ready.

My mother tried hugging me, but I shrugged her away. When the others had packed, we caught a shuttle bus to the airport. Tori squeezed my hand on the way. I didn't respond. My entire body was numb. I asked my father where the car was, and he explained that the best way to lose a vehicle was to park it at an airport in long term parking. We were being met by a friend once we landed in Boston.

I sat on the shuttle staring out the window. I needed to cry, but I couldn't. I needed some pot, but I had no more. After checking three suitcases at the airport, I sat waiting for our flight, and thinking about Steph. I couldn't ease the pain in my chest. My temples throbbed, and my stomach was sour. Tori had ditched the last of the moonshine before we left the resort. I needed a drink. Instead, I stared into space and waited.

Chapter Fourteen

The flight back to Boston was uneventful. I had a window seat, and stared out the glass for a half hour. I read a few chapters from Strohmeyer. Nothing helped. I closed my eyes and fell asleep. When I woke up, we were instructed to prepare for landing. Tori handed me a can of ginger ale which I chugged, and a bag of pretzels which I gobbled down. Free is free, and the airlines overcharge.

After we'd exited the plane, we made our way through the terminal to the baggage claim area; and we waited for ninety minutes. I was already depressed, but this was the last straw. The airline had lost all of our luggage. My parents checked everywhere, but remained cool and composed about the situation.

I staggered to a row of chairs along a wall -- my body convulsing -- my knees pulled to my chest -- as tears streamed, leaving a salty taste in my mouth and snot flowing out of my nose. I was helpless to stop. Tori dashed over, grabbing me. She held me, and made ineffectual soothing noises.

My parents were oblivious to my plight. They entered an office with glass walls. Through the haze of tears, I saw my father shaking his arms and gesticulating. I downshifted, and tried some controlled breathing. It helped.

"What's with you, bro'? I know they lost our stuff, but it'll be found eventually. And, I realize that your heart's crushed, but you and I both know that they had to lam. None of this worked out the way you wanted it to. Sobbing like a bitch doesn't help. Brace up." Tori hugged me, and I returned it.

After a visit to the restroom, I emerged to find my mother and father standing there with several sheets of paper to fill out. We walked outside with our carry-on bags.

A woman met us, and was introduced as an old college friend of my mother. Her name was Pat Melendez. She was my parents age, and looked to be South American, or Hispanic. Pat led us to a new Buick Enclave that was parked in a short term garage. Next to it was an older looking Datsun.

"Thank you for everything, Pat!" my mother gave the lady a hug. "I'll send you a big batch of oatmeal raisin cookies next week."

We climbed into the Buick, and Pat climbed into the passenger side of the Datsun. The man behind the wheel of the Datsun pulled off, and they were gone. I climbed into the back seat of the Buick..., and saw our missing luggage. My parents had done it again, only I didn't know what they had done. I was momentarily distracted from my depression.

As we drove away from the airport, I started laughing, which set Tori off. "OK, Mama, dish. How in the hell did you do that?" Tori laughed so hard that tears filled her eyes.

"It's a simple matter, dear." My mother smiled back at us. "I had your father call Pat and describe our luggage. She grabbed it the minute it came down the chute. After stashing the luggage, she waited. We didn't find it on the conveyor because it was already missing. The idea is to wait until the last of the bags have ejected. Then make a fuss, and a report. The airline will search in vain for our bags before declaring them lost. In the meantime, we fill out forms indicating what was in the bags. Items such as cash and jewelry aren't counted, but clothing, electronics, and so forth are. Each bag will net us a bit under two thousand dollars if we fill the forms out correctly."

I was awed. "That's got to be one of the coolest things you ever taught us. How long before the money shows up?"

"Takes about ninety days if I call every day and put on the pressure," my father chortled.

We drove home, circling around Pardmest, and pulled up as dusk was hitting Harvest Junction. There was a for sale sign in the Baker's yard. Two unmarked Crown Victoria cars were parked between their house and ours. I climbed out, and Billy Bob Fisher came running over. He hugged Tori.

"About time you guys got home. Welcome back Mr. and Mrs. Il-Cazzo. This entire town's going crazy. Police have been all over. The Bakers disappeared, and Myron left a suicide note. He can't be located. Sorry, Vinnie, but your girlfriend is gone. Police think either Mrs. Baker and the girls left town, or that Myron may have murdered them. If so, the bodies haven't been found." Billy Bob started as if to help us move the luggage inside.

Tori gasped in horror, clutching Fisher. I was already depressed, and it took no real skill for me to slump against the van and start bawling again. My mother came over and sat holding me. "Oh, honey, they probably aren't dead. That's something the police have to check. They probably decided to move. Myron must have gotten a better job. You know how secretive they are." My mother held me as I got my sobs under control. "Tori? It'll be fine. I'm sure no real danger exists."

My father had always taught me two certainties about giving facts. One was to include the kernel of truth and embellish it to suit your audience. Misdirection and mirrors is what magicians call it. The second was that under interrogation one starts with a whopper. Then whittle the lie down. In time everyone can be broken, but when you're forced to tell the truth how will the police even know?

I stood up and Fisher chucked me on the arm. "I'm sorry, Il-Cazzo. If I can do anything to help just let me know. Hey, after you guys unpack come by my place, Il-Cazzo. Tori, you come too. You can tell me about your summer vacation."

I nodded and went inside. My mother and father walked downstairs to their bedroom, and Tori and I went to our rooms. After I unpacked, I took my glass pipe out of the baggie I had taped to my boxers. I peeled a hundred dollar bill off of my small stack of money behind my underwear drawer.

Tori met me in the hallway. "I'm sure you noticed that the neighborhood is under surveillance, Mr. Barrymore."

"The two bears in brown wrappers? Sure. Would we do less than act surprised, Miss Hepburn?" I paused. "But you have a good idea, Tor." I returned the pipe to my drawer.

"OK, I'm clean now. I have my lucky hundred dollar bill, but nothing else." I bowed regally.

Tori laughed, and gave me a pop on the ass. We left through the back door and cut across several yards. We exited from the Contreras' yard and walked another block to Fisher's house. His parents were away at a business conference for three days. He poured us each some raisin mash, and nothing could have tasted better. I drained the glass and asked for a refill.

"Easy there, bro," Tori giggled. "Ah hell, numb your ass. You need it. Slow the roll, though, you don't want those Crown Vics seeing you drunk."

I slid Fisher the hundred, and he nodded. He informed me that in two days there would be something at the baseball field near third base. We all sat and talked about nothing in particular. Fisher said he was considering trying for a GED, and going to the state university a year early. Tori asked about how that worked. I sat sipping my second glass, and staring into space.

After another couple of hours Tori and I returned home. I was lucid, but exhaustion had set in. That was a perfect situation because, upon arriving at our house, we found that the undercover cops were talking to my parents.

"Vinnie, Tori, this is detective Loszar and detective Rooter. They have some questions. Your mother and I already indicated that we've been on vacation." My father looked agitated.

"What do you want to know, sirs? I'm tired." I tried to look irritated and tough at the same time,

"Where did you guys go on vacation?" Rooter tried for conversational.

"To visit our older sister, Gina. Then we drove through some country towns, looked at some used bookstores and antique shops, and came home." Tori stood with a hip arched at an angle, weight on her left leg, arms crossed.

"Yeah," I sighed, "want to see my books? Oh, and we stopped at an uncle's house. He loaned us a van when we moved earlier this summer and took our Buick. We traded back. So, you can quit harassing our neighbors, thanks."

"Vincenzo!" My mother snapped. "Show some respect."

"Yes, Mama. I'm sorry, officer, sir." I yawned heavily.

The detectives ignored my attitude and asked my parents a few more questions before turning back to me. "A couple of people at the church attended by the Baker family indicate that you were seen there with them several times." Loszar looked down at me with challenge in his eyes.

"One time. I admit their older daughter got my carburetor flooded. She's a real knockout. That being said, I wasn't very secure with Mr. Baker as a driver. He was heavy on the pedal and I was sure we were going to have an accident. I didn't join them again. A few weeks later, at my request, my family attended one other time. I wanted to see if I could get permission to see Stephanie Baker socially. I figured the formal approach might work. But it seemed like bad timing. Mr. Baker looked depressed and agitated. He seemed restless." The prevarications were coming naturally. "Anything else, officer, sir?"

"Well, thank you for your time. We'll be in touch if we need anything else."

After the detectives left, my parents looked at us. "How'd you know to mention the car?" My mother inquired.

"Fisher told us that everyone is being interrogated. He was asked what sort of car we drove and the license plate. He didn't know the license, and mentioned the minivan." Tori sat at the kitchen table.

"I figured that mine was the simplest lie. Those goons from Saskatoon didn't even ask what uncle. Straight from the fridge, Gina will alibi us. They don't have warrants, or cause to get them. We're covered." I yawned again.

"Smart thinking, kids. But, there's more involved here. I can't tell you anything. Not yet. if matters go south, we have a plan to stay in the clear." My father hugged us and suggested I go to bed.

The next morning, after doing my kata in the back yard, I saw my mother sitting in the kitchen with four other ladies eating marble cake, drinking coffee, and discussing the PTA. They also reminded her about a meeting at the local ladies club to swap recipes and discuss ways to improve the town. I introduced myself, gave my mother a kiss, and took my coffee to my room. I spent the day finishing my books on the steel industry, and sorting my clothes. The books were well written and informative. I hoped to find time to ask my father or some teacher at school about how the closures of the steel industry shaped the current events of our nation.

Tori had gone to Fisher's for the morning and when she came home, she had a stack of documents about the GED and early graduation. After the neighbor ladies left, I listened to Tori and my mother discussing various topics while they prepared a chef salad for lunch.

My father spent the day locked in his office. He was distracted and grumpy. I wasn't certain of the reason. He didn't join us for lunch and my mother told Tori and me that there were problems with his computer and he was working on them. I didn't think much of it.

Life changed for me that day. Over the next year my parents became entrenched in the societal happenings of Harvest Junction. They took part in everything from PTA, and the local assembly meetings, to the decoration of the streets for the holidays. When celebrations took place, or block parties were arranged, my parents took a lead role. They'd help out if any neighbor needed assistance. I was conscripted to mow the lawns of older residents. My parents insisted that I not accept money for the task. Our family became well known in the area. The involvement was necessary for a number of reasons that I learned later. At the time I found that getting involved was therapeutic. It took my mind off of missing Steph.

Chapter Fifteen

In the week before school commenced, I spiraled into a deeper depression. The detectives had come by twice more with questions. I was in no mood to deal with the interrogation, but I had no choice. The more they questioned me, the more my raw, psychic wounds over losing Steph were reopened.

"Understand that we aren't accusing you of complicity in a crime. We aren't even certain a crime has occurred. But the timing of your family vacation and your return from vacation is suggestive." Loszar tried for conversational, and achieved nothing close.

"The timing is coincidental. If anything, it's a nuisance as well. Not because of the questions so much, but our son is at that interesting age where girls are crucially important. He's been infatuated with the older daughter of the Baker's, and with them gone he receives no closure." My mother was trying for aggravated, and hitting her mark dead on.

Each interrogation session drove me deeper into my reverie. I developed a great distaste for the police. "Detective, sir, I admit that I had, and continue to have, carnal interest in Stephanie Baker. I was never able to follow up with her in that regard, and it troubles me. I had one try at church, and it wasn't a success. I suppose one day I might meet some other doe-eyed, pouty-lipped beauty who will oil my gears, but at the moment I doubt it. I wonder if I even have what it takes. Is that clear enough, sir?" I scowled.

Tori took on a position of complete ignorance. "I didn't even know the family. I'm in the tenth grade and don't have a thing in common with the children of the neighborhood. I spend my time with Billy Fisher. Our activities are immaterial, and none of your damned business. So, detective, other than my pain in the ass baby brother behaving like a rutting mooncalf, I have nothing for you."

Detective Rooter seemed less interested in the Bakers. He did seem unusually interested in my father's relationships with a number of other individuals both in the neighborhood and from other cities.

"So, Mr. Il-Cazzo, we are looking at various scenarios. If, for some reason, Myron Baker did disappear then there must be a reason. We have indications of extreme violence where he's concerned, and serious infractions involving drugs and alcohol. Suppose Heather Baker and her daughters needed to leave a violent situation. Where might they go?" Rooter began. "There's a shelter not too far from here. The police in that jurisdiction keep a watch on the place, but they try not to get involved. There was an incident a few days ago wherein they suspected that Heather Baker and her daughters might be there. Myron Baker had called in a report of an abduction. He was inebriated when he called. The matter was followed up, but no evidence was found. We tried making contact with Mr. Baker the next day, but he had disappeared. It may well have been a drunken spat. The thing is that while we were exploring this path, we found out that a person of interest named J. W. McCool is a major donor to the shelter."

"And?" My father shrugged.

"And we know that McCool is involved with businesses that are connected to you as well. He's also connected to a Louise Cook and a Linda Pang. Those women are persons of interest in other matters that concern us. Furthermore, we know of three other individuals connected to the computer business with McCool who also are invested in businesses where you are, likewise, invested." Rooter was driving his points home, but my father remained nonchalant.

"That sounds complicated. I'm on disability, as is my wife. I'm not working for anyone. I'm not employed. As to my investments, I'm certain untold numbers of people invest their money. I don't know anyone by the names you mentioned."

"Do you know a Vasily Mogilevich? We believe you do know him." Rooter demanded

"Vasily? Of course. He and Natasha are old friends. We're invested in many of the same companies. We talk daily over social media, discussing our best options with regard to buying and selling of stock and commodities." My father brightened. "Which in turn means that anyone else in those cyber rooms would appear connected to us, whether or not they were. The web is a huge and unwieldy mechanism, no?"

Detective Rooter nodded, and thanked my father. He let himself out our front door.

I was confused by the line of questioning, as it seemed to be tangentially connected to Myron or Heather and her daughters. The people at the shelter in Pardmest had no doubt denied knowing anything about the Bakers, and later my father assured me of this fact.

Clearly there was an obvious link to us if people who were financially supporting the shelter were also involved in stock trading with my father. I knew my father was giving misinformation, and I assumed that it was to protect Heather, Steph, and Caroline, as well as the women running the shelter. I couldn't begin to imagine anything else that could be going on.

After that final interrogation the surveillance cars left our block. However, there were plenty of other cars driving by checking out the Baker's property. Mixed in with those looking at the property were no doubt various undercover officers.

I sat for a day watching three trucks pull up and remove every item of property from the Baker's house. The drivers had signed documents from Heather and Myron. That added a confusion to the investigation, since there was no evidence of any crime, and the documents were clearly not forged. Myron's signature matched the signature on his suicide note, and from his bank information,

After the house was cleared, and had been cleaned, the line of prospective buyers increased. I knew that my father was planning to channel the funds from the house and the sale of the estate. I asked if he could also include a message from me. He told me no, and to forget about trying to find Steph. He stated that my continued interest was creating difficulties.

I fought my growing resentment the only way I knew how. I attacked in the only manner available to me. I would daily go to Polidore's diner on Washington street, and remove the toilet paper rolls from the men's room. On a shelf behind the toilet, Polidore always left a stack of extra rolls still in the packages. Stashing them in my knapsack, I would bring the rolls home. Polidore, the lanky African-American man, with a greying afro, and a broad smile, ran the diner. That made it a mom and pop kind of place, and therefore I skated the edge of the pirate's code. I figured that it wasn't so terrible. In short order I had filled Tori's and my entire bathroom closet. It was a penny-ante plunder but it was only the tip of my spear.

I also started hitchhiking to Sweetbriar each morning. Tori was spending her every waking moment with Fisher, and my parents were busy with their own activities. The other kids in the neighborhood were nice enough, but I didn't feel like being social. I took off every morning, and returned before dinner. In Sweetbriar I found everything to take my mind off of my depression. There were twenty-five recovery meetings, and I hit them all once. I even hit the biggest meetings a few times. My roll of cash increased, although I used the last of my fake twenty dollar bills.

After meetings I would explore the thrift shops and supermarkets. I began exchanging my clothes at the second hand clothing stores, and soon had a new wardrobe for school. One afternoon I picked up all my school supplies, and Tori's, at a supermarket along with sodas and chips. Walking out was easy since the back doors were open for deliveries. The bathroom was located against a wall near the loading docks. After relieving myself, I walked away and cut down an alley. I hit up every fast-food restaurant I could find if only for a free cup of coffee. I took mugs, condiments, and silverware from several restaurants. One day, while exploring, I spotted some open trucks behind a liquor store. No one was around, and a few cases of alcohol were open. I put two bottle of Bombay gin, and a bottle of Jameson into my knapsack before anyone noticed.

I beat a hasty retreat, and returned home where I hid my stash. I had grabbed several one liter bottles of water on the way home. I poured most of the water out, and refilled them with gin. The Jameson I kept for bedtime.

School was starting soon. I was unsure how that would go. I wasn't in the mood to be around people and school was all the time a huge bore. That night I started reading *King of The Gypsies* by Peter Maas. I didn't enjoy it as much as *Marie, Serpico,* and *The Valachi Papers*, but it was a solid read. I grabbed the Jameson, had a good pull, and in time drifted to sleep. It had been a crazy summer, and despite my ambivalence about school, I was glad it was over.

Chapter Sixteen

I woke up on September first to weather that was unseasonably hot. After my morning rituals, a shower, and a shot of gin to calm my nerves, I pulled on my black designer jeans and a silk shirt that I had recently found at a Salvation Army. I slipped my feet into a pair of Italian loafers that uncle Vasily had sent me, and looked in the mirror. I was ready to make the scene. I brushed my number two crew cut with my fingers, put on a straw boater, patted some aftershave into my face, and proceeded to the kitchen. Tori walked in dressed in a plaid skirt, red fishnet tights and a sleeveless pink top. She poured coffee, and sat across from me.

"Ugh. I can't believe school's starting again."

"At least it's something to do. I hope the teachers are better here." I spread blackberry preserves on my toast.

"I'm hoping I can get my equivalency soon. It seems pretty easy. After the past few weeks, and this harassment from the cops, I want to get away from here. You realize that those detectives questioned everyone in town? Literally, everyone. From what I hear no one said anything important, but I feel a bad vibe. Something's rotten in the state of Bismarck."

"Savvy. I feel the same way. Why the deep interest in Mama and Papa? And, since then, Papa's become preoccupied. There's stuff being unsaid, but what? By the way Bismarck isn't a state. It's the capital of North Dakota."

"Smart ass." We headed outside. Al Contreras met me there along with Mike Casey and a few other guys from the block. Tori walked ahead of us with Fisher. As we walked toward school Al kept giving me the fisheye. The other kids did too. I stopped in my tracks. "What? What's with the looks? I feel like a damned specimen in the zoo."

"Nothing, Il-Cazzo. I mean, well, do you know anything about massage parlors? Or, Asian-American buffets? Or, truck stops and low budget motels? When the Bakers disappeared, cops came around asking about Myron. They were pressuring us, and asking our parents about human trafficking. They said that your pops is a partner in a bunch of places across the east coast, and they hinted that the places traffic in illegals." Al looked at me nervously.

"Bullshit! My parents are on disability. We barely have any scratch outside of some investments. Legitimate stocks and bonds kind of investments. I wish my parents were business owners because we'd be groovy with the gravy. We clearly aren't the frigging Corleone family. Jesus! Yeah, we lived near New York City before we moved, but we were scraping by there too. Hell no my father doesn't traffic humans!" I scowled fiercely.

"I had to ask, man. My parents are concerned because they know I hang out with you. They also know plenty about illegal immigrants, and the stuff people do to them. I'm not sure how they know so much, but they get hot about the subject." A few other Hispanic kids nodded.

"What are you all planning to do for friends when your brains give out? Seriously! You really want to stand here accusing me and my family of this? Stow it and rope it down before your mouth writes a check your ass can't cash." I stepped back into a low stance ready to take on all comers.

"Calm down, dude. No one dimed out your family, but that night when Myron Baker came flying through town, almost killing everyone with his truck, you and your dad were seen going over to that house. People saw your dad and you leaving with the Baker girls and their mom. Later a car pulled up, and your mom and sister left. The cops think you're involved with the Baker's disappearance." Mike gave me an intense look.

"If you have anything interesting to say, let me know. I have plenty of other ways to spend my time than to listen to this crap, dudes." I was pissed. "It isn't like I'm waiting to kidnap people at gun point and sell them to the nearest pimp. That action doesn't happen anymore in America. Hell, we're about to elect a Black man as president.

"Yeah, that stuff does happen. More than you know." Al shook his head. "I wasn't accusing you of anything and neither was anyone else. I had to ask."

"Mike, thank you, and whoever, for keeping it under the lid. I can't tell you anything. I know nothing. My family went on vacation and had nothing to do with any disappearance of anyone. That's all I am going to say. Savvy?" I gave Mike a stone cold look.

I needed a drink and a smoke, but clearly that wasn't going to happen. Agitation sprang from the accusations, and an unspoken fear gnawed at my stomach. It was similar to my angst about piracy. Could my father be involved in more sinister activities than simply taking on corporate America? On many occasions I'd heard my father and various family friends discussing the business of helping people escape to America. The subjects in question were escaping totalitarianism and despotic regimes. My sister Gina was in the know about people who made fake ID cards that looked authentic. That might have been part of helping people get established. I had no clue. Uncle Vasily and my father dealt in counterfeit money, but that seemed an ancillary issue. Was it such a stretch that they would be involved in other ventures outside the law? The thought made me want to vomit, so I formed a conclusion on the spot. My parents weren't involved in anything that hurt actual people. Not deliberately, not if it meant that square johns were being endangered. I decided to table my internal deliberations on the topic.

We arrived at school, and Mike showed me the front office. I made sure that everything was squared away with my records, and picked up my schedule. Homeroom was also my first period room. I had English with Fred Barker who monitored the homeroom. In the rear of the room, I spied rows of desks occupied by cats and chicks I didn't recognize. They sported leather jackets, or military OD jackets, off-the-rack jeans, and wore work-boots or cheap sneakers. The group looked uniformly tough. I felt a sudden camaraderie with them.

Moving to the back and taking an empty seat I noticed Al looking at me askance. He and some other neighborhood kids had taken seats to one side, nearer to the front of the room. I looked at some of the chicks who were sitting near me. They were as ripe a crop of tomatoes as a cat could want. Straight up sweater girls with ample racks, or augmented to appear so, heavily made up, and cute in a hard edged way. Something inside drew me like a moth to a flame. The feeling was akin to the arousal that overcame me when I thought about Steph Baker, but it was different as well. These girls were different. Except for certain moments on the trip to Spectacle, Steph was an innocent. The sort of innocent a guy could take home to mother. These chicks surrounding me were temporary and feral. I decided to feel out the game before dealing myself a hand.

Turning toward a girl at the desk next to mine, I gave her a wink and dipped my head slightly. She was a tough looking doll, about four-foot-eleven and no more than one-hundred and twenty-five pounds soaking wet. She had long black hair, black eyes, and a tan figure that made my breath catch. Her name was Julie Dimitrion and that she was from the far edge of town beyond the train tracks that divided Harvest Junction. Most of the kids sitting around me in the back of the room were from the east side. She informed me that she wasn't spoken for. I gave her my cell phone number, and suggested she call me. Something told me that she could take my mind off of my troubles.

She was there at lunch, and again that afternoon in math class. Our teacher, Tony Porcaro, was explaining the stock market to us. He gave us an assignment to pick and purchase four stocks with a virtual thousand dollars. We were to follow our stocks and keep a journal. We could sell a virtual stock if we wanted, but we had to buy another stock in its place. I was fascinated by the possibilities. I asked Julie to come home with me. She agreed to meet me after school.

Mike Casey approached me as the final bell rang. "Hey, Vinnie, I've seen you all day in classes hanging out with the east side trash. You need to be careful, man. Those dudes are bad news, and the chicks are worse. You could catch things from them."

"Who asked you for your contribution, Clyde? You really think you're better than they are? Let me carve your dome, dude, and you can send the word. I grew up around cats like that. You seriously think that because a chick is on the skids that she's some kind of slut? You really think every down and out cat is a hoodlum? Maybe their caravan fell on hard times? Our economy isn't flushed out, you dig? Those kids you're calling trash might not have two nickels to shake, and they might live hardscrabble, but they seem righteous." I shook my head in disgust.

When Julie walked out of the building, I approached. She smelled lightly of perfume. I gave Mike and some other dudes a hard look, and hooked Julie's arm in mine. We walked toward my house, talking about school and our teachers. Julie was not only molded from the neckline south; she was stacked in the attic. A doll might be the hottest swell to ever back into a mattress, but without the knowledge box loaded, the other box isn't worth my time. Julie was worth knowing stem to stern.

When we got home my mother was all smiles. She had two platters of fresh baked cookies laid out in the table. There were also brownies and muffins. In the center of the table were fresh cut flowers in a vase. She wore a gingham apron, and sounded positively airy.

"Hi, honey. How was your day? Who's your friend?" My depressed and disengaged mother had been abducted by aliens and replaced with June Cleaver.

"Her name's Julie, Mama. We're going to go study in my room. Is Papa around?" I gave my mother a hug, took some cookies, and poured a mug of coffee.

"In his office. I think it's OK to knock. He shouldn't be too busy. Tell him I put the pot roast in, and will put in the potatoes about five. Dinner will be about six. Care to join us, Julie?" My mother was either on something, or had suddenly found Jesus.

Julie accepted the offer and called home to let her mother know. After she shut off her cell phone, we knocked on my father's office door.

"Come on in." My father turned from his laptop and smiled. "Hey son, Uncle V and Uncle Paulo send their regards. They said to tell you to study hard and that they found some Bugatchi shirts and Armani jeans in your size. They're sending them special delivery."

I introduced Julie. "Papa? If they can find any dresses or jeans and blouses in Julie's size I'd make it worth their while. Maybe some Oakley shades and a few pairs of Air Max 90s or some JS Wings." I smiled at Julie.

"Damn dude! You trying to impress me? No need if you are, because I already like you." Julie laughed.

"Nope. I know people who work in the garment industry and they get major discounts. I figured why not see if they have anything you could wear." I gave her nonchalant.

My father turned and typed for a couple of minutes. He turned back smiling. "A truck delivered both styles of shoe last week. They said they can get two pairs of each. Also, five pairs of Amo cropped jeans and seven blouses from some designer called The Row. They received a shipment from The Gap, as well, from which they will send some samplings. The shades they don't have, but they'll ask around."

"Thank you, sir. That's incredible. Uh, here." Julie wrote some sizes on a sticky note. "Whatever they can get is fine. What do I owe you? I only get ten dollars a week allowance, but maybe you need some yard work done?"

I was insulted. "You owe nothing, babe. This is between me and my uncles. Savvy?"

My father closed his laptop and inquired about school. We spent the next hour discussing stocks. He was a fount of useful information. We chose three blue chip stocks and one tech start up that was making an initial opening.

"For practical purposes, blue chip is the solid and boring way to go. You make a little bit and lose infrequently. By putting a quarter of your money in a start up, you risk losing big on that one. I would never advise that with real cash. On the other hand, the startup might be bought by a major company and you make a fortune overnight. I think you made good choices, seeing as this is only a school project. Personally, I find Wall Street repulsive. They represent everything that's wrong with our nation. More rich bastards screwing the poor." My father shook his head.

"I need to ask you something later, Papa. I heard about some businesses that aren't stocks. I want to know about them" I hugged him.

We left my father to his work and walked to my

room. I shut the door and locked it, looking nervously at Julie. I wanted to take her right there, but I wasn't sure how to ask. "Do you drink? I mean like beer and stuff? Because I really need one. If you don't mind."

"You have anything? Your parents seem kind of square to let you drink." Julie laid down on my bed. I laughed. Whatever was going on with them, my parents were definitely not squares.

"I have a bottle of whiskey, well part of a bottle. I have gin too, if you want. Do you smoke out? I have a quarter of buds, but we'd have to go for a walk." I reached into the bottom dresser drawer under my sweaters. I pulled out the Jameson.

"Damn, Il-Cazzo, you're a wild boy. You sure aren't like the other dudes that live around here." Julie chuckled. "Pour me some of that."

"I don't get it. Here on the west side the kids act like their better than everyone else. The east side cats act like toughs. It doesn't seem like one side is that much richer than the other, though. I mean, we all attend the same schools." I poured Julie a double shot and had one myself.

"You have to know the history. My side of the tracks, we're mostly white and politically conservative. There's more crime over there for sure, more junkies and drunks too. But even the people who aren't into that shit in my neighborhood can't imagine this Obama dude being president. I mean a Black Muslim? Me, I don't care. But, a lot of people do." Julie tossed off her whiskey. "Over here you might have noticed that a lot more people are ethnic. My neighbors say the Mexicans are why so many white people lost jobs lately. I don't know if there's any truth to that, but my parents say that the foreigners, especially the Hispanics, are mostly illegal or the children of illegals. There's some social crossover between the areas, we play on the same teams at school and stuff, but what you're seeing is political mostly. Parents dislike parents and kids follow that."

"I got it, but I don't want it. Racist white trash on one side and multicultural on the other." I shrugged. "Small town politics. Whatever."

I drew Julie into my arms, soft and warm, and we necked for a while. After a half hour or so, we lay on my bed together reading *Catcher in The Rye*. I had read it a few times already, and told Julie my impressions. An hour later, she turned and gave me another kiss. A passionate kiss. I returned it with vigor. In another moment our shirts were off and we were necking pretty heavily. Her firm round breasts pressed against me through the filmy material of her black brassiere as I started undoing her pants. She grabbed my hand.

"Easy there, tiger! I don't know about you but I don't go that far on a first date. Kissing, yeah, even laying here with my shirt off. But I don't want to go all the way. I like you, but let's take it slow." Julie sat up and pulled on her shirt. "I'm in no hurry, dude. We have lots of time for that. And we should get started on the science homework."

I sighed and excused myself to the bathroom. Fifteen minutes later I returned to study. Somehow, I made it through another hour before my mother called to us that dinner was ready.

When Julie and I walked into the dining room, Tori and Fisher were already at the table. Fisher looked momentarily surprised and then smiled. "Hey, Julie. I didn't know you knew Il-Cazzo. How's your brother doing?" Fisher looked at me, shaking his head slightly.

Julie blushed. "Vinnie and I have some classes together at school. My brother's home for now. There was no way he was going to be convicted, and you know that. I didn't know you knew Vinnie either."

I looked a question at Tori and she shrugged. "Your

brother? What happened?" I gave Julie curious.

"Yeah. My brother, Dino. He was picked up a few months ago on suspicion of dealing meth. But he never has. Not as far as I know. If he was dealing, he's too smart to get caught. The cops harass us because we have friends who they want information on." Julie sighed and shook her head.

"Cops around here are knuckle draggers. Hey, since we all know each other, how about we double date sometime?" I tried changing the subject to a more pleasant topic.

"Maybe we could. I need to talk to you later, Il-Cazzo." Fisher had a strange look in his eyes. I nodded.

My father emerged from his office and came to the table at the moment my mother appeared with dinner. The pot roast smelled heavenly and there was a giant bowl of homemade applesauce flavored with brandy and raisins, little potatoes, and fresh bread. It was the fanciest dinner we'd enjoyed for a while.

"What's the occasion?" Tori helped herself to pot roast. "This is delicious but..."

My father gave her a look. "What? You act like your mother doesn't always keep a nice home. It's dinner time. So, eat." He winked at her.

The meal was followed by hot cherry pie and coffee. We all sat and talked about school and current events. My mother was playing the Martha Stewart role to the hilt that evening. I was in the middle of my second piece of pie when she floored both Tori and me.

"Julie, is your mother on the PTA? I signed up this morning. Also, I'm hosting the book club next month. That's Wednesday afternoons with a light lunch afterward. In case she'd care to join us, we're going to be reading *Change of Heart* by Jodie Picoult." My mother didn't look like she was on happy drugs.

"I volunteered to help with the barbecuing during the big block party next month. I'm having a pig delivered to spit-roast. Carols Sanchez is coordinating things along with the Wolf's and your father, Billy." My father sounded more alive than he had in a year.

"My dad told me, sir." Fisher took a sip of coffee. "You folks will definitely get to know everyone in the entire region if you keep volunteering that way."

"I'll be sure tell my mother" Julie smiled pleasantly.

After dinner I walked Julie to school. Her father was waiting in a red Ford pick-up truck. He was wearing a Stetson, and a tight grey t-shirt. His arms were as big as my thighs and knotted with muscles. He tipped his hat wordlessly at me as Julie climbed inside the truck.

I was walking home and spotted Tori and Fisher. They waved me over. "Hey, what's the scam, Sam?" I gave Fisher curious. "What was all that at dinner?"

Fisher laughed without humor. "You really know how to pick 'em, Il-Cazzo. First the Baker girl and now a chick from the other side of the tracks. Do you enjoy heartbreak or are you into white trash?"

"Who the hell are you? What makes you any better? Steph was definitely not trash, and Julie and her friends seem cool. From what she tells me her parents are bigots, but so are a lot of people? So what?"

We walked to the town square and sat on a bench. Tori coughed. "Get your flaps down before you take flight, bro. From what I hear around school those east side kids aren't like us. Not even close. I'm hearing stuff about cooking meth, about stabbings and shootings, about selling heroin and crack. That isn't piracy or brewing a little moonshine, that's serious." Tori looked over at me.

"Julie doesn't do that stuff. I doubt anyone else in my school does either." I was pissed. "It's uncool to judge those cats if we don't even know the score."

"But their families do sell drugs. That isn't up for debate. And a lot of them do worse from what I hear. Please be careful. Something's going on around here. I'm not entirely sure what. I got weird questions from some of the girls at school. Fisher's folks were questioned about some crazy shit too." Tori stood up with Fisher and headed back toward his house.

I walked home and went to my room. After finishing my history assignment, I took a healthy swig of gin from a water bottle and lay down to sleep. My parents were up to something, my sister was being judgmental, and my life was spinning out of control.

Chapter Seventeen

The next morning, I woke up early, made breakfast, and took it with me. I wasn't interested in hearing stupid questions about my parents, or stupid comments about my choice in friends. I couldn't force my mind to shut up, and the more I thought about the possible scenarios, the more my stomach churned.

After a long day of boring classes, I went straight home. My mother was laying out three sweet potato pies to cool, and baking a casserole. I gave her a hug, took some butterscotch cookies and a cup of coffee, and knocked on my father's office door.

"Papa? If you aren't busy, I need to talk."

"Certainly, my boy. What's going on? I hope nothing's wrong."

"I hope not, too. First of all, yesterday, on the way to school, a couple of cats from the neighborhood were asking some loaded questions. Apparently, while we were on vacation, the cops were asking about you and Mama. Like did you know anything about people being trafficked into restaurants or massage parlors, and like that." I looked at the books lining the walls. "Billy Fisher's parents were questioned, as well as who knows how many other people."

"Vinnie, there are things you need to understand. No, your mother and I are not directly involved in anything like that. Nothing is ever straight forward, however; things aren't black and white. That's not reality. For example, you hear in the news about certain people demanding certain rights and privileges because they're a specific race or choose a specific sexuality. The fact is that minorities were oppressed for years. The other fact is that certain groups carved out a niche, and fought blood filled battles to get ahead. Other groups chose to form gangs, create questionable music, and bitch about the ills perpetrated upon them by the majority. In the middle of that is the truth. Cats survived, and got ahead, based on their own drive and desire. Look at Nicky Barnes. He built an empire, and stayed competitive, despite his melanin. The entire issue is a shade of grey." My father looked solemn.

"OK. What does that have to do with what I asked? I'm not being rude, but this has me worried. I told the other kids that the cops were idiots." I twisted my fingers.

"Son, I help people come to America. I contribute to organizations and invest in businesses that hire refugees from other countries. Countries that are not exactly known for treating their own citizens well. You mother helps where she can. As I said, there are shades of grey. Nothing in this world is truly free. Yes, we take plunder as pirates, and that's free, but somewhere a price is paid. We don't pay it. That's all that matters. The refugees and immigrants have to bribe border guards, cover airfare, pay for lodging, food, fake identities, and so forth. The illegals don't have much cash, if any, so they work to pay off their costs. They do so willingly. Nobody is forcing anyone to come here." My father leaned back in his chair.

"The cops say that these organizations engage in slavery. That people are forced to work without pay or benefits. I thought pirates were against that."

"The workers don't receive a paycheck, no. Their paychecks go to pay for their expenses until those are paid off. Then they're free to work anywhere they choose. As to benefits, they receive medical care, and they're in America now."

"I dig the riff, but it's discordant. The next thing is that Mama is being unusually social and interactive with the community. I'm glad for that, if she's happy. Also, what happened to Myron Baker?"

My father looked stern before quickly smiling.

"Your mother and I decided that we should join in with the community, is all. It provides a good buffer against outsiders being nosy. I think you should get involved as well. I'm pleased that you're making friends from both sections of town. I raised you to notice everything, and trust nothing without questioning it. Now, though, you're asking some questions because of that; and the answers are far from easy." My father sighed.

"Well..." I prompted

"Remember how I told you and Tori that if you wanted to lose a car, the best way was to park it in long-term parking at the airport and remove the plates? Well, similarly, if one wishes to lose anything smaller in a permanent way, one can put the item in a car and send it though a compactor. The crushed metal is then put in back of a semi-truck and dropped into a river, or taken by boat, and dumped into the ocean. The item is never found again. The same works well with corpses." My father gave me matter of fact.

I blanched. "Savvy. I won't ask anything more about it. Except, why? Wouldn't it make more sense to arrest a person than...that?"

"There's more involved. Sometimes people are involved in matters, and involving the police would cause undo hassle. Furthermore, some behavior causes potential for headaches. So, there's a need to remove the issue permanently. That's a part of piracy that you needn't be involved with yet." My father stood and hugged me,

I went to my room and put away my homework. I grabbed some gin, my smoking supplies and *The Great Gatsby*. I walked to my circle of trees, lit up, and soon the warm cocoon enveloped me. I took a swig of gin, and sat thinking about what my father had said. Clearly the whole matter was as complex as any soap opera. There were other people involved. I decided that the best thing to do was nothing. Not yet. I needed to watch and wait. But if anything did occur which necessitated action, I would be ready.

I sat for an hour reading before heading home to a dinner of leftovers. After dinner I completed my other assignments and fell asleep. The next day I invited Julie home again, and started doing so every day. We even spent weekends hiking on some trails, and having picnics complete with buds and booze. It eased my anxiety, at least for a time.

Chapter Eighteen

Over the next year, life took several twists and turns. School was as boring as ever, but I compensated by learning life lessons instead. The first came from steadily dating Julie. The clothing I had asked my father to have sent arrived a few weeks later. One Saturday morning I opened the front door, and a package was there addressed to me. It had no return address, no indication as to whom had delivered it. I texted Julie, and she hitched a ride to my house.

My parents were at a meeting about upcoming community events, and Tori was at Fisher's house. I invited Julie into my bedroom, and showed her the clothes I'd received.

"I got some new threads from my uncles in New York. I got you some stuff, too. Like I said I would. Shoes, designer jeans and skirts, blouses, even some stuff from a lingerie boutique. I was hoping you might model it all to see if it fits." I winked.

"You're a wild man. No one spoils me like you do, or feeds me like your parents." Julie and I kissed. "I'm sure you want me to model for you. Especially the bras and panties. I'll try everything on in your walk-in closet, and let you know if it fits." She winked back at me.

I tried for nonchalant. "What? Come on, babe. You keep playing hard to get. What do I have to do in order to make you dig the riff?" I was irritated and flustered. I needed a drink or several of them.

"If you bought me this stuff as an exchange for sex, then keep it!" Julie started to leave. "I'm not a whore! I don't go all the way with a guy unless I know he's serious about me."

"I ordered those clothes because I thought you

might look nice in them. The wanting sex is because I find you irresistible. You have a great chassis, and an even better mind. You can take the clothes. Don't feel obligated by my gifts." I was frustrated. I reached for one of my water bottles of gin, and had a good pull. It helped.

Julie looked at me, and then walked into my giant closet. She closed the door, and, after some rustling around, emerged dressed in JS wings, a pair of tight, black jeans, and a baby blue blouse that was cut low in the front. I whistled.

"I like how these fit. And the silk lingerie is out of this world." Julie beamed at me. She modeled a few other combinations over the next half hour.

After she was done, she pulled me close, and we necked for a while. "Vinnie," she gasped for air "I know you like me. I like you too. You treat me better than anyone in school. It's that I never actually have…"

I held her close. "Me, either. Not really. I had a girlfriend, and we almost got there. It was fantastic being near her, you know, but I've never had sex before." I blushed.

"Maybe we should wait then. But, if we still want to at Thanksgiving break, we can go to the fields near the tracks, have drinks, smoke some buds, and see where it goes." Julie undid her blouse. She had on a red silk bra. She took my hand, and ran it over her firm breasts. I stiffened.

"That would be out of sight! I can procure a nice bottle of wine." I moaned and buried my face in her neck.

We lay on my bed, kissing and cuddling for another hour, before going for a walk. I filled half a bottle of Coke with the last of my whiskey, grabbed my bowl and buds, and headed into the kitchen. We packed a bag with cookies and brownies before hiking to my circle of trees. The afternoon took care of itself.

I smiled at her, feeling loose and relaxed after a few

hours of smoking and drinking. "Hey, would you be my girl?"

"How about settling for us being each other's." Julie smiled at me.

"Is that the best offer I can get?" I held her close.

"That's the best offer anyone can get." She kissed me.

A week later Julie couldn't come over. She said her father was returning to town after a few weeks of trucking. He would be home for a few days, and she had a lot of chores to catch up on. That worked out, because Tori and I were corralled into helping sort books at the library for a sale they were having. Several of the kids from my neighborhood were helping as well. My father and mother were glad-handing the library staff, offering to make a sizable donation to a building fund. I had a sense that the volunteer work, plus this obsequious friendliness, had a purpose. I was determined to find out.

Over the two months between school starting and Thanksgiving, I started reading articles online about human trafficking, drug deals, opiate epidemics and other matters. One subject led to the next. It was through reading that I began to connect some pieces of a puzzle. There were large cyber networks that operated in a shadowy place called the dark web. It was like the regular internet, but highly protected. These networks engaged in certain activities I recognized as urban piracy. Counterfeit money, FOT goods, discussions about how and where to obtain free food, clothes, and housing.

However, the dark web networks also dealt with discussions of bringing immigrants over the borders and handing them over to employers who abused them and enslaved them. Like old time slave auctions, there were sites that literally allowed people to bid on other humans. One article I read dealt with people who helped fund women's shelters as a means of locating suitable workers for strip clubs and the sex trade. Another mentioned hiring men to work in unsafe conditions scrapping metal, clearing fields, and other hard labor.

A thought occurred to me that if someone like Myron Baker was involved in enslaving illegal immigrants to work crushing cars, and if that person was also risking police attention by abusing his wife and kids, then it might be necessary to make him disappear permanently. That thought drew me back to my conversation with my father. Could Uncle Vasily and other people I knew be involved in such crimes? Could my parents?

The more I studied this subject, the surer I became. And, the more I needed to drink in order to calm my nerves. I've never been stupid, and it was crystal clear to me why my parents had become pillars of society. If the cops came back and questioned anyone, they would hear how sweet and wonderful Frank and Antoinette Il-Cazzo were. How they helped out with the community activities. *"Certainly, they would never be involved in such dealings, officer."*

I developed digestion troubles, and my headaches increased in frequency. I visited a doctor, but he found nothing physically wrong with me. He posited that it was tension, and recommended breathing exercises to help me relax. I already performed daily kata, and a part of that involved controlled breathing.

As Thanksgiving approached, I began teaching Julie some kata. My skills were limited, however. I thought about trying to find somewhere in Sweetbriar to study again on the weekends, or maybe to learn Krav Maga as Otis LeMar had suggested. That would have meant losing time with Julie though, and we were growing closer. She and I often hitchhiked to Sweetbriar together, but that was for other reasons.

One of the first lessons I had learned in life was to pass on my knowledge, and to help others less fortunate than myself. I used our trips to Sweetbriar to educate Julie about piracy. At first, she was uncertain, but she grew to become quite accomplished. I made a quick trip every two weeks, with or without her. I was almost a teenager, and a couple of fifths of whiskey or gin was needed if I was going to function.

By the week before my thirteenth birthday, I had developed a routine. I would wake up, take a hot shower to clear my sinuses, have a shot of whiskey to steady my nerves and help my headache, do my kata workout in the backyard, have breakfast, and shower again. At school I kept several twenty ounce bottles of Coke laced with whiskey in my bag. It was easy to grab my sack and take a pull. On the weekends I occasionally played at sports with the neighborhood kids, and once in a while had some of Fisher's raisin mash. Mostly I kept to myself, with the exception of time with Julie.

There was a big party for my birthday, bigger than I wanted. It wasn't that I objected to a large party, but I suspected that everything my parents did was part of a larger con. My mother and father started preparing several days in advance with the delivery of several giant smoked turkeys, a whole pig on a spit, and two cases of Chateau Montrose. My mother was baking cakes and pies, preparing hors d'oeuvres, and making salads and cold cut platters.

The day of the party I was helping to set up tables on the block. We had set up cones to close off the street, and guests were arriving with presents and food, The Dimitrion family, minus their son, showed up early with Julie in the lead. She was dressed in a long, grey, Dior wool skirt, a tight, black sweater, and grey, suede boots. Her father, James, and mother, Luella, helped set up food and drink stations, while Julie and I mingled with the other guests.

Julie had become accepted by the cats and chicks in my neighborhood, due in large part to her being around more often. Fisher and Tori had invited us to go to the movies the next week. Al Contreras arrived with his parents, and six cousins who were visiting. It was a block party for the ages. I was the nominal guest of honor, but it seemed more like a huge gathering of everyone from the west side of town,

I was talking to Natty Wolf when a car pulled into a driveway down the block. It was a sleek, black jaguar, and emerging from it was Vasily, and his wife Natasha. My sister Gina was in the back seat with her fiancé. I ran over and hugged her as soon as she had climbed out.

"Well, look what wanders in when we leave the gates open." Tori came running.

"I wouldn't miss this for anything! Happy birthday, Vinnie!" Gina handed me a card. I hugged her again. "Open that later. Alone."

Gina introduced us to Nicky DiNapoli. He and she were engaged, and he was a computer programming major with a minor in business. I noticed that his nails were beautifully manicured, he wore a silk shirt, opened at the collar, designer jeans, a long leather coat and expensive Nike shoes. His black hair was brushed back and slicked. The guy had a swarthy look, and an air about him that made me think of mob movies.

An hour later, everyone gathered around as my father made a toast to my future. Guests helped themselves to food, and I managed to sneak a bottle of Jack Daniels from the open bar, stashing it in my room. As I was walking out of the house Fisher approached me.

"Hey, Il-Cazzo, I brought you something. But you need to put it on ice, if you catch my drift." Fisher handed me a quarter ounce of buds and a quart jar of mash. "I wasn't sure what else to get you, man. You seem to really enjoy chilling with this stuff."

"Thank you. I really appreciate that." We walked back inside and I hid everything, "So how's that GED thing going?" We rejoined the party.

"Not bad. I think by New Years I should have it. Tori too, maybe. We have to ask Frankie about that." Fisher smiled at me.

I nodded, and went to mingle with the guests. I received a stack of new books, several DVDs, and a closet full of new clothes. I thanked everyone and was putting the gifts in my room when I opened the card from Gina. It contained a Florida ID card in my name, but listing my age as fifteen. There was also a Social Security Card in my name, but with a different number than mine. I walked back to the party and found Gina and Nicky,

"Thank you. But, why?"

"Later. We need to talk. Tori too. But, not here." Gina hugged me.

That evening the party was winding down, and I helped clear everything away. I was feeling the effects from having taken a few good swigs of raisin mash. As I was carrying in the last of the covered dishes, Gina and Tori came outside dressed in black turtlenecks, cashmere sweaters, and jeans. I walked into my room, changed into jeans and a hoodie, grabbed my sack and pipe, and joined them. We walked quietly to my favorite spot.

"Hey, we got trouble. Well, not yet exactly, but we will soon." Gina wasted no time. "The cops are nosing around the old neighborhood, and they've already called in several family friends for questioning. Vasily and Natasha, Marco and Tatiana, Lucas, Carissa, Vickie, and some others."

"Questioning about what?" Tori looked nervous.

"Mostly about stuff that goes far and away from the

short cons on which we were raised. I got dragged into the middle of it, although Mama and Papa didn't want that." Gina lit the pipe I'd loaded.

"I hope I'm wrong, but I'm pretty sure I can guess what the cops want. Some guys I attend school with started running their sewers about human trafficking and about drugs. I can't accept that Mama and Papa would engage in that deliberately. But maybe they're invested in businesses that engage in more sordid activities. Maybe Myron Baker was trafficking for people who are engaged in that. Maybe he brought down heat because he was a scumbag. Maybe he had to be removed." I looked at Gina with a steady gaze.

"You have more than marshmallows in your head, bro. You almost have it right. A lot of people we used to know are involved. They have been for years. It's a lucrative business and they justify it because in the end people get to live in America."

"So, how are we in trouble from this? What's the pitch, bitch?" Tori was mellowing.

"Mama and Papa are planning to sell the house. As it is, they scammed their way onto disability and moved here in order to lay low. It hasn't worked, though. So, they'll sell and move away. Sis, you and Billy are almost ready to get GED's. Then you're free to attend college. Baby bro', that ID lets you get a GED as well. You need to study for it, though. You're academically ready, anyway. Socially, not so much. I'm not sure you'll ever be ready socially. Once the house is sold, you should head south. I have a plan and we can discuss it."

"Travel how far south, and stay with whom? Or do you mean I'm on my own here?" My guts tightened despite the pleasant cocoon of the marijuana.

"You can figure it out. You always do. If you really need help, Nicky and I will be available. We can talk tomorrow before I leave. I have some ideas." Gina hugged me tight.

Chapter Nineteen

The morning after my birthday I walked into the kitchen at a much later hour than was my custom. An extra portion of Fisher's raisin-mash had precipitated my falling asleep. My head throbbed slightly, so I chased some Ibuprofen with coffee. Gina joined me, along with her fiancé. Tori was at Fisher's studying. Gina poured coffee and made toast. She sat and looked at me a moment.

"Nicky and I have to get back to academia, bro'. We have some work to get done. After our talk last night, I think you'll have concluded that we help Uncle V and others by providing ID cards. There's a DMV near the campus, and Nicky works there. He knows someone who helps us out. We can cover any of the fifty states." Gina sipped coffee.

"Why do you help with that? Isn't that antithetical to our code?" I gave her quizzical.

"To you it might be. But, dig this, Vinnie, no one asks the illegals to come to America. The jobs are scarce as it is. Money's tight. That's why we plunder businesses in the first place. No jobs means no money. So, we take what we need. There'd be more jobs if we had less competition. Not enough more, but more. The illegals insist on coming here anyway. In order to make money, people facilitate their journey. I don't ask about the details, because I don't need to know. I'm getting through college debt free by helping out. If it bothers you to be involved, then don't." Gina's face registered irritation. "I didn't figure you'd care so much. You certainly aren't a saint."

"I dig the riff, but the cops are getting involved. That's some serious shit."

"Baby blue, by next Summer it'll all be cleared up. You'll be free to make your own life. Mama and Papa will be safely out of reach. Me and Tori will be regular college students. Trust me, this all ends for me next Summer." Gina poured me more coffee.

"Next Summer I won't even be fourteen. I can't just hang out all day and not go to school without drawing attention to myself. How am I supposed to swing it being on my own?"

"The same as you always have. Only you won't come home every night. You're the smartest kid I know. You have the ID, your wits, you know how to survive. You'll be fine."

Gina and I spent an hour discussing The Gulf Coast of Florida. We formulated a plan for my survival and discussed various scenarios that might arise. I started making plans for whatever might happen.

One plan involved Julie. She hitchhiked to my house the next day. It was the day before Thanksgiving and her parents were preparing for arriving guests. I packed my supplies including a pint of Fisher's brew and grabbed my sack. We walked a mile to where some hiking trails wound through trees and fields.

"I might have to leave next year, doll. My father landed a gig. I was wondering if maybe you and I could take off together. Get out of this place and head somewhere sunny and warm," I broached the subject as we walked

Julie looked at me with an odd expression. "No way my parents would go for that. I like you. I really like you. But, I'm not ready to go start a life together. I'm only fourteen and a half. You scare me sometimes, Vinnie. You act like you're already an adult."

"I feel like one most of the time. No choice. I can't explain everything, but my life isn't what you think. Anyway, it was a stupid idea. Sorry I asked." I shrugged.

"You might be surprised at what I understand. But, I'm still not ready to run off. In fact, for me, that might cause worse problems. I want you. I wish we could escape. My home life isn't pretty. Not everything your neighbors say about my side of town is completely false."

"I dig. We're both treading water so we don't drown. The waves keep crashing over us, and every time we spot dry land it's only a mirage."

"And in my case, I'm surrounded by sharks."

"I'll teach you how to out-swim them."

We walked another mile on the paths until we came across a field that was hidden from view by a thicket of trees. We maneuvered back and found a maple tree on the far edge. After a couple of hours of smoking, drinking, and necking we decided that the day after Thanksgiving we'd return and see how far we wanted to go in our relationship.

The day after Thanksgiving I packed a large picnic, included a bottle of Moscato d'Asti I'd boosted from a store, and met Julie by the path. We hiked in feeling timid and bubbly all at once. After a smoke, a few drinks, and some kissing, we slowly helped each other undress. We started slowly anyway, feeling each other, and getting excited. It was easy enough to pocket a box of Trojans at a drug store, and though putting one on was uncomfortable, I was not going to make an issue out of things. The experience ended faster than it had started.

We stretched out on a blanket in an open field, beneath a maple tree. We had managed to pull on enough clothes to look decent. It was like riding an out of control roller coaster – exhilarating, exquisite, and wild. After a half hour we went for a second round. I thought about Steph, and wondered what it would be like laying pipe with her. After we caught our breath, Julie drew closer to me and we kissed. It was a mild day for November, so we sat up and dressed. I held Julie in my arms for a long while before we packed everything and returned to my house.

While heading back, a euphoric glow surrounded

me. The feeling was even better than the warm cocoon of pleasure I got from smoking buds. I stopped several times along the way to swap chews with Julie. She smiled brightly.

"I love you, baby. May…maybe we could find a way for you to stay around here. If you do have to move away, though, then we can have until next Summer. I hope you want that too." Julie blushed and looked away.

"More than anything, doll. More than anything. Can we get together next weekend? I want to fill you in. On my life I mean. I think my parents are going out of town. Tori practically lives with Fisher these days, so we'd have the place to ourselves."

That evening, after a dinner of Thanksgiving leftovers, my father and I gave Julie a ride home. Her house was on the far end of a road that was more potholes than asphalt. The surrounding houses weren't completely decrepit, although most were in need of paint and some landscaping.

As my father and I drove home, with Perry Como playing on a CD, I began a discussion that I had been planning for four days. "Papa? I was talking to Gina a couple of days ago. Is everything OK? I mean if you need me to do anything to help out, I'm here."

He turned and looked at me with soft eyes and then returned his eyes to the road. "Everything's fine, son. It's nothing your mother and I can't handle. I would have spoken to you and Tori but I really hoped that matters could be dealt with. This whole situation has spun out of control." His voice was soft and despondent.

"What's the situation? Am I allowed to ask? Can you please tell me straight?"

"Vinnie, there's more to surviving than simply plundering free food and necessities. I needed to invest our money in order to make a decent life for you kids. I had to work around the edges of the system. Damned if I was going to invest in Wall Street, though. Instead, I invested in some businesses. I and some friends gave them seed money to get started. But, some of these Clydes I invested with are engaging in behavior that leaves everyone federally liable. The jerks running the businesses aren't the sharpest tools in the drawer, either. In the end, your mother and I devised a way to move to a quiet community and lay low. Unfortunately, you fell in love with Stephanie. Myron worked in a business that was operating outside of the law. He put a bunch of people at risk with his drunken abuse."

I turned my head, tears flowing. "So, this is because I fell in love?"

"No, you did nothing wrong. We had to help them." My father ruffled my hair gently. "But things became far more complicated. In order to secure the help Heather and the girls needed, certain people required some quid pro quo. Myron had to disappear. That drew the attention of the police, which in turn brought back pre-existing issues." My father sighed. "The only thing to do is for your mother and I to disappear as well. We know some places outside of the country where we can live comfortably for the rest of our lives. You kids will survive. We raised the three of you to survive. Gina can focus on her education. Tori and Billy can get married, and attend school. You'll have a large safety network if you need it. That's the whole enchilada."

I stared out the window until we arrived home. I had more or less deduced everything weeks before, but I hadn't understood the depth of the problem. Fear overwhelmed me, but I had to stay tough. I went to my room, locked the door, and had three fingers of Jack Daniels, before changing into my pajamas and laying down to read *Columbine* by Dave Cullen. It did nothing to make me feel better. At some point, I put the book down and fell asleep.

The following day I woke up before dawn and went to the back yard. I started with judo kata and transitioned into the Zui Quan. I pushed myself fast and hard, working up a major sweat. If I was going to be thrust into the world alone, I had to get prepared. After the kata, I dropped and recovered twenty times briskly, executing ten push-ups on each drop. I rolled onto my back, performed fifty flutter kicks, and stood.

After my shower, and three cups of coffee, I made my way to school. The neighborhood kids walked beside me, but I felt alone. At school I smiled at Julie, but kept my distance so that no one would suspect anything was between us. So many emotions flooded me at once that my stomach hurt. I had no one to talk to about my feelings. I had to play the hand as it was dealt. I had to bluff as best I could.

Chapter Twenty

The whole week was a repeat, each day like the day before: A hard workout, breakfast, school, return home and landscape the garden and a few shrubs, another strenuous work out, followed by dinner and homework. I read in order to keep my mind occupied, and drank almost an entire bottle of Chopin vodka.

On Friday afternoon, my parents left to attend a wedding in New York. Tori was spending the weekend with Billy Bob Fisher. I was sitting on the porch swing finishing up *Columbine* when Julie arrived. We walked inside, shed our jackets, and turned to kiss.

"I told my mom that I was staying at a friend's house. Her sister will cover for us if anyone calls. I said we were working on the project for history." Julie gasped after our extended kissing session.

"That works. We have the crib to ourselves. Tori won't be home until Sunday, and neither will my folks." I put Julie's backpack in my room.

"You got any of that wine left?" Julie looked in the fridge and took out sandwich fixings.

"No, sorry. But I can make martinis. If you prefer, I can make Rum and Coke."

"I've never had a martini. My dad would peel my ass and take a switch to me if he knew what you and I were doing. He'd beat the hell out of you, too. He isn't around that much, though. Mom is usually out of commission in front of the TV." Julie made sandwiches and chips. "They pulled it together for your birthday party, in order to impress your folks, but that isn't really them."

"Can I ask you something? Are people really dealing meth and heroin on your side of town? The other kids say it, but I don't believe everything I hear." I took a bite of sandwich, a sip of dry martini, and turned on the TV to a Christmas movie about kids in an airport.

"Yeah." Julie gave me matter of fact. "My brother was almost put in jail for dealing. He doesn't deal, though. He helps move the money. So does my dad. I'm left out of things. My mom doesn't want to know anything. She'd rather drink, and watch soap operas,"

We ate, drank, and snuggled together on the couch. It felt terrific having Julie near me. The knots in my stomach began dissipating.

"I was wondering, did you know Steph Baker?" I took a sip of martini.

"Yeah, she was in some of my classes since kindergarten. Real shy. Kind of awkward. I tried to make friends with her, but she never wanted to hang out. Then suddenly her family disappeared last summer. Some cops came around asking questions, but no one on east side is going to get involved. Not with cops, and not with her dad." Julie took a bite of sandwich.

"I met her, sort of, when we first moved to town. There are things I have to tell someone. I'm trusting you to keep it to yourself."

"Please! I wouldn't dime on you, Vinnie. You can tell me anything." Julie leaned in and wrapped her arms around me.

"First of all, Steph wasn't shy, or awkward. She was being hurt. So was Caroline and Heather. Myron was a violent drunk, and he beat them. I didn't know either, for a while. One evening her mother called me on my cell phone -- in hysterics -- and my family helped them get away. I have no idea where they went, though." I sighed, swallowing hard so that I wouldn't cry.

"You did that? Your family did?" Julie gave looked shocked. "You really are something, Vinnie. I've never known anyone who cares so much about people." She kissed me and held me closer.

"There's more though. Worse stuff. Myron was apparently involved in some crimes. Something about hiring undocumented labor. The people who he answered to were pissed that the cops were looking at him for domestic violence. I think people I know made him disappear, permanently." My chest heaved and my face flushed. I took a slug of martini which helped.

"Dude, that hairball was involved in everything. He was hiring Mexicans, and stealing their wages. He sold drugs and prostitutes, too. He was a scumbag! I'm glad if he got killed."

I nodded. "I dig. Thing is my parents are mixed up with people who do those things. I thought that the extent of their action was running some heists on big businesses. Plundering corporations that screw the poor. But, this, this involves square johns getting hurt. Regular people are being targeted and Papa always taught me never to target them. It pisses me off!"

Julie held me and listened.

"And because of this thing with the Bakers, the cops started sniffing around again. Apparently, they were looking into my parents before, which is why we moved. I can't figure it from any angle. Everything is spinning out of control." I took a bite of sandwich.

After we finished eating, and washed the dishes, Julie turned toward me. "You've been. through the wringer, huh? How the hell do you stay so calm with all that going on?" Julie started unbuttoning my shirt.

"I'm tough. I've always had to be. I wouldn't know any other way. The guys help, too -- Jim Beam, Jack Daniels, Johnny Walker, and Jose Cuervo." I slipped off my shirt and started unbuttoning Julie's.

Fifteen minutes later we were standing in a hot shower soaping each other up and exploring each other's bodies. The steam filled room felt wonderful with Julie in my arms. We turned off the water, and dried off. She put on a pink velvety robe. I put on my boxers, and a silk smoking jacket. We sat in my room, relaxed and quiet, snuggling. At some point we drifted into a nap.

Three hours later I went to the kitchen and took out two steaks to defrost. Julie sat in her robe, feet tucked under her, and flipped through the channels before settling on some show about a family with sixteen kids.

I poured us each a glass of Coke with a shot of Bacardi in it. "Here you go. Steaks will be ready in a while."

"Vinnie? That stuff you told me earlier, it isn't your fault you know. You fell in love with Steph, and you did what you had to in order to help her get away from being abused. The rest of that has nothing to do with you," Julie leaned against me. "Did you and her...uh...you know." Julie sipped her drink.

"I wanted to, but no, we never got the chance. She never smoked out with me either, or drank. We did get a chance to be alone, but only once. It didn't feel right at the time, though. Did you ever have any other boys?" I held her closer.

"Not really. I told you that you were my first. I don't like the boys in my neighborhood, and you're the first from west side to stick up for me, and care about me." Julie snuggled closer. "I mean, when I was eleven there was a birthday party, and we were playing truth or dare. I got dared to moon Bobby-Rae McGraph. So, I did. That's the closest I ever came.

We watched TV and snuggled for an hour before I put the steaks on to grill with slices of sweet potato. While they cooked, I made us a salad and poured us glasses of Peligrino. We sat eating, and watched a movie called *Lies My Mother Told Me*.

"I wish I could run away with you, Vinnie. My life isn't so great. It got a lot better after I met you, but it still isn't great. My dad drives truck down to Florida and back all week. He's not home much, and when he is, he gets pissed about everything I do. My brother is friends with people I don't want to be around. And, my mom, she drinks herself into a stupor every day, and watches soap operas. I have to clean the house and cook." Julie ate some steak.

"You can come with me when I take off next Summer. I'd protect you." I smiled at her.

We ate and watched the movie before walking back to my bedroom. I turned on some Charlie Parker, and we held each other in the quietude of eventide. After a half hour we slipped off our robes and messed up the bedsheets. With practice we had improved, and the effects were spectacular.

After another hot shower, we curled up together in our pajamas and watched TV until we fell asleep. At dawn I changed into my shorts and t-shirt. I was working through kata in the back yard when Julie opened the sliding glass door.

"There you are, lover boy." Julie laughed. "Wow, you really know that stuff."

I finished a judo kata, and motioned Julie to come outside. She shook her head and pointed to her pajamas. We ate breakfast instead, before I showered off. She cleaned up while I dressed, and we sat doing our homework.

That afternoon we walked to the tree circle and smoked a bowl. As the pleasant feeling surrounded me, I held Julie's head close to my chest.

"I need to call some people later. Is there anything you ever wanted for Christmas, but never got? Serious question, babe." I leaned down and kissed her.

"Some nice perfume. A big teddy bear. Like those

giant ones that are four feet tall." Julie laughed. "I want a new laptop, too."

"Well, maybe if you're a good girl Santa will bring you those things." I winked.

"I love you, Vinnie. You're the craziest boy I ever met, but I love you for it." Julie stood and we walked back to my house. '

After eating a whole tray of cookies with milk, we sat on the porch swing. An hour later we walked the four miles back to her house. I watched her go inside before walking home. On the way back I saw Al Contreras and some of the other kids tossing a football. I joined them. It was a crisp autumn day, and I felt better than I had in a long while.

The next day I sent emails to people I knew in New York. I put in an order for Julie's Christmas gifts. After that I ran my bed clothes through the laundry, washed the dishes, and sat around reading *Huckleberry Finn* until my parents came home.

Chapter Twenty-One

Christmas brought with it frigid air, and heavy snowfall. I spent most of the weeks leading up to the holiday on my laptop. I had doubled down on requesting coupons and scoring vouchers. I found one that worked like a dream. There was a brewhouse that also served sandwiches and burgers. I emailed locations across the nation, and each franchise sent an e-card worth twenty five or thirty dollars good at any location. Inside of three weeks I had over five hundred dollars in vouchers.

I was sitting in the living room, reading *No Angel* by Jay Dobyn, when some packages arrived at the house. The delivery man was driving an unmarked white panel truck. I helped him unload the boxes, and tipped him $50.00. Inside one box was an Apple MacBook. Inside another were six bottles of perfume, three Chanel and three Versace. The last box held a five foot tall teddy bear. I took the gifts to my room and wrapped everything except the teddy bear.

That weekend I met Tori and Fisher at his house. Julie was with me, and we had brought a thermos of cocoa spiked with Baileys, a bag of buds, and a huge container of cookies and fudge. Fisher had a bucket and a specially reconstructed soda bottle. We walked to our favorite spot

"So, you both passed your tests? Except the math?" I smiled at Fisher and hugged Tori.

"Yep. It was tough, but we did it. You'll do it too, soon enough." Fisher began loading snow into the bucket. He took a quart of water from his backpack and made a slurry.

Julie cleared an area on the ground and set up the snacks. While she was getting things arranged, I stood talking to Tori. We'd spent the first week of vacation making plans. I had resigned myself to the inevitable fact that my parents would lam. They were in over their heads with people who were scumbags. My emotions were everywhere, but I was ready to take care of myself. I knew Julie couldn't come with me, but we had each other until June.

After the snacks were set up, Fisher demonstrated the use of a gravity bong. My first try on the device was so cold, and gave me such a large hit, that the cocoon of pleasure was instantaneous. I took two more hits, and was laughing, loose and silly. I tuned in some Sinatra on the Pandora app. Julie and I started slow dancing, and soon Fisher and Tori were as well.

After eating our fill of cookies and fudge, washed down with spiked cocoa, we walked Julie home. The cold air felt incredible. I was happy for the first time in months. I walked Tori and Fisher back to his house, and returned home. My mother was reading a romance novel in the living room, and my father was working in his office. I went to my room, and, for the first time in a long while, fell into a deep dreamless sleep.

Life relaxed once I accepted that the situation was going to play out as it had to. I could prepare for what was coming, but I couldn't stop it. The preparations were not all initiated by me, either. My father began teaching me some necessary skills.

Christmas morning, I woke up to find dozens of presents under our tree. The previous night had been spent with Gina, her fiancé, Tori, and my parents, eating cookies and watching TV together in front of the fireplace. It was a family Christmas tradition. Having everyone together again was wonderful. I fell into another peaceful sleep.

At eight in the morning, Christmas day, I made the coffee and sliced a pumpkin pie. I put in a CD of Perry Como singing carols, and set out the food and drinks. That also was a family tradition. Tori came out of her room dressed in her terrycloth robe, Gina and Nicky emerged from Gina's room dressed in jeans and sweatshirts, and my parents came upstairs dressed in matching red pajamas. We all sat by the tree eating pie and drinking coffee. I started the festivities by giving my father a box of Cuban cigars and my mother a bottle of Chanel number 5. I gave Gina and Nicky an Xbox for their new apartment complete with a dozen games. Tori had been more difficult to shop for. I ended up buying her a monogrammed leather luggage set. None of the items had been damaged when they fell off of the truck.

The majority of the gifts I received from my parents came from a big catalogue store to the north. The store had a lifetime guarantee on everything they sold. If a pair of jeans wore out five years after purchase, they replaced them free of charge. That arrangement was tailor made for my family.

My parents had purchased a top of the line mummy sleeping bag for me, a backpack that could hold a week's worth of clothes, plus food and camping gear, and some high quality, waterproof hiking boots. They also bought me a military grade flashlight, several pairs of jeans, and two weeks' worth of double thickness cotton t-shirts. Tori bought me a stack of books. Gina and Nicky bought me a cargo vest, and a new monogrammed wallet.

That afternoon my father gave me a ride to Julie's so I could deliver her gifts. She was overwhelmed by the size of the teddy bear. I brought her parents some scented candles and a giant tin of cashews. My father and I joined them for some eggnog and we sat around talking.

"I was in the scouts as a younger man. I've been planning to take my son camping in the mountains. You know, teach him some survival skills. Your daughter's welcome to join us." My father gave them his best Robert

Young.

"That's right neighborly of you. Let me think on it."
Her father drawled.

Julie and I sat sipping our eggnog. We had both passed all of our final exams with high scores. I listened to my father extol the virtues of camping and getting back to nature.

The next six days I spent hiking in the snow with Julie, having snowball battles with neighbor kids, and reading. I kept up with my exercise routine, and wrote to restaurants and manufacturers, but as I relaxed and accepted life, I found my need to drink had decreased.

On the eve of 2010 I rang in the new year with Tori, Fisher, my parents, and Julie. Julie's parents were at a party of their own, and her brother was out of town. My parents went to sleep moments after the ball dropped in Times Square, so Tori, Fisher, Julie, and I went for a walk. I had brought a pint of spiked eggnog and four paper cups. We toasted the new year and our futures.

After the holidays I began learning about camping and survival skills. My father gave me an old scouting book of his, and though I never joined the Boy Scouts, he taught me everything he knew.

Sometimes Julie joined us, other times not. These trips provided me with a terrific education and insight into non-urban survival. They also provided my father with a needed escape from his worries and stress. During those trips where it was he and I, the feeling of paternal love resonated. My father began telling me about his childhood, and in his way making amends in advance for leaving me to fend for myself.

We would pack up tents, sleeping bags and warm clothes. After driving north, we would hike a dozen miles to a campsite near a lake. During the hikes I learned what berries were safe to eat, and how to tell poison ivy and poison oak from regular leaves. Once we arrived and pitched our tent, we would live for a few days on the fish we caught and a few basic food staples. I also learned how to shoot a gun.

My father would set up cans and plastic bottles full of water. After teaching me how to check a pistol and reload, he began teaching me basic gun safety. I was always to assume that a gun was loaded. I was never to point a gun at a person unless I planned to shoot them. If I did need to shoot, I was to aim at the chest and fire the gun empty. Once I learned the rules, he taught me to fire straight, and hit what I aimed for.

The trips where Julie was permitted to come included Tori and Fisher as well. We fished, but we also brought hot dogs and marshmallows. It was more camp out, less survival skills. And, although we couldn't have sex, Julie and I spent a lot of time by the fire holding each other and snuggling. When Fisher came, we would leave my father to have a nap in a hammock. Tori, Fisher, Julie, and I would go for hikes and sip raisin mash.

These trips became a bi-monthly event. I was savvy enough to look toward the future and incorporate the new skills into my plans. I had no idea where I might end up, and it was good to know how to survive anywhere until I could get back to civilization.

As springtime came to Harvest Junction, my father and I began doing some home improvements. We resurfaced the driveway, replaced the rain gutters, and installed a lighting system in the yard that activated itself once the sun set. After we finished, my father listed the house for sale. My mother put out platters of cookies, and a big urn of coffee whenever there was an open house. I would escape the scene and meet Julie to go hiking, smoke out, and make love.

Summer fast approached, and, despite my stresses, I

had gotten straight A's. My mother and father purchased a small home in the Dominican Republic. I asked about joining them, but they said it wasn't a place to raise children. They had trained me to take care of myself, and now it was time to do that. I was almost fourteen. I was a man.

Two weeks before school ended, the house transferred to new buyers, furniture and all. I took my personal possessions and packed them into my backpack. With that, my parents hugged me and Tori, gave us the number of a burner phone in case we needed to talk, and were gone. I was officially alone.

Tori was staying at Fisher's house, and I was given a guest room there. In exchange, I helped his parents with the grocery expenses. It was a fair trade. I spent every minute I could with Julie, but good times have to end. On the last Friday of school, we ended as well. I promised to text every day. We kissed, and she walked home. The air was thick and sour like a bad late movie, my chest hurt, and my eyes throbbed. The feeling didn't last long.

Book Two

"All in the wild March-morning I heard the angels call,
It was when the moon was setting, and dark was over all;
The trees began to whisper, and the wind began to roll,
And in the wild March-morning I heard them call my soul."
Tennyson

Chapter Twenty-Two

On the last Friday of school, I packed my backpack. I had given the majority of my book collection to Julie as a gift. I tightened the straps, hugged Tori and Fisher, and walked out the door of his house. Down the street in both directions, younger siblings of some school friends played in their yards. Where the Bakers had once lived, Bobby-Ray McCoy and his son Jethro worked on a car, oiling the rods, tightening the nuts, and like that. Our house was now owned by an elderly couple. I'd miss the place. The smell of succulent roasts, chicken, stews, fresh pies and bread wafted through the summer air as I headed into an uncertain and precarious future.

I hitched a ride west for a while, and caught the greyhound bus to New York. The trip was spent sleeping and reading *Beat the Dealer*. I bought junk food at every stop, and where there was time, had a toke and a drink. After a day, I began practicing a basic card count, if only to keep my mind occupied.

Returning to the old neighborhood, I spent two days and nights with a pneumatic blonde named Mirella Kiskurva. She was Venus in a four foot eight inch package, with a smooth, blemish free face, a perky chest and a slender body. We had an encounter in a corner bistro. She was having trouble with her debit card and I paid for her meal. Her parents were out of town so we took a couple of days to get acquainted over take out Chinese food and many bottles of plundered merlot. She seemed eager to study my every nuance. Mirella was seventeen and thought I was as well. Why ruin a good thing by volunteering unnecessary information?

Spending a couple days inside of a cozy apartment was just what the doctor ordered. I was stressed, my sinuses were throbbing, and other than the love of a lady, a stiff drink, sleep, and comfort food was all I craved. Mirella and I napped and watched a Law and Order marathon in between coital sessions. I found a bottle of single malt in the rear of her parent's liquor cabinet and helped myself. My stress eased.

After a couple of days, I looked up Vasily and Natasha. They were in the process of moving to the south seas. My parents were settled in the Dominican Republic. I took Vasily out for lunch at a steakhouse on East 46th.

"I need something before you light out, Uncle V." I took a bite of potato.

"Anything for my favorite nephew." Vasily's voice was strained, but his eyes were sharp and focused.

"I have this girl I like. I want to get her something nice, but she's sort of big. Could you get some bottoms in a fifty? Oh, and maybe some tops in a twenty as well?" I passed him an envelope with thirty Benjamin Franklins in it. Before moving, my parents had given me and Tori each five thousand dollars in our bank accounts. I also had six grand left from after our move to Harvest Junction. I was set.

"Give me until tomorrow, young man." Vasily and I spent the rest of the meal talking sports and politics. The next day he gave me the bills. I stashed them in the inner pocket of my backpack.

The following week I travelled to see Gina and Nicky. They informed me that Tori and Fisher had been accepted at a college in New Mexico. After providing me with letters from my "parents" indicating permission to take the GED a year early, and buying me a heavy canvas courier's sack, they drove me to the train station and put me on an Amtrak. The courier's sack had a removable piece of stiff canvas covered cardboard on the bottom inside, so I stashed the bills from Vasily under it.

I was sitting in the club car, eating an overpriced hot dog, and drinking coffee laced with bourbon, when this voluptuous English girl approached. She was heavily made-up, and wore fishnet stockings, a mini-skirt, and a low cut blouse. I had seen hookers who were less obvious.

"Hi, you alone? My name's Cherry Bakewell. I have a private sleeper car if you'd care to keep me company."

"Yes, I'm alone. Was just reading the newspaper. Sure, I'd enjoy keeping you company, as long as there's no obligations with the offer."

"No obligations. You're handsome, and I'm lonely."

We walked back to her compartment and let nature take its course. I shared my bottle of Jack Daniels, and she shared her food. She was eighteen and heading to college. I had experience with Julie and Mirella, but Cherry was at a whole other level. I learned some new techniques before departing the train in Tampa, leaving her to continue south.

After texting Julie, and taking a short bus ride, I arrived in Clearwater, Florida. I caught a city bus downtown, and got the lay of the land. Within a few blocks of the main station were several recovery meetings including a twelve step club. The club had well attended meetings, and better yet they had a booklet that listed every meeting in the area. I bought a cup of coffee with an ersatz twenty, received change, and cut out on the double. I resupplied my food needs at a grocery store, hiked over a bridge, and found the beach.

Walking along the beaches I scouted for the best location to set up base. Clearwater Beach was too crowded and commercial. It looked acceptable for purposes of activity and social networking, however. The string of beach communities heading south were entirely too upscale for my needs. By midnight I hit Treasure Island. The area was perfect. The beach was all but empty, the housing mid-level expensive. I'd fit in.

I had my backpack full of threads and toiletries, a large towel, and my canvas courier's bag that held my books, money, electronics and my stash of weed and alcohol. After a week I confirmed my suspicions that this was the right beach for my needs. Each morning the cops scouted the beaches, harassed the homeless campers, but they never noticed me. I texted Julie every day. She'd maintained some relationships on the west side of Harvest Junction, and was dating Victor Wolf. I felt better knowing she was doing well.

My schedule on the beach was to sleep on my towel from seven in the morning until three, and ride the busses until five. I would hit a series of AA meetings, grab free coffee and snacks, and exchange my money from Uncle V. Around ten at night I would go to a local college to sit and study for my GED. At five in the morning, I would ride back to the beach and start over. That allowed for plenty of time to hit up restaurants, use my coupons at the grocery stores, and sneak tokes in alleys or behind buildings. Even better were the outside bars. People would leave a drink unattended and I would grab it and finish it off. I also managed to kite bottles of liquor, or to pay a homeless person to buy them for me.

On the busses I read a series of articles about a trial in Missouri. A cat they dubbed The Boonie Hat Bandit was up on charges of bank robbery. Bank Robbers held a special place in my heart. I had neither the smarts, nor the testicular fortitude, to pull off a bank job, but if ever a class of people handed the wealthy their asses back. I checked, but there were no books written about the man.

I managed to locate some thrift stores and trade worn out shorts for swim trunks, and older shirts for tank tops. The look, plus a pair of canvas sandals, was the denouement of fitting in as a tourist.

I slept well and the sun on my skin felt terrific. My first day I'd discovered some outdoor showers. With an abundance of hotels, it was easy to lift some mini soaps, and, dressed in a swimsuit, I was able to clean myself while remaining discreet. After using a restroom to change into a polo shirt, designer jeans, and Nikes, I used two vouchers at a McDonalds, and paid cash for a large cheese pizza from a place called Britt's. I took the pizza on the bus, and explored St Pete. It was hospitable, but not quite the place for me except for finding meetings. The area was gritty, and a bit harsh, for being that near a coastal environment.

In Clearwater, as I've mentioned, I found a small college which had accessible buildings. I staked out some places to study and got to work. The coursework for the GED was basic. I studied to be sure of the material, but, in fact, I knew most of the information cold. I went to the public library if the weather turned soggy, or if I needed a change of pace. I'd read until I fell asleep in one of the oversized chairs. I even located the brewhouse that had sent me so many vouchers through email. I ate steak at least once a week. I sat in on recovery meetings at various locations. Over time I became established at a few of them. They believed that I had three years of sobriety.

A couple of younger girls I met at some St Pete meetings even had their homes to themselves when the parents went out of town or worked the graveyard shift. I was invited over and spent time in carnal enjoyment. The action came in spurts. As was my custom when I found myself spending time with a female friend, I would be sure to raid the refrigerator in between activities, and take long hot showers, with or without the flavor of the moment. Drinking wasn't part of the deal, since we met in the recovery meetings, but that was the only downside.

A season passed, and fall was as much like summer

as anything I had ever known. Florida is not the place to go if one enjoys separate seasons. They have three. Hot, hurricane, and tourist. The warmth eased my depression, although I've never understood the mechanism for that.

As August turned toward September, I met an older cat named Cìkè Cheng. He was standing in the surf one morning performing kata. I stood a polite distance away and practiced Zui Quan. This caught his attention.

"Where you learn this?" The old man approached. "You quite good. But, must breathe more." He imitated the move I'd executed, with greater force and less exertion.

"I studied with a sensei years ago." I bowed. He returned the bow.

"You like to learn more?"

"I'd dig that. Straight from the fridge, gate, I want to learn Krav Maga at some point."

"Shi! You want to learn practical application of styles. I can teach."

Master Cìkè observed the kata I knew, and led me into kata I had yet to learn. Soon I adjusted to learning a style that was simultaneously offensive and defensive. I was sodden, and exhausted, but Master Cìkè looked refreshed when he departed at eight that morning. We agreed to meet the next morning.

That afternoon I managed to plunder a fifth of rum from the back of a truck. I spent the rest of the day sunning on the beach and sipping spiked Coke. The next morning, I had a tremendous headache when Master Cìkè showed up.

"You don't look so good, young man. You not sleep?"

"Yeah, I slept. It's a boomerang effect from some Captain Morgan."

"I see. I was young once too. So, we train, and then we go back to my motel. I teach you perfect remedy."

We began training in earnest. I incorporated Judo,

Kung Fu, Karate, and basic street fighting. The effects were salutary for cleansing the toxins out of my system. Ninety minutes later we took a break. I followed Master Cìkè down the beach to an older building. We entered a standard looking room that included a refrigerator and a microwave.

Master Cìkè pointed to a chair. "You sit and observe. I take a tall glass, add two ounces of gin, a few drops of orange water, some egg white, a bit of cream, some Sprite, and stir. Here you go, a Ramos Gin Fizz."

I took a sip. "On my word, dude, this is out of sight!"

"Is best remedy, other than strenuous workout. Cream lines insides, gin clears brain." Master Cìkè bowed.

I transcribed the recipe before cutting out. That afternoon I located a shop that carried orange blossom water, and purchased some fresh lemons and limes, as well as a bottle of liquid sugar. Next, I purchased a plastic shaker and a tumbler. The rest of the ingredients were a matter of heisting things at a grocery store, and paying a cat to buy me a bottle of gin.

By Halloween I was far more supple, and far more deadly. A sense of dormant anger had been replaced by a cool, almost existential calm. Master Cìkè was returning home after a sabbatical, and I had reached a point where Florida had run its course.

A few days before Halloween, 2011, I passed the GED. I had the certificate mailed to Gina and Nicky's apartment. I was a high school graduate. Instead of excitement, a momentary sense of hollowness developed. I wasn't ready to attend college, I wasn't interested in slaving for the Woolworth's, and as I stated, Florida had run its course for me. I thought about hitting Disney, and yet doing so without a chick sounded like a waste. I didn't even feel like finding a girl at that moment. I sat on the beach thinking about Steph.

I needed something, but was unsure what that was. Master Cìkè suggested returning to New York. He and I had discussed our birth homes one morning after working out. Everyone associated with my family had moved from the old neighborhood, and yet there was still plenty of excitement in the city itself. I planned to explore the museums, the parks and double up on my reading. Maybe some ideas would come.

Two weeks before my fifteenth birthday, seventeenth according to my fake ID, I hooked up with a girl named Ashton. We had met on the beach that afternoon. She was five-foot-two-inches tall with black hair to her collar, brown eyes, and glasses. I took her for a tourist due to her twangy, aww-shucks accent, and her simple-minded demeanor. We drank enough beer that for one of the first times in my life I got quite drunk. We stripped each other, and waded naked into the Gulf of Mexico at eleven at night. After playing chase, and laughing quite a bit she got dressed and staggered back to her motel. I spent a small fortune eating pancakes and bacon with black coffee. The next morning, I slept off a major headache stretched out on the beach. I shook up two Ramos Gin Fizzes and drank to my future.

Chapter Twenty-Three

I hit NYC a week before Thanksgiving. The air was crisp, the crowds were dense, and the lights at night were amazing. I wandered fifth avenue and dug the scene, but gradually. I strolled through Central Park admiring the shapes in drapes, spent several hours in Rockefeller Plaza, and took in some art at the museums. When the mercury dipped, I bought coffee and rode the subways. There were still contacts of my father's in the garment district, and I introduced myself. One evening a visit to a bar led to my meeting a cat named Ralph Morelli. I was on my second club sandwich and third vodka martini. With my five o'clock shadow, my height and build, and my thick roll of bills, the bartender never asked for ID.

Ralph walked over and copped the barstool beside me. After ordering a beer, he looked at my sandwich and ordered a duplicate. "How about those Mets, huh?" He looked at me and then towards a corner TV. "Name's Morelli. Ralph Morelli."

"I don't follow sports, Morelli. I guess the Mets are as good as any other team" I drank martini, enjoying the smooth taste of Chopin. "Vinnie Il-Cazzo is what they hung on me in the maternity ward."

Ralph bit into his sandwich, and I stared into space feeling the effects of my drinks.

"I'm up from Queens. I was buying gifts for my family, and saw you sitting here looking like you could use company." He wiped foam from his mouth.

"Not really. I'm pretty good by myself. I enjoy the solitude."

We ate in silence for a while. I paid my bill and was departing when Ralph approached. "Hey, Il-Cazzo, where you live around here?"

I shrugged, and continued walking down the block looking for somewhere to rest. "Here and there. I sort of hang my hat wherever."

"So, what are your parents like? I mean, don't they worry if you aren't home?" Ralph was giving me the once over.

"Look, Morelli, what the hell do you want? I don't go for other dudes, and you're pushing it. Shove off unless you want problems your cranium can't tolerate. If you got something to say then spill it, and work your ground smashers back the direction you came." I got testy.

"OK. Yeah, right. I do have something to say. Look, I work for some people. I'm always looking for other people who might fit in to the business. You have the look, and the build."

"Savvy. So, what's the job? Oh, and my parents are nowhere. As in, I don't know where they are. They took a powder. I'm seventeen and can take care of my own"

"The job's simple. It's all about deliveries. You pick up packages from a neighborhood in the South Bronx, and take them to different neighborhoods each day. Usually Bronx to the city, but sometimes it's Brooklyn or Queens. Almost never Long Island. It pays five hundred a day, sometimes double that." Ralph gave me a hard eye. "I have one concern. I saw you putting away the martinis. You aren't a drunk or nothing, right?"

"So, you mule hot goods or narcotics. Savvy. I engage in certain operations as well. Not muling, but other things. I prefer to stay low key. I admit that the bread you mention has my meter running." I stopped at a bench and sat. "And, no, I'm not in the grip of the grape. I attend twelve step meetings, but for other reasons. I don't consider myself to have a drinking problem. I've met plenty of drunks, and I'm not like that. I know people who'll serve me, as long as it isn't prime time. If the clothes are right, and the roll sufficient, no one asks questions."

"I think you might work out. Yeah, Il-Cazzo, you seem almost tailor fit for Mr. Pipes' outfit. Hey, if you don't have anything else going on, let's catch the train to Queens. I can tell you about Mr. Pipes, my boss. You're welcome to join my family for dinner, too. My pops runs a bakery, and Mom is the best cook ever."

I agreed, and we walked to the station. I was unsure about the turn of events, but I had nowhere else to be. Something told me that Ralph and I might hit it off. I stopped along the way and lightened a store's weight a couple of Cokes worth. I poured a shot of Beam into each bottle, pitched the empty pint container into a trashcan, and we sipped on the train.

Several chicks walked by, stopping to chat with Ralph. They dug his hip to the tip form, from the slicked back DA, flipped up and curled in the front, to the sharp creases in his navy slacks, and dark purple dress shirt, complimented by oxblood brogues, and a coffee colored dress leather. He was a hepcat's hepcat. The dolls were not immune to my charms either, and they were of an age and style that put them a few notches above my usual.

"Mr. Pipes is a hard guy. Hard like calculus, and hard like a lead pipe. He runs his deals, and no one with any sense tries to interfere. You and I show up on the corner near an apartment building he owns. We pick up a case and instructions on where to make the delivery. Once we make the drop, we pick up another case and bring it back to where we started. It takes about four hours round trip. If you perform well, you sometimes get extra money. The minimum is five bills. I have to introduce you in a few days, and see if Mr. Pipes agrees, but I suspect he will. Wear something nice if you have it. But don't overdo it, either. Dress like you were going to a private school, and get a shave. You want to look high school, not college.

"You're coming through cool and clear, gate. I've got the threads for any situation. I'll have an outfit ready. Like I said, I've got activities of my own, and they likewise require the right threads," I sipped some Coke.

Ralph lived in a three floor townhouse with his parents and younger sister. His sister, Jess, was ten, with long flowing black hair. She had thick eyebrows, narrow eyes, and more nose than her face required. The kind of girl who would grow into her beauty, but was nowhere near the finish line. Mr. Morelli, Charlie he told me to call him, was built like a middleweight boxer. He'd been one in early life. His hair was receding, but his face was far from soft. And Ralph's mother, Betty, was a short, vivacious beauty right out of an old TV show. She wore a blue and black blouse with a pleated skirt, a pair of blue flats, and had her hair done in a bouffant.

We washed our hands and sat to dinner after Ralph introduced me. The caprese salad was served with wine for everyone except Jess. She had seltzer. There was a plate of fresh baked bread as well.

"You go to high school with our boy, Vinnie?" Charlie took a bite of salad. "You studying business, as well?"

"I'm interested in the markets, and I like studying currency fluctuations." I sipped white wine and tried to sound studious.

"That sounds like a career in the making. I'm hoping Ralphie can help out at the bakery in a few years." Charlie sipped wine.

The conversation went like that for a time. After the salad we were served fagioli soup, gnocchi Alfredo with prosciutto, broccoli rabe, and more bread. We had sfogliatelle for dessert with espresso. The food was phenomenal.

"Thank you for the meal. I hope to see you more

often." I hugged Betty, and shook Charlie's hand. "Morelli, I'll meet you tomorrow for breakfast. Maybe we can hit the Guggenheim after school." I departed and walked to the subway.

I found a copy of The Times, and sat reading the whole way. The story of the Boonie Hat Bandit had died down, but there were political happenings that caught my eye. After returning to Union Square Station, I went for a walk and smoked a joint. I looked through my backpack and selected a pair of stone-washed jeans, a cashmere k-jacket and a dark blue shirt. I took the outfit to an all-night dry cleaner, and arranged a six in the morning pick up.

With that tended to, I went shopping for some Italian loafers, and a dark blue fedora. I now had contacts in the garment district who provided good deals from the rear of their trucks. It was ten, and I had the rest of the night to kill. I spent some of it on a bench under a floodlight in Morningside Park reading *Slave Girl* by Sarah Forsyth.

It was a mild night for autumn, and two dolls about my age were practicing some martial arts. The shorter was a brunette with an a-cup chest, and the taller a blonde with a nice c-cup. As they worked out, one attacking and the other defending, I looked from my book. I tried not to stare, but something about them pumped my pistons.

Forty-five minutes into their workout I was watching them with a critical eye. The smaller of the two was the superior fighter, but neither was in my class. After another fifteen minutes they turned to leave.

I tipped my hat. "You're not too bad at that, but you both hook your feet at the end of the kicking sequences. You'd do better to snap the kicks."

They stopped and turned. The smaller girl's nostrils flared as her eyes narrowed. "Yeah? Can you do any better?"

I shrugged, and returned to my book. "Straight from the fridge, gate. None of my concern. I should tend to my own."

The beauties glared. "Yeah, right."

A few days later I was in the park reading *The New York Post* when the chicks returned. The taller of the two sat on my right side, and the other sat on my left. A group of pussycats passed by. They looked passion driven but fierce, with full blown lips, mascara and long eyelashes. The chicks beside me glared at the intrusion.

The blonde cleared her throat to speak when from another direction came a herd of mugs dressed in motorcycle boots, tight jeans, and black vests over tight black shirts. "Mighty Musclers" had been designed into a patch on the back of the vests. They all sported sunglasses despite the late hour. They were joking and laughing with each other. The chicks eyed them hard, and they returned the glare.

Blondie cleared her throat again. I marked my place in the book, and turned to give them my attention. "Hi there." Blondie gave me a disarming grin. "We've been seeing you around. My name's Destiny Wilbury. This is my girlfriend, Mackenzie Guevara."

"Hello ladies, what can I do you for? Yes, we have been crossing paths of late. Name's Vinnie Il-Cazzo." I winked at Mackenzie. "Any relation to Ernesto?"

The waif-like brunette called Mackenzie stared into space, speaking to no one in particular. "Guevara is my mom's last name. I don't know any of my relatives."

"Forget it. I doubt you and Che ever met." I shook my head, and let the joke fall flat.

Destiny took a breath. "You have any spare change? Anything? We're hungry, and we can make it worth your while. We need to get a room for the night too. I'd do anything."

Mackenzie re-animated, and turned, batting her eyes. "Could you spare enough money for coffee? We're so cold, Vinnie." Her hand reached for my back pocket -- and stopped short as she registered that no wallet was there. I resisted the urge to pull her across my lap for even trying.

I froze them both with a stare. "I'm not about to lay any bread on either of you until I know you better." I focused the glare on Mackenzie. "Nice try, chick, but only a total Harv keeps his wallet in the rear." Returning to Destiny, I winked. "If you're hungry, I would dig buying you both some eats. I dig what you offered, but I'll ignore the solicitation, ladies. Not that you aren't both hot dishes, because you are."

Destiny's mouth quivered. Her words came out in a rush. "Sorry, sir. I got kicked out of my house almost six months ago, and ended up in New York. I met Kenzie in the park, and we hit it off. We've been doing OK, but we ran out of funds. We need help. You look like you're doing OK for money."

I stood up and grabbed my sack. "Well, allow me to feed you then. I can even get us a room for the night, and you can get cleaned up and crash. But say another word about offering me sex in exchange for that, I'm going to have to get strident." I glared, and then smiled at the chicks. "If you find me attractive, and want to spend time together, that's a horse of a different color." I adjusted my backpack, and we started walking with each of my arms draped around one of the dolls.

Mackenzie looked up at me. "I'm sorry for my part, too. You're a nice guy, Vinnie. Thanks for helping us out."

I tried not to laugh at that comment. "Don't count on me being nice, chick, but don't sweat it either. I help where I can. It's the way I've always been. I care about people. Maybe too much."

We crossed an avenue, and promenaded toward a

diner I enjoyed. "This place has decent grub for a greasy spoon. The prices are next to nothing, and you get your money's worth."

Our servers name was Lucretia. I'd had her before. She was a stocky, older lady with glistening skin, and over her hair a bandana that was knotted in the front. Her face was round, with cherubic cheeks, and she had a white toothy smile. Mackenzie and Destiny ordered cheeseburgers with fries, coffee, and apple pie. I ordered a piece of pumpkin pie and coffee.

"If we head uptown, I can get us a room. Nothing too fancy, but it should be clean. Have to be somewhere by seven in the morning, but I can pay for two nights. That way you can sleep as long as you like before leaving. I'll give you my cell number in case you want to hook up after my meeting." I watched the girls eat like they hadn't had a meal in days.

"You're unbelievable." Destiny sipped coffee. "I'm sorry I offered you sex like that. We've never done that before, it's just that we're desperate right now. For shelter, not for sex."

"We'll discuss that later, chick. And if this job interview works out, maybe we can see what's what." I ordered another piece of pie. "You dolls have moxie, I'll give you that, and moxie is a righteous turn on."

Mackenzie looked across the table. "You sound like a street dad. You got a family?"

"I have sisters, but they don't live around here. I don't know where my parents are. I'm not a papa yet. At least I damned well better not be. There's been no word indicating such." I shuddered at the thought and sipped coffee.

Destiny shook her head. "She doesn't mean family like that. Some kids we've met are part of street families. They have an older teen who acts as the street dad. Like those ladies and guys in the park earlier. Most of the time an older girl acts as mom. The family protects each other. The dad's in charge."

I took a forkful of pie. "Oh. Yeah, I dig the flip. Solid. No, I'm not part of that scene. But if you want me to watch over you, and take care of you, I mean sure. Why not? But only if you want." I shrugged, unsure of what to make of the offer. "One thing, though. I'm not too hot on that dad term. I like you both, but not with a dad sort of vibe. That'd be straight creepy."

"I'm sorry about what I asked." Destiny blushed. "We haven't been doing so well with the busking lately. Must be the cold weather. Last month I was knocking them dead with old school rock and country mixed with gospel tunes."

Mackenzie yawned with a small coo. "It's all good about the dad thing. You can just be in charge."

I motioned the waitress for a third piece of pie. "Yeah, I dig that. Why label these things? Ladies, about the busking scene, you have to change up the riff to fit the seasons. I'm sure that music you were swinging in the summer, and even into the fall, was solid jive. The cats and kitties always dig that riff. Thing of it is, it's the holiday season now. Tomorrow you should try swinging some traditional carols on that ax of yours, Destiny. Your pallie here should join in on the backup vocals, get the crowds singing with you. You'll rake in next to a heap of bread."

We finished eating, and I paid the bill. I winked at Lucretia and slipped her a twenty dollar tip. She'd charged me for one piece of pie, and the dinners. I hailed a cab, and we rode fifteen blocks to a moderate hotel. It was one in the morning when we were secured in a room. The desk manager was happy to take cash, and my word that I was nineteen. The room was more than adequate. We set our gear down, and I eyed the chicks. At first, I considered giving them each a swell fanning for trying to solicit me. Then I decided to scare them as a warning.

"OK, you both, get stripped, and into a hot bath. You need it, trust me. Then we're going to make sure you don't try soliciting again, and get you to bed." I yawned, and started taking off my jacket and shirt. I was removing my loafers when I noticed Mackenzie having what appeared to be a mild seizure. She had her back to the wall, and was frozen in place. The corner of her mouth was twitching, and her eyes were glazed over.

I looked up at Destiny. "Is she alright? Should I call 911?"

Destiny hugged Mackenzie from behind "She'll be fine in a minute. It isn't your fault, because how could you know, but the comment about getting undressed and into the bath triggered her. Give us a moment, please."

I'd blown it, but big time. "Please accept my deepest apologies. I wasn't clued in. I can let you both have the room. I'll catch some shuteye on a bench, or on the trains. Or if you'd rather, I can crash in the chair until the early bright."

Kenzie relaxed in Destiny's arms. She paused and after a moment the corners of her mouth turned up. "No, you paid for the room. I'm sorry. I freaked out."

"It's cool. I dig the riff. Some cat caused you distress and now your gauge gets blown when certain notes go discordant with your mental circuitry." I had momentary visions of Steph and Caroline.

"Huh?"

"You were hurt by someone and it sets off an alert in your brain when circumstances remind you of the incidents surrounding the hurt. I've seen it before."

"Oh. Umm, yeah. Before I took off from home, my mom had men around. A few wanted to watch me and my sisters have a bath and stuff." Kenzie relaxed a little.

"I dig. Well, if you'd rather, you and Destiny change in the bathroom and boil up."

"Would you really have slept somewhere else?" Kenzie began untying her shoes.

"I still will if you'd rather. Don't want to blow my girls' radiators What kind of a caregiver would I be if I ignored your distress?"

Destiny aimed a finger in my direction. "That right there is why we trust you. No one we've come across gives a damn about that. They just want sex."

I took out my cell phone and texted Morelli. Kenzie and Destiny stepped into the bathroom, emerging a half hour later pink and glowing with vitality. I set down my book and scowled as they stood naked and shivering, wrapped in towels.

"If memory serves, and it does, you both tried to prostitute yourselves. Don't let it happen again."

"It won't. I promise, sir." Destiny stared a hole in the floor.

"I assure you that it better not. That kind of jazz is a one way ticket to Doomsville. You said you want me in charge. Well, now you have it. You ever go that route again and I'll roast your butts! Get your pajamas on, vixens."

Kenzie's eyes glistened with tears as they grabbed clean pairs of panties from their backpacks.

"It won't happen again, I swear." Destiny was beyond petrified which wasn't the reaction I expected. "We don't have pajamas. We usually sleep in our clothes or our panties and t-shirts."

I handed each of them one of my shirts which fit them like dresses. They changed in the bathroom, and I tucked them into bed and kissed their foreheads. I settled in the middle, and they curled up beside me. Holding them felt far more comfortable than it should have.

Chapter Twenty-Four

Three hours later I climbed out of bed, dressed, and took a pint bottle of bourbon from my backpack. I swallowed a double shot and retrieved a photograph of Steph from my backpack. I kissed the picture and returned it. Prior to leaving I wrote a note and left it on the desk.

Here's fifty dollars for each of you plus my cell number. Get dressed and take your backpacks to the following address. Get change on the way by ordering breakfast. Do your laundry and put on clean clothes. Wash what you put on this morning and rewash anything that's extra dirty. Have a nice lunch and meet me at the dinosaur exhibit in Natural History at four. Be good, V.

I cut out and caught a subway to meet Morelli for breakfast. On the way I stopped and picked up my dry cleaning. After changing clothes in a restroom, I left my old faded jeans and my tatty sweatshirt on a bench for whomever might want them. While having my loafers polished, I reached into my backpack and took out the watch my father had gifted me a couple of years prior. My appearance was razor sharp. I was hip and swinging.

"Hey, Il-Cazzo! I was wondering if you'd show. Check you out, dude! You're looking mighty fly!" Ralph was sitting in a booth. I joined him. He was dressed in brand new Nikes, tight black chinos, a long sleeved rugby shirt, and his leather jacket.

"You said seven. It's ten after. Sorry for pulling a White Rabbit. I had an interesting night." I motioned to a server, and ordered a bagel with a lox schmear and a coffee.

"White Rabbit?" Ralph gave me confused. "Oh, like *Alice in Wonderland*. Yeah, no problem. We have time to eat before the car gets here. By the way, what's with that watch? Lose that, please. You look perfect, but no high school kid wears that kind of blingage. A necklace with a cross or something, sure. Maybe even an earring. But a gold Rolex? Not a chance. Not unless they want everyone to know they deal, or that they're a pimp."

"My father gave me this watch, Morelli! I happen to like it. I'll put on my other watch, though, if you think it matters that much." I switched to my cheaper Casio.

"This is all about appearances right now. If Mr. Pipes likes how you look, and believes you won't draw attention to yourself, then the job's yours." Ralph sipped his coffee.

We discussed the job some more, and then talked about girls including the two I had met. I told him about Julie and Steph, and a bit about my background. He told me about his family, and his current girlfriend.

"My parents were impressed by you. They don't know about me working in this business, but they know that I intern for someone. You have an open invitation anytime you want to come over for dinner. That means you, not anyone else you hook up with."

"Savvy." I nodded.

Ralph threw a couple of twenties on the counter, and we exited at the same moment a black limousine pulled up. The windows were tinted. We climbed inside, and sitting across from us was one of the most severe looking men I have ever encountered. He was well into his thirties, dressed in a navy silk suit, crisp white shirt open at the collar, pointy black shoes that shone like mirrors, and a homburg. He had on mirrored sunglasses, and a diamond pinky ring. He looked me up and down.

"My name is Antonio Giuseppe Cantante. Raffaele has informed me that you are seeking employment, Vincenzo." Mr. Pipes didn't show any expression.

"Yes, sir. If you have any to offer."

"I do. I understand that you are familiar with my lines of work. Please understand that once hired you may not quit. You will work for me until I feel that you no longer fit the necessary profile." The man was stony.

"Savvy. I dig the riff. I'm collecting items to be delivered. I show up every morning at ten. I travel to a specified location, and have a specified exchange of words, before easing the case of product to the receiver. He eases me a similar case full of cash in return. I bring that back to your representative, and he slides me some bread. Doesn't sound difficult." I gave Mr. Pipes my own stony look.

"Correct. Please do keep the hipster parlance to a minimum when addressing me, Vincenzo. I prefer straight talk. If I wanted hipsters, I would look for the boys above one hundred and tenth." Mr. Pipes offered me a drink which I declined. I wanted one, but sometimes discretion is best. He poured himself a screwdriver.

"Very well, sir. I shall await your decision." I sat looking straight ahead. I noticed Ralph hadn't moved a muscle.

"No need to wait. You are what I need. I gather you enjoy reading? You enjoy music?" Mr. Pipes sipped his drink.

"Yes, to both. I prefer light jazz and soft rock over the modern junk. I enjoy reading almost anything." I remained cool, and kept my gaze even.

"Good. You should listen to music while traveling, and bring one of your school books, or a novel that might pass for assigned reading. You need to look like nothing so much as a student heading to class. If anyone appears to be following you, or you suspect that there is undo attention being paid, send a text to this number. Memorize it. Do not save it on your phone. If you text, someone will meet you to handle the matter." Mr. Pipes had his driver pull to the curb. "Here is a three hundred dollar sign on bonus. Be on time tomorrow. Raffaele will show you where. Welcome aboard, Vincenzo." We didn't shake hands.

I climbed out, and Ralph followed me. We were at the top of Union Square Station. It was eight-thirty in the morning. I waited for the limo to drive away.

"That went well. I guess I'm in." I shrugged.

Ralph smiled. "He scares me. I mean that. He terrifies me. He pays well though, and that helps out my folks. You handled yourself well. I have to get moving, and you need to come with me. I'm going to show you the way that this works, but after that you cut out until tomorrow. We'll meet at eight thirty near the pickup location. There's a place that does a decent omelet."

We took the subway most of the way to the South Bronx and then caught an uber to within five blocks of the pick-up location. I hung back at the corner across the street and read the New York Post. Out of the corner of my eye I watched Ralph approach a large man dressed in a leather overcoat. He shook hands with him, and took a case that looked to be a leather book satchel. Ralph walked away in the opposite direction with the satchel under his arm. I walked to a subway and rode to Central Park. I stopped, and had three Chicago dogs, before texting a girl I knew. Her name was Penny Jackson. We were friends with benefits.

At four I was sitting looking at the dinosaurs in The Museum of Natural History when the chicks arrived. They had on their worn out shoes, but the rest of their clothes were clean, if tatty.

"Hey there, Daddy-o." Mackenzie side hugged me, "We slept until noon, and then did our laundry like you told us in your note. I hope you don't mind, but we took all the toilet paper and an extra bar of soap from the room."

"Thank you for everything. I didn't know if you'd show up or not?" Destiny smiled at me, and stood on tiptoe to kiss me on the cheek.

"If you still want to hang with me, I got my job. I think we should get some food and confabulate. We didn't have a lot of time last night. Also, we need to find somewhere to stay tonight, and turn in early. I don't want to stay at that same hotel." I stood up and took one of them on each arm.

As we walked, a surge of emotion overwhelmed my mental circuitry. I was a year and a half older than Mackenzie, roughly the same age as Destiny, but there was a definite protective vibe. It was a feeling with which I was familiar, and for which I never had adequate words. At times I wondered if the caring for others was an act I put on to justify my pirate ways. But I had to admit that Destiny and Mackenzie tweaked something inside of me when they asked me to be their street-dad. No, the helping others in need was no act. It was visceral. I filled a need in the world that far too few were willing to fill. I'd plundered food to feed kids at school, I'd aided in the escape of the Baker ladies, and I'd helped Julie fit in with the west side cats. I couldn't not help. In return, those I helped depended on me. They were beholden to me. That was my reward. I wasn't sure if that was the only reason, though. I couldn't imagine not helping others. It was my raison d'être as a pirate.

I looked down at Mackenzie to my left, and Destiny to my right. They looked tired, but content. Did I love them? I barely knew them, but, yes, I loved them. I thought about Julie. I thought about Steph. I thought about the other swells I had met and spent time with over two and a third years. Did I love all those chicks? Sure. I loved Steph first, and most, however.

Where love was concerned, Mackenzie and Destiny were something else. They needed protection, although I wasn't certain from what. They needed to be home, wherever home was. They deserved a warm bed, hugs, and forehead kisses. They had no business running around day and night, alone and at liberty, in the fetid city. For that matter, neither did I. That thought sent my mind reeling off the tracks. I needed a drink; I needed several drinks.

We entered a Turkish restaurant that I had known as a child. I got us a table with minimal waiting by slipping the host a ten-spot. The girls looked around the place, and then at the menu. Destiny peeked up at me, obviously concerned about the cost.

"Order what you like. If there's leftover food we can take it with us." We ordered several appetizers and entrees. I was hungry, and the girls looked famished. "Let's get to it, dolls. Where are you from, and why are you running? Also, why did you pick me to ask to be your guardian? From what my friend Ralph tells me, there are countless street families around. Why not join one of them? Or, did you run from one? How much danger am I in by taking care of you?"

"I'm from Florida, sir." Destiny looked down. "My parents are conservative and strict believers in The Bible. They don't understand that I'm bisexual. When I was younger, they forced me to sit on a blanket, and if I moved off of it, or even put a hand off of the blanket, they hit me. Their church tried to re-educate me about what they call sexual sin. It didn't work. On the day I turned fifteen, my clothes were packed and on the porch. My father told me I wasn't allowed to come back unless I submitted to his beliefs. So, I hitchhiked to New Jersey, and caught a ferry to the city."

Mackenzie looked at me with sad eyes. "I used to live in Jersey City. My mom had eight kids by eight men. I was the third. I got tired of being pushed around and yelled at. I got tired of being told to get out in the middle of the night because she was entertaining. I finally left for good. My mom said that she's fine with that, because I'm an ungrateful bitch."

I sipped seltzer, and thanked the waiter when he brought the appetizers. We ate in silence for several minutes. I coughed. "Why me? Why not the other cats who group together?" I sighed. "I'm a loner, dolls. I like to read, and work out in my own little bubble. I'm glad to help you, but why me? I have to know."

"We've looked at other street families, but it isn't as good as it sounds. Most of them are criminals. I'm talking purse snatching, beating up old people, shooting up drugs kind of criminals. We don't want to get arrested again because some thug stole an old man's wallet. We don't like that most street-dads think of their daughters as sex partners, either. Except for my offer last night, we aren't sluts." Destiny bit into some borek.

"I saw you in the park, and told Destiny that you looked like you had money. The way you dress, you must be doing pretty good. I thought we should chance it. It worked out too, except you threatening to spank us. We earned that; I know." Mackenzie ate some begindi.

"Savvy. Well, you dealt the cards so let's play the hand. I'm glad to find us places to crash, and to look out for you. I'm not much older than you, just been surviving on my own for too damned long. I was forced to grow up fast. Sounds like we have that in common. My life hasn't been an easy road so far, but I got a job, and I'm going to be working part of every day except Sunday." I paused to eat. "After the Christmas break you chicks need to be in school. Either that, or we need to get you GED certificates. Not being in school, or something of the like, could attract attention from cops. That I can't allow. I already have a GED. I expect you to lay low and stay out of trouble when not in school. I won't bail you out of jail if you do anything stupid, and if you get into any serious trouble that brings attention my way, you'll think what I said last night was nothing. Don't test me on that. If you agree to my terms, I'll teach you what I know about survival skills. Take it or leave it."

"We'll take it. We know that we have to do what you say. You're the guardian." Mackenzie smiled so warmly as to soften my tone.

"Mind if I call you Kenzie?"

"Why would I? It's my name." She giggled.

Our entrees arrived and we dug in. I didn't realize how hungry I was until I got into an eating rhythm. I wanted some beer, but felt uncomfortable asking in that establishment. The girls were focused on their share of the comestibles. We ate without further conversation. I paid in cash and left a fifty percent tip.

"Want to see a movie? Go skating at Rockefeller? What sounds good?" I was overcome by a burst of energy. "I could get us a room instead, and a bottle of something. You two smoke out?"

Destiny's eyes widened. "We both smoke pot when we can find it. I was afraid to ask if you did."

We walked to a different hotel than we had used the previous night. I proffered two pictures of Benjamin Franklin in exchange for a room with a king sized bed on the fourteenth floor. The desk clerk agreed to forgo needing a credit card if I put down an extra bill for security.

"We should go shopping before we head upstairs. You need pajamas, and other things." I pocketed the key-card.

We caught a cab. I purchased toiletries for them at a drug store, and kited a new hairbrush and a folding toothbrush for myself. Afterward, we headed to Macy's. I bought Destiny a pair of pink Hello Kitty pajamas. Mackenzie opted for a long nightshirt with Winnie The Pooh on it. I let them pick out some underclothes, as well. It felt strange paying full price. On the way to the hotel, I stopped at a dry cleaner and left an outfit. A homeless man sat on a bench nearby. I gave him thirty dollars to buy me a bottle of Jack Daniels.

In the room again, I poured glasses of bourbon, and lit my bowl. We smoked some pot, blowing the hits out an open window. The pleasant effects hit quickly. It was nine-thirty, but I was exhausted. I had a shower, texted my sisters and Julie, and fell asleep with the girls wrapped in my arms once more.

Chapter Twenty-Five

I awoke at four-thirty in the morning. After slipping out of bed without waking the girls, I rose and had a good stretch. I stood watching the chicks cuddled together in the void I had left on the bed. In the pre-dawn darkness, my thoughts started racing. I was sixteen and had two dolls depending on me for security. Kenzie was at the middle section of fourteen, and Destiny was at the middle section of fifteen. I was playing guardian, although our ages were closer to siblings. They needed me, that was for damned sure. I thought about my new job. My heartbeat raced, and my belly tightened. Opening the bottle of Black Jack, I took a swig. I kissed my picture of Steph, and sent out a silent message to her wherever she was.

After dressing in an outfit that was wearing out, I slipped on socks and loafers, brushed my hair, grabbed my fedora, and left a note.

Girls, be out of the room by ten. Here's food money. I'll meet you at the Stillwell Ave. station at four. You might look at some stores, and see if you can find any backpacks you like. You need new shoes, too. If there is any change in plans, text me. Papa V.

I left them fifty dollars, and slipped out the door. Exiting the hotel, I grabbed a cup of coffee before retrieving my clothes from the cleaners, changing, leaving the worn out threads on a bench, and boarding the subway toward the Bronx. I reached for my sack and plugged in my iPod. Soon Elton John was filling my ears. I closed my eyes and relaxed.

The job went off without a hitch. I strolled past a squat, chiseled, bald, African American named Daquan. He was leaning against a wall, draped in high style. I paused, looked at the map on my phone, and backpedaled.

"Excuse me, sir? I was looking for this address. I'm supposed to meet my tutor there." I set down my sack.

Daquan gave a curt nod. "Two blocks up, on the left."

I walked away, and bought a cup of coffee and a cheese danish at a corner deli. While eating, I realized that I had forgotten my courier's sack. I dashed back. "Hey, mister. I left something…"

Daquan nodded. "Sure did, boy. I figured you'd come back."

I grabbed my sack, and headed to the subway. After tuning in Coltrane on my iPod, I extracted my copy of *Taming of The Shrew*. Sticking out like a bookmark was a card with an address. I memorized the information and shredded the card.

I was finishing act one when the train arrived in Union Station. The A train took me within a few blocks of my destination. Grant Houses looked nice from the outside, but I'd been warned about the area. I approached and a man on a bench looked up.

"Is that *Romeo and Juliet*? I read that in high school."

"*Taming of The Shrew*." I replied. "Same author."

"They made a musical of that, didn't they?"

"Of both. *Kiss Me Kate* and *West Side Story*."

He patted the empty seat beside him. I sat and read. He grabbed my sack and walked away. Fifteen minutes later he returned.

I departed without acknowledging him, reversed course, and two hours later strolled by Daquan. "Oh, hey. I wanted to thank you for returning my bag this morning. My folks would kill me if I lost my schoolbooks." I smiled. "I hoped you'd be here. Bought you a turkey sub, chips, and a Coke as thanks." I handed him the brown paper bag from my courier's sack.

"No sweat, grey meat. The reward is unnecessary, but appreciated." We shook hands. I felt a fold of cash in mine.

That evening I sat across from the chicks in a restaurant with soft lighting, and the quiet murmur of surrounding parties. I'd made reservations for a Thanksgiving feast. The first course was autumn squash soup with citrus yogurt, and a pear and pecorino salad.

"Last night we told you about ourselves, but what about you? Where are you from and what's your story?" Destiny took a bite of salad and a sip of mineral water.

"I was birthed in a suburb two shakes and a shimmy outside the urban blight. My bodily metamorphosis took place there until I was neigh on twelve. My parents are cool. My father's sharp enough to shave with, and he's flushed out in hearts where compassion is concerned. My mother, she's always stayed back and kept it mellow. Thing of it is, they grew up watching our nation take repeated body slams economically and socially. Their own parents were a real mixed bag and that sort of shaped them."

I paused to eat before filling them in on the details of my life. The waiter brought poached turkey with mushroom leek stuffing, cranberry relish, and gravy. There were traditional sides of candied yams, mashed potatoes and a broccoli rabe risotto to go with it. The chicks eyes were saucers, their mouths turned up at the corners, as their wigs were blown by the quality and quantity of comestibles.

Once I had the details of my life laid out, Destiny blushed. "Is Steph Baker the picture you kiss every morning? Yeah, I've seen you."

I chewed some turkey. "I assumed you both to be asleep in the early bright. Yes, that's her photograph. The only one I have of her. Damn she was hot. I miss her like crazy."

The waiter served maple-bourbon pumpkin pie and coffee. Destiny looked away, then at me, then at her pie, then at me. "Were your parents involved with the human trafficking you mentioned? Is that why they ran?" She stared a hole into the table as Kenzie ate some pie.

I sighed. "Not directly, doll, no. Part of how they operated involved being closely connected to people who had their fingers in it, though. It was explained to me that the people who came to America were only paying back the cost of the trip plus housing and their document papers. I'm a quick study, however, and I know the truth." I shrugged. "Once life took a southward turn, I started dating several different chicks. Julie Dimitrion was just one of them. When I moved to western Florida and obtained my GED, I not only made plenty of bread but I had arm candy by the dozens. After moving back to my original neighborhood near the city, I met a guy who hipped me to a gig that pays decent. I thought life was perfect being alone, and easy breezy cool. Then I met you. Once more someone needed me, and again I couldn't say no." I raised my coffee to them while wondering to myself what the hell I was doing.

We finished dessert, and had more coffee. "Do you know where Steph moved to?" Kenzie inquired.

I paid the check with a pre-paid MasterCard I had scored, and left two c-notes for the server. "I don't. That was necessary in order for them to escape. I have a vague knowledge that Heather Baker was from a small town in Nebraska. One day I might beat my kicks eight to the bar, and give it a look-see."

"That was the best meal I've had ever. Thank you." Kenzie sipped coffee.

I yawned. "I'm glad I had you to share a meal with. Three days ago, I turned eighteen, according to my ID. I was alone and blowing the blues. Now I have you chicks in my life, and that's the most swinging gift ever." I side-hugged them both "So enough of my depressing story, what kind of action did you chicks get into today?"

Kenzie finished her coffee. "We watched the Macy's parade, played some music, and looked at some stores. The backpacks are expensive. So are the boots."

"Savvy. You can pay me back half of it when you earn the bread," I winked, "or, I can hep you to how I operate. Then it won't cost a dime." We stood.

Kenzie looked shocked. "Hold up, hold up! You saying that you can get that stuff for free? I don't want to be involved with robbing a store or anything like that."

"You won't be involved. I know some people who get stuff F-O-T. I duke them a fraction of the shelf price. In this case I might can suggest that with the holidays coming up they could help me out on this deal." We donned our jackets and hats, and I walked between them. "It's part of what I was telling you about how my parents operate."

We walked toward fifth avenue to look at the window displays. "What's F-O-T?" Destiny gave me concerned.

I laughed. "It means the items fell off of a truck."

Kenzie looked up with irritation. "I'm not the smartest girl who ever lived, but if the items fell off of a truck, then shouldn't the driver pick them up and put them back on the truck?"

I laughed heartily. "I asked that same exact question when I was five. The term is an expression. For the most part the store's upper management turns a blind eye when a truck driver pulls in and items vanish from the inventory. They collect insurance on the stolen items, plus they get a cut of the bread on resale. The drivers get an extra couple hundred clams to take a powder for a few. It's a well-run part of most retail businesses."

"So, the items are stolen. But the evidence trail leads nowhere because no one actually wants it to lead anywhere. Therefore, you're buying hot merchandise for less than market value, and have probable deniability if it comes to any questions being asked. Is that the gist?" Kenzie smiled a little.

Destiny gawked. "Look at you with the big words all of a sudden"

"I watch *Law and Order*. I understand these things." Kenzie shrugged, smiling.

"Give the girl a cigar." I ruffled Kenzie's hair playfully. "Not hot merchandise, though. Lukewarm items at best."

The city was decked out in its finest of gaiety, with lights, tinsel trim, and lighted trees. There was a Santa on every other corner ringing bells and hustling bread. The glittery department store windows were a sight to behold. I dropped a sawbuck in every Santa's kettle, and duked a few homeless people some bigger bills. I'd make it all back in spades, I was sure.

After strolling down fifth avenue casting our glimmers on the iconic window displays, we bought hot chocolate and went in search of a hotel. As we walked briefly through the park, I reached into my backpack and took out a bottle of Chopin vodka. I poured two shots into each cup of cocoa.

Kenzie's face lit up as she drank. "Where do you score on the booze? You always have a bottle on you, but you aren't old enough to buy it. Not even with your ID. You just ask someone in the park or what?"

"I don't need to go that route, often. I have other means by which to procure whatever libation I might require." I checked the marquee of a middle of the road hostelry. It would do if I could talk the manager into lowering the price. "I'll introduce you to some cats tomorrow night."

Destiny side-hugged me and gave me a kiss on the

cheek. Kenzie smiled and followed suit. "Before we go in, I want to do something. We didn't know you then, but we do now." Destiny undid her guitar case.

They performed a soulful version of Happy Birthday. My eyes began leaking, so I donned my shades. We secured our gear, I paid for a room on the twelfth floor, and we took the elevator. The room had a king sized bed, a desk and chair, a dresser with a TV on it, and a large bathroom with nicer towels than expected. Destiny turned on the tub to get the water hot. The girls emerged from the bathroom in their pajamas a half hour later. I poured Jack Daniels and Perrier into three glasses. We drank and fell asleep.

The next morning, I was up before the sun. I dressed, kissed Steph's photo, and composed a note to the chicks.

Girls, I have to make the scene with a cat in Queens later. I won't be back until after midnight. Either we can hook up tomorrow, or you can meet me somewhere tonight after my appointment. Text me and let me know. Here's fifty dollars. Get cracking on the schoolwork today. Thanks for the great birthday present. Stay gold, V.

After my delivery was complete, I hooked up with a chick I met at MOMA. She was an art student, and we killed several hours at her studio in the east village. While I was dressing, I received a text from Destiny and Kenzie to meet at midnight in Rockaway. That night Ralph, I, and four other cats had an evening meeting with Mr. Pipes and a few of his associates. The six of us were noted for our outstanding job performance. I received a grand in cash as a holiday bonus. Ralph likewise received a grand.

After saying our goodbyes, I caught the subway and arrived at the station in Rockaway Beach. The girls were locked in an embrace and swapping chews. I had to call their names a couple of times before they sat up.

"Evening, gates. Let's percolate. Hope you weren't waiting too long."

Kenzie covered a yawn. "Long enough. We showed up and had some immediate trouble. There's an assclown around here calling himself Contagion. He thought we looked like easy marks, but our pit bull here told him where to shove it." She kissed Destiny. "One of his bitches took offense, but we made it clear that we wanted to be left alone."

I scanned the area while retrieving a pair of brass knuckles from my right pocket. A gift from Ralph. Contagion and his crew didn't return, and no one else showed up for the train. The fourth car was a third full. We found seats and sat half-sleeping.

During the ride to Harlem and back to midtown Manhattan, Kenzie used my lap for a pillow and Destiny caught some shuteye leaning on my shoulder. The paternalistic feel of the situation was disconcerting. I was falling in love with these two chicks. That had potential to ruin what we had. Furthermore, I had several broads across the city, and Steph was still out there somewhere. I pulled a water bottle of gin and tonic from my pack and had a swig. It cooled my pistons.

As false dawn approached, I escorted the chicks off the train, and stopped at a corner store. While the girls used the restroom, a can of Sapporo slid up my sleeve. We walked to an all-night corner deli for breakfast, and as we arrived I three pointed the empty can into a dumpster.

I chewed a biscuit contemplatively. "This arrangement we've set up is a solid gasser, chicks. I had a notion, however, that might work us from a three aces hand to straight flush in hearts if you dig the flip. But I need your input." I chased the biscuit with some coffee. "I'm making plenty of bread at my job. I even get bonuses, which that was part of what tonight was about. If we can find a hotel that's not a complete dive, or a pay and lay, I might can get us a monthly rate. That way we don't have to always be on the move. We can stash our gear and you both can have a permanent place to crack the books."

"That'd be awesome!" Kenzie smiled. "We can help out with the costs."

Destiny nodded. "We made four hundred and fifty dollars last night. Most nights is around two hundred, maybe three hundred on the weekends. These two girls stopped and asked to play with us. It made a big difference. I never realized how much a violin and clarinet could improve my performance."

I removed my mirrored sunglasses and folded them. "That's far out! I'll allow that you both can perform and help out. But homework and schoolwork first. Savvy? You need to tune your dials to the GED certificates." I slid Sally-Mae, our server, a ten dollar bill and requested more coffee.

"We can't even get GEDs for a couple of years." Kenzie shrugged. "We're too young. We don't have ID cards like yours."

I gave them suave. "Give it time, ladies. As you grow closer to the goal a path may appear. There's much to discourse where that's concerned."

"I'm tired." Destiny yawned. "Can we talk about it tonight?"

I paid the bill. "Plan on it. I'm going to make like a newborn and head out. You chicks stay safe." I gave them a thumbs up and clicked my tongue.

Chapter Twenty-Six

The chicks needed better backpacks, shoes, and clothes. They were clean enough, but raggedy as compared to my stylish drape. I made arrangements to purchase items for them. In return they introduced me to a doll that almost made me forget my quest to find Steph.

Her name was Veronica Louise Englekut, and she was a sweater girl for the ages. More than a mere shape in a drape, she was everything plus. Long red hair, light freckles, a nice chest, flat belly, long legs, and she kept her claws sharp. She was one inch shorter than me, and dressed in such a way as to accentuate her curves and folds. Her jeans were tight, her shirt made a nice display of lifting her bust, and she wore a hint of perfume. Her intelligence matched her looks.

I was seated in the rear of a pizza parlor enjoying a pitcher of beer and two large pizzas. The place wasn't a red onion, but it wasn't the Ritz either. I spotted the chicks, waved, stood, and kissed Destiny and Kenzie on the cheek.

"Vinnie, this is our tutor, Ronnie." Destiny introduced me. My throat caught for a moment as I stiffened. "She says we're doing well with our studies."

"They sure are. So, you're the Vinnie they speak so highly of." Ronnie sat next to me with her back to the wall.

Taking Ronnie's hand, I turned it palm down and kissed it. "Yes, ma'am. Vincenzo Cassiel Michelangelo Il-Cazzo at your service."

Ronnie blushed. "So elegant you are. That's a lost art. Most guys don't know the proper way to greet a lady."

We all served ourselves, and poured glasses of stout. "Dolls, I have action most Saturdays, but there's some sort of executive to-do about supply and demand tomorrow. My services aren't required, and I thought we might take the opportunity to go shopping and replace any threads that are down at heel. I have new backpacks waiting for you with a friend of mine. Please feel free to join us, babe." I winked at Ronnie.

Kenzie drained half her glass of beer in a gulp. "Our friends Rory, Sheila, Jeanie, and their son Rainbow are coming to the city for a day. They invited us to join them for breakfast and a walk in Central Park. You're included. I'm sure they'd join us to shop afterward."

"Copacetic." I smiled. "Are they cubistic or would they be hep to urban piracy?"

"Piracy?" Ronnie looked shocked. "You mean like stealing?"

"No ma'am. I mean piracy. Yes, I am known to help grocery stores reduce their overstock, but in this case what I have in mind requires a bit more finesse." I draped an arm around Ronnie and she didn't object.

"What's the plan?" Destiny poured another beer.

"The plan is to trade-in older threads for newer items. It involves a technique my father taught me." I wiped foam from my mouth and explained the rules.

Ronnie laughed. "You're a real hustler, buddy." She turned her face and kissed me.

"Must you return home tonight, Ronnie my dear?" I left a twenty on the table "The ladies and I shall be retiring to a hotel, and I invite you to join us. Also, prudence requires me to ask if you're seeing anyone on the regular."

Ronnie blushed again. "I don't have a boyfriend, no. I should go home, but I guess I could tell my mom I'm staying at a friend's place tonight. She pulled out her cell phone and dialed.

Two hours later we were sitting together in a Brooklyn hotel suite. Between the four of us we managed the price. Kenzie and Destiny had the foldout couch in the main room. Ronnie and I were sharing the queen sized bed in the bedroom.

As Kenzie and Destiny flipped through the TV channels, Ronnie and I headed into the bathroom. She looked even more sensational without clothes on. I soaped her up, not ignoring any fold or crevice. She returned the favor. We kissed and held each other under the steamy water. She knelt down, and in less than five minutes I was skeeting. After she finished, I reciprocated as she moaned and gasped.

We rinsed off again, dried, and dressed in our underwear. Kenzie and Destiny were watching an old Woody Allen flick on TV. After the movie ended, we sat on the queen bed drinking Jack Daniels with a splash of soda.

"So, other than clothes swapping and five finger discounts, what other acts of piracy do you engage in?" Ronnie rested in my lap.

I spent a half hour detailing the various hustles that I ran. They laughed and listened.

"You chicks want to see how it works?"

"Yeah." Kenzie's eyes lit up.

I fired up my laptop, and typed as I read aloud. *Dear sirs: I was in your location in Missoula the other day with my wife and three kids. We each ordered strip steak with a baked potato to go. We asked for rare but the meat was much too well done. Also, you forgot some condiments. Yours, Julius Marx.*

Ronnie snuggled closer. "You turn me on like no other guy I've ever met."

"With the PO Box address included, I'll expect an e-card in email or a gift card in the mail. In either case we can head to Jersey one afternoon and chow down. It isn't a certain guarantee, but the odds favor my receiving some sort of a comp."

"Destiny and I lift food at church every week. We

bag up the cookies and fried chicken." Kenzie giggled.

Fifteen minutes later, Destiny and Kenzie retired to the main room. I gave Ronnie a soft kiss, but events grew heated quickly. The chick had ways like a mowing machine. She definitely knew her way around the block. We fell asleep wrapped in each other's arms.

The next day Destiny and Kenzie introduced me to a tall, jovial, Irish cat named Rory, a sweet southern knockout named Sheila, and a short stack of pancakes with blue hair who went by Jeanie. We enjoyed an exquisite meal together and became fast friends. During breakfast, and a brisk walk in the crisp fall air, I learned a great deal about ancient Christianity, homosexuality, and the literature of the Harlem Renaissance. I was able to contribute to the last topic. The first two were more or less centered around the self-doubt that tormented Destiny.

I filled in the group on certain places my family had plundered in the city. Everyone enjoyed the stories, although Rory gave me sideways glances from time to time. A fun morning was had by all. Rory and his family returned home, and I took the girls shopping.

With the addition of Ronnie to our threesome there came the addition of church on Sunday. Ronnie and the girls were regular attendees at church services in Brooklyn. I hadn't been to a church since the debacle with Steph, but I figured it might not hurt to make the scene.

Pastor Affenhoden was a superior minister compared to Pastor Gaphals. Affenhoden was both a born orator and a liberal cat. I dug his style and the message he espoused. I also dug playing footsie with Ronnie and holding hands.

As I've indicated, Ronnie wasn't merely a physical turn on, she was a mental challenge. I hadn't met too many chicks as well read, or as cosmopolitan. There was a definite pain behind it all, and I knew that education had provided an escape from her home life. So had church. That education, however, also created a whole package of beauty that was as rare as finding a taxi at rush hour.

With the approach of Christmas, Destiny, Kenzie, and I decided to jungle up in a hotel room that charged by the month. Ronnie helped us select a place within easy walk of both the church and a subway station. I handled the preliminaries alone with the manager.

"You the manager?" I asked a shell of a man dressed in a rumpled suit, with a grey fringe around his head.

"I am. What can I do for you, son?" He had a raspy voice as if he smoked too much.

"I need a room, month to month. I'm attending NYU, and my kid sisters are doing the homeschool thing. Our parents are gone, may they rest in peace." I crossed myself.

"You have ID?"

I showed him my ID, and he nodded. "Twenty-five hundred a month, and no parties."

"I can swing that. No parties ever. I have to study. My sisters'll behave, trust me. If not I have pops strap that used to hang in the den."

The man gave me a half-hearted chuckle and accepted cash. "Son?"

I turned back to him.

"Whatever the real story, as long as you pay, I don't say a word to anyone who asks."

I nodded man to man and cut out.

That night we set up house while Ronnie sat on the king sized bed. It was a perfect set up, except one matter that couldn't be helped. Next door to the hotel, so close I could have hit a window with a pea shooter, was an apartment complex. Several dining rooms and kitchens faced our window. If we had the shades up while undressing, the neighbors would get the full monty.

Another issue cropped up the next day. Destiny and Kenzie left to go busking while I was having dinner at the Morelli's. Destiny texted me at ten o'clock that they were planning to return to the room by one.

I texted back *"Must discuss curfew."*

At a quarter to one, there was the snick of a key card, and the door opened. I was still awake, reading *Black Widow* by Ramona McDonald. I placed the book on the side table.

"I'm still getting the hang of this guardian gig, dolls, but I see no reason for you to be rolling in this late. Even with studying, you can still do your music, and whatever, and be back by ten. Unless you have a good reason to be back later, do that."

Kenzie pouted. "We've been busking until one in the morning for months. We're used to staying up late. We make more money after the shows let out."

"I make plenty of bread. I'm more concerned about your safety than you're ability to bring in the do-re-mi. Anyway, you didn't know me before. You asked me to be in charge, I agreed, so curfew is ten unless we're together, or there's an emergency."

Destiny nodded. "Yes, sir. That's fair."

Kenzie sighed. "No. No, that isn't fair. We can handle any trouble. We've been handling ourselves for months, dammit!" She started sulking.

I channeled my inner Charles Ingalls. "I said ten, young lady! Do I need to take down your pants and we can discuss this across my lap?"

Kenzie looked down, shaking her head. "No. Fine. But It isn't fair."

The girls grabbed their pajamas and changed in the bathroom while I closed my eyes and fell asleep. Presently they crawled into bed on either side of me and snuggled in.

The clock read four-thirty when I opened my eyes. I stripped, kissed my photo of Steph, opened a bottle of Pepsi and drank about a third. The empty space in the bottle was replaced with Jim Beam. After dressing, I slipped on my loafers and adjusted my homburg.

I stood watching the girls sleep, and wondering why I cared how late they stayed out. Did I have any right to be so concerned? The question was immaterial; I was concerned. I loved them. I also loved Ronnie. I had given up all my other dips around the city, and was coming to terms with the fact that my search for Steph might not bear fruit. It was possible that she might have met another guy, or would before I found her. In that case, Ronnie was more than a fair substitute.

While Kenzie and Destiny shopped for Christmas gifts and busked a few days later, Ronnie and I sat in a quiet café enjoying cheesecake and wine. The waiter was happy to both serve us, and give us a table in the rear. A pair of Hamilton's can do that. A minor commotion up front drew our attention.

A broad with green hair cut into a severe butch, dressed in a flannel shirt, jeans, and boots was having a conniption. "Dammit, I told you not to call me ma'am! It's sir! I identify as male, OK? I can take my business elsewhere you know, and put you assholes on blast all over social media!"

The server was on the verge of tears as an older man stepped out from a back room. "My apologies, Mr. Feinstein. She didn't know. She's new."

The broad who identified as a cat lowered the thermostat and ordered some food to go.

"It's what philosophical cats call antinomy, doll." I poured Ronnie another glass of sweet Riesling. "We're born with the equipment that makes us male or female. Yet gender has become as much a matter of choice as of biology."

"If it is, in fact, a choice."

"You don't think it is?"

"I think a lot of people are starting to accept that it is in order to not be considered out of synch with the so called woke people."

"But, you. What do you think?"

"I think you're born how you're born. I think if a person with a dick walks into the bathroom I'm using, he's getting hurt."

"I dig the flip. I understand that some people are born gay or bi or whatever plethora of terms they use. Like Destiny and Kenzie. I love them how they are. This gender thing, though, it's a step too far for me."

"You ever read anything by Quentin Crisp?"

"Can't say as I have."

"You should. He was very astute and ahead of his time when it came to these things."

"I'll look into his writings. I try noodling out this being woke business, but anymore it's a drag trying to stay two steps ahead of the most hip."

I had to admit that I was falling hard for Ronnie. Things were not all biscuits and gravy, however. There were hints of problems on my job, problems that risked exploding in every direction.

A week before Christmas I was up at four as usual. After a shower, shave, and a quick breakfast, I approached Daquan in the usual spot. He was surrounded by four cops who were questioning him, and searching a backpack he had with him. I walked past on the opposite side of the street, and ducked into a greasy spoon. The emergency number worked, and a raspy voice told me to order coffee and sit tight.

An hour later Daquan entered and business transpired as usual.

"Good moves, grey meat. You handled yourself well, and Mr. Pipes is pleased." Daquan ordered coffee and a crueler.

"What's with the five-oh, or may I ask?"

"They're fishing. No way is any product on me or near me. After I grab your sack it gets passed through three other stations before I return it."

"Understood."

Daquan handed me a medium sized paper bag. "You forgot your lunch, grey meat. I brought it to you."

"Thanks." I put it in my courier sack and headed out. On the way I paid for both of our coffee and food.

Chapter Twenty-Seven

Despite such stress inducing shake-ups, life away from work was pleasant and cozy. Three evenings before Christmas I joined Ronnie and the girls at a French restaurant. Destiny and Kenzie had managed to procure tickets to *Godspell*, and to a Christmas Eve matinee of *Porgy and Bess*.

I stood outside the restaurant draped in black from tip to toe, breaking it up with a silver tie. As the threesome approached, dressed in evening gowns, hair professionally styled, I bowed gracefully and took Ronnie by the arm. We entered, and I slipped the Maitre'd a picture of Benjamin Franklin.

We began with a salad that had watermelon and feta cheese with a mint garnish. I ordered each of us a pear prepared with bleu cheese, and split an order of escargot with Ronnie. Our main entrée was Cornish game hen which was worth the cost. The wine was phenomenal, and no one questioned out ages after I parted with another C-note.

After the meal we proceeded to the theater and admired the breathtaking architecture. Ronnie provided a quick art lesson and explained that most Broadway theaters of any renown were once part of the vaudeville circuits. I knew some of the information from reading, but some was new to me. After a few minutes we found our seats and the performance began.

The show was outstanding, the music upbeat and joyful. I had seen the movie of Godspell, but the stage production was above and beyond. I wasn't a pious, bead jiggling cat, but the way the story was presented left me believing that a bit more church was in order.

Afterward, I took the chicks to a corner restaurant for coffee and cheesecake. "So, what'd you think, dolls?"

"That was so cool! I've never seen a show like that!" Kenzie bubbled.

Destiny sipped her coffee. "I agree. It makes believing in Jesus fun, and joyful. The way I was taught growing up was scary and judgmental. But this was like they were testifying to the audience of how interesting and exciting life can be as a believer."

"Yeah, I agree." Kenzie nodded. "They were telling us about being more than a church Christian. It's about forming a community which carries on the teachings of Jesus. Kind of like you talk about doing, Vinnie."

I chewed on that for a moment. "My methods aren't always Christ-like, but they're whatever they must needs be to hold the corporate marauders at bay. I dig the riff, doll. The end result is helping the poor and downtrodden. If that's the mission of The Lord, then so be it."

"So, you girls are saying that it's the effect Christ has on others which is the story, as much as it is the blood atonement and saying the words of a believer. That's insightful." Ronnie gave the girls a big smile and nodded. "And sometimes the ends justify the means."

"Exactly," Destiny pushed away an empty plate. "Jesus was crucified, but through the agony and pain of seeing that, we are more drawn to carry his message of community and caring, not judging others."

Kenzie smiled at Destiny. "Not judging ourselves." Destiny looked away and shrugged. Kenzie squeezed her shoulder.

I paid the bill and we took Ronnie home in a cab before returning to our hotel room. Kenzie and Destiny hung their dresses, and climbed into bed. We curled up together and fell asleep.

There was a reprise a couple of days later with a soul food lunch instead of French fare. Attending a

Christmas Eve matinee of *Porgy and Bess* was incredible. I had grown up listening to it, but had never seen it performed.

After the performance Destiny and Kenzie left to make last minute purchases and busk. Ronnie and I planned to meet them at church for midnight services. Prior to that we returned to the hotel and spent the evening together drinking wine and making the beast. Ronnie was in excellent shape, and after ninety minutes we took a nap wrapped in each other's arms.

The candlelight service was exquisite. The choir sang carols and Pastor Affenhoden read from Luke. After the sermon, the entire congregation joined in singing Silent Night. There was a cake and coffee gathering, and Destiny bagged up extra cookies to hand out on the way home. I was proud of the chicks for their compassion toward those less fortunate.

After services, Ronnie returned home, while Destiny, Kenzie, and I walked to our hotel. As we perambulated, the girls handed fistfuls of cookies to every homeless person we happened upon. At one corner sat a man dressed in a rumpled, tan, shadow stripe suit. By his feet sat a Doberman. Kenzie reached down to pet the dog and the man looked up at us.

"Don't." He murmured. "Her name is Karma and she'll bite you in the ass."

A half hour later, we were in our room. After cleaning up, I poured eggnog with rum in it, and lit a bowl of pot. The effects came fast and the girls began to yawn. Kenzie and Destiny climbed into bed falling asleep in each other's arms as I set out their gifts.

By eight in the morning, I was sitting in the desk chair reading *A Christmas Carol*. Destiny and Kenzie sat up in bed. "Merry Christmas, dolls! It looks like Santa came." I motioned with a thumb to a huge pile of presents.

I'd gone all out, with bottles of Acqua di Gioia, giant black teddy bears. matching leather jackets, and black leather, calf high, lace up boots. The girls had purchased a robe for me, two kinds of cologne, and a dozen fancy cigars.

For Kenzie I had also purchased a copy of *The Motorcycle Diaries* by Ernesto Guevara. Inside I inscribed, *I doubt you're related to Che, but you should read this anyway.* She hugged me and we kissed. For Destiny I purchased sheet music to *Godspell* for guitar. Her hug like to cracked my ribs."

The final gift was from Ronnie and me together. We had purchased Apple laptops for the girls from a guy I knew.

After exchanging gifts, the three of us stood looking out the window and hugging each other. Across the way children played with toys, as parents cooked breakfast.

Ronnie was waiting when we arrived at church. She was a sight to behold with her hair done up in a chignon, her cheeks glowing from the nippy air, and a big smile for us.

"Merry Christmas, girls. Merry Christmas, Vinnie my love." She kissed us each on the cheek and led us inside. She informed us that she had made reservations for our Christmas dinner, and a carriage ride through Central Park.

The service was full of carols and discussions of renewal in the spirit. Pastor Affenhoden suggested that the congregation seek to do more for the poor and deprived. After we were dismissed, Ronnie called a cab and took us to eat. She and I sat together playing footsie, as did Kenzie and Destiny.

Christmas dinner was an English feast and the mood was festive. We cavorted to Central Park afterward, and climbed into a classical English carriage. Our coachman was dressed in old fashioned riding boots, knickers, a topcoat, and a top hat. We rode through the park looking at the trees and feeling the brisk air on our faces. After the ride, the four of us returned to our hotel and rested while watching Christmas movies on TV.

Chapter Twenty-Eight

Between Christmas and New Year's Eve I began schooling Ronnie, Kenzie, and Destiny in the finer aspects of urban piracy. As I came around to accepting the possibility of a long-term life with them, hipping the chicks to my family's knowledge felt necessary.

I helped Destiny and Kenzie set up their laptops for studying, but I also taught them how to create dedicated email accounts, and likewise how to delete those accounts. The accounts were a channel to requesting vouchers and coupons in the mail. If anyone ever got wise, unlikely though that was, better that they find dead accounts scattered throughout cyberspace.

I also began taking the chicks to recovery meetings. I never let them pass the phony bills, but they filled up on coffee and snacks. The same was more or less true of the places I scored items FOT. I told them never to approach the trucks themselves. They benefited well from the process, but I preferred a layer of non-culpability between them and the actual process.

One afternoon I scanned some real estate ads in Long Island. There were four open houses within a two mile radius. I typed the addresses into my cell phone.

"This is something my parents taught me and my sisters. These swanky residences often. put out a small spread to encourage real estate agents. But anyone can attend."

Ronnie laughed. "Fantastic. I can use the car service my family pays into. We can arrive in a town-car."

I gave her a kiss. "That'll seal the deal. Don't dress like you're going to the prom, but don't dress sloppy either. It has to look like Ronnie and I are in our twenties. Destiny, you and Kenzie are our nieces along for the ride."

Three days later I trimmed my goatee, thinned my mustache, and draped myself in a pinstriped Versace suit, black loafers and went without a hat. Ronnie wore a long blue dress, and matching pumps. Kenzie and Destiny looked the part in blue jeans, pink Oxford shirts, and boots.

At the first house, we toured the rooms and filled up on finger sandwiches, crackers with cheese, and crudité. At the other three, we devoured mini-eclairs, cheesecake, and cannoli. We decided to forgo the wine and stuck to water and pop. There was nothing available that we could afford a mortgage on, even with the money I made.

New Year's Eve was a gay affair. Ronnie had her brownstone to herself because her parents were gone for three days. She invited us to join her there for a celebration. Destiny and Kenzie invited Rory, Sheila and Jeanie.

The afternoon before our party, Destiny, Kenzie and I hit four AA meetings. I dropped twenties in three of them. The fourth meeting was a speaker meeting in a church and had well over three hundred people in attendance. I was low on fifties, but dropped one of them and took eighty dollars in exchange.

"You know," Kenzie looked up at me as we walked toward a subway, "if you let us have a few of those twenties, we could hit more meetings at the same time."

"That tune wouldn't play the hit parade, sweet-cheeks. I'm the assistant treasurer at a meeting as of two weeks ago. I exchange fifties there before the cash goes into an envelope for the bank. The rest of the ersatz bread will be exchanged soon. You dolls lay low and play your cards straight. Let me deal the doubles." I ruffled Kenzie's hair which caused her to purr.

That night everyone sat around in jeans and t-shirts eating caviar, pâté and crackers, assorted cheese with bread, and drinking flutes of Moscato d'Asti wine I had procured. Soft jazz played in the background as we sat rehashing the past year and conversing about our aspirations for the new one.

"It's hard to believe that it was eight months ago when we first met you, Destiny. You were terrified and couldn't even meet my eyes when we talked. Look at you now, kid." Rory's eyes lit up as he sipped his wine.

"I'm still scared sometimes, but Kenzie's helping me learn how to survive. And I'd never have stuck it out if it wasn't for you three teaching me the truth about my faith. Ronnie, Vinnie, what can I say. You give me the boundaries and structure I need. And, Vinnie, you're a natural teacher when it comes to survival skills."

"All I ever did was make suggestions." Ronnie chimed in. "You girls took the ball and ran with it. I'm proud of you."

Kenzie downed her glass of wine and filled it again. "I wouldn't have made it without you, Destiny. I was ready to give in and become another loser on the street when you showed up. You brought these three into my life, introduced me to church, which brought us Ronnie. Vinnie, I love you. I love you so much you don't even know. I bitch a lot, and sometimes you have to put my ass back in line, but you're just so...I love you Daddy-o." Tears trickled from her eyes.

Sheila cleared her throat. "I'm glad to have you all in my life. I put in an application for graduate studies in New Mexico. So did Rory. Jeanie can finish her undergraduate there. If it comes through, well, you all have an open invitation any old time."

Jeanie looked at each of us. "I love each of you. You're my strength, and my hope for a better tomorrow. Seriously, I mean it."

I sat listening, contributing little, but soaking in what everyone else was saying. My thoughts were racing, kaleidoscoping, and formulating a plan. I lifted my glass.

"Seems to me that we none of us came from great shakes. We all got a first-hand dose of dysfunction, but early. Now we have each other. We're a perfect family of imperfect souls. Street families, from what I'm finding, all have names. My suggestion is that we dub ourselves the FEBU family."

Kenzie sipped her third glass of wine. "Feh-boo? What's that mean?"

"It's an acronym. Stands for fuck everybody but us! It stands for complete loyalty and unconditional love amongst our members. The rest of this world can get knotted." I raised my glass once more.

Rory raised his glass. "That's strong. Quite powerful. I like that, indeed."

"I think I have something in my eye." Jeanie rubbed away a few tears.

Sheila raised her glass. "Happy New Year my beautiful FEBU family."

We drank and ate, the ambiance radiating coziness. After the wine was gone, I brought old fashioned glasses from the kitchen, filling them with Jack Daniels and a splash of soda water. We watched the ball drop and drank toasts to each other. Ronnie brought up Barry Manilow on her phone, and we all listened to him croon "It's Just Another New Year's Eve"

At three in the morning Ronnie brought out blankets and pillows and everyone fell asleep in the living room. Ronnie led me to her bedroom and in short order was naked in my arms. We ushered in the new year with a bang.

The next morning everyone was worse for wear. I didn't have much of a hangover, but the others were groaning and complaining.

"There is a solution, gates." I stood surveying the scene. "Ronnie, darling, might I have a look at your larder? If you have the right ingredients, I have a sure fire remedy." A half hour later I emerged with a tray and seven tall glasses. "The Ramos Gin Fizz is the hissing hair of dog to cure all your ills, gators." I passed them around. "A friend in Florida taught me about these. His name was Cìkè. This has lemon juice, egg whites, powdered sugar, cream, orange extract, and gin, with a dash of soda water. Lines the guts and sends pixilated juniper to the brain. After having one, I suggest a hot shower with plenty of steam."

A half hour later I stood naked under a pulsating stream of hot water with Ronnie washing my back. We reversed position and then rinsed. Before we dressed, Ronnie kissed me and held me in her arms. "Would you marry me? We could take the girls and move north. Attend college."

I kissed her and squeezed her butt. "Let me chew on that, doll. I have several options I'm considering right now."

Everyone emerged from their showers, and Ronnie prepared ham and scrambled eggs with toast and guava jelly. I ground fresh coffee and used the French press. Once breakfast had been consumed, Rory, Sheila, and Jeanie cut out. Looking in the paper, I found a classic movie festival at a nearby theater. Ronnie, Destiny, Kenzie, and I swung by our hotel to grab snacks and sodas before catching the subway to midtown.

I hadn't been playing coy with Ronnie, I did have several ideas knocking around in my skull. The biggest one was that if I could find Steph, I might be able to bring her to New York. It was Heather who might draw legal heat, not Steph or Caroline. With permission, easily forged, I could marry Steph. We could form an honest and true family with the others. If she and Ronnie could learn to share, it might be the best possible hand I ever drew.

I reverse engineered the situation next; realizing

that finding Steph was a long shot. Who knew if she was still interested in me? She was a real tomato, and plenty of guys likely waited to peel her. Ronnie's idea might be the best option.

There were four movies showing: *Bonnie and Clyde, The Getaway, Dog Day Afternoon,* and *Going in Style.* All classic, all well-acted, and all pieces of the modern artistic landscape, they put my musings to rest. After the movies we stopped at a deli before retiring to the hotel. I had never felt so family oriented in my life, not even with my own family.

Chapter Twenty-Nine

Two months after our New Year's party, on a Sunday after church, Destiny, Kenzie and I were taking a walk on Van Cortland Avenue enjoying the spring weather. Ronnie had business at home. The three of us headed toward the subway station. Ahead of us a large group of African American youths were strutting along looking fierce and proud. They were dressed in electric blue dress shirts, grey slacks, and very shiny dress shoes. On their heads they wore matching grey wide-brimmed hats. A young, buxom brunette was standing in their path holding a package containing a laptop. As the group approached, she clutched her box. The group of teens sidestepped the lady, tipping their hats and laughing. They were a tough bunch, but not a threat unless first threatened.

As we approached the station, a group of Caucasian teens with shaved heads approached. They were dressed in brown t-shirts, suspenders holding up jeans, and combat boots. The group of African Americans was still in front of us. *Neither my farm, nor my jackasses.*

I zigged the zag, sweeping the chicks along, running with instincts born of necessity. Dashing down the subway stairs we swiped our cards, clicked through the turnstile, and waited for a train while keeping our eyes on the stairway, Destiny unsnapped the sheath on her left inner calf to free a stiletto. Kenzie took a collapsible steel baton from her purse. I motioned them to stay cool.

Ten minutes later the black youth were descending. Some of them had fresh marks on their faces and hands. There were some tears in their shirts. They had won the skirmish. I nodded to each of them as they clicked through and stood near us. Kenzie put her weapon away, and Destiny closed her sheath.

"Hey man. Thanks for staying and helping out." One of the cats shouted, his voice dripping with sarcasm.

I gave him cold menace. "Like I told you before, Trey, I was born with a crack in my ass. I do not, absolutely do not, need you or those Nazi bastards finishing the job of breaking it. If they start trouble with me or my chicks here on a personal level, it'll make national news. They know it. You need not to forget it."

"Yeah, maybe. Or, maybe you're chicken shit." Trey laughed.

I lowered my center of gravity and stepped into a T-stance with fists raised. "Want to test that out? You and me one on one. The boys hang back and do nothing. Same for my girls."

The rest of the group moved into positions to attack. Destiny grabbed her stiletto and Kenzie popped open the baton. Trey held up a hand.

"Like hell if this needs to turn into a massacre. I saw what you three did the other night to that old dude who was hassling your chicks. You a'ight for being white. And watch who you calling boys." Trey smiled as everyone relaxed. The rest of Trey's army started laughing as the tension eased.

We boarded the train one car ahead of Trey and his crew. At one end of the subway car a radio was blasting ACDC's "Wild Child" Destiny leaned on me, and I ruffled her hair. Kenzie kept her eyes on the connecting doors, but no one came through. Yeah, I was growing quite fond of those two.

The following Saturday I was arriving back from a meeting with Ralph as all three girls approached. "Feel like pizza, chicks?"

"Sure. Sounds good."

I sat on a bench and put my phone on speaker. "Gino's Pizzeria. Is this delivery or carry out?"

I gave the man my best hillbilly accent. Howdy. My name is Dwight and it would be delivery but I need to speak with a manager first."

"This is. What can I do for you?"

"Well, you see buddy, I was in a few days ago and I got two large pies with mushrooms and pepperoni. But the person making them only gave me pepperoni. I got back to town from visiting my sick aunt this morning so I wanted to call. Never had this happen before."

"Sorry to hear that, Mr. Dwight. Do you have your receipt?"

"Well, golly. I reckon I threw it away. Is it necessary?"

"Oh, it's OK this time. But in the future, we require a receipt to replace food."

"Thank you kindly. Yes sir, I'll surely keep the receipt next time."

I gave an address a block away from our hotel and disconnected the call. "OK chicks, head on up. Destiny and Kenzie, pajamas on. Honey, if they give you any lip, paddle their butts." I winked.

As I arrived with the food, Kenzie took four bottles of Shock Top out of the mini fridge. We watched some action movies on TV before I tucked in the girls and took Ronnie home.

The next day Ronnie wasn't at church. As Destiny, Kenzie, and I exited after services, a pack of dark clouds moved in. We caught a bus toward Queens as rain deluged the city.

We sat on a row of seats and I gave three girls sitting across from us my best smile. They had fair skin, multiple pierces in their ears and long hair dyed in various shades.

I affected a British accent "I'm a bit lost, ladies. Is Rockaway hard and far to reach? Can I catch a ride on this bus to Rockaway Beach?"

The girls stood up and moved toward the back. Kenzie and Destiny looked at each other trying not to giggle. They failed, and the raucous laughter pierced the silence of the afternoon. I reached for my sack and took out a twenty ounce bottle of bourbon and Coke, sipped some, and passed it to Kenzie. Kenzie had a swig, and passed it to Destiny.

A boy boarded with an iPod. Oblivious to us, he sat singing "Goodnight Saigon."

"Hey, Vinnie, you know everything about everything. Was Billy Joel having a gang bang in Vietnam?" Kenzie's eyes crinkled with mirth.

I shook my head laughing. "No, that's not what he meant about going down together."

Chapter Thirty

Three weeks later Kenzie turned fifteen. Destiny woke up with the sunrise, dressed, and slipped out of the room. The previous night we'd stayed up late watching old movies.

While Destiny was out, I took the opportunity to hold Kenzie close and snuggle with her. She cooed, and pulled me closer. We fell back asleep cozy and warm. I heard the snick of a keycard, and snapped upright with a switchblade in my hand. Seeing Destiny, I glared and climbed out of bed. We hugged and kissed before making coffee. Destiny had purchased a few custard filled pastry known as bombalone, and we put a candle in the center of one.

Standing at the foot of the bed watching Kenzie saw logs, we crooned. *"Happy Birthday to you. Happy Birthday to you. Happy Birthday, sweet Kenzie. Happy Birthday to you."*

Kenzie opened her eyes and groaned with a smile. "Oh man! You two! Geez!" She climbed out of bed and hugged us.

Destiny lit the candle, and Kenzie blew it out. Tears dribbled down Kenzie's cheeks when Destiny handed her a wrapped copy of *Black Robes White Justice* by Bruce Wright.

After church, followed by a sheet-cake for Kenzie at the potluck, we walked through Central Park. Many trees were starting to blossom and the air was fragrant. Despite the celebratory day, work was on my mind. Undercover cops were making a regular appearance and casing the scene. Ralph and I were monitoring the situation.

That evening, I sat across from Destiny and Kenzie at a bar and grill. The bouncer, Eric, and the bartender, Mac, were acquainted with me. The chicks and I were shown a table in the far back where the light was soft. We each had a ribeye steak with fries and a vodka gimlet.

I had been in contact with my sister Gina and her boyfriend, and had waited for this moment to give the girls a special gift. Kenzie opened her birthday card, and inside were two authentic New York State ID cards. One had Destiny's name and picture, the other had Kenzie's. The difference was that they were now eighteen years old according to the birthdates.

I ate a bite of steak. "My oldest sister, Gina, sent me those. Her boyfriend works in an office next to a DMV down south, and he knows a guy. They have access to a computer system and can get these from any state. There's another way, but it's complicated."

Kenzie squealed in delight. "Thank you! This is so cool! Now we can get our GED certificates." She drank some gimlet.

I gave her a wink. "Don't dive into the deep-end, but yes, yes you sure can. Play it cool, though. Don't use those for anything too nefarious."

Destiny sipped her cocktail. "In my old church, the men offered a girl special words of wisdom on her eighteenth birthday. You have any?"

I reflected for a moment, chewing on a steak fry, thumbed my chin and nodded. "You've got to love living, dolls, because dying is a pain in the ass. They say you only live once, but the way that we've lived these past few months, baby, once is enough. We're not like those complicated mixed up cats looking for the secrets to life or the answers to life. We just go on living day to day taking what comes. Sure, we have our dilemmas, our struggles. Who doesn't? In the end, we take forever a minute at a time. But if you want some sage advice to surviving in this big bad world, sweet cheeks, I'd have to hep you to what my papa always told me and my sisters. You have to play everything big, wide, expansively. The more open you are, the more you take in. Your dimensions deepen, you grow, you become more of what you are." I sipped my gimlet.

"That's how I want to be. Like you. I want to help everyone around me, and always look out for the underdog. I want to do it with style, like you." Kenzie finished her gimlet and was brought another. "I want to be a lawyer like Jack McCoy so that I can help others."

"That's the only way to do anything in life, doll. Do it with style, or it isn't worth a damn. I mean look at Frank Abagnale, or Richard Marcus, they managed to be the best because they had savoir faire. It set them apart. As for being a lawyer, why not be a lawyer like Mackenzie Guevara? You have a lot to offer being yourself." I pushed my plate away. "Hey, we have to meet Ronnie at the hotel for cake."

We boarded an F train and rode to our stop. After taking the elevator up and letting ourselves in, Kenzie was grabbed by Ronnie. She sat on the end of the bed, pulled Kenzie over her lap, and delivered fifteen feather-soft swats.

"Happy Birthday, my sweet girl!" Ronnie hugged Kenzie and kissed her on both cheeks. "Open your presents."

Kenzie unwrapped a calendar with a new vocabulary word for each day of the year. She also received *True Stories of Law and Order* a book that details the actual cases used in the show. Her final gift from Ronnie was a DVD of *Gideon's Trumpet*. She hugged Ronnie and couldn't speak for a moment.

Kenzie's mouth turned up so far that her face like to split in two. Tears trickled down her cheeks. "I never had a birthday party before. I mean not a real celebration. Today sure as hell made up for that."

Destiny handed Kenzie an envelope. Inside were

tickets to a Robin Williams movie festival. Kenzie squeezed her tight. Words couldn't get through the smiling tears, but her face said it all. We had chocolate torte with coffee, and after wrapping the leftovers, the four of us caught the subway to midtown where the festival was showing. Kenzie and Destiny sat holding hands and kissing as we watched the movies. Ronnie and I sat snuggled together feeling each other up.

The following day we slept in. I had a day off. We spent the afternoon in the park reading and enjoying the passing parade. We were preparing to leave, when a group of teens approached. Destiny froze a moment as the teens glared at us.

Kenzie turned to face them "Well, shit. It's that douchebag Valiant, and his gang of pansies. Vinnie, this asshole is the one we told you about. He's the scumbag who got us arrested before we met you."

Valiant sneered. "We got eighty-sixed from our park because of you bitches. We owe you an ass kicking!"

I shoved the chicks behind me. "Slow your roll, gate." I raised my hands in a gesture of surrender. "We're cutting out."

Valiant snarled. "Don't think so, faggot. You can leave but..."

My right hand slap interrupted the arrogant puke, rocking his head. A side kick to the groin dropped one of his boys, and a front snap kick to the knee brought Valiant crashing down. No one else approached.

I gave the punk a disarming smile. "I'm their street dad, cats. You come near them again, they'll find pieces of you from here to Oyster Bay. You goons from Saskatoon catching my signal?"

Kenzie and Destiny backed away, but Valliant's crew were already moving in the reverse direction. Valiant hobbled after them, leaning on his girlfriend. The boy who'd been kicked in the manhood staggered behind them.

We pounded our ground smashers, caught a subway to Little Italy, and ordered a large anchovy and mushroom pizza. I was already having job issues, and attention from cops wasn't on my agenda. I didn't have a choice but to end the fight before it began. As we sat, I received a text message from Ralph.

Picked up a shadow. Ditched him. Caught another. Let's talk. Tomorrow. MOMA.

Kenzie paused mid-bite. "Something wrong?"

"I'm not certain, doll. There might be a big problem. It doesn't concern you chicks. It's a job hassle."

Destiny reached across the table and held my free hand. "We're FEBU family. If it's a problem for you, it concerns us."

"I've schooled you chicks well, but in this case, I can't involve you. It's just..." I paused. "I can't discuss my job. But as with my parents, I may have gotten in over my head. Stupid on my part, but so far, I'm safe. Thing of it is, dolls, if there's even a chance I could get jammed up, I'll have to clear out fast. Should anyone ask, you don't know me."

Kenzie cocked her head sideways. "What's that all about? You kill someone? Knock over a bank?"

Destiny rubbed her temples with her thumbs. "We don't need details. If we have to run, then let's run. You name the destination; we'll get Ronnie and go with you."

I sighed "No, you won't. Ronnie needs to stay out of this, too. Look, I love you both, like with all my heart and soul, but I told you from jump street that I'm better off alone. I took a job because the bread was sweet, and I figured it wasn't hurting anyone who wasn't willing to get hurt."

Kenzie finished her last slice, and another glass of beer. "If you have to go, I'd suggest finding that girl you told us about. Call your sister, get a new name, and go find your soulmate."

They read me like a dime-store novel. I settled up on the check and we walked outside. I hit an AA meeting with them and traded in my last bogus twenty, collecting twenty-five in change. I tried to relax, but a sense of finality crushed in on me.

Chapter Thirty-One

Two months after Ralph texted me, Destiny turned sixteen, nineteen by her new ID. Ronnie joined us after school let out, and the four of us had dinner at a soul food restaurant in Harlem before attending a production of *Harvey*. It took my mind off of the issues at work

After the play, we returned to our room. Destiny was standing in her panties, getting her pajamas out of the dresser. When she bent over, I grabbed her and held her in place. Ronnie picked up a hairbrush and delivered the gentle birthday swats. We gave her a book of sheet music to Bob Dylan's greatest hits. I'd cut a deal with a delivery man for a jewelry warehouse, and gave Destiny a gold, ladies wristwatch with diamond chips on the bezel. She hugged us both.

Ronnie cleared her throat. "Guys, I have something to tell you." She looked around the room searching for the words she needed. "In July I'm moving. I was accepted to Urbana. My mom isn't happy with that choice, and neither is my step-father. I'm going anyway, and paying for it myself. I want to study education. I'm thinking about being a teacher."

Destiny gasped. Kenzie stood staring at us, and then turned toward the window and stared at the apartments across the way. I walked over, embracing her from behind. Kenzie began shaking as tears flooded from her eyes.

Destiny moved to one side and held her. "What's wrong with you? I thought you'd be excited for her. Mom's finally free!"

Kenzie grabbed Destiny in an embrace and bawled. "She's abandoning us. We need her and she's leaving. She's dumping us."

Ronnie sat on the bed and pulled Kenzie into her

lap. "I have to go to college, baby girl. I have to live my life. You know that." Ronnie rocked Kenzie like a small child as I snuggled with Destiny. "You're almost ready for your tests. I'll help you get that set up. You'll both have your certificates before I leave."

Kenzie sniffled and blew her nose. "I'm sorry. I know it isn't fair of me, but everyone who's supposed to love me ends up abandoning me."

I kissed Destiny and took out four glasses from the refrigerator, filling them each with three ice cubes, a splash of club soda and scotch. "To new beginnings."

Kenzie gulped her drink and I poured her another. "I hope you enjoy college, mom. I'll miss you more than you know."

"We can text and email. And by the time you're sixteen you'll be in college too." Ronnie sipped her drink. "I love you, Kenzie. I've been trapped for years, though, and you know it. I can finally escape the grand dysfunctionality I call a home."

Kenzie's eyes flooded as she sat holding her giant teddy bear. Destiny rubbed her shoulders. They could work through their grief without me, and I needed to take Ronnie home.

Ronnie and I left together after finishing our scotch. We rode in a cab, necking the whole way. I returned an hour later and Kenzie was asleep. I tucked in Destiny and fell asleep between them.

The job situation headed south with increasing speed. I wasn't sure how to handle matters, but I was damned if I was going to go to prison for anyone. I knew that my role was to place another layer between Pipes and his product, but my loyalty to him started and stopped at the dollar sign. I was loyal to the girls, to Ronnie, and to a certain degree I had loyalty to Rory, Sheila and Jeanie. I was loyal to Ralph and his family because they treated me well. Loyalty to Pipes and his crew was all but non-existent. They were playing it stupid, or someone was. Cops were around on the regular, and it was difficult to make the pick-ups without being tailed.

One evening I invited Ralph to a bar so we could discuss matters. He had a chess board set up, and took white because it was his board. I sipped a Chopin martini as he moved king's pawn to king's pawn two.

I moved queen's bishop pawn two spaces and he looked up. "Sicilian defense?" He moved his knight, trying for a Fegatello attack.

As in life, piracy, and chicks, forethought wins the game. I stared at the board with deep concentration. "I'm not sure what's going down, Morelli, but four days straight the five-oh is interviewing D when I show up. I don't plan on wearing a number across my tits."

We exchanged moves in silence. He sipped his lager and moved his rook, taking my bishop. "You and I both, Il-Cazzo. Thing is, I know a guy, who knows a guy, who's in with the supplier. We could make our move and go straight to the top. Move it ourselves."

The game was getting interesting. I took his rook, and dangled my queen as bait. "You're about two steps out of synch with the beat, gate. Neither of us is that good, and on you a busted head wouldn't look becoming."

"There is another possible." He took my queen, but left himself exposed. "I'm set to be accepted at three universities in the Midwest. How's about making a drop, and walking with the green."

"Count me out on that one, too. If I'm forced to walk, I'll walk clean. I don't want my chicks, or my other family, taking a hit. If you pull that rope-a-dope, those Guidos will sell your sister for the cash. They'll leave your parents in a car with their heads removed. For a real down cat, you can be awfully dim. Checkmate."

We finished our drinks and left one at a time. Morelli cut out east, and I caught an A train. The chicks met me at the Rockaway station and we rode back to the hotel. The next day was Sunday, so we ordered a late dinner of Chinese food. I poured the martinis, and the four of us watched a western.

The next morning, we attended church. I was growing accustomed to the services, but they caused a resurfacing of guilt pangs about the way I conducted my life. Not that I planned to change, or even thought I could. I had the fine threads, the bling, the residence, the women. Giving up my lifestyle meant giving up everything else, and that wasn't in the cards.

Ronnie had something cooking at home, so Destiny, Kenzie and I attended a movie marathon at a nearby theater. Steve Martin was good for some laughs. I had spiked some bottles of Coke with bourbon, and the spirits eased my troubles.

The next week everything changed on the job. I arrived Monday morning at six, and Daquan was being arrested. I kept walking and stopped at a mobile phone store. Dialing from a test model, I was given an address in Long Island. I showed up, and a man motioned to me from a cab. I climbed in the back. We drove away.

"You called for a pick-up, Jack? It should be about fifty from here. Hey, I dropped my pack of Camels, see if it's back there."

I reached toward the floor and lifted a brown paper bag. Sliding it into my courier's sack, I shrugged. "Doesn't seem to be here."

"It's cool. I'll look after I drop you."

On Tuesday and Wednesday, I walked to Central Park. An older man sat beside me and read the paper. I scooped the bag he set between us.

Thursday, all Hell broke loose. Morelli called me as

I was on my way to Queens. "Check, and mate." The phone clicked off.

I exited the train, and caught one to Manhattan. There were four men in the garment district with whom I did regular business. I gave them descriptions of Ronnie, Kenzie, and Destiny. After picking up a case of burner phones, I returned to the hotel. Destiny and Kenzie were half naked, getting their freak on.

Deciding in a hurry what to keep and what to ditch, I began packing books and clothing into my backpack and courier's sack. "I've got a major hitch in the get-along, and we need to talk. As soon as possible." I looked at the chicks.

They sat up, pulled on t-shirts, and zipped their jeans. "What's wrong? What can we do to help?"

"There's nothing you can do. I got word that someone I know in the Bronx was arrested. Before they toss his computer, I have to make tracks. If anyone asks, you don't know me. No matter what."

Kenzie's eyes widened and her mouth turned down at the corners. "Of course we won't dime you out, but it's a huge city. Why don't we change hotels?"

I sighed. "It isn't the hotel. I can't tell you what this is about, but I have to get moving. You have another three weeks paid for here. I'm leaving you three grand as well. You can get another place next month."

They enveloped me from each side, weeping. "If you have to leave, go find that girl you lost. You changed our lives. You taught us so much. You deserve happiness."

I walked with them out the door. "Then my work here is done. Let's go tell Ronnie."

Ronnie didn't take it well. "Damnit, Vinnie! I love you. We love you. Marry me, and we can head north. You can get into college with me. So can they.

I sipped a straight Jack Daniels, and looked at a spot

a thousand yards away. "I'm sorry, doll. I wish circumstances were different, but this is the tune the fiddler played, and we must needs jig to it."

Ronnie blinked back tears. "Can't you please hang on for a bit longer? The girls are almost ready to take the tests, and they'll pass. I'm sure of that. I'm almost ready to head to college. I swear you three could get accepted there too. We can all live together. Let's get married. Please?"

I kissed Ronnie hard. "Would that it could work that way. I can't do it. I have to cut and run quick, fast and in a hurry. I should already be gone now. One day maybe I'll find you chicks again. We'll stay in touch anyway. For a while."

Ronnie hugged me, and forced a smile. "You going to be alright, Daddy-o? Because we can find a way to help. I'd do anything, and you know our girls would."

I hugged them each in turn, and gave each a smack on the ass. "I'm not flushed out, chicks, but wrap your ass in a sling and bet it that I'll be a'ight."

I walked out the door knowing that everything was arranged. Rod Allen and Lou Gonzalez had pictures of the chicks, had burner phones I'd paid for, and had cash for the girls and for Ronnie. Everything was set. I still had four grand in my clip and another twelve grand in a bank account. I checked a map on my cell phone and decided on Chicago. It was a perfect place to hole up and research the whereabouts of Heather Baker's family.

Chapter Thirty-Two

I exited a train at Union Square. Heading to midtown and west thirty-ninth street, I grabbed my sack and extracted two bottles of spiked cola. I opened one and sipped it, placing the other in my pocket. After buying my ticket for the ferry to Hoboken, I drank the second bottle. My eyes puddled up as I second guessed my decision. I turned back four times before steeling my resolve. I had to leave; The safety of my entire FEBU family was at stake. The ride was uneventful, the air thick and putrid, as I sat watching NYC become part of my past.

Exiting the ferry, I headed to the nearest busy street and spotted a place to catch a ride. While waiting, I used a burner phone to text Ralph.

College? I decided on a vacation. Thank your parents for everything.

PING College. Yes. One day we'll meet again. Checkmate.*

After standing a while with my thumb out, an elderly gentleman in an old, green, dented Buick pulled over. "Where you be headed?" He had a thick accent that was almost English but not quite.

He motioned to me, and I climbed in. "Nebraska, eventually. For now, anywhere west. Chicago looks good." I looked out the window as the man pulled off.

"Aye, lad," the elderly man stated, "used to travel a lot in me younger days. Best bet for a long distance ride would be a truck stop. I'm traveling through Mahwah, and you've got a big one there." He turned on the radio and "Love on The Rocks" by Neil Diamond crackled through the speakers.

A half hour later I climbed out and proceed toward the truck stop. Cutting across the highway, I spotted both the stop and a diner. Truck stop diners are not standard restaurants. They are some other species, and notable for gas inducing food in large quantities, as I was soon to find out.

I had never plundered a place like that, and I took a moment to plot a strategy. After a few minutes I entered the dining area and took a casual look around. The lighting was artificial and dim. There were booths along every wall made of cheap synthetic material that was designed to look expensive. At the front was a long counter with stools. The smell of grease and food mingled with sweat and cheap perfume. A jukebox blasted "Coal Miner's Daughter" by Loretta Lynn. I registered three names on the shirts of the servers.

After my initial foray, I proceeded into the truck stop itself. The change in atmosphere was startling, and a shock to my eyes. Instead of being dim and low-key, the lighting was bright and fluorescent. The area produced the sensation of continual daylight. There was a great deal of noise and push to the place. I wandered over to check out a series of tables where truckers were congregated awaiting orders from their mother companies.

"Anyone heading to -- or near -- anywhere in Chicago?" Several truckers turned and gave me their attention.

"I'm hauling machinery to Chicago. Leaving in an hour. You need a ride?" A short, squat man who looked older than the rest spoke up.

I looked him over as men often will with other men. Simple question, can I take him or not if necessary. The man had a huge red beard, and long red hair, which was in my favor. He looked powerful in the chest and arms, which was not. In the end I opted to take the risk that the guy might ask for money, or that he might be predatory.

"Sounds good. I need to down some groceries.

Please, feel free to join me when you finish up here. Least I can do is buy you one on the dark."

"Make that dinner and we have a deal. I already gassed up on the company dime so no worries." The trucker offered a hand. "Name's Bull."

I took the hand and we shook. "Name's Vinnie." With an abrupt turn I headed for a payphone. I dialed the truck stop diner and requested a manager.

"Yeah? Help you?" Came the tired voice that resembled gravel in a food processor.

"Yes, sir. My name is Desmond Jones. I was in last week with my buddy and we got dinner. About ten. Great waitress named Melinda. I got the chicken fried steak and he got a burger and fries. But see the steak was sort of greasy, and his burger was over cooked. Plus, it had onions, and he can't eat them. Stomach problems."

"Yeah? Hey, if you are in another time, tell them Big Ernie put your name in the book. Two meals on us. Anything you want. Sorry for the problem Mr. Jones."

"Matter of fact, I'm staying in my rig tonight. I can pop in, and my buddy will be by as soon as he gasses up."

"Sure thing, Mr. Jones."

I hung up and headed to the restroom. After washing up, and changing into jeans and a hoodie, I entered and sat at the counter. A waitress approached, and it wasn't Melinda. I asked to speak with Ernie. He came out leaning on a cane. A grizzled, drunken old man, with a red, vein-lined face, bloodshot eyes, grey hair in a comb over, and a heavy stubble, he shook my hand and said the meals were on him.

I ordered a lumberjack breakfast for dinner anchored with a pot of black coffee. While drinking the coffee, I reminisced about Steph.

My food came, and I began eating it without noticing how it tasted. Somewhere in the process I dozed off. I came to, realizing that the truck driver, Bull, was tapping my shoulder.

"You look bombed." He looked concerned. "You don't take drugs, right? Because, if so, then forget it. I don't need trouble like that."

I shook my head. "I'm kind of worn out. Was thinking about my girl. I appreciate you giving me a ride."

Bull shrugged. "You buy me dinner, it's a deal."

I nodded and Bull summoned a waitress. He ordered a double cheeseburger with fries, coffee, and blueberry pie. After consuming my food, I ordered blueberry pie, and more coffee.

"So, you said something about your girl. You mean a daughter or a girlfriend." Bull. tucked into his food while making conversation.

"Old girlfriend. I met her a couple years back. She moved, and we lost touch. I'm trying to find her again."

"I see. You're what, eighteen? You look about that. Recently out of school? Looking for answers and adventure?" Bull took a bite.

"Something like that," I shrugged.

"None of my business. I said I'd give you a ride, and I will." Bull laughed. "I was young and horny once too."

We finished up, and I left a forty dollar tip. Once we were arranged in the cab of the truck, Bull told me about the nearby area of Patterson. I hadn't made the connection to Bob Dylan's "Hurricane," but Bull not only knew the entire backstory, he lived five blocks away when the murder occurred.

I dozed off after Bull finished his tale, and the static and crackle of a CB radio provided a vague white noise backdrop to the lonely country tunes on the radio. I came to four hours later. There's a place between asleep and awake where you still remember dreaming, and yet can hear everything transpiring in the nearby vicinity. The place, I'd heard, was similar to a coma or a drug induced haze. Hearing one speak to you, but being unable to answer, this was a realm with which I was familiar. I sat in the passenger seat, head tapping against the window, and continued to sleep off my dinner, and the bone-weary exhaustion that was coming on strong and sudden.

The truck came to a stop two hours later. I regained a fuzzy consciousness, and climbed out. After some coffee, and draining the main vein, Bull motioned me to load up. I felt less anxious with the coffee in my system. I opened a bag of Hershey's Miniatures and handed it over. "Help yourself." I looked out the window. "You know, this is kind of cool. I've never seen this part of the country, except in pictures. It's peaceful out here."

Bull handed back the bag of candy, and I put it away. He looked at me. "That's one of the great things about trucking. It's peaceful, and solitary."

After a few minutes, Bull continued. "I know a guy in Washington, fellow named Billy. He has a large property out there that he runs with another guy. They take in lost people, and people who need help off the books. I don't know what your real story is. Maybe you are looking for a girl. But if you need anything else, I can give you an address."

I felt a tweak in the base of my spine. Helping people off the books. *Maybe, nah, too far-fetched.*

"I really am heading to find a girl I met, but, carve my dome, what's this cat like? I mean, is he cubistic? Is he woke? There's no telling where this chick ended up, and Washington's as possible as anywhere. Does this cat take in anyone or what?"

"For starters, he doesn't make the decision on his own who to accept. There's another fella, Doc, who also has a say. They rely on a committee of other community members, as well. If one needs help, they rarely say no. As to what Billy is like, that depends on who you ask. There are people for whom he would bend the very gates of Hell to assist. There are also people whom he would send to Hell, and lock the gates behind them. It depends on loyalty, and whether the person is willing to help himself. Billy is no pushover. His friend, Doc, though, that man has a serious compassion for lost causes. He's seen some hard traveling, and it clouds his thinking."

I pondered this information a few minutes. "How did you meet them?"

"Billy and I go back a while. We met as teens in a place on the eastern part of Oregon. I try not to think about the place too much. Bad memories." Bull shuddered. "One day, while I was taking a couple months break from driving trucks, I was hired by three ladies in Wyoming. They were former members of a different type of community. They escaped from becoming child brides. Now they work to help others. There was a lady with infant twin sons whom they were helping. I was hired as a bodyguard. After freeing the lady, Lydie Barlow, I transported all four ladies, and the two babies, to a place in Washington. Lo and behold, Billy was there to receive them. Since then, I've stayed in touch."

"Small world, I guess. So, this place, is it like a cult or what?"

"The one in Wyoming? Sort of. More of a religious order. Magic drawers, and following a guy they believe to be a prophet. If you mean Doc and Billy's place? No! Absolutely not a cult! Doc would never allow that. He was in a cult for two years prior to meeting Billy. Some pseudo-intellectual place in the northeast based on the teachings of a Gerry, or so he told me. Said it was a bunch of people hiding from reality. That those in the inner circle had the biggest brood of spoiled brats he'd ever seen." Bull cleared his throat. "Doc made sure this current community was nothing like that. There's no inner circle. Everyone works to make the place run. Speaking of that, be prepared to tell them what services you can offer. One thing Billy and Doc insist on is that community members help out. I was there last winter, and they even had four-year-olds on hands and knees scrubbing the dining room floors."

I pondered this information as I drifted back to sleep. At ten in the morning, we reached Chicago. Glen Campbell's "Rhinestone Cowboy" filled the cab. Bull pulled into a truck stop that seemed to lack much in the way of amenities. Reaching for my sack, I pulled out two cards entitling the bearer to a free value meal of their choice at McDonalds. I also removed a coupon for a free large pizza of choice at Pizza Hut.

"Here, Bull. Thanks for the ride. You might find use for these vouchers. Keep the bugs off the glass and the cops off your tail." I shook his hand.

"Vinnie. It was a pleasure. I hope you find whatever you're searching for. I have a feeling it's more than a girl. Here's my business card. On the back is the address of the place I was telling you about. If you find yourself needing anything, or if your plans fall through, give me a call. I know some people, and you might could get into a trucking academy and make a good living." Bull patted me on the shoulder. I waved as I walked away.

The air was mild for June. I brought up the GPS app on my phone, and requested nearby parks. The robotic feminine voice was difficult to hear over the traffic. Following the directions, I meandered toward Washington Square Park. I once read about the historical significance of the park with relation to free speech rights. I caught a city bus, walked for another fifteen minutes, spotted the park, and noticed a library across the street. The architecture of the building was stunning. I took it in before entering and reserving a computer.

I began by searching for information on Heather Baker in Harvest Junction. I got three hits, two of them requiring money. The third gave a maiden name of Tanner. Not as generic as Smith, but it wasn't going to be easy to track.

Next, I read articles on Joey Pipes and Daquan being arrested. They were both out on a half-million bail, but police continued looking for associates. Neither my name nor Ralph's were mentioned. I suspected that I had been paranoid. We were low level, and insulated from the real action. On the other hand, there was no way that I could put my new family at risk.

I texted Julie, Tori and Fisher, and Gina and Nicky. *Had trouble in New York. Travelled north to Chicago to give the area a once over.*

Julie texted back first. *Hey, Vinnie! I'm doing well. Got a 4.0 first time ever in school. Not much changes here except the faces. Miss you. Vic says hey.*

I got another message. This one was from Destiny. *I love you. You changed our lives. Please stay safe. I'll never forgive you. Love, Destiny.* My eyes puddled up. A moment later my phone pinged again. *I mean I'll never forget you.*

I sighed, and texted her. *I think you were right the first time, doll. I'm sorry. I wish things had been different. But hey, if my grandma had balls, she'd be my grandpa.*

Thinking about Steph I had a memory of Otis Lamar. I recalled his mentioning the Navy. If I couldn't find Steph, it was an option. Certainly no one could link me to my parents, to Myron Baker's death, or to Joey Pipes if I used a fake ID and enlisted. I used the computer to look up BUDS. The search brought up books on flowers and Navy SEALs. I searched Navy SEALs and, after some scrolling of various authors, settled on some titles. I'd already read *Rogue Warrior* by Richard Marcinko, but I wrote down

Hell Week and *One Perfect Op* by Dennis Chalker. I recalled him as being one of Marcinko's boys. I also hit upon *The Warrior Elite* by Dick Couch. The reviews for that were excellent. I'd left almost all my books with the chicks, and I needed reading material if I planned to stick around Chicago for a while.

I walked toward a reading room and sat in an overstuffed chair. In a matter of moments, I was sound asleep clutching my sack. I enjoyed blissful slumber for about four hours dreaming about Steph, Ronnie, and Julie. At first, after waking, I cast furtive glances as if people might be staring at me, but everyone in the room was either reading or napping. I stood up, grabbed my sack, and worked my way toward the exit.

After exiting the library, I was looking around for a place to get coffee when I noticed a gathering in the park. I walked across the street, wandered through Washington Square Park, and saw men setting up equipment and a makeshift stage. There were about one hundred people milling around and talking to each other. I saw a small stand where ladies, dressed in long, plain colored dresses and frumpy hair-dos, were selling bibles and various religious books and tapes. I already owned a bible and had no desire to read commentaries on Paul. The people reminded me of how Destiny described her parents and their church.

I located a hot dog stand and ordered four Chicago style footlong dogs with a root beer. The air was rheumy and thick, and yet the sky offered little chance of rain. I looked over toward the gathering and noticed the crowd size had doubled with more people arriving on chartered school busses.

Walking over, I worked my way through the crowds toward the far side. An ear piercing shriek split the air as a guitar sounded and some drums rattled. In a matter of seconds, a group of men were playing a variety of brass instruments, and ladies were banging tambourines. I watched the crowd swaying and raising their hands toward the sky.

The musicians started with a fast number that had something to do with their right to shake church foundations with praise songs. They segued into singing "I Shall Call Upon The Lord" and then took it down several notches with "In the Garden"

After this raucous introduction that left me feeling invigorated and manic, the preacher came running from the side of the stage with his arms raised like a football player after a touchdown. He was five and a half feet tall, overweight, dressed in a powder blue leisure suit, and his dark brown hair was sprayed into a straw-like coif that would sustain gale-force winds. After a long and repetitive opening prayer, he commenced his sermon from a makeshift pulpit.

I listened to the man with great discomfort. Much of his opening sally was bigoted, xenophobic, and against everything I believed. I wanted to leave, but the crowd had me hemmed in. I was raised to believe that people are entitled to live their lives as they saw fit so long as it didn't hurt anyone. This schmuck was anti-choice and a gay-basher. The crowd was eating up the message.

Despite my unease with the general message, I found myself getting sucked in by his hypnotic voice, and the wild gesticulating and shouted "Amens" of the crowd.

The zealous fervor of the congregated bodies, combined with the fact that I couldn't move, left me in a state of awed confusion. I had heard preachers before. Gaphals was OK. Affenhoden was superb. This guy was alluring, but dangerous. He was a politically conservative muckraker, but he offered up his poison wrapped in layers of scripture about love.

As the preacher finished, I thought that I might have a chance to leave, when from the front of the crowd I saw some girls who flooded my carburetor. They stepped up onto the makeshift stage. As the guitar and drum sounded, they began to sing a soulful rendition of "The Battle Hymn of The Republic." I tried to edge forward. The soloist was a chick with ringlets of dark hair cascading past her shoulders. Her breasts heaved and undulated as she sang. As the group finished the song, I saw several older ladies near the front raise their hands in the air and begin breathing strange utterances. The ladies mouthed a creed which it would seem no sane mortal could understand. As I worked my way toward the stage, hoping to talk to the girls, those around me began to cry and make howling noises into the night. The crowd was running, jumping, shaking, shouting to the top of their voices, spinning around in circles, falling on the ground, jerking, kicking, and rolling all over. I was afraid someone would get hurt. I had never witnessed such histrionics. These people were mentally deranged, or under a spell. The preacher claimed them to be filled with the spirit.

"Yes, my people! Hallelujah! The Lord is having a movement in this park!"

I stopped in my tracks and started laughing out loud. I bit my tongue so as not to yell "You're going to have to clean it up. I think they provide baggies for that." I had worked my way to the far edge of the crowd near a street.

My laughter was mistaken by a couple of men who thought I believed in all of this hokum. One of the men took an outstretched palm and smacked me on the forehead.

"The Holy Spirit is upon you brother!" The man screamed.

I was startled, and responded by throwing a hard right jab into the man's bread basket. "Hit me again, asshole, and I swear you'll meet Jesus tonight!"

Before anyone could react, I bolted away. This was too much. I wanted to talk to the girls I had seen singing, maybe hook up with one later, but this was ridiculous.

Chapter Thirty-Three

As I moved away from the crowd, and out of the park area, anger surged inside of me. Those people were scared and formed religious groups for protection, but the crap that jerk was laying down, followed by someone hitting me on the head, was beyond the pale. I needed a drink. A cat in decent threads approached from behind. As I turned to defend myself, he held up his hands.

"Woah! I come in peace my brother. Nice punch back there. I think you might have cold cocked Colton Draeger. I stand impressed. My parents used to drag me to those sideshows, although I never cared for it. I mean it's entertaining, but I don't buy into their jazz."

I nodded. "I'm going to get a beer. Want one?"

"Sure. Hey, you got ID? I can get the beer if you want. I'm twenty-one." The guy smiled.

"Mine says I'm nineteen, but most bartenders ignore that when they see a pile of lettuce."

"Oh. Well, I am twenty-one. I go to the University. Hey, if you have ID, you ever gamble?" The guy looked me over "By the way I'm Eddie. Eddie Germinis. Friends call me Eddie G."

"Pleasure. I'm Vinnie Il-Cazzo. If you mean cards and stuff, well sometimes, but I don't have a lot of money." I gave him a straight face.

"No. I was thinking about a casino. There's one about three hour drive. I was planning to go earlier, but I got sucked into this freak show." Eddie and I entered a corner tavern.

We got a table and ordered a pitcher of stout. The waitress didn't even ask for ID. I asked if they had any peanuts. She returned with a basket of semi-fresh popcorn. I drank beer between handfuls.

"So, what made you decide to attend the festivities?" Eddie nursed his beer.

"I was having dinner and saw the crowd. Next thing I knew I was trapped on all sides. I tried to escape until I cast my eyes on those chicks who were singing at the end there. They caught my attention. I was hoping to introduce myself to one of them. Maybe lay something down later." I poured a second glass of beer.

Eddie started laughing. A real laugh, with his head thrown back. He almost choked on some popcorn. "You sure know how to pick them, man. Those are the Draeger sisters. You punched their oldest brother. The one who did the solo is Cinnamon Draeger. They appear at these revivals a couple of times a year. Something of a draw, I guess."

"Yeah? Cinnamon was the main chick I had my eye on. I shot down my chance, huh?" I swallowed beer, and poured Eddie a second glass.

"You never had a chance, man. First of all, their father decides who they can associate with. Second of all, you'd need a crowbar to get her legs apart. Any of those girls. They're the tightest you ever saw." He shook his head still laughing.

I flushed a bit, angry and embarrassed. After a moment I realized he wasn't making fun of me. He was amused by the situation.

"Changing the subject, you mentioned a casino? I have a decent pile of bread on me, but I don't noise it around. I've never been to a casino, but I'm all for new experiences." I finished my beer, and put a twenty dollar bill under the pitcher.

"Yeah. I was planning to shoot some dice. You interested? You can either build your money, or lose it all. Either way it's a great way to kill a few hours. You live near here?" Eddie stood up. I grabbed my sack and followed.

We stepped outside and walked toward a side street. "I'm interested. No, I'm from New York. I'm planning to case the scene in Nebraska, but gradually. I met a doll a few years back, and I want to follow up with her. Her people are from there."

Eddie reached into his pocket and extracted a keychain. He pushed a button, and the lights on an Audi flashed. "That sounds like a great time. I always think about traveling across the country. Maybe after I finish my degree in political science, I will." We climbed into the car. "Dude, you better be careful, though. You're chasing after one chick, and on the way stop to try for another?"

"You study political science?" I ignored his comment about my desire for the softer persuasion.

"Yeah. Mostly the Daley machine, and the various aspects of politics leading up to that." Eddie picked up speed and turned on the radio. Irish folk music filled the car.

"I read about him. I think it was Daley. I heard about him in a movie, too. About a couple whose daughter was killed."

"Could be anyone. That's sort of vague. Daley was about as crooked as any politician. The more you study politics the more you realize that success is based on a lack of scruples, combined with a crooked mindset." He opened a Coke. "If you don't like NPR feel free to change the station."

"I dig this, gate. Dowaliby. That's the name. The couple in that book. *Gone in The_Night* it was called. The movie too." We took an exit to a smaller town.

"Ah. Yeah, I know something of that case. A tragedy. It did involve a Daley, peripherally. He was running for office and the timing of certain events was suggestive. It was before my time, but I read about it in my case studies for one of my classes." Eddie looked at me. "You know how to play craps?"

"I've read about it in books. You roll the dice and get a seven or eleven. If you roll anything else, except snake eyes, three, or twelve, get that same number again before rolling seven or eleven." I shrugged.

"Not bad, but I better school you in the game before we get to the casino. You have to know how this works. I mean, we could play other games, but I like craps. Blackjack and poker require a lot of skill, and roulette is boring." Eddie merged.

"I know blackjack, too. I've read *Beat the Dealer*. I can count cards a bit." I pulled a bottle of Pepsi out of my pack.

"Thorp is the most basic card counting. There are far more advanced techniques these days. Let's stick to dice for now. Your first roll is called a come-out. If you roll a seven or an eleven on the come out you win. If you roll two, three or twelve you lose. After that, it gets more complicated. If you roll any other number that's called your point. Then, like you said, you have to roll that number again before you roll seven or eleven. If you do you win. Roll seven or eleven after your point and you lose. If you roll snake eyes you lose. Except that you can bet on rolling two or twelve, and, if you bet that, and hit it on the next roll, you get thirty to one odds. Other bets have odds too like hard way eight and hard way ten."

I was listening. "I get it. You make more for point bets, right?"

"Sure do. The dice are wonky, though. They might not favor us; or they might. Lady Luck is a fickle bitch."

"Sounds fun. If I lose everything, though, I'm screwed, so she better smile on my hands."

We rode in silence for an hour and listened to the radio. I offered prayers for luck. Eddie jerked across two lanes to turn on an exit for Peoria.

"So that park in Chicago, do you buy into any of that?" I looked over with curiosity.

"You mean because I drink and gamble? Well, Vinnie, yeah. I do buy into some of it. Not the way they sell it, though. My feeling is that Jesus was, and is, and always will be real. He told us to feed the poor; help the destitute; care for the needy. He would barf on his sandals if he saw the crap people preach in his name." Eddie shrugged. "Do you believe, or were you in fact following your penis?"

"Both. I believe what you said. I've read a lot. From what I can dig, The Bible jibes with what I know of other religions. It all comes down to taking care of others and trying to do the best we can. What we can't do as people is what Jesus does."

"You're pretty smart. You get the real message far better than the Draeger's. Far better." Eddie grinned "My personal belief is this. Some folks walk a straight and narrow path. They're Simon pure. Those people are saints and they get statues of themselves built. The birds come and shit on the statues. Other people do anything to get ahead. They couldn't care less who they hurt or destroy. They want theirs, and screw us. Those are sinners..."

I interrupted. "And politicians."

"Hey! Watch it buddy." Eddie guffawed. "Fair enough. Most politicians today, too. In between saints and sinners are me and you. We live our lives, we do our deals, and we try to balance our walk through the mire against what it benefits those we care for. We keep our good intentions in front of us."

"My parents would dig you. That's more or less how they raised me. Also, you just helped me with a dilemma I've been having."

"Sometimes I get lucky. Everything cool? What's this dilemma?" We pulled into a huge parking lot. The casino was in front of us.

"I got involved in a bad situation back home. Well, a string of them over the last couple of years. Everything involved helping others, but, well, you wouldn't dig it all. Let's go break these bastards."

Eddie chuckled, got out, and had a stretch. "You'd be surprised by what I'd understand. For now, let's table the dilemma. Time to make or break."

I grabbed my sack, and then decided to leave it with my backpack in the back seat under a pile of clothes. "So how do we get in here? I've never taken on a casino before." I matched my pace with Eddie.

"We show ID. Then we get chips at the cage. I need the money you're putting up. It's easier if we combine. I have three grand."

I peeled three grand off the stack of bills in my clip. "I'll match you."

"Shit dude! You're loaded. Good-o. We can get six large in chips. Let me bet and you roll the dice when it's your turn. Either we lose fast and leave, or we stick around until about six in the morning. They have a great breakfast buffet here. Then I'll take you back to wherever you're staying." Eddie stopped and dusted off my black T-shirt. "You look like a college guy out for a night. Not too professional, which helps keep anyone from getting anxious if we win big."

"I have other threads in my pack, but tonight felt like a jeans and t-shirt deal." I shrugged. "Win or lose, I want to get back to Chicago. I haven't found a hotel yet. I was planning to get a monthly place and do some setting up tomorrow." I opened the door and was hit by loud noise and bright lights. The atmosphere was a disorienting and sybaritic utopia of nubile flesh.

"Monthly motel in Chicago? You could, I suppose, but most of those are in bad neighborhoods. You can stay at my apartment for a while, if you like. I have a couch. Call it a reward for sucker punching that ass-clown at the freak show. If we lose everything you may need my place anyway." Eddie was shouting over the noise.

"I'll take you up on that, but I'm OK for money, win or lose."

We showed ID which was scrutinized. I got nervous at first, but as usual my ID passed muster. Eddie approached a caged in desk. I put fifty cents in change into a slot machine. There was no pull handle, but a button was blinking. I pushed it. Various pieces of fruit appeared in spinning rows. After the rows stopped, lines appeared through certain ones. I heard bells, and quarters came out. I collected them. Forty quarters. Ten bucks.

"Hey, lucky you." Eddie clapped me on the right shoulder. "We might do OK tonight."

I motioned to a passing waitress and asked for two cokes. She directed me to a bar where I bought the cokes and tipped five bucks. I followed Eddie, handing him a glass.

We edged over to one of the larger crap-dice tables. Ten bettors and five casino employees, stood around it. Some of the bettors wore semi-formal attire. One guy had on a tuxedo. A few were wearing jeans and t-shirts. Various bettors placed chips in the boxes marked on the green felt surface. The man in the tuxedo threw two dice up against the padded end of the table.

"EEEE-eight!" Shouted one of the casino employees holding the dice trapped with a curved stick.

Two other employees collected and distributed varying quantities of chips. When the new bets were placed, the stickman released the dice to the man in the tuxedo. He rolled them again.

"Nine!" Yelled the stickman. "Point is nine!"

More bets were placed. Again, the dice were

thrown.

"Seven! Crap Dice! Next shooter!" The stickman bellowed.

The dealers swept away bets and paid a few. The stickman shoved five dice in front of where Eddie had placed our chips in a holder. I selected two. The other three were swept away. "You betting?"

"Sure am." He put four fifty dollar chips on a spot marked 'pass line.' "I'm betting you win. Throw the bones nice now."

I threw the dice in the air hesitantly, and they rolled half way across the table.

"Fi-ive" the stickman called out. "The point is five!"

"Now roll us a five before you roll a seven or eleven." Eddie patted me on the back. "Hey, what odds on five?"

"Three to two, sir." One of the dealers replied.

"Great. I want to put five hundred on five."

The dealer pointed to a spot behind our wager. "Can only bet two hundred. No more than your initial bet when taking the odds, sir."

Eddie put four more fifty dollar chips where the dealer had indicated. The stickman pushed the dice toward me. "Sir, could you throw the dice so they bounce off the wall on the far end of the table?"

"Cuts down on cheating" Eddie whispered.

"I can sure try. Is it still my turn?"

The stickman nodded, and I grabbed the dice and threw them hard. They bounced off the padded end of the table and caromed back at me.

"Ten. Easy ten" the stickman intoned.

I threw again and the stick man yelled "Six!"

I threw once more and there it was. "Five" shouted the stickman "Pay the line"

"Atta boy! Keep doing like that!" Eddie smiled.

"Winner, winner!" I kvelled. "I am the dice-master!"

"Damn straight!"

A dealer put a small stack of new chips in front of us. Eddie moved a tall stack of chips on to the pass line. "Five hundred says my boy has a magic wrist."

The stickman pushed the dice at me. "Still your turn, sir."

I smiled, kissed my hand, and threw the dice.

"SEVVV-EN! Pay the line!" The stickman shouted.

"Vinnie! Baby! You're doing fine my friend!" Eddie collected the winnings.

"I thought seven was a loser." I was getting confused from the noise and lights.

"No. After you make the point the game starts over." Eddie shoved another five hundred into our pile. "A grand says he can do it again!"

I took the dice and flung them. The caromed back.

"SEVVV-EN! Pay the line!" The stickman shouted.

A dealer put a different colored set of chips in front of us.

"You're hot! Dude you are smo-kin!!" Eddie looked as excited as I felt anxious. He put the thousand on the line again. I rolled.

"Yo-leven!" The stickman intoned.

"Uh oh I..." The dealer gave us chips. "Huh? I thought we lost."

"No, man! Remember? Seven or eleven out on first throw is a winner. Each time you win is like a new throw." Eddie was riled up.

"I see. I see." I nodded.

"Don't see nothing, brother. Keep on burning those dice." He put two grand on the pass line.

"Sorry, sir. One thousand is the limit." The dealer

pushed back the bet.

"You got to be kidding! What is this, a kids game?"

"Sorry, sir, a thousand dollars is the limit. You may bet as many numbers as you like, plus the other spaces, but no more than a thousand on each," the dealer was apologetic.

"Fine. Two hundred on all the numbers, and a grand on the hard-ways!" Eddie placed his bets, and a lady matched them as did several other people gathering around.

"What's that mean?" I looked at my new friend hoping he wasn't getting greedy.

"I'll show you. Two hundred on the four, five, six, eight, nine and on the ten. A grand on hard-way eight and hard-way ten" Eddie pointed at me. "Roll double four or double five. Then roll any of those numbers before you roll a seven or eleven."

I rolled and two fives appeared. "Hard way ten! Point is ten!" The stickman shouted. The dealer shoved a huge stack of chips at us, "I thought we had to make a ten again."

"That's a line bet. Now we're betting numbers. Plus, we got eight to one on a hard-way bet." Eddie whooped.

"Keep rolling?" I picked up the dice.

"Roll them bones!" He fist-pumped the air.

After an hour of rolling, my arm ached. Eddie motioned me to quit rolling. I looked at him surprised.

"Like they say. Bulls make money. Bears make money. Pigs lose."

"If you say so." I yawned. I was out of gas.

"Ladies and gents, it's been a thin slice." Eddie tossed a multi-colored chip to each dealer and the stickman. "Buy yourselves some new shoes."

We approached a cashiers cage and pushed in the chips. The cashier counted our chips at lightning speed, adding sub-totals on a calculator. Her professionalism had a hypnotic appeal.

"$25,350.00." The cashier informed us. I almost passed out.

"Holy Mother! How'd we do that?" I was in shock.

"Fortune smiled on us. We'd like to cash out ma'am." Eddie was cooled out.

The cashier entered data into a computer and in a few minutes passed us a check. Eddie put it in his wallet, and led the way to a restaurant. We were seated near the back with menus.

"You have a magic arm, Vinnie! I have a proposition. What say I give you ten thousand and I keep fifteen. The fifteen would cover my rent for a year."

"Sounds great. I can use that money to get a place in the city for a while. What about the other three-fifty?"

"We eat and get gas for the car. I know several old men who live on the street. The remainder of the three-fifty would be a fortune to them." Eddie closed his menu.

A waitress approached the table, tall and all angles, about fifty. "What'll it be guys?" We ordered, and sat yawning. When the food came, we ate without a sound. After the meal we returned to the car. It was three in the morning.

Eddie started the car. "I haven't had a night like this in a while. But dude, please, promise me you won't try going into casinos alone and playing. First of all, you most always lose. Second, it's better to have another person for back up. If they even suspect cheating, or if you win too much, they'll beat the hell out of you."

I closed my eyes and was gone. Some light jazz played on the radio. When I opened my eyes, the dawn was breaking. We were parked in the garage of a large building. I stretched, and reached for my sack.

"If you want, as I mentioned last night, I have space in my apartment. It's a small studio, but you can crash for as long as you need. Later we can hit the bank and get some cash," Eddie stepped out of the car. "There's also something I need to ask you later."

I climbed out and followed Eddie to an elevator. We exited on the fifteenth floor and entered through one of the four doors. The place was small, and smelled faintly of incense. I set my pack on the floor in an empty corner.

"Thanks, man. I feel rough. I think I'll crash in that corner."

I laid down, using my backpack as a pillow, and was gone in minutes. I don't recall dreaming or even moving. I woke up to the smell of coffee and checked my watch. It was three in the afternoon. I took a moment to recall the previous evening before asking if I might take a shower. Eddie said to feel free. After a long hot wash, and a change of clothes, I stepped into the living room. Coffee had been poured, and fried ham with scrambled eggs served.

"I'm glad I met you, man. You seem like a decent guy. This city has everything and I'd enjoy showing you around. Also, my friends would enjoy meeting you." Eddie ate his food.

"Copacetic. I hope we can hit that casino again. That was off the hook." I shook my head still amazed at our winning. "Hey, where can I find a good used book store?"

"Hitting the casinos again is what we need to discuss. Let's wash these dishes; then we can go deposit this check, cash you out, and find you a store."

An hour later we exited a bank. I had ten thousand dollars in cash in the false bottom of my courier's sack where I'd once held my fakes from Vasily.

Eddie and I walked a few blocks and I found several used bookstores. I began perusing the shelves in one and found a number of books about Navy SEALs and Delta. I also bought another copy of *Gone in The Night* by David

Protess. I paid, and broke one of the hundred dollar bills. Afterward, Eddie and I visited a clothing store. I bought a belt with a zipper on the back of it for hiding money. I stashed fifty C-notes, and kept the rest in my sack.

"Hey man, you ever have a Chicago pizza?" Eddie pointed to a restaurant. "It's not like regular pizza. This has a thicker crust. Real deep-dish."

"Never have."

We entered and I recognized Dean Martin's voice crooning from the ceiling speakers. The atmosphere was candlelight and strong aromas. We sat at a table, and were brought water and an enormous basket of bread. I looked at the menu but Eddie was already ordering.

"A medium deep dish, and a pitcher of lager." Eddie looked at me. "Trust me, you're in for a treat."

He wasn't kidding. The three pieces I consumed were each as thick as a real piece of pie. The cheese was rich, and the sauce hearty. I chased pizza with beer as the flavors lulled me toward a soporific haze. I was on my second piece when a chick joined us.

She was dark, fleshy, and tough looking, with big brown cow-eyes that could melt a guy into a puddle, or narrow with intensity and freeze him like a cube. She had fluffy, teased, black hair, thin penciled eyebrows, and luscious full blown lips. Her cheeks were dusted with pancake and rouge. I eyed her, from the open-toed shoes and flaming red toenails, to the hips that kicked out at an angle, up to her prominent and accentuated breasts. My first instinct was that she was a hooker, but then Eddie made the introductions.

"Vinnie, Becky. Becky, Vinnie."

"So, is he on board?" Becky had a husky, sultry voice.

"We haven't got there yet." Eddie looked at me. "You told me that you've read Thorp. You know anything about team play?"

I nodded. "It's where a group plays blackjack. One cat counts the cards. He signals the others when the cards are right. It's imperfect, but it gives a small edge."

"You're well read, Vinnie." Becky took a piece of pizza. "Your information is a bit out of date, but you have the gist. Edward and I, and some friends, work our way through college by playing blackjack. We're no geniuses, but we get by. Thing is we lost two players recently. They graduated."

"Savvy. You want to teach me to count cards?"

"Not a chance." Eddie shook his head. "We don't have that kind of time. You'd sit at a table, bet the minimum on every hand. If you even suspect security is approaching, you signal the others. We have someone to run blocker if it comes to that."

"I'm in. How much do I make?"

"Well, Vinnie, to be in you'd need to invest. We'd ask five grand up front. You'd make ten percent of the nightly winnings." Becky gave me a soft smile that made my heart flutter.

"I'm in. It sounds like an extension of urban piracy, and I'm always game to learn new techniques."

"Piracy, dude?" Eddie cocked his head.

"Right. Taking on the entities that screw over the little guy in an effort to fatten the billfold of the rich."

"Taking them on how?" Becky gave me interested. "If you're in trouble with the law, that could be a liability for us."

"I'm not. Not yet anyway. I've stayed ahead of such entanglements, thus far."

"So, if you don't mind my asking, what have you done that could have the law after you?" Eddie looked at me with a stern gaze.

I spent an hour telling Eddie and Becky about

Steph, my efforts at plundering, my muling for Joey Pipes, and my upbringing in general.

"It sounds like you've had a rough go of it." Becky batted her eyes at me. "It sounds like you're also of a mindset to help us break the casinos."

"I'm willing. If you hip me to the moves, I'll dance to whatever tune you blow."

Becky took my hand and stroked it. "I'll introduce you to the others tomorrow."

Chapter Thirty-Four

Six months later my life had taken several sharp turns. I resided in a monthly hotel on North May Street, and spent my days at the library researching and reading. The hotel wasn't top of the mark, but neither was it bumsville. As far as my research went, Scotts Bluff, Nebraska was a large area, and Tanner was a common enough name. However, I was drawing a bead on the location of Heather Baker's parents.

Once the sun gave way to the night rhythms, I filled the hours with dating Becky, playing blackjack, and shooting dice. My income had increased astronomically, and so had my alcohol consumption.

As promised, Becky had introduced me to two other players. Lilian Guzman was a short Latinx with serious eyes and a toned body. She was pre-law, and dressed like it. The other player was Mel Pate. He was a light-skinned African American with wavy black hair, slicked down and parted in the center. His eyes and smile gave lie to an intense inner fire. He was a business major.

My role involved playing the minimum bets while watching the giant staircase and the elevators. I'd spent hours studying pictures of the security staff, and memorizing the uniforms. If there was even a hint of trouble, I was to use the word scramble in a sentence. It could be anything from requesting that a server bring me some scrambled eggs and bacon, to discussing how that last drink had scrambled my brains.

Although that was my singular role, Becky began teaching me to count cards while we dated. I became proficient in counting an eight deck shoe, but I wasn't perfect. Perfection was the cutoff point. Becky, Eddie, and Lilly had those skills.

The deeper my involvement with the team, the more I began having frequent cluster headaches, abdominal issues, and was overcome with aches in my joints. I saw a doctor, but was given a clean bill of health. Comfort food helped ease some of the issues, alcohol and pot helped more. When not breaking the casino, I would pull at a bottle of Coke that was spiked with Jack Daniels. I was never drunk, but the steady infusion of bourbon settled my system.

At night I'd meet Becky at a restaurant near her pad. We'd consume large quantities of pasta and sauce, bread, and salad. Other nights we'd opt for burgers, pizza, or steaks near my place. As I had in New York, I found an area where men unloaded trucks for stores.

Most of my wardrobe, while suited for a debonair cat on the make, was unsuited for a person wishing to keep a low profile in a casino. I kept my four Bugatchi shirts, but traded in most of my silk dress shirts. Instead, I opted for polo and rugby shirts as well as double-thickness cotton t-shirts in neutral colors. I upgraded my slacks, bought five sports coats, and purchased a pair of black jeans. I kept a pair of Italian loafers, but also purchased three pairs of suede Nikes from the back of a truck. The overall effect was that I presented as a conservative college student. For the times in between casino play, I purchased a black mohair suit, a grey pinstriped suit, updated my collection of hats, and purchased a new pair of mirrored shades.

Becky turned me on to an author named Lee Child. His Jack Reacher series was a perfect antidote to my constant stress. The weather was pleasant; perfect for reading in the park. I practiced kata every morning, showered, researched and read from noon until three, practiced a basic count for two hours, and either met Becky for the night, or connected with the team to hit the casino.

The casino situation was easy enough. Either Becky

or Lilly would take the role of big bettor. The other would back-spot the table. Eddie would sit at first base and bet the minimum while counting. Mel would vary his bets according to Eddie's signals. I either stood and watched the game, or sat and bet the minimum all while watching for security.

As the months progressed, Mel became proficient enough to count, and Eddie eased into the role of chauffeur and getaway driver. I had trouble following the count at first, but Becky suggested I match up cards and cancel out the numbers. My count improved. I hoped to move up the ladder by the following year.

None of the action, however, allowed me to forget Ronnie, Destiny, Kenzie, or Julie. I certainly never forgot Steph. I still kissed her picture every morning. One night I was coming home from a lucrative casino run when I got a text on the last of my burner phones. It was from Ronnie.

Hey, Daddy-o. The girls passed their GEDs. We had a party with Rory and his chicks. You were missed.

Tears trickled down my cheeks as I smiled. My current situation wasn't world class, but that deal had worked out in spades. My three chicks had the future at their command. I bought a martini at a corner bar and toasted them from afar. So much had happened. Most of it had been out of my control, and yet even that which was in my control remained out of control

I asked for a bowl of peanuts, and sipped a second dry martini. The self-assessment began flowing. While my family was helping Heather, Caroline and Steph to escape, Heather had accused me and my family of duplicity. Despite my sister Tori's appraisal of Heather as a half-hipped goody-goody, the word duplicity was correct. The difference was that I and my sisters played for immediacy. My parents were playing a much longer game. That made sense in terms of generational maturity and needs, but long game or short, it left a bad taste in my mouth.

I drank my martini and grabbed a handful of nuts. From everything my father had told me on our camping trips, my grandparents on both sides had led lives of quiet desperation. The times had dictated that. They were from a generation that had seen wars, and still remembered a stock market crash. My parents, in turn, lived lives of quiet duplicity. The times dictated that as well. They were cleaning up the previous generation's messes, and had watched cooperate America grow outsized while screwing the little man. For those reasons, they had raised me and my sisters on short cons and hustles. I was good at the con games. I enjoyed the results. Still, something inside gnawed at me and refused to let up.

That brought me to martini three, and thoughts about my amorous conquests. There was nothing duplicitous in my love for Steph, or Julie, or Destiny and Kenzie, or Ronnie. There was no duplicity in my feelings for Becky, either. My love for these chicks was the most honest thing I had going. Maybe the only real thing in my life.

I could hear my father in the back of my mind telling me to figure what others wanted, and to use that to further my own needs. I didn't object to the idea in principle, but when it came to the chicks I dug the most, I couldn't use them as pawns in a chess match. They were my queens.

Was my obsession with finding Steph even rational? We had known each other for less than three months. The circumstances were traumatic and volatile. She and I had enjoyed each other's pleasures, but more out of desperation than any real sense of love. I had more of a bond to Julie, Destiny, Kenzie, and Ronnie. I was beginning to build something with Becky, and that wasn't a bad thing. My need to know if Steph and I had a chance was persistent, however. I had to follow that path. If it didn't work out, the navy held options. So did finding a suitable female replacement.

I finished my third martini, settled up, and returned to my room for a nap. The next day I made a few phone calls to some churches in the Scotts Bluff county of Nebraska. I also laid out some cash and checked public records. There were three couples named Tanner associated with Heather based on an approximation of her age. Of the three, two couples might be her parents. The other would likely be an uncle and aunt. The third almost had to be cousins.

Having the information, I was ready to move on. If I found these people, odds were I would find Heather, Caroline, and Steph's location. My understanding of people, minimal as it was, indicated that even on the run a person was incapable of not making contact with family. It had been four and a half years; they must have settled somewhere.

So why didn't I take off? To be honest, I froze. If you don't bet you can't lose. I pocketed the information and remained in Chicago. I was clearing five to ten grand a month at the casino, had Becky, and was enjoying life. I didn't know for sure that Steph still wanted me. What I built up in my mind emotionally was easily torn asunder by logic. When the feelings got too strong, alcohol cooled my radiator.

Over time the introspection and agony became unbearable. One evening I walked into a café and sat in a booth. Crosby Stills and Nash were singing "Wasted on The Way" through the corner speakers as I ordered cake and coffee. The café was seedy and down-at-heel, the sort of place I enjoyed when the blues wrenched my soul. After chasing the last crumbs around my plate, I left a twenty dollar tip and caught a bus toward Becky's pad. The ride was uneventful except for a guitarist singing Willie Nelson off-key. I threw him ten bucks anyway. He reminded me of Destiny and Kenzie, struggling to survive. Arriving at my destination, I made a stop at a bodega for a pint of Jim Beam and a case of IPA. The bodega owner was happy not to ask questions in exchange for a picture of President Grant.

I called a local pizza parlor, used my standard ruse, and gave the manager an address. Next, I dialed Becky and told her I was coming over. She said she'd be expecting me. I walked to the building I had mentioned to the manager and waited. I tipped the delivery guy a twenty and entered a different building, one that had never seen better days. Mounting the stairs, I smelled the mingling of spicy food, cheap booze, sweat, and tears reeking from the walls. Becky was waiting for me dressed in a tank top with nothing under it and a pair of flannel pajama bottoms. She smiled at me, noticed the look on my face and motioned me though the door of her apartment. I set the food on a coffee table, and we sat on the sofa. Becky straddled my lap and buried her face in my neck. Sitting there, locked in an embrace, her breasts pressed against my ribs, something clicked into place. My introspection dissipated. I rubbed my hands on her rump. I'd been to this rodeo before.

Fifteen minutes later we let go. I leaned over and kissed her upturned face. "Hey, babe. Thanks for letting me come by."

"You could come by anytime. You don't as much lately, but you could." She smiled and rubbed her hands on my ass.

"Yeah, well, you know, I have cobwebs and junk cluttering my attic. You're always here when I need you, though." I held her and sighed. "I appreciate that."

We took the pizza and booze, and walked into her bedroom before crawling through the window. After climbing the fire escape, we sat on the roof eating and drinking? I did most of the drinking. We watched the skyline and Becky put her head on my shoulder.

At ten I looked around at the lights in the distance. "Nice out here. Really a nice night."

"I think it's better with you here, but the weather isn't on your mind. Talk." Becky took another slice of pizza and opened a beer.

I alternated between swigs of beer, bites of pizza, and sips of bourbon. I heaved a sigh. "It's been a good run. The team's worked out like nobody's business, but I have to get gone. I mean eventually. I have to move along."

Becky shook her head. "May I ask you something serious?"

"Sure. Anything, doll."

"Why did you ever get involved with muling drugs? You're too smart for that. The other stuff, it's minor. Who cares? But the drugs? I mean after what you told me your parents were into, why?"

I shrugged. "The bread was sweet. I had Destiny and Kenzie to help out. There was Ronnie, too. I mean you don't keep a class doll like her if you don't got the roll."

Becky leaned on me. "If you split, you going to see that girl? Steph, isn't it? Have you found out where she lives?"

I shook my head, which made me dizzy from the alcohol. "When my family saved her, and her mom and sister, I remember they mentioned relatives in Nebraska. I might have a couple three leads out there."

We collected the dinner remains and Becky led me back to her bedroom. We sat on her bed and she pulled a book off her desk

"Is this your high school yearbook?"

"Yeah. You want to see a funny picture?"

"Sure."

She flipped through the book. "This is me in the school play. I played Juliet. Reuben Feingold played Romeo. Look at my hair. Lordy!"

"You look cute. Sometimes I wonder what I missed by getting a GED." I finished off the last of the whiskey.

Becky and I kissed a while. She stroked my cheek. "Vinnie, You're a lovely guy."

"Lovely?" I laughed, lubricated from the alcohol.

She pouted at me and snuggled in closer. "Don't worry about it. It's the best thing I've ever said to anyone. Why'd you stop coming by? I've missed seeing you outside the casinos."

"Yeah, doll, that's why I came here tonight. I think about you all the time. I'm considering leaving town and I just, well I..."

Becky interrupted. "You wanted to leave your options open. You expect me to always be available. If you're breaking up with me, I think it's only fair to tell you that we've never had an actual date. We've had hook-ups."

I smiled and brushed my lips over her cheek. "I'm not breaking up with you, necessarily. I need to see where this other thing goes. Anyway, you and I are so good we don't need dates."

"Why don't we sleep together tonight, and then break up?" Becky removed my shirt.

"Listen, there's stuff. Let's not get into it. I have to find Steph. I had to see you to tell you I'm thinking about leaving. I might not be back. Then again, I might." I lifted her tank-top off and we sat together bare chested. I kissed her breasts.

"Neither of us is crying. Everything's okay. You're the strangest person in The Windy City. That's why I love you." She started unbuttoning my jeans.

"Oh, you shouldn't. No, don't fall in love with me. What we have is great already." I slid off my jeans and lay in my boxers.

Becky clung to me. "You're holding me and kissing me. In my bedroom. With what you drank, you may be clearing up my sinuses."

Becky slipped off her pajama bottoms and snuggled in my arms, soft and warm. I held her for a while and touched my lips to her hair. After a while her arms tightened about me as she turned her face upward for a kiss. I leaned down and the lips that found mine were fierce and adult. It was a grown-up, knowing body that moved hard against mine. The hands that drew me against her were those of one who had been down this path. We collapsed onto her bed and began the exercise in earnest.

An hour later we were both exhausted, naked, and sweaty. The bed was in disarray. Becky handed me a cigarette and lit it. She lit one for herself. We sat there a while holding each other and thinking about life.

"How old are you really, Vinnie?"

I threw my mind into it. "Sixteen and change. My oldest sister got me my ID. I'll be seventeen three days before Thanksgiving."

"Could you wait until your birthday to leave? There are some other things I need to tell you, too."

"I could. What other things?" I put out my cigarette in an ashtray.

"Eddie went to the casino the other night to play some dice. He sat in at poker for a few hands, as well. Thing is, he thinks that some security people were following him. It's not serious yet, but our team might be made."

"I dig. This isn't Atlantic City or Vegas. We've hit that one spot hard. Only a matter of time before they caught on."

"Yeah, and the place is owned and run by big business types. You of all people know that they don't have follow the same laws that others follow. If we get caught, it could get ugly."

At some point Becky and I both fell asleep. After a few hours I heard her murmur "Please." It was a sleepy faraway voice and I wasn't sure if she was addressing me. I drew her closer and allowed my body to obey the sleepy instructions issued by hers. There was no outburst of coital emotion this time. It was a friendly and satisfying act shared by two lonely people in the middle of the night.

The clock read 7:30AM. We'd both dozed off again. We got out of bed and took a long, steamy shower. After drying each other, and putting on a decent amount of clothes, we walked to the kitchen. I made coffee. She made toast and eggs with bacon. We sat eating and gazing at each other.

"I could get used to a life of this real easy." Becky sipped her coffee.

"Yeah. Me too. I was starting to with Destiny, Kenzie, and Ronnie. But I can't settle down yet. I need to figure out some stuff before I can go there. Doll, if it doesn't work out with Steph, or if I can't find her, you're first on the list. I'll send for you."

"You'll stay until Thanksgiving?"

"I'll certainly try."

We finished getting dressed and I kissed Becky. We walked, holding hands, to a place that did a nice brunch buffet. I was still hung over, and Becky was clingy. Over eggs Benedict and melon, we talked about college and the navy. Clearly there were options aplenty if the deal with Steph fell through.

Chapter Thirty-Five

A week before Thanksgiving, false dawn broke the horizon. Lili Guzman appeared on the verge of passing out. Not that I could see outside. The casino had no windows, and the lighting was such that time became irrelevant. Eddie had schooled me that this was true of most, if not all, casinos. The idea was that if you didn't know what time it was, you couldn't judge how long you had played. Not knowing, you continued playing until your mental circuits quit, or until you lost everything you had.

There were three empty martini glasses on the table in front of Lili, and she was leaning forward on both elbows, her gaze focused on the cards. The undersized, Asian dealer was still feigning patience, in deference to the pile of rainbow-striped chips in front of the martini glasses. The other players were beginning to get restless. Well, except for Mel Pate at third base. He looked bored, fingering a small pile of red chips. The rest of the table wanted Lili to make her bet already, or pack it in, grab the leather satchel under her chair, and head back to Chicago. What was a college senior going to do with fifty grand? The dealer, sensing the mood at the table, tapped the blackjack shoe. "It's up to you, Miss Guzman. You've had a great run. Are you in for another round?"

She reached for three five-hundred-dollar chips, then glanced around, pretending to look for the cocktail waitress. Out of the corner of her eye, she waited for my signal, and Becky's.

I was close enough to see the table but far enough away not to draw any suspicion. Lili caught my gaze, then waited for the signal. If everything was copacetic, I'd scratch my chin. At that point Becky would signal the bet from ten feet behind me and to my right. For the first time, everything was not cool. As Becky had warned me, the heat was on.

I approached the empty seat at fifth base and thunked down hard. "I need two grand in chips, buddy. You're gonna have to sort them for me, I get the colors scrambled." I slurred my words, playing the inebriate.

Lili looked irritated. "That's it for me," she said to the table, slurring her words as well. "Should have skipped that last martini, I guess,"

Lili grabbed her satchel, and jammed the chips into her pockets. The dealer was watching her. "You sure you don't want me to color up?"

The suits were making a bee-line for the table. Three of them, coming around the nearest craps table. Burly, dark toned men with narrow eyes and perfectly coiffed hair. Security. I had seen them on the staircase.

"That's okay," Lili said, backing away from the table, "I like the way they jiggle around in my pocket."

She turned and darted through the casino. I knew they were watching her from above, the "Spy-cams." Becky was already at the craps table making five-dollar line bets. Mel played another hand, won thirty dollars, and left. I played for another half hour and broke even.

We were lucky. I made it outside without anyone looking my way. A minute later a cab showed up and took me to a divey bar two miles away. I entered, had a beer, and left. Walking a half mile, I spotted everyone sitting on a bench at a corner park. The satchel was on Lili's lap.

Mel lit a cigarette. His hands were shaking. "That was too close. They came straight at us from the stairs. Four more were guarding the elevators. They must have been upstairs watching the whole time."

Lili nodded. She was breathing hard, and her chest was soaked in sweat. "You handled that perfectly, Vinnie. The scramble signal, spot on."

Becky took the satchel and put both hands on it, feeling the stacks of bills inside. A little over a quarter of a million dollars. All in hundreds. Twenty-five grand of that bankroll was mine.

I looked at everyone, smiled at Eddie, kissed Becky. "Guys, I'm out. Nothing to do with tonight, but I found the chick I've been looking for, or anyway people who will know where she is." I sighed and rubbed my throbbing temples.

"I think we're all done for a while." Eddie looked ahead into the darkness. "That was too close, and this isn't Vegas. There's no other places to hit. Tomorrow we divvy."

Becky cleared her throat. "Before we split the winnings, and before finals hit, would you guys like to get reservations for Thanksgiving dinner at somewhere upscale? Vinnie's leaving town, and Lili's graduating. Seems like a nice way to end."

Eddie nodded. "I'll make the reservations. Dress up sharp. We're going deluxe."

I caught a ride back to my neighborhood and found a park bench near my hotel. My mind refused to shut down. I had one more week in Chicago, and then I was going to make every effort to find Steph. I'd been playing blackjack and shooting craps for over a year. I knew that Ronnie was in college, and from her discovered that Kenzie had come unglued. Apparently drinking wasn't something Kenzie could control, and she needed the meetings that I had once hit up for cash. Furthermore, another event was also forming an odd circle. Rory, Sheila, Jeanie and their son had moved to New Mexico, two hundred and fifty miles from my sister Tori and Billy-Bob Fisher. Kenzie and Destiny had cleared out a week before Hurricane Sandy and were heading to see Rory and family.

There was a strong temptation to travel in that direction instead, but I couldn't give up on finding Steph. If I did find her, I didn't want to mess up what might be my only shot. Over twelve years I had become an accomplished pirate. I had tried my hand at muling narcotics to great success. I had played look out for a low-grade gambling team. None of that was acceptable in terms of being the sort of man Steph deserved. Her entire childhood had been shattered, and for all I knew she'd been on the run for five years. I had to change my ways. But, could I?

I walked back to my room and changed into my boxers and smoking jacket. I poured three fingers of Chivas Regal and sipped as I let my thoughts flow. I was almost seventeen, no matter what my ID said. If Steph didn't work out, and if I joined the navy, I needed to be in the best shape of my life. My daily kata workouts in the parks were fine, but I needed more. That would have to be figured out at a future date.

Finishing my drink, I made some decisions. For the next week I was going to play tourist. Furthermore, I was going to trade in my backpack and a pile of clothes for new items from the store in New England. They had a lifetime, no questions asked, guarantee. That wasn't cheating, that was taking advantage of a benefit that they offered. I would donate all but one dress outfit and my Italian loafers to a Salvation Army. I would purchase outright some warmer weather drape that was more suited for Nebraska.

Having decided these matters, I fell into a deep, restful sleep. The next morning, I purchased a large box, printed out a return and exchange slip, included the price of rush delivery on my new merchandise, and sent the box overnight mail. I caught a bus to the Wicker Park-Six Corners area and shopped for clothing. On the way I spotted a homeless encampment and hopped off to donate some of my finer threads.

The next day Becky and I met across the street from Water Tower Place where we boarded a motor coach. A guide narrated a tour of Chicago's famed criminal and historical sights. This was the turf of Al Capone, Tommy O'Conner, Spunky Weiss, and Bugs Moran. I had read about it, but seeing Chicago's most notorious crime scenes, including the courthouse where many famed mob cases were tried, and the site of the St. Valentine's Day Massacre was a dream come true. You can take the boy out of the piracy game, and all that jazz. We took in the Biograph Theater and Holy Name Cathedral, had lunch at an authentic speakeasy, and returned to the spot where we had begun.

After spending the night together in my room, we took in The Art Institute of Chicago. It rivaled the art museums of New York City, and that's saying something, if you dig the flip. We took in such iconic works as Georges Seurat's A Sunday on La Grande Jatte, Pablo Picasso's The Old Guitarist, Edward Hopper's Nighthawks, Mary Cassat's Child's Bath, and Grant Wood's American Gothic. Having a permanent collection of over a quarter million works of art to see, we spent a second day enjoying the exhibits.

My head stopped hurting, and my stomach issues improved over the three days. On the fourth day we enjoyed chamber music performed at the university. I fell asleep that night with a sense of peace that had eluded me for several years.

On Thanksgiving Day, I dressed to the nines, and met the team at a swanky restaurant on the top floor of a high class hive in midtown. The Thanksgiving buffet was to die for, with maple roasted turkey, pineapple ham, sturgeon, shrimp, butternut squash soup, mashed potatoes, candied yams, sage and cornbread stuffing, five kinds of bread, a variety of cheeses, and an assortment of desserts.

Eddie ordered three bottles of Cristal to go with the meal, and we dined in a private room.

"Guys," Eddie raised his glass, "here's to the winners who know when to quit. Here's to Vinnie, one hell of a spotter. Happy birthday, brother. May your future be golden. Here's to Lil, may the odds be ever in her favor. Here's to us all."

We toasted and ate. As dessert was being consumed, the group sang happy birthday to me. Eddie gave me a first edition copy of *On the Road* and *Dharma Bums*.

"Oh my Lord, cats and kitties, I am nonplussed. I wasn't expecting any gifts. Certainly nothing as wonderful as this."

"Well, we didn't know what to get you. You're always reading, and you have a distinct way of communicating. We figured that Kerouac might resonate with you.

I sipped Cristal and looked at my friends. I'd miss them, but this chapter was over. It was time to move on.

The next day several large packages arrived from the clothing store in New England. I laundered my new threads, and packed my new backpack with all my supplies. On the way back to my hotel, I donated my mohair suit and a shirt to a homeless shelter.

I rose to a crisp, autumnal morning, left housekeeping five C's, checked out of the hotel, and texted Becky. By force of habit, I also texted Julie, Tori, and Gina. I stopped on the way to the Amtrak and purchased a burner phone. Texting Ronnie was bittersweet.

Ronnie replied. *Hey, hey Daddy-o. I'm in school and free. It seems like a dream everything that we went through. I met a guy. He's a gentle soul. Looks a bit like a mountain man. We room together. Glad you're well. I miss you.*

I was glad Ronnie was happy, but it felt as if an opportunity had been lost. I had no right to expect her to wait for me to get my act together.

Julie texted that she was graduating from High School, and had been accepted at Oregon State for Psychology. Vic was accepted there for Business. Al Contreras had been accepted at Universidad del Guadalajara. Natty Wolf was heading to USF for Marine Biology. Mike was heading to Minnesota on a football scholarship.

Tori texted an hour later. *Hey, bro. NM is the best. You're welcome to come visit. I miss you. Happy seventeen, again.*

Gina texted me that she was pregnant. I was going to be an uncle. The news didn't make me as jubilant as it might have. There was a sense of disconnect from everyone. It was time to head west.

Chapter Thirty-Six

On the way to the Amtrak, I decided to blow myself to a sleeper car. The price was beyond outrageous, but I had money to burn. After purchasing my ticket, and arranging for the added amenities, I sat waiting. The room was spinning slightly, but I wasn't drunk. I closed my eyes and tried some deep breathing.

Once on board, I started reading *The Dillinger Days* by John Toland. I didn't get far before the nausea and vertigo resumed. Instead, I took a few sips of Jack Daniels and fell asleep. I slept on and off for the rest of the trip, and chased my meals with heavily spiked Coke.

The train rolled to a stop as I woke up one last time. I grabbed my sack and exited the sleeper car. I'd reached Nebraska; A smaller town from the feel of it. I knew that I had to find somewhere to jungle up. Breathing was an exercise in futility. My sinuses were clogging, and each cough was a sledgehammer to the chest. I located a highway three blocks from the stop and allowed my ground-smashers to carry me forward without much consideration for where I was heading. I hoped to either catch a ride to a hospital, or to find a motel. A half hour later the sky turned dirty gray as an exit and another small town appeared before me. I edged my way along the shoulder until I found a grocery store and next to it a liquor store.

Entering the grocery store, I purchased a box of herbal tea bags that said they were for cold relief. I also bought three cans of beef broth, a bottle of aspirin, and a jar of honey. Not bothering with the coupons, I paid in cash. At the liquor store I purchased a fifth of Bombay Sapphire gin. The clerk gave me a hard eye, but she took the cash I proffered plus an extra twenty.

A half mile down the road I spotted what appeared to be a small cabin of some kind. It was at the edge of a field that was surrounded by a fence. I was starting to vomit from coughing too hard, and made a spot decision to turn toward the cabin and see if anyone was home. I knocked. The door swung open on its own. No one was inside. I entered and closed the door as the sky burst open, and a torrential rain cut loose.

My eyes, adjusted to the outdoors, tried to focus. The dim light of the cabin was made dimmer by a thick coating of grime and dust on the sole window pane. The cabin was made of two rooms. The smaller room was cave-like with a packed dirt floor. The dirt apparently held some clay because heat had baked it until it was hard as brick. The mud mortar between the logs was just as hard. At the far end of the room was a fire place that had been built into the rear wall. I found a lighter, kindling, and a few logs in a corner. I had no idea who lived here but I was freezing. I lit a fire hoping that whoever belonged to the place might come home and take me to an emergency room. My cell battery was dying, there was no outlet in the cabin, and I was far from lucid. I needed help. I had never been without some sort of support system, even if I chose not to utilize it.

In searching the cabin, I found that the second room was occupied by a bed made of sturdy wood logs that had been split and lashed together. There were heavy blankets made of sheep skin, and a quilt that had been left by whoever occupied the cabin last. I saw a notebook that had dates, numbers and some indications about animals of some kind. I placed the quilt on the floor near the fireplace. Looking around the cave like room, I discovered that a small gas stove was functional, and that there was a supply of cookware and utensils. I took a pan and put it outside the door. After using another to boil broth, I collected the pan of rainwater and boiled that.

I ate the broth and made herbal tea with honey. I spiked the tea with gin and after three cups my coughing subsided. I took the blankets and covered myself on top of the quilt, closed my eyes and slept. Four hours later the rain was still going strong, no one had appeared, and I was shivering spasmodically. I took a few pulls on the bottle of gin and fell back asleep. When I came to, the rain had decreased to a trickle. I had no idea what time it was. I was about to try leaving when I heard voices outside. Two female and a male. They sounded young but not like children. I tried to call out but the coughing started again.

The door opened and a young cat, about sixteen, was standing there holding a .22 rifle. He had a rust colored mullet, and sported dark blue Levis, a red, western-style shirt, a sheepskin coat, and black boots. On his head was a black Stetson. He stared at me as an older man entered. Seeing me coughing and wheezing, the older man knelt down with a stern gaze.

"Who are you, son? What in tarnation are you doing in here? Don't move. You need to lay still." The man had a drawl and a bit of an accent that I couldn't place. He checked my pulse assisted by two girls my age who had entered behind him. The older man was an expanded version of the boy but with a heavy, salt-and-pepper beard and mustache and very short cropped black hair. The girls looked like twins. Strawberry blondes, hair in braids, draped in jeans, red gingham blouses, blue quilted jean jackets, and boots. They held me still as the man checked me.

"My name is Vinnie. Vinnie Il-Cazzo. I was looking for a motel, and the sky was about to deluge. I saw this cabin so I ran over and knocked. No one was here but the door was open. I need help. Like a doctor. Like now." I crackled and coughed.

"Lucky you did get inside. More like you were

blessed. I'm a doctor. My name is Hiram McFarland. The boy there is Zeke. These girls are Pearl and Elsa. We don't mind that you used the place, but from what I am hearing, you're ailing. I need to get you over to our house and check you out, son."

I managed to stand, and as the girls started cleaning the cabin, Zeke and Hiram helped me outside and into a pickup truck. They drove me to a three story house where I was introduced to Miriam, Hiram's wife. We walked through a large room with a decorated Douglas Fir, and assorted Christmas decorations surrounding a crèche. Hiram led me toward an office in the back, and shooed away Zeke. Hiram listened to my chest and looked in my ears, nose and mouth.

"How long have you been sick, son? A while I suspect." Hiram looked stern, but not angry.

"I've had sinus pressure off and on for a while. Doctors suggested it was stress. I was doing better. Had good eats, a few drinks, plenty of sleep, and like that. The problems subsided. I figured I was OK. On the train I started to hurt again. It got worse." I was hoarse from coughing. I tried to stand, but Hiram put out a hand as if to say stay put.

"Son, you have a sinus infection. Where are your folks? Please don't tell me you been traveling around out there in this condition. You need medicine, boy, and rest." Hiram sat in a chair.

"I have no idea where my parents are. They left. I've been taking care of business for years. There's a girl I used to know, and I'm looking for her. Her people live in Scott's Bluff, Nebraska." I coughed. "Uh huh. Well, you aren't going anywhere for another week at least. If you've got no one else, I reckon you can use our guest room. I guess Jesus sent you to us, and it would be a crime not to accept the chance to bless another. Especially this close to

Christ's birthday." Hiram helped me up, and I staggered past a fireplace lined with stockings toward a room off the living room. "By the way, Scott's Bluff is a small piece south of here." As we were walking the twins returned. They looked me over, unsure about something.

"Pa? We don't want to get Zeke and his friends in the jam pot, but we found a half bottle of liquor in the cabin." They looked nervous.

"Not your brother's gin, dolls. It's mine." I rasped. Same for the pack and other stuff I left there. I need it back."

Elsa looked at me askance, and Pearl put her hands on her hips. "You oughtn't be drinking at your age," Pearl scolded, "or at any age."

I shrugged. "Opinions vary."

Hiram scowled at the girls. "Tend to your own, ladies." He gave me a peculiar stare, like he was taking my measure. "You drink often, son?"

"Now and then. It helped with the coughing anyway," I coughed.

Hiram led me into the guest room. "I reckon it did. Most cough syrup is nothing but dandified liquor." Hiram gave me stern.

The girls walked out of the room and returned in moments. Elsa held my sack and Pearl had my other gear in her hands. They set everything down on a chair. Hiram got me settled on the bed. "Son, you rest up. We can talk later. It sounds like there might be plenty to discuss." I closed my eyes as the three filed out of the room. I slept a dreamless slumber, and when I awoke Miriam was bringing me breakfast.

"Morning, Vinnie is it? Hiram said that's your name. We didn't have much of a howdy-do." She set a hand-carved bed-tray on my lap. On the tray was a plate of toast, a dish containing three soft boiled eggs, and a mug of ginger tea.

"Yes, Vinnie Il-Cazzo. Most call me Vinnie. Some call me Il-Cazzo." My voice sounded normal again. I coughed and wheezed.

"My name is Miriam. Welcome to our ranch. Not much of a spread really, but we have some sheep and horses. That cabin you were in is where the young'uns sleep during certain seasons. We have to keep track of the stock."

"Thank you for the hospitality. I was looking for a motel, but I had to get out of the rain." I dipped toast in the egg yolks and ate.

"Now don't you fret none about that. The Good Lord provided you a safety and us a blessing." Miriam turned as the door opened. Hiram entered.

"Son, I went to the pharmacy and got you some medicine. You're not allergic to anything are you?"

"Not that I know of." I took the proffered pills.

"That there is C-chlor. The other is a multivitamin. You take the C-chlor twice a day for ten days." Hiram sat beside Miriam. "Now that you feel better, how about you tell us where you hail from. My guess is New York."

"Good guess. The accent is a dead giveaway. I was born there, outside of the city. I've traveled some, but went back for a while. Things got squirrelly, so I cut out to Chicago. Then I came west looking for this chick I used to know.

Miriam smiled and Hiram nodded. "I take it you mean a gal, not a fuzzy yellow bird. You said your parents abandoned you? When was this? I'm not trying to be nosey, but if it turns out you were a fugitive, or something, it would cause trouble."

"No, sir. I'm not a fugitive. Not that I know of. Not yet anyway. I'm not a runaway either, or anything else. I'm a regular guy looking for someone. My parents had some problems and took off. Fact of it is that the doll I'm looking for had to cut out with her mom and sister because of a bad scene. Helping them get clear is what precipitated the problems for my parents."

Miriam took my tray, and Hiram kept talking. "Well, that doesn't sound good. You seem resilient, though. I had to look through your gear. Mind if I ask how a boy your age gets that kind of greenbacks? Also, what's with the envelope of coupons, and all the weapons. You in trouble? You be straight with me so we can help you."

"No, sir, I told you I'm not. There's a casino outside of Chicago, and the cards and dice treated me well. I have more in the bank. The coupons and vouchers are something I collect. My weapons are for protection. If it's a big deal to you, I can pack and leave." I started to stand.

"Son, you stay put. I believe you. Thing of it is that I had my own troubles once upon a time. By the by, how long have you been drinking?" Hiram patted my shoulder.

"I drink from time to time. I can stop, and I do. Sometimes I have too much energy and I can't sit still or keep a thought in my head. Other times I feel anxious, or sick. I have a few pulls. Sometimes I smoke herb too. It helps. I relax and get some sleep." I yawned.

Hiram looked at me a few minutes and nodded. "You get yourself a nap. Later I have some friends you ought to meet. My kids are anxious to visit with you, too."

I nodded and closed my eyes. I fell into another deep sleep and remained there until I smelled the faint scent of lilacs. I opened my eyes and the twins, Pearl and Elsa were sitting in silence, crocheting and watching me sleep.

"Hi." Elsa murmured with a blush.

"You need anything?" Pearl looked at me with a soft smile.

"I could use a beer. Maybe a burger and some fries?" I looked them over.

They were dressed in full length denim skirts, white t-shirts that accentuated their positives, and baby blue sneakers. They had their hair pulled back with clips. The gentle scent of perfume filled the room.

"Mama said you need a softer diet than burgers and fries. Beer is out of the question. We can get you some eggs and toast." Pearl stood and exited. Elsa set her crocheting on the side table and moved closer.

"You gave us a scare yesterday. We don't get many strangers out here. No one but us ever camps in the mating field." Elsa smiled.

"I'm sorry to scare you, doll. I had to get out of the storm, and then I started getting the shakes." I took her right hand in my hands. "I would never wish to scare one as beautiful as you, or your sister."

"Thank you," she blushed, "but we have boyfriends. Pa said you were heading to see your girlfriend."

"Well, a girl I met. I don't have a girlfriend as such. You might say that this country has been my mating field." I let the hand go "I meet broads wherever I go, and they always take an interest. I had a steady chick in Harvest Junction, and one in New York. I had several short flings in Florida, almost met some girls in Chicago, and found a steady chick there. Through it all there's one who got away."

"Oh. So, you're like Damien, huh?" She giggled.

"He's our best ram. He's popular with the ewes."

"I suppose. I do enjoy the company of the softer flesh."

Pearl entered with a tray of food and a Sprite. "Here you go, Vinnie. Mama said that if you feel better this weekend we might be able to go to the drive-in."

"Careful, sis. Vinnie has a lot in common with Damien." Elsa blushed.

"Oh? Do tell." Pearl giggled.

"Nothing to tell. I don't go looking for dolls. They seem to find me. I've met a few that oil my gears, but one in particular. You two are beautiful, like these girls I tried to meet in Chicago. Their name was Draeger. They didn't show any cards, like you two don't. That's a total turn-on." I ate the eggs and toast.

"If you mean that we don't wear shorts with our naked butt-cheeks showing, and peek-a-boo shirts, I'm glad you approve." Elsa gave me a chilly look. "We believe in modesty around here, and if we forget it, we get reminded in a hurry."

Pearl nodded. "Pa and Mama say that if kids want to expose their rears, then their rears need smacked."

I yawned. "I don't know. I like chicks in tight shorts and shirts that show cleavage. I grant you, there's something heady and mysterious about a chick who reveals nothing, however. Hey, I'm getting tired again. Thanks for the food." I closed my eyes as the twins took the tray and shuffled out.

When I woke up a couple hours later it was to a knock on the door. Zeke entered with Hiram, and three older men.

"Hey there, son." Hiram nodded at me. Sorry to wake you, but I invited some friends of mine over to talk with you."

I sat up and looked at everyone. Zeke gave me a smile. "I 've been wanting to meet you official. I mean other than when we found you. But Pa said to leave you rest."

I nodded. "Pleasures all mine, gate. Call me Vinnie. Sorry to cause so much chaos."

Zeke started to say something but Hiram cut in. "Please stop apologizing. The Good Lord led you here. There's something going on with you, or several somethings. I'm thinking we should all talk. These three men are Lincoln Hollister, Jethro Mulhaney, and Elijah Steeds."

"Allow me to start." Lincoln Hollister stated in a rich basso profundo voice. He was six and a half feet tall with wide shoulders, a barrel chest and a narrow muscular waist. He had long black hair, a leathery complexion, and sun darkened skin.

"My name's Lincoln and I'm an addict. My drug of choice was whatever I could find and as much of it as I could get. I stopped using almost twelve years ago."

I sat up straighter. I had no desire to be rude to these men, but was hoping they didn't think I was an alcoholic, or worse, a junkie of some sort.

Lincoln spent the next fifteen minutes talking through his drinking escapades. He'd been a falling down drunk for most of his life, starting at the age of twelve. His family were migrant farm workers, so he never made friends easily, and felt as if he didn't belong with his peers unless he had a few drinks in him. I related to parts of his story. He disliked school; got more out of reading. He finally gave up drinking after being arrested for assault.

The part about migrant work reminded me of Myron Baker, my parents, and several families in Harvest Junction. "You stopped drinking? Solid. Sounds like you were behind the cork in a big way."

"Behind the cork? Oh, yeah, my friend, I'm a drunk. I stopped in time, but it wasn't just stopping the drinking, and smoking. I had to learn a whole other way of thinking. I had to realize that I ain't less than no other man. I'm simply gifted in different ways than some."

I nodded. "I dig the riff with that school crap, sort of. I had no problem with doing the work, but I sort of feel like I learned nothing of value. I got a GED instead. Most of those cats and kittens going to public school are clueless of what's important in life. If you can dig it, none of the bullshit they teach has anything to do with surviving day to day."

"Survival, huh?" Elijah spoke up. "I guess reading *Beowulf*, or studying geometry has no relevance to regular life, unless you're a writer or an architect. School does help one to think, though. I mean, look at it this way; if you can think about angles, velocities, and pressure, then you can more easily crush an opponent in a fight, no?"

I nodded. "Never considered that."

"Well, boy, my turn, I guess. My name, as you were told, is Elijah. I stopped drinking and drugs fourteen years ago. Mostly I used because I was bored, but to the way my mind works I couldn't stop when I wanted to. I have an obsession with using and an allergy to alcohol. That my family is the law in this town never won me a lot of friends as a kid. I was bored. I would sit, and read, and drink. In time a found a small section of a farm that was unused. I began growing pot. At some point I realized that there had to be more to life. I took off and traveled. Nothing worked out too well. In time I came back here and decided to get help because I couldn't stop drinking. Some friends were rebuilding a barn. I helped them. The hard work kept me straight for a time, but I went back to my bottle soon after. I started attending meetings, and now have fourteen years clean, a steady job, and a family."

I sat pondering this narrative. "I dig the riff about boredom. I grew up near one of the most active cities on earth, but I was bored stupid at times."

Elijah patted my shoulder and turned to the man called Jethro. Jethro spoke up. "My name is Jethro. I have a year on me. I got released last year after a long hitch for dealing meth. I don't have a lot to say about that except that I grew up poor and I found a job that paid a lot. I got into using, as well as selling, and that don't mix."

I nodded. "I know people who deal in stuff. It's

crazy dangerous. Glad to meet you all."

Hiram looked at me. "Son, I hope you see where drinking and drugs can take you. We aren't here to tell you if you should or shouldn't drink. We aren't telling you how to live. I am going to suggest that if you feel like you have too much energy, that there are medications to help with that. If you feel like you don't get enough out of school you can always learn more in your free time. Drinking isn't the only answer."

I yawned. "I take your point. I'll admit that when I stop drinking, I start to want a drink after a day or three. I don't think I'm an alcoholic, but I see how I might end up one given time and pressure."

The men all stood, shook my hand, and filed out. I closed my eyes and fell asleep again. I woke up an hour later. I started thinking about what the men had said. I saw bits of me in their stories. If there were medicines that helped with having overdrive energy, then that was a good deal. Furthermore, I could save that money. I wanted Steph, and the more bread I had, the better my shot at edging out any other dudes. The conclusion I came to was that, at least for a while, drinking was not for me. I needed to give it up.

I took out my copy of *Rogue Warrior* and read some. Several people had suggested the Navy to me, and if serving was anything as enjoyable as Marcinko described, I was all for it. I was in the middle of a chapter when Pearl entered with a pot of tea.

"I thought I heard you. You should drink some of this. It helps clean you out." She smiled at me. "If you feel better this weekend, they have a Christmas marathon at the drive-in in the next town. The guy who owns the place, Old Man Wilkins, used to teach courses in cinema and screenwriting. Now he shows a lot of older movies every weekend until the snows come. Me, sis, and Zeke usually go once a month."

I sipped the hot tea and nodded. "Sounds good. So how did you guys come to ranch sheep? I mean is it a family tradition or what?"

"It's all us kids have ever known. Maybe you better ask Pa about that." Pearl bit her lower lip. "I have some chores to finish." She left.

Chapter Thirty-Seven

Two days later I was sitting in the early bright reading *One Perfect Op* by Dennis Chalker when Hiram knocked and entered. "Vinnie? I saw the light on, and wanted to check on you. You appear to be improving and I hear you've been eating well." He cleared his throat. "My kids tell me you're interested in our ranching operation. If you want a job, I have plenty of work."

I paused a moment to consider. "That's a nice offer. I was wondering how one becomes a rancher. I mean was the land passed down or what? Been thinking about the future some."

"I reckon it can occur that way. In my case, I came out here because of something bad that happened. I was a big time gambler. I ended up owing a lot of money to certain people. I couldn't pay it back. I was in big trouble. Plus, I was heavily into drugs and drinking. Then something happened, and The Lord intervened. I was approached by a government agency who agreed to get me into a rehab and save my medical license. They set me up here. In exchange I had to give them information about certain people." Hiram's face registered the pain of his memories. "They changed my name as well."

"I dig. I know the type of people who make those loans. I know a few anyway." I shrugged. "I suppose all of us have our problems."

Hiram chuckled. "That we do. One never knows what The Lord has planned, either. It was here I met Miriam, and we had three children. So, now my wife and kids and I live out here. We tend to the sick, raise our sheep and horses, and spend time with The Lord. A more peaceful life I couldn't imagine."

I nodded. "Sounds like it."

Hiram rose and left the room. I grabbed my sack, and headed to the guest bathroom for a shower and a shave. I was turning into Grizzly Adams, and smelled ripe. After cleaning up, I resumed reading. The more I read about SEALs the more that sounded like a solid path for me. I was strong, and the action they saw seemed constant. I was starting to realize that if I could focus, maybe trust people a bit, that maybe there was a future to be had. The farm work would hone my body like nobody's business. The trusting people was a big if. So was not drinking. If things worked out with Steph, another big if, would she be willing to deal with my being on assignment. Making it through any training was no issue in my mind. The chiefs would kill me before I quit.

At ten I joined the family for breakfast. Good morning, young man. How's your head feeling?" Miriam motioned me to the table.

"Copacetic, ma'am. Feeling better. You and Hiram are aces in my book. I wish I could do something to even the score." I drank some pulpy orange juice that Miriam set in front of me.

Zeke entered, followed by Elsa and Pearl. "There is something, actually." Miriam cracked eggs in a pan.

"What? How can I repay you all? Anything, barring nothing." I sat up straighter.

"You can't pay us back, son. You can pay it forward. Someday you'll find people in need, and you'll have the means to help. When it occurs, please remember us. And pay our hospitality forward." Miriam set platters of food on the table.

I thought about Heather, Steph, and Caroline. I said a silent prayer that they were safe. Then I prayed for Destiny and Kenzie, Ronnie, and Rory and his family. I even found myself praying for all the street families, and desperate losers I'd encountered in my travels.

Hiram looked a question. "You alright? We lost you there for a minute."

"Yeah. I was talking to the spirit in the sky. I've already been in several situations where I helped people. I figure that given my track record; I'll meet plenty more. That girl I'm looking for, I helped her, her mother, and her kid sister. My family helped them."

Everyone served themselves from the platters, and Hiram handed me a few bottles of pills. "That's Strattera. It's non-stimulant. Take one at breakfast. There's Effexor which is an anti-anxiety and anti-depressant. Take that at breakfast and at dinner. The third bottle is Alprazolam. You take that at night, and only if sleep won't come. You have ten of those and no refills. I'm hoping that you won't need it."

"Thank you. I think I'll be OK for sleep. The bed is comfortable."

"Glad to hear it. I see that they have a great show at the drive-in tonight. I'll let Pearl drive the car. Elsa can drive it home in the morning. Son, I expect you to get a good nap today. You're better, but not in perfect health."

I nodded as I ate. "What's playing?"

Pearl looked up from her food. "Thanks, Pa. They have a Christmas marathon."

"Excellent. Hiram? Am I allowed coffee?"

Hiram poured me a mug. "The kids don't care for it, so I never thought to ask you."

"Thank you. So, yeah, I was wondering something. Those guys I met the other day. Do you attend meetings? I was thinking I might like to attend one. I, well, I need to talk to you about that later. Privately."

Hiram smiled a broad smile. "How about Monday morning? There's a speaker meeting at ten. We can talk in my office after breakfast."

"Sounds great." I finished my third helping of food,

and assisted the girls in clearing dishes.

I walked with Hiram to his office. "What's going on, son?"

I looked around the room. There were medical books on wall-shelves, stacks of wrapped presents in a corner, a razor strap hanging on the wall, a mahogany desk, and a large window that was decorated with paper snowflakes and holiday cards. I sighed. "I'm going to lay something on you, and you might not want me around anymore."

"You kill someone?"

"No, sir. Those meetings, I used to attend them. A lot. I had friends of my family who could pass me fake money. Perfect replicas. I traded in the fakes for real money."

Hiram swallowed, nodded, and swallowed again. "You still do this?"

"Not for two years. I haven't had the fakes. Thing of it is, I feel bad about it. I thought the people attending to be weak. Now, well, damnit…"

Hiram threw back his head and laughed. "Now you need those meetings, too. You sorry son of a bitch. I'm not angry, son. Might be better, though, just keeping it between us."

I smiled, man to man. "Yes, sir. The money I have now, it really is from gambling. Part of the stakes, though, was from the meetings."

"Don't do it anymore, got it?" He gave me a stern look.

"Yes, sir."

We walked out of the office and I turned toward the guest room and lay down. I read some of my book on the Dowalibys. It was dense subject matter. I was getting into the story, but couldn't stop yawning. I closed my eyes for a nap. Two hours later, Zeke woke me up.

I took a hot shower, dressed, and brushed my hair. I was tying my boots when Pearl walked into the room. She was dressed in tight jeans, a pink top, black cowboy boots with a glossy shine on them, and a leather jacket.

"We thought we'd take you out to dinner before the movies. There's a place between here and there that we like. The Rainbow Café. We'll meet our friends outside afterward and convoy." Pearl sat and gave me a stern gaze. "None of us drink, or smoke, or anything like that. I hope you understand."

"Savvy. I've given it up myself. Do you mind if I ask though, why do you have such a hard-on about alcohol? I mean I get that your father is in recovery, and his friends are, but you, your sister, and brother are tighter than a fishes sphincter." I shook my head.'

Elsa and Zeke walked in. Zeke was dressed in jeans, a western shirt with a bolo tie, boots and his sheepskin jacket. Elsa was in an outfit that matched Pearl's.

Pearl adjusted Zeke's tie. "Vinnie was asking why we're so straight laced. Why we don't drink and party." She looked at Zeke.

"We've heard the stories about what can happen. And we've seen people come in all mangled from auto wrecks, fights, and sometimes abuse." Zeke looked pained by some memories.

"I can testify to that. Plus, it makes you look stupid." Elsa smiled. "Last month, Ma's brother came riding across our property on his stallion. He was so liquored up I was surprised he could mount a horse. He certainly couldn't get down. Pearl and I had to help our Uncle Jack off his horse. It was a mess. He went south last week to enter a rehabilitation center."

I took her hand. "I'm on the wagon, too. At least for a while. I can't say forever, but for now."

Pearl beamed at me. "Take it one day at a time.

That's what Pa says."

The four of us entered the kitchen and told Miriam where we were heading. She kissed her kids, hugged me, and walked us to the front door. We climbed into a red Buick sedan, with me and Elsa in the back.

"Chattahoochee" by Alan Jackson was blasting on the radio. Zeke harmonized with Pearl. It got me thinking about Destiny and Kenzie. I looked at Elsa, and a familiar sensation stirred deep inside. It was pleasant to be active again. Fifteen minutes later Pearl pulled the car into a space at The Rainbow Diner.

The exterior of the diner was sensational. There was neon lighting and the parking lot was crowded with various groups of teens hanging out and talking, or making out against walls. These weren't the sort of cliques I saw in the cities. The teens were more like the friends I'd made in Harvest Junction. Stetsons and baseball caps were a big item, as were dressy looking cowboy boots and tight jeans. The whole outside of the building was awash in rainbow colors, and a giant neon rainbow arched across the roof.

The interior was decorated in pastel colors. There was a counter that ran across three sides of the diner, and high tables with stools on all four sides. A giant screen TV adorned each of the four walls. A re-run of an old show called *Love Boat* was starting. A sign next to each TV listed days and a corresponding topic. *Sit-Com Mondays...Game Show Tuesdays...Crime Scene Wednesdays...Medical Thursdays...Fifties Fridays...Romance Saturdays...Spiritual Sundays.*

"You guys come here often?"

"A couple times a month. Most of the time we're busy with homeschooling and chores. Ma and Pa let us cut loose now and then." Zeke motioned to a waiter that we had four people.

A tall, angular, platinum blonde man, dressed in a

pastel lavender shirt, a pink and purple scarf around his neck, and skinny jeans sashayed over to us. He handed out menus and led us to a table. We sat on the high stools and perused the menus.

"Welcome," the waiter gushed "I will be your server, Phil McCracken."

"What's that?" Pearl asked me. She was absorbed in the menu offerings.

"He's being friendly." I replied.

Elsa smiled at me. "Enjoying yourself? Probably not what you are used to."

"This place is fantastic. I admit this isn't my usual type of hangout anymore, but there was a time. I used to live in a sort of rustic area, and joints like this existed. Heck, in New York and Chicago I used to enjoy some all-night dives that came close." I smiled back.

Phil approached, and we ordered. A half hour later he brought our food. "Here you go. sausages in lightly toasted buns for the men. The ladies have fish sandwiches."

We sat eating and watching the television screens.

"What did you do for fun where you lived?" Pearl inquired.

"I read a lot, sat in the park, did kata, worked some, gambled some, spent time with girlfriends. Once I hit Florida it was beaches, babes, and studying. Then in New York City and Chicago, the activities were never ending. Broadway, museums, concerts, opera, like that."

"I'd like to visit New York." Zeke said. "Sounds like an exciting place."

"It can be. You need a decent roll, though. Where I hung out was rougher, sort of ghetto and hard. The better areas require plenty of cash. I made enough bread that the nicer side of life was available as needed. One of my chicks there had money, and I needed to live up to her class and style."

"You've had more than one girlfriend? How do you manage that?" Zeke was impressed.

"From what he told us; the same way Damien does." Pearl giggled as Zeke blushed.

"Oh! I get it. I'm strictly a one woman guy. If I could find the woman."

"I found my one woman when I was twelve. Then I lost her. I've met others, mostly chicks who need help, or need me to fill the void. It's complicated. I was looking for the first doll I mentioned when I ended up in your cabin." I leaned back and digested.

"Complicated how?" Elsa asked.

"Well," I clicked my tongue, "I enjoy reading, working out, and staying in my own bubble. I'm no good as a solo act. I need company, and I need action. Not too much of it, though. I like to run the controls."

Pearl nodded. Elsa sipped her Coke. "Go on."

"Thing is, I would have given all my control up for a decent shot at this chick, Steph. I mean we had what we had, but she turned my insides to mush. I can't explain it. She had an effect on me like no other chick, except maybe one."

"What happened to this Steph?" Zeke was fascinated.

"Her mama had to lam with her and her sister. Myron, her father, was a total scumbag." Phil refreshed our drinks and I drank my Coke. "Steph's grandparents are from around the area, or I believe so anyway.

"Who's the other girl?" Pearl finished her sandwich.

"Her name's Ronnie, and she's an everything plus."

"Everything plus?" Zeke tilted his head.

"Solid sender looks. Stacked in the knowledge box."

"Man, I wish I could find one like that."

"Isn't hard. To put it in your language, I'll lasso a

herd of fillies, and you cull them."

Elsa and Pearl giggled. "Oh yeah? How?"

I pulled a fold of bills from my pocket and made the five-hundred dollars flap like a bird. "Attention, all single ladies, attention. If you come park it over here, sodas are on Big Z."

Eight chicks ambled over and took spots in the booths around us. I folded four twenties, and surreptitiously slid them to Zeke.

"Buy them sodas and burgers. Chat them up. Take your pick and wet your..."

"Vinnie Il-Cazzo!" Elsa blushed and interrupted my patter.

I sat nursing my Coke and observing Zeke. He was stiff and awkward. He needed lessons. A half hour later he stood by our table with a tall, leggy, blue-eyed, pale-skinned blonde. She came up to his shoulder and looked corn-fed and pure. Her name was Macy Engerhintern.

"Let me settle up with the server and we'll make the scene by the screen."

"We have cash, man. You don't have to cover us." Zeke offered me a twenty.

"Put that back. Better yet, use it to buy Macy here something from the snack bar later. I got a nice roll. I built it on my way west. I stopped in Chicago and met a guy. We went to a casino. The dice were on our side. Big time. Cards too." I followed them to the car.

"You drink, gamble, smoke pot, you're a real bad boy, aren't you?" Pearl looked back at me annoyed.

"I told you I'm giving up drinking and pot. Anyway, I promised my buddy Eddie I wouldn't go into any casinos alone." I shrugged. "Besides, I didn't know you then or maybe I would have mended my ways sooner."

Elsa laughed. "We don't mean to be judgey-judgey. We haven't lived anything like that. We hear about it, and read about it, but we've never experienced it."

Pearl pulled out of the parking lot. We drove around listening to music and chatting. I started feeling something similar to my experiences with Ronnie, Kenzie and Destiny. I missed having a family. I'd never had an older brother, except maybe Ralph or Eddie. I needed a beer or some bourbon.

"I've been wanting to ask you something. When we first found you out in our cabin you had an envelope in your backpack stuffed with coupons. I looked through them, sorry. Um, why do you carry those? Don't your parents do the shopping?" Elsa held my hand as I was lost in thought.

"They aren't around – haven't been in a few years – and you have a knack for asking complicated questions."

"Where are they? Sorry if I'm being nosey. You fascinate me."

"Not a problem, doll, but I don't think you're going to dig the riff, or care for the answers. It isn't exactly straightforward, either."

"Start with the coupons." Elsa gave me a smile.

"I was raised on the hustle and the short con. My parents made it a way of life." I took a few minutes to educate the group.

"You amaze me." Pearl scolded. "You're a total miscreant. That's stealing you know."

"No, doll, I don't think it is. I tell them I had a bad order. They offer me the vouchers. I don't ask for anything, and they are under no obligation to provide. Often enough the managerial cats thank me for telling them about the problem and hang up without offering a thing. I move on, or let their corporate office handle it. It might be that I offer an untruth, but it doesn't rise to the level of theft." I shrugged again.

"What else do you do. I mean those store coupons

you have aren't like the ones I clip from Sunday's paper." Elsa looked interested.

I explained about the coupons.

Elsa was laughing, and for once so was Pearl. Zeke was sitting making eyes at Macy. "Sound like you have it all figured out. Imagine what you could accomplish if you put that brain of yours to use for good things?" Elsa side-hugged me as Pearl pulled up to a gate at a field. On the far end was a giant movie screen.

I paid for our tickets, and after we parked, I offered to buy the sodas. We settled in as a group of teens approached. They apparently knew the girls and Zeke. "Vinnie? This is my boyfriend, Martin. Elsa's boyfriend, Joe." Pearl introduced me.

Martin was my height, but broader, with thick, knotted muscles. He had long reddish hair tucked under a John Deere baseball cap, a thick, brown coat, Levis, and boots. Joe was six feet tall and wiry. He had glasses, a pointed nose, and could have passed for a banker or an accountant.

"Pleasure's mine." I shook hands. "I'm a family friend, I suppose."

"Something like that." Zeke chuckled.

Martin and Joe climbed in the back seat with Pearl and Elsa. I was left in the driver's seat, and Zeke sat next to the window with Macy between us.

"Vinnie is from New York City. He was telling us about life out there. He's something of a hustler and a bad seed." Elsa giggled.

I tried to look cooled out, flipped up my collar, played the rebel looking for a cause. "By the way, do you ever have any open houses around here?" I asked Elsa and Pearl.

"Why? You looking to buy a house? My dad's a realtor in town." Joe commented.

"Not really. Not quite that old yet. Plus, I don't know for sure if I'm sticking that long. I have to discuss a job offer with Hiram. I was telling the ladies about how I manage to obtain vouchers and coupons for food when cash runs short. There's another fun activity if you have open houses around."

"Do tell." Elsa shook her head in amused exasperation.

"Well, you see, I usually put on a nice sport coat and slacks. My chick of the moment puts on a skirt and blouse. Then we attend whatever open houses are going on. On certain days there are more realtors who show up than other days, but the public can still attend. On those days, the homeowners put out finger sandwiches, pigs in a blanket, drinks, desserts, and so on. One can literally help himself to as much as he wants." I put my feet on the dashboard and leaned back.

"You're a con-man." Pearl giggled. "I've never met anyone like you. If Ma caught either of us, or Zeke, pulling stunts like that we'd be taking a trip to the barn."

"At least she cares enough to care enough." I swallowed something caught in my throat. "Hey, movie's starting."

The first feature started. We didn't bother pulling in our speaker because we could hear from the speakers around us. The soundtrack was like a disembodied voice from beyond. I looked in the rearview and saw Elsa and Pearl snuggling into their dates. Martin was rubbing his hand on Pearl's butt and she had her face buried in his neck. Elsa was in a tight clinch with Joe. So much for them being pure and perfect angels. I had no date and became engrossed in the movie.

I started thinking about Steph again. I whipped out my cell phone and began texting my sister Tori. I texted Gina next. I hadn't kept up frequent contact, but with the holiday nearing I missed them. Gina texted back. There was a lot of chaos and drama at her new job. She asked if I was doing OK. I replied that I was fine. I watched the climatic courtroom ending of the first movie and then climbed out of the car. I wasn't all that fine, but I couldn't put a finger on why.

I headed to restroom. I saw Elsa and Pearl following suit. After taking care of business, and washing my hands and face, I stepped outside as a large, heavily bearded, and tipsy man hovered over Pearl and Elsa. They looked uncomfortable. Other kids were gathering, but they all looked scared.

"Come on girls. I can pay the price. You two are too pretty to be all alone. Come on with me. I promise I pay well. Now don't look at me like that. Come on. Been too long for me. I need it." The man reached out to stroke Pearl's hair when Martin came running over.

"Hey! Get your damned hands off my girlfriend, you big ox!" He stepped up and shoved the man. A moment later Martin was on the ground having been floored by a gut punch.

I stepped forward and grabbed the man by the right wrist. Twisting him off balance, I kicked his right knee in the wrong direction. The force might have driven the man down if I hadn't been holding him. He screamed in pain. I let go and he backed off, limping, but still game. He was stronger than he looked.

"Watch how you address the ladies. You dig? My cousins are ladies. Not whores, not pieces of meat, ladies. You read me, you ugly son of a bitch?" I was ice cold, and in my element once more.

I bounced around on the balls of my feet, fists raised. Like a pugilist. The man limped forward, focused on my hands. That was my intention as I aimed a full force kick to his groin. The best way to execute that kick is with the shin. I aimed my shin to kick a spot a centimeter above the middle of the man's eyes. He barely moved, then his brain registered, and he crumpled to the ground vomiting. I stepped in to finish the job permanently when Martin grabbed me from behind.

"Stop! Back off. He's finished. If you kill him it'll make problems and the cops are here." Elsa pleaded as she turned me around and hugged me in a tight embrace.

Pearl ran over and hugged me too. There was a stunned silence, and then applause and cheering from the gathered crowd. I saw the lights of four police cruisers pulling up. I moved from the girls and stood alone, hands behind my head interlocked. Kneeling, I crossed my ankles and sat back. An officer approached me with his gun drawn. Seeing me kneeling and compliant, he re-holstered his weapon.

"What happened here? Who are you, boy?" The officer was tall, muscular, and sported a black crew-cut. He looked around at everyone.

"His name is Vinnie." Elsa stepped forward. "That guy there, he came out of nowhere. He started harassing a bunch of us girls. Then he tried to take privileges with my sister and me."

"That what happened?" The officer looked at me.

"Yes, sir. I thought he was about to rape one of them. He punched out Martin. I didn't have time to dial nine-eleven. Not that you officers don't do a great job, I'm sure." I started getting aches in my legs but I remained still.

"Get up, son." I stood. "You have ID?" The other police officers were checking on the drunk guy.

"No, sir. I have a school ID, but I left it in New York."

"You have anything on you that you shouldn't?" The officer looked me in the eyes. "No, sir. I have a pocket knife. But the blade is only four inches." I tried to look pleasant

"Where you staying?" He inquired.

"With the McFarland's. I might be helping on their ranch." I replied.

"All right, kids. Go back to your movies. Stop rubbernecking." Two of the officers cleared the crowd.

"Son, I'm going to let you go. You did a serious number on this fella, but he has several outstanding warrants." The officer looked stern, "Son, in the future we don't like vigilante justice around here. Let us do our job. Got it?"

I nodded, and walked Elsa and Pearl back to the car. "That was fun. You OK there, Marty?"

"Yeah, thanks to you. You're a real karate kid."

"I guess. I can handle myself if necessary. I don't go looking for it."

"Hey, I owe you a big one."

I gave him cooled out as the second movie commenced. The chaos had delayed the start. Joe motioned to three girls to come over toward the car.

"Vinnie, this is Linda Mulvaney, Valerie Antonelli, and Bridget Custer. They attend our school. That creep was coming on to them too."

Before I could reply, Bridget and Valerie pointed to an empty convertible. I wandered over and climbed into the front seat situating myself between them. As the movie rolled, they rested their heads on both my shoulders and Bridget pressed her face into my neck. I held the chicks close and watched the film. For the first time in my life, I was uncomfortable with the affection for which I would normally have killed. The vibe was wrong. I kept thinking about Steph.

After the movie ended, I excused myself. I walked toward the rear of the field and sat on the swing-set. I kept running the past few years through my mind; Steph, Julie,

Ronnie, Destiny, Kenzie, and Becky. Piracy, drug muling, and gambling. I had survived, but I had survived because of my wing-men, Jack Daniels and Jim Beam. I choked up as tears cascaded down my face. I hoped no one would come walking by as I tried to come to terms, once and for all, with this hollowness deep inside me that ached constantly and never went away. It didn't go away when I was romancing my girl of the moment, it didn't go away when I was reading, or at a museum. School sure as hell never filled the void, and after the alcohol or pot wore off, the feelings returned more intensely. I needed something stable away from fighting, piracy, cheap romances, and always playing for the minute. I thought about the chess games I played with Ralph. Chess was about the long game. You could lose a few pieces, even sacrifice critical pieces, but in the end, you won by playing with a longer vision.

I was tired of my life as it was, and unable to envision life any other way. I wanted a steady life. That was why I had to find Steph. She could be that solid, steady, rock of a soul that I needed. Then again, she might not be. In that case the Navy could offer stability.

The third movie was a quarter way through when Elsa, Pearl, and Zeke walked over. They had their dates with them. I wiped my face as if to clear away some sweat.

"You all right?" Martin tipped his Stetson.

"Yeah. I needed a moment. I have Weltschmerz, and sometimes I need some air."

"That like an allergy or something?" Joe looked concerned.

"Nah. It's a chronic condition I was born with."

"Hey, we're all kind of tired, and were thinking about heading home. That cool?" Zeke helped me stand up from the swing. "We have the last movie on DVD."

"Sounds good. I need to talk to Hiram, anyway."

We all walked back, and the girls kissed their dates.

Zeke took Macy's number, and Joe offered her a ride home.

Elsa drove us back to the ranch. Hiram was working on some reports. He was surprised to see us home early. Elsa and Pearl filled him in on the events of the evening, leaving nothing out.

"Vinnie, thank you! I appreciate you protecting my daughters. I think we need to have a long chat. You kids will excuse us." Hiram motioned me to a chair.

I looked at Hiram, man to man. "I wanted to talk with you also, sir. I have something going on, but I can't figure it."

"I reckoned that might happen. Let me guess, there's a big hole in your guts. A hole that never fills no matter how much action you find, nor how many women you sleep with. Alcohol fills it, but not for long."

"Straight from the fridge, gate. You nailed it. I even had two dolls tonight, and the furthest thing from my mind was getting busy. I have this ache that won't quit, and I've sworn off the only solution."

Hiram leaned back in his chair. "There really is only one solution, and it isn't found in a bottle or a pipe."

"I'm tuning in your signal, so carve my dome. What's the solution?"

"You'll have to figure that out for yourself."

"But you found the solution? You've had this problem?"

"Everyone has this problem. In addicts it's exacerbated. Yes, I found a solution. My solution. You'll have to take time and find yours."

We sat in silence for several minutes. I yawned. "So, what kind of work do you need done?"

"You ever shovel stalls? Cleaned a chicken coop? You ever do any carpentry?"

"No to the first two. Yes to the last."

"Well, son, tomorrow you'll be shoveling out sheep

pens. After that you'll shovel out the horse stalls, and clean the chicken coop. Once that's done, we can start rebuilding the barn and preparing things for the spring. I'll pay you a fare wage, same as I pay my kids."

"Copacetic." I shook Hiram's hand to seal the deal.

Chapter Thirty-Eight

The next twelve days I spent working, using muscles that I didn't know I had, and enjoying myself immensely. I shoveled manure into a wheelbarrow, and dumped it in large piles that would be treated and used as fertilizer. I helped brush and curry horses, fixed fences, cut boards to repair walls on the barn, and painted the shack where I'd first stayed. The days flew by, and the work helped me to forget my need for alcohol.

I also attended several recovery meetings, and for once I paid attention to those speaking. I put two twenties in each basket, and took no change. At my fourth meeting I asked a man to sponsor me. He agreed, and we began meeting every day to read the basic text. The issues pertaining to alcohol didn't trouble me, but the discussions about character defects hurt. I began realizing that alcohol was a symptom of a deeper issue. I wasn't a nice guy. I wasn't cool. I was manipulative and self-serving. When I tried asking about how to address this, my sponsor, Ammon, told me to take things slowly.

Two days before Christmas I made some headway toward clearing the wreckage of my past. The circumstances weren't planned, but the result would have pleased my parents sensibilities. At least I hoped so. I was able to help beat a major corporation at their own game, and do so without causing further chaos.

I woke up at six, dressed, and proceeded toward the kitchen. I stopped short, and overheard a conversation between Hiram and Miriam.

"No other choice, dear. We have to sell half the sheep, and three horses. I might even need to sell the car. The truck we need to run this place." Hiram set something heavy down on a table.

"The bank won't give us another few months?" Miriam sighed

"No. I have fifteen, but they want the whole thirty-five. Otherwise, they'll auction off the land. We have no choice."

Like hell they didn't, but I wasn't ready to interrupt. I crept back to the guest room and fired up my laptop. I had eighteen grand in the bank and six grand stashed with my gear. I checked the address of the bank branch closest. My plan would kill most of the bread I had made in Chicago, but, for the first time in months, the hollowness inside of me dissipated completely.

I returned to the kitchen and had a pile of biscuits, eggs, and bacon, anchored by a pot of coffee. Afterward, Hiram secured the sheep, and Damian the ram, behind a fence surrounding a field. I began shoveling the pen and wheeling sheep dip to the fertilizer pile. I had developed a technique for shoveling that used my whole body. The burning sensation as I worked was different than when I performed kata. The muscles I used were different.

At noon I looked up as Zeke approached. "Dang, dude, look at you go. You really fly. Stinky job, huh?"

I chuckled. "It's alright. Gives me a workout. I should be done here in an hour.

"I'll help clean the chicken coops tomorrow. We need to repair one of the walls. I have to run into town and get my haircut. You need anything while I'm out?"

"Yeah, actually. I'd like to come with you. I can look around town, buy some Christmas presents."

"Fine by me. I'll tell Pa. You should knock off soon and come get supper. This looks better than it usually does. You don't have to polish the walls and floor; the sheep don't mind."

I paused a minute, caught his joke, and laughed. "I figure a day's pay is worth a day's labor."

"Between us and Pa, with help from the girls, we might finish the barn before March. You really help out."

At three in the afternoon, I was standing outside a bank. I had a Christmas card in my courier's sack, and in the card was a cashier's check for twenty grand. That left me slightly less than four grand of my life's savings. It was more than enough. I had purchased some other gifts, as well.

Zeke appeared, his hair trimmed and neatened. I crossed the street. "Howdy, gate, let's dissipate."

"I need to pick up some groceries, but then we'll head back." Zeke said.

"Copacetic. Can I kick in toward the cost?"

"Not necessary. Ma and Pa pay for the groceries," Zeke gave me a sideways glance. "I've never met anyone like you. One minute you're talking about con games and picking up girls, the next you're offering to pay for everything."

I sighed. "I take your question. The answer, it's how I operate. It's all I know. I've never done anything half assed, and I've never failed to operate in survival mode. My parents weren't busted, but we weren't Rockefeller class either. So, I learned to help out."

"Well, learn to chill. Relax a little. We like you, and you don't have to worry so much about taking care of everything. Like at the movies. My sisters and I get a good allowance. We can handle our end. My parents pay the household bills. Just relax, dude."

While Zeke shopped, I bought a cup of coffee at a gas station and sat reviewing my life again. I couldn't stop. Potential answers were appearing, though. I only hoped that my ideas would bear fruit.

After helping to unload groceries, I walked back to the fields and put things away. I stood by the fence watching the sheep, lost in thought, when a loud noise interrupted me. I looked up to see Damian charging the fence. I jumped back, spun, and ran for the house.

Panting and out of breath, I stopped in the foyer. Pearl and Elsa came by and gawked. "You OK, Vinnie?"

"I'm...I'm...I'm fine." I gasped while catching my breath. "Damian charged me. The fence was between us. It scared me."

The girls laughed. "He can't hurt you unless you're in the field with him. He doesn't know you yet, so he was protecting his ewes."

"I dig the flip. Even so, I don't need to be perforated by an angry goat."

"Sheep. He's a male sheep."

The girls walked to the kitchen and I took a shower. I read my book on the Dowalibys until Miriam called out that dinner was served. The smell of chili and sweet cornbread hit me and I double timed to the table.] "This looks sensational." I scooped chili over a dish of cornbread, and poured milk.

Hiram looked at me. "I'd like you to take tomorrow off. Rest. You're working us under the table. I appreciate it, but you need a break."

"Yes, sir. I had a break. I went to town with Big Z. You're paying me, so I work hard."

"Big Z, huh?" Hiram chuckled. "Well, tomorrow I thought you and I might hit a meeting. After that I have some patients to see."

"Sounds good. I can get to the coops after the meeting."

"No, son. I want you to rest. You're going to get sick again if you don't slow down. The kids have schoolwork, and Miriam has a ladies quilting group. You should read and rest."

"If you insist. I'm fine, though."

"I insist. I don't expect my children to work half as

hard as you've been working, and as long as you're on payroll you'll do as I say."

I nodded. "Copacetic."

Hiram began discussing homework with Pearl and Elsa, and I ate another helping. A strange feeling was washing through my body. Not a bad feeling, but a new one. I'd felt love, at a certain level, when I was around my parents, but they weren't the most tuned in cats where me and my sisters were concerned. So long as we didn't bring trouble to our doorstep, they gave us a free reign. My FEBU family was full of loyalty and caring, but that was more about survival. The strange feeling of warmth and compassion that the McFarland's exuded was a different level. I had never experienced a family like them, and I wasn't sure how to react.

A looming snowstorm hit on Christmas Eve afternoon. I sat by the window, eating sugar cookies, drinking coffee, and planning how to pitch an idea to Hiram. Pearl and Elsa were wrapping presents, Zeke was studying geometry, and Miriam was making dinner.

After a dinner of root beer glazed ham, potatoes, biscuits, salad, and three kinds of pie, we all sat around the table digesting. I had coffee, Zeke and the girls were drinking hot chocolate. I cleared my throat and reached into my pocket.

"Hiram, Miriam, I have a confession to make. A few days ago, I overheard you discussing the finances about the farm." I looked away. My stomach felt hollow despite the enormous meal.

"Well, son, don't fret none. We'll find a way." Hiram sipped his coffee.

"I'm sure. The thing of it is, I'm learning plenty in the meetings. I'm not at step nine yet, but..."

Hiram interrupted me with a chuckle. "Not hardly. You're barely at step two."

"Yes sir, but there is an amends I owe to society at large. One I should make now rather than later."

"Go on, Vinnie." Miriam smiled at me. Zeke, Pearl, and Elsa looked curious.

I handed Hiram the Christmas card. "I never earned much of an honest living, and I don't know what need I have for a big pile of bread right now."

Hiram opened the card, did a double take, and passed the card and check to Miriam. "Lands sake, son! That must be everything you have to your name."

"Almost, not quite. I have enough to get by, for now. Thing of it is, I was figuring that when the ranch starts showing a profit, and it will, maybe I could get an annuity. A yearly check to help me out. Also, if things work out with my finding Steph, maybe in time I could build a cabin and a garden in the lower forty."

Hiram nodded and rubbed his chin. "That's good thinking, son."

Pearl looked at us. "What's this about, Pa?" Elsa and Zeke looked at Hiram with curiosity in their eyes.

"It's nothing I wanted to worry you about. The bank note was due, and your ma and I were figuring out a way to pay it. Instead, Vinnie chose to pay the lion's share of the loan for us."

"It buys me some serenity and good health." I shrugged. "I can always make it back."

We helped clear the table and retired to the living room. Zeke started the fireplace, and Elsa began playing piano. We sang carols, and Hiram read from Luke. The feeling of familial love was strong, and I soaked in as much as I could.

The next morning, I awoke to the sound of giggling. I sat up quickly, and reached under my pillow. I no longer kept my knife there, and I realized that the sound was coming from the hallway. I dressed in jeans and a t-shirt, stepped into the hall barefoot, and watched Zeke and his sisters eying a pile of gifts by the tree. I had a good stretch, and joined them.

"Merry Christmas, Big Z. Merry Christmas, dolls." I sat on the couch.

"Hey, Vinnie, looks like Santa found you here. There's a stack of these for you, too."

We sat in the glow of tree-lights and waited for Hiram and Miriam to make an appearance. After a few minutes I headed toward the kitchen and started the coffee. I found Hershey's cocoa powder, sugar, and cream. In three mugs I made hot chocolate, and put a peppermint stick in each. I poured a mug of coffee for myself and carried the drinks in two at a time.

"I used to make the coffee and divide a pumpkin pie on Christmas morning in my family." I sipped the black gold and felt warmth and energy surge through my system.

"We have our traditions, too. First we have to wait for Ma and Pa." Zeke drank cocoa.

A half hour later Hiram and Miriam entered dressed in bathrobes and slippers. "Well, looks like you kids were good this year. Either that, or Santa is awful forgiving." Hiram chuckled and sat with Miriam.

I fetched them each a cup of coffee. "They said Santa found me here. He didn't need to do that."

"He surely did need to, son. You're living here." Hiram began handing out presents.

Zeke received clothes, some gift cards, and several CD's from his parents. Pearl and Elsa had knitted him some dark green slippers. The final present was from me. I'd purchased a bottle of Aramis for him.

Zeke looked at me. "Thanks, dude. This stuff smells nice."

I winked. "More importantly it attracts the chicks."

Zeke blushed and dabbed some on.

Elsa and Pearl received clothes, yarn, knitting needles, crochet hooks, and a book of sewing patterns from their parents. Zeke had made them each a wood carving with their names burned into the wood. I had purchased them each a bottle of Chanel.

"I didn't know what to get you. This is what I always bought for my sisters." I shrugged.

"This is perfect. We don't do makeup, but a little perfume is always nice." Pearl gave me a smile.

Everyone looked at me, so I opened my gifts. Pearl and Elsa had crocheted a long scarf in burgundy and forest green. Zeke had made me a new leather sheath for one of my knives. Hiram and Miriam bought me the first three in a series of books by Eliot Wigginton titled *The Foxfire Books*. I had never heard of them, but after a quick perusal I understood. The books were a direct link to true Americana. They were, more or less, instructions on simpler living. Hiram had also purchased a copy of *As Bill Sees It,* a collection of short writings by Bill Wilson.

The girls and Zeke had purchased a hand-stitched quilt for their parents. I handed Hiram and Miriam a wrapped book. I had purchased a leather bound coupon book. After sorting my coupons and vouchers I filled the pages by expiration date.

"Well, if this don't beat all. Thank you, Vinnie." Miriam was touched.

"I figured it was time to play the cards straight -- to quit stacking the deck. You have more use for those than I do, anyway." I shrugged. "I do have a favor to ask."

"Ask it. I can't say no unless I know what you want."

"Could you teach me to cook?"

Pearl and Elsa giggled. "You want to learn cooking?"

"I do. One day I'm going to find Steph Baker. If not

her, another doe eyed, pouty lipped doll. I can't be a stand up man for Steph if I don't know how to cook and take care of her. I'm accomplished at fighting and surviving, but I know very little about domestic arts."

"That makes rare good sense, son." Hiram nodded at me. "A well rounded man is the best kind of catch for a woman. I hope my girls are lucky enough to land a man with your sense."

I shrugged. "I'm sure they will. I still have a long ways longer to go before I am worthy of someone as good as Steph."

"One day at a time, son. Take it easy. Give yourself a break."

I winked at Hiram, "yeah, I read the wall hangings at the meetings, too."

"Smart ass." Hiram chuckled.

The family moved to the dining room, and Miriam gave me my first cooking lesson. The waffles we made were fluffy and light. The secret is in beating the egg whites stiff with a bit of lemon juice. I almost burned the maple syrup warming it, but Miriam saved me from disaster. The sausages were easy to grill, and I knew how to brew coffee.

After breakfast we retired to our rooms to put away our gifts. I texted my sisters and Julie. I considered texting Ronnie, but I wasn't certain. The news I found indicated that Pipes and Daquan had beaten the charges. There would be no repercussions on that front, but I still had a sense of paranoia.

I checked on some churches in Scotts Bluff and located three that had possibilities. I made plans to attend one the following Sunday. The Tanner's would be members, or not. If not, there were two other churches to explore.

Chapter Thirty-Nine

Three years sounds like a long stretch, and looking at it forward it is. Looking east from the westward end, the time moves far too quickly. I built a steady schedule for myself, and days became weeks. Nine months passed. Oldest trick in the book, time passing us by. Zeke, Pearl, and Elsa spent most of each weekday studying, and taking courses on their laptops. They attended actual classes in a building, but only three classes a week. While they studied, I attended meetings, and worked on the ranch. I began rebuilding the barn, tended to the sheep and horses, and cleared an area where I hoped to one day lay down a stack of bricks and create a domicile. My muscles responded to the work, and combined with daily kata I gained thirty pounds and lost two waist sizes.

Every Saturday I spent with my new family. We either worked on the ranch, I helped Miriam with the cooking and learned to sew, or we went into town for various reasons. Every now and again Zeke, Pearl, Elsa, and I went to the drive-in or attended a dance. We had no more reoccurrences of violence or molestations. I'd sit in a car with a couple of girls, but I focused on the movies. My interest in constant priapic activity was replaced by my desire to find Steph. The McFarland clan were as close as I'd ever felt to being part of a stable family. My desire for alcohol and drugs dissipated. My medications helped me to remain on an even keel.

Sundays I would walk to the highway and hitch a ride to Scotts Bluff. I joined a church that was strict and stodgy. Their beliefs and mine were definitely not in synch. However, one of the lead elders was Joseph Tanner. The head of the ladies auxiliary was Lydia Tanner. I had found Heather's parents. It had taken six months to finally get a look at some old church records in a book from well before I was born. Heather's baptism was recorded as was her wedding to Myron. It had taken another three months to approach Joseph Tanner. Sometimes the best bet is to scope out the game before drawing yourself a hand.

I sat in the back of the church each Sunday and half-listened to Pastor Svante Fitta preach. His texts were at best misogynistic, at worst abusive and xenophobic. I usually read from the Big Book of AA or The Basic Text of NA instead of focusing fully on the message being preached. I sang the hymns, and listened politely during Sunday School, but the sermons didn't resonate. I dug why Heather Baker pulled a fade.

Nine months into church attendance there was a potluck. I made a quart of ambrosia salad and brought it along. By that time another congregant was giving me a ride each week. His name was Niels Pflueger, and he was my age. He took the opportunity during our drives to discuss his plans to leave town once he graduated and to join the Marines. I listened and decided that maybe the navy wasn't my only military option.

At the potluck I finally approached Elder Tanner. Short of my encounters with Myron, I can't recall a time when I was quite so nervous. I placed my plate of food at a seat across from Elder Tanner and his wife.

"Sir, I've been attending for a while now, and I've been working up the nerve to approach you."

He gave a curt nod, "About what."

"My name is Vinnie. Vincenzo Cassiel Michelangelo Il-Cazzo. I, well, I think I used to know your granddaughters, and your daughter."

That got not only Elder Tanner's attention but his wife's as well. They quietly put down their utensils and stared at me. "Repeat that."

"I met them six years ago. They were living down

the street from me. There was trouble with your son-in-law"

Lydia wept. Joseph gave me a cold stare. "You tell the truth. Heather mentioned your family to us. We haven't seen them in five years."

My heart tried escaping out of my mouth. "Do you know where they live now?"

"We do. You don't. I think for now that's how I'll leave it. If you'd care to come around our home, I have repairs I need help with. We can talk and get acquainted. Once I'm sure of you, young man, I might tell you what you want to know."

That's what happened. I began working every morning on the ranch, and then traveling to the Tanner's home in the afternoons to chop and stack firewood, help mend fences, rebuild a back porch and mow the lawn with a tractor mower.

Two months in, Joseph Tanner walked into the yard with two glasses of lemonade. "Take a break there. Come sit a spell."

I approached a bench that sat in the middle of the yard. Thanksgiving was just around the corner as was my nineteenth birthday. "Yes, sir. You have more work to be done?"

"Vinnie, I want to talk to you. I'm an old man. I've made my share of mistakes. The biggest was in how I raised my little girl. I'm not saying there wasn't wrong on both sides, but there was maybe more on mine. I tried to control my daughter by asking people too many questions and requesting updates on her activities. I'd steer conversations with her friends in such a way as to coax them to divulge matters she likely wished to be private. Lord knows I'd browbeat her into telling me everything. A body needs people to confide in that will keep their mouths under lock and key. I drove Heather into that man's arms."

Tears fell from Elder Tanner's eyes.

"That's the past, sir. I'm sure she's forgiven that." I stared straight ahead. "She didn't seem like the grudge holding kind."

"You knew her all of a few weeks, yeah? How do you know what kind she was? I know she hasn't forgiven me or her mama. I aim to make one thing right, however. Here's my offer. You tell me everything you can about finding that low down skunk who hurt her and my grandkids. I'll tell you where they are. I trust you. I've seen how hard you work and I've seen how honest you are."

I shook my head softly at the last comment. He didn't know, and what he didn't know couldn't hurt me. "That's a nice offer. I think it's a bit lopsided, but you couldn't know that. I have things to explain."

Joseph nodded. I spent the next hour laying out all the details about Myron's demise and the reasons for it. I held nothing back.

"If you find a chance, tell them people who sealed his fate that I appreciate it. As to the other matters, I don't much care what he was doing, or anyone in that regard. I had some beaners working for me a while back. They stole from me, kept looking at the white girls in town, and were drunks. Only thing worse is the uppity colored folks who want me to pay money because their great-great-great-grandpappy and mammy were taught Christian values and civilized in exchange for working the land."

I bit my tongue. There was no sense in losing my chance at information. I felt sick to my stomach, but I held my peace. "I don't have contact with those people, but if I ever do, I'll pass on your thanks."

Joseph stood, and collected the glasses. "They're in Washington State. I have the address somewhere. I'll get it to you tomorrow."

I put the yard equipment away and headed back to

the ranch. As I walked, looking for a ride, my temples began to throb. My heart raced. My skin grew warm and sweat oozed from my pores. The ground was spinning and weaving. I spotted a tree stump and sat. I don't know how much time passed after that. Day turned into evening -- evening into night.

A truck pulled up. I tried to stand, but couldn't. I would've thought myself drunk; except I hadn't had a drink in almost a year. The driver took me by the arm and helped me into the cab of his truck.

"I best call someone or get you to a hospital." The concern was palpable and brought tears from nowhere.

"Call this number," I handed him a piece of paper with Hiram's number on it. "Please get the address and take me there. That's my dad."

"You don't know your own address?"

"Right now, I barely know my name, sir. Help me."

He helped me. He called Hiram, and took me back to the ranch. I offered him a picture of Ben Franklin, but he declined. Instead, he lifted me as if I was a feather, carrying me to the door. Hiram took over and helped me to his office.

Zeke, Elsa, Pearl, and Miriam entered the room and stood looking at me with concern.

Miriam spoke up. "What happened, Vinnie? We got worried when you missed dinner. You look like you've seen a ghost."

"I've seen worse. I'm seeing worse." The words came hard. "I've told you some about my past, but there's stuff. Stuff I don't speak to. Not even to myself."

"Dear, if you'd feed the kids some dessert or something. We might join you or not. He and I need to talk." Hiram tilted his head toward the door.

After the others left, he sat at his desk. "Son, have you ever heard of PTSD?"

"Yeah. Soldiers get it after the war."

"That's true. They aren't the only ones, though. Science has come to understand that many people fight wars that are as tragic as any combat a soldier sees. I fought most of my childhood. It doesn't matter how or why, but until I made peace with myself, asked my higher power to remove the pain and guilt, the past was still my present. I was fighting wars that had existed decades ago."

"I've accepted my past. I've even told my sponsor about it. Everything."

"I know this, Vinnie. I want to know one thing, however. How does Vinnie feel about everything that happened?"

"It had to happen. Myron Baker needed to be removed. The things I did, I did to survive. My parents wanted me and my sisters to survive, and they taught us well."

"Son, I didn't ask you to justify your past. I asked how does Vinnie feel about it?"

I sighed, "I don't know anymore."

"Yes, you do. When you're ready, you'll tell yourself."

Hiram guided me to the guest room which was now my room. I climbed into bed without undressing and fell into a fitful sleep.

Chapter Forty

There's an old saying, you aren't a real hustler unless you can lose everything and win it all back. A Biblical parallel is that a man must lose the whole world to gain his soul. Over the next two years I worked with my sponsor, Ammon, to break down my life and register my feelings. I worked with Hiram as well. As for Zeke, Pearl, Elsa, and Miriam, they gave me as much love and support as they could.

One immediate change that took place was that I began attending church with Ammon. I had received the information from Elder Tanner as to Steph's whereabouts. She was living at a community in Washington. The community the truck driver, Bull, had told me about. I wasn't ready to move forward, however. Had I rushed to Washington, the results may have proven disastrous for both myself and Steph. She deserved the best. I deserved to heal. That had to come first.

One day, a year after my panic attack, I sat at a newly constructed picnic table on the back forty of the ranch. Ammon sat across from me next to Hiram.

"Hey, Vinnie. You've told us both how you were raised. You've told us about the human trafficking, the murder, the drug muling, the girls, all of it." Ammon rubbed his chin. "We're getting closer to the truth all the time. So, how are you feeling right now?"

I shrugged. "I'm OK. If you want the unspeakable truth, my parents are jive jerks. So are my sisters. So am I. I taught others to behave that way. It doesn't taste good to admit it, but I'm a manipulative bastard."

"You mentioned that this Heather Baker once called you a scoundrel. That she accused you of being a con artist." Hiram chimed in.

"She did. It bugged me. I've questioned my pirate ways off and on since I was little. At some point I stopped feeling anything negative about my activities."

Ammon chuckled. "No, you drowned the feelings. You numbed them. Then, when you stopped, all it took was the right trigger and you lost your senses. The feelings ganged up on you. You have always known somewhere that what you were doing was wrong."

I nodded. "I dig the riff. I'm not stupid. But…"

"No. Don't rationalize it. Feel it. You're a manipulative asshole."

I sighed. "Screw you! But, yeah, I am."

"So, what do we do about it?"

"We?"

"Yeah. You, me, Hiram. We."

"I believe the book suggests being willing to have these defects removed and asking that we be granted relief from our shortcomings

"I believe it does. I'll see you tomorrow morning in church." Ammon stood up, hugged me, and walked to his truck.

I stood watching his back. "Dad, have I thanked you for saving my life?"

"Dad? Careful son, I could get used to hearing that," he chuckled. "Yes, you've mentioned your gratitude."

"Well, I'm saying it again. Thank you." We hugged and walked back to the house.

The next morning Ammon picked me up and drove us to church. The McFarlands didn't attend church often, and Hiram followed his spiritual path while working on the ranch. As Ammon and I sat in the front row of pews, a lady in a flowing, powder blue gown began to sing. Her hair was like gossamer, her face shining and radiant.

A tall man in his late thirties ambled from the back

to the front shaking the hands of every congregant on the aisles. In his hand was a battered Bible, and his words were hushed. "I'm not going to preach over-long this morning, I just want to give you some good news. How well you listen could determine the rest of your life and all eternity.

I looked up at the man and his words grabbed me. Something in his tone aimed for my heart like a bullet. "I want you to know that repentance is required to get right with The Lord. Without sincere repentance there can be no relationship with a higher power. Doesn't matter if you're Jewish, Buddhist, Catholic or Baptist. Heck, when I did time back in ninety-three, sixty percent of those incarcerated were Baptists.

The audience laughed. "Salvation is not guaranteed because you belong to a church. You best believe that most decisions to join a church take about the same consideration as joining a civic club. Joining the church won't save you. You can quit drugs, quit alcohol, quit playing the field, quit stealing, join a church, and still not be saved."

Each word was a dagger to my subconscious. I wanted to run, but a greater force than myself kept me pinned to my seat. "If you enjoy life without The Lord, then you simply are not saved. Whatever your vision of The Lord is, and I doubt any human alive today has the exact handle on that one, you'd best come to know him personally. I can hear some of you saying, 'but I'm a church member.' Guess what, being a church member no more makes you saved than joining the Elks club makes you an elk. If you want to be saved, I'll tell you how to do it."

I tuned in his signal. I had never listened to anything more closely. "You have spent your whole life running the controls. You have set the lighting, arranged the choreography, and written the script. When that didn't work out you blamed the world. In short you have walked your own path and justified it as being righteous. If you would find salvation you must stop where you are right now. You, from this point forward, must do what The Lord wills for you to do. You do it to the utmost of your ability."

Tears filled my eyes. I convulsed in a way I hadn't since the day I thought an airline had lost my family's luggage. I fell to my knees sobbing. Pastor Goodlove's message drilled through the calloused layers of my soul and left me exposed. He continued as Ammon placed a firm and loving hand on my shoulder.

"If you are ready to give your will and your life over to the care of The Lord as you understand him, then do this. Feed his sheep. Give the thirsty water and the hungry food. Clothe the naked. Visit the destitute and imprisoned. Just do it honest. Don't cheat Peter to feed Paul. Do these things to the best of your ability and you'll find salvation. You'll be more Christ-like than the most holier-than-thou televangelist could ever hope to be."

I stood up and began walking toward the altar as if in slow motion. It wasn't a conscious choice. Some greater power was moving me. I approached and looked up at the pastor. He looked down at me.

"I want this. I want this like nobody's business. Please ask The Lord to forgive me."

"Brother, you just did. I'll agree with you on it, though. Where two or more are gathered there The Lord is. You have a whole church behind you so that's a sight more than two. Your sins are forgiven you. Go and sin no more."

I sat by the altar for another hour. The choir sang, the announcements were made, church was dismissed and I sat there. Ammon came and sat with me.

"How are you feeling, man?"

I shrugged, "Confused. Kind of weird"

"Weird how?"

"Weird like, I feel like a huge weight was lifted off my chest. Thing is that rationally it changes nothing. I'm still Vinnie. I'm still the pirate I've always been."

"That's the truth. We can change the future but we can't erase the past nor forget who we were. Welcome to step eight. It's time we made a list of people you hurt. I sense you're already willing to make things right if you can."

"Of course. Straight from the fridge, pallie."

We returned to the ranch and I commenced the list. Next to each name I made a proposed amends. In a great deal of the cases there was no amends to make except to agree never to plunder businesses, whatever the cost to my own needs or wants. I had made a major financial amends by helping the McFarlands, and that would have to do.

I texted Julie and explained in some detail what had occurred in my life. I apologized for teaching her methods of urban piracy. She replied that she didn't blame me for how I was, but that she never used my methods.

I wanted to text Destiny and Kenzie, as well as Ronnie. I decided against that. I didn't want to interfere with Ronnie's new relationship, and every indication was that Destiny and Kenzie were already on a better path.

The hardest part was forgiving myself. It took another year to internalize the damage I had done to myself and to separate that from the damage others had done to me. I came to realize the futility of retrieving an inner child that never existed, but I began finding pleasure in simple activities like board games and the movies. Life lived without looking for an angle or an edge became more natural. I started the process of healing.

Chapter Forty-One

In the spring of my twentieth year, I left Nebraska. I had given up my fake ID, ordered a birth certificate, and claimed a driver's license. I had a copy of my original social security card. I was ready to find Steph, whatever was to come of that.

With everything going well spiritually and temporally, I assumed that life would remain on a steady track of recovery. Despite the recent election of a reality television twit with a cheap toupee and a bad spray on tan, my serenity was ever present.

I spent a week with the McFarlands watching movies, helping Miriam cook, and helping Hiram with ranch chores. We had a feast the day before I left, and I promised to stay in touch. I kept that promise. I finally had the family I needed.

I spent two days on the train west after leaving the McFarland's. I reread *Warrior Elite* by Dick Couch. It was nothing like Marcinko or the two by Chalker. They presented the SEALs in a much more exciting and dynamic way. Couch was dynamic, but far more informational. This time I saw reasons why the military might not be a good fit for one of my temperament.

My second night on the train I sat in the club car eating hot dogs and drinking coffee. The thought came to me that a beer would be tasty. I instantly thought through the reasons I had stopped drinking. I took out the NA basic text and read the first two chapters. I fell asleep in a booth. The next morning the train reached Seattle. I grabbed my sack and disembarked. The area was damp, wired, and different than anything I had ever experienced. In a funny way it was a place I could call home.

I looked for somewhere to charge my phone, and

suddenly realized how many coffee shops lined the streets. It looked like three coffee shops to every block. I picked one that had outlets at every booth. After plugging in my tablet and phone, I ordered a sandwich, a piece of pound cake and a large coffee with three shots of espresso.

I texted Tori and Fisher. *You'll never believe it. I found the Bakers. Anyway, I know where they are. I'm in Washington right now.*

PING *You're relentless. Glad you might find closure. I'm in therapy now. Gina is too, she tells me. We really need to hook up and talk. All three of us. PS, Fisher and I are making it legal next year.*

I smiled at that news. I ate, and texted Gina. *In Washington. Found that family you met when we visited.*

PING *Word to the bird, baby blue. We're doing great out here on the Bayou. Life honest is life best. Think about that.*

I sat for a while as my phone charged. After unplugging, putting things away, and settling up, I exited into a fracas. A group dressed in black face coverings, jeans, combat boots, and heavy jackets were squaring up against a group of skinheads, and people who could have been members of a biker gang. They held signs either for or against the current administration. I tried locating a path around them.

As I backed away, a teen dressed in a brown shirt, tight black pants, suspenders, and boots charged at me. He smelled of alcohol. Instinct took over and I tripped him. He started to rise and I backed away. His punch came out of nowhere and caught me on the left shoulder. My left arm went numb. I responded with a right hand to the Adam's apple. He gasped for air and fell as his right knee collapsed in response to my kick. Others were crowding in from both camps. I turned to run. Three police officers in riot gear grabbed me and pulled me toward a car. My arms and shoulders shrieked in pain from their grips.

I relaxed my entire body against their force which confused the officers. They cuffed me and shoved me into the backseat of a car. As I watched through a window, police officers battled the protestors. I ducked when a soda cup full of cement smashed the windshield. A hole surrounded by spiderwebbing was created on the passenger side. As I remained near the floor, my prayers were those of one not expecting to live long.

A police officer climbed into the driver's seat and pulled off. Eight blocks later I was transferred with great hostility into a van and taken to the station. Every aggression of the police was met with silence and compliance. That's the only safe response. I wound up in a ten by ten concrete cube, without handcuffs, sitting on a metal bench bolted to the wall.

Two hours later the door to the cell opened. A stout, bespectacled man in uniform stood a safe distance from where I sat. He held a small container of some sort in his right hand.

"Stand. Turn to face the wall. Arms behind you fingers interlocked. Try anything and you will be pepper sprayed." He was curt, but unemotional.

I complied and was again handcuffed. The officer led me to a room painted bilious green, and helped me into a chair at a table. The cuffs were removed again, and the officer stood by a wall. A male officer entered, dressed in slacks and a matching jacket.

"I'm detective Yamin. This is detective Rollison. We have questions, and it would be in your best interest to respond. At this point I am required to remind you that you have the right to remain silent. Anything you say can be used against you in a court of law. You have the right to an attorney. Do you have a lawyer we can call for you?"

"No, sir. I only just arrived in the area. There's

someone in Nebraska, but he's not a lawyer?"

"You'll be given a call later. We can bring in a lawyer if you wish, but that might take longer."

"I have time, sir. I won't answer anything without a mouthpiece."

He gave a curt nod and both detectives left. I sat in the chair and recited "The serenity prayer," "How it Works," and "The Twelve Traditions." I followed up by praying quietly. I figured that I would be released and sent on my way. I was wrong.

After a three hour wait, I was transferred to another cell. My watch, wallet, belt, and shoe laces were taken from me. They already had my backpack and courier sack. The new cell had a concrete bed, a thin mattress, and a combination toilet and sink contraption. I remained there for eighteen hours. It dawned on me that life had come full circle. I had started out in a politically crooked world and deserving of arrest. I had fought my way through scrapes and situations. In time I had given up drugs and alcohol, found a spiritual path, and settled down. Now I sat in a jail cell charged with assault because of politics. This time I wasn't at fault, but I had more than earned it for all the times I had escaped justice.

My thoughts were interrupted by the cell door opening. A man entered dressed in a charcoal suit and well shined brogues. He had bushy grey hair, and a salt and pepper beard and mustache. "Mr. Il-Cazzo? My name is Jerome Baron. I've been assigned as your legal representative."

We shook hands. "Thank you, sir. I appreciate it."

"Let's start with what happened."

I recounted the story of the fight. I was in the middle of the part about being arrested when he cut me off.

"Let me get this straight. They read you your rights prior to questioning you, but not prior to arresting you?"

"Correct."

"Did you say anything in the interim?"

"I wouldn't talk without a lawyer. I'm willing to take a deal if you can get me out of here."

"I'm pleased that you chose not to speak. It'll save us time sorting out what is admissible and what isn't. As far as deals go, you'll be offered a deal; A very nice deal. I advise against taking it. There's no law against the police lying to you, so they will."

"When can I get out of here? I have somewhere to be upstate."

"Suck it up for a day or two. It might be longer, but most likely twenty-four hours."

"I've survived in worse places."

I sat and resumed my internal dialogue as my lawyer departed. I was tired, and although I fought sleep, it came. I sat with my knees to my chest and dozed off. The next morning at four I jolted awake. An hour later an officer came by with a tray of oatmeal and withered apple slices. There was a carton of orange drink to wash it down, but no utensils. I drained the carton and fashioned it into a makeshift scoop for the oatmeal.

At four that afternoon I was handcuffed and taken to a courtroom. After being ushered to a seat beside my lawyer, I listened to other defendants being granted bail, or not.

Jerome shuffled some papers. "You are advised to plead not guilty. We have several videos of the protest. You appear in three at least. You were clearly moving east, away from the fracas. The assailant rushed you, and you are seen turning to the side, whereupon he fell. He then assaulted you, and you defended yourself. By definition, you are not guilty."

"Yes, sir. How much longer will I be incarcerated." I stared straight ahead, exhausted.

"Possibly until trial, but I doubt it. You'll have to remain in Seattle, however. At least until trial."

That's how it happened. We were called forward, I pled not guilty, and I was released on my own recognizance until trial.

"Thank you, sir. I have thirty-five hundred dollars to my name. It's yours."

"The county will cover my fee. You need to find somewhere to stay that you can avoid trouble. Do you have anywhere?"

"Are there any AA meetings around?"

"I'll give you a ride to a recovery club.

Chapter Forty-Two

I attended three meetings that first night, and shared my story at each. After the midnight meeting I was approached by an older man named Lennie Wheelhouse. He was a tall, thin man, with a mop of curls, and a gaunt face. He offered me a couch to sleep on, and I accepted.

The apartment was small, but the couch was comfortable. I showered off the stink of jail, and discarded the clothes I had worn. As I exited the bathroom with a fresh shave, feeling myself again, I saw a televangelist on TV. Lennie was strumming on a guitar and watching the faith healer do his act.

That was life for the next year. I received updates from my lawyer, and reported to the station for UAs and questioning once a week. The assclown who'd attacked me was recovering, but the throat shot I'd delivered had done damage. There were threats of attempted murder, felonious assault, and other like charges, but Jerome laughed those off. The biggest risk I faced, he claimed, was a civil suit.

I spent my days reading, either in the apartment or at the library. I even found a book on Amazon titled *Bank Notes* by Caroline Giammanco. It was the full story of The Boonie Hat Bandit, the guy whose case I'd followed in the news. The book was terrific, and I gained even more respect for the subject. He regretted his choices, as I regretted mine. He also didn't deserve the harsh sentence he landed. I deserved far worse, but I was free. Fate was a fickle shrew.

There was a coffee shop on the same block as Lennie's apartment. While enjoying coffee each morning, I talked to my new AA sponsor. His name was Emil, and he was an affable Sicilian. We started at step one and worked through a book called *The Grey*; the original basic text of

NA.

I also texted Hiram the details of my arrest. He understood, and informed me that if I ever felt ready, our agreement still stood as regarded the ranch. I discussed that option with Emil. He agreed that ranching was likely the better portion over military service.

As I worked through the steps, something became clear to me. My problem was not simply that I drank and smoked pot. I had a volatility that was often out of control. Whether threatening Destiny and Kenzie with punishment for their behavior, or defending myself in fights, I was far more aggressive than the situation called for.

"So, what the fuck is really going on?" Emil asked me daily.

"Too much to sort out."

"We have all day. All week. Start from the beginning."

"OK. So, it's like when I was a kid. I was bullied, sure. My reaction was to end the fight brutally, if you dig the riff."

"Sure. I get that."

"With Destiny and Kenzie, so they solicited me, so they stayed out later than I thought best, was it necessary to threaten violence?"

"You didn't hit them, though, you said." He drank his cappuccino.

'No, I didn't. But, why was that my first go to?"

"Good question."

"The drive-in with Zeke and the chicks. I almost killed a man. It was only Pearl telling me not to that stopped me."

"I'm seeing a pattern"

"I might have to do time because I almost crushed a man's windpipe."

"Yeah. What do we do about this?"

"I don't know. I need help. Help that the program and steps don't provide. I need them, too, but I need more."

"I think you're getting the main thrust of the program. Congratulations."

Eleven months after my arrest, I appeared in court again. A jury was convened, and the next day I was released by His Honor, Jeremiah Ezelkut. The video footage was enough, but testimony from eye witnesses helped. I even managed to forestall the civil suit by agreeing not to file a counter suit for assault upon my person.

The following day I paid Lennie seven hundred dollars for the use of his apartment. It only covered a half month of his rent, but it was the best I could do. I walked to a highway and hitched a ride with a guy with several piercings in his face. His girlfriend sat beside him, her hair pink and shaved on both sides to form a puffy looking mohawk. I agreed to pay fifty dollars in exchange for a ride to my destination. The music they listened too was a lot of screaming and cussing to no purpose. I was starting to get a headache when we pulled over at a rest stop.

"Here you are, dude. The address you told me is like twenty five miles down there, but I ain't going that far. I shouldn't even be this far, but we needed the cash. Gotta get back before my PO freaks out. Later, dude!" The guy sped off.

I followed the old logging road for five miles before stopping to sit on a boulder. I was so close to finding Steph that every fiber of my being wanted to push ahead. My stamina, however, was faltering. A pick-up truck pulled over; the driver close to my age.

"Need a lift, buddy? Not much up this road except one place."

"I'm looking for some men. I only know the names Doc and Billy. Someone I met some years ago, he told me about this community they run."

"I figured. I can get you as far as the front gate. One of them can meet you there."

I climbed in the truck, and the guy pulled off. AC/DC screamed through the speakers. Forty minutes later we stopped at a large gate made of logs. I stepped out and stood to one side. The driver reached an arm out the window, made a circular motion in the air, and pumped his fist. He stepped out, pushed the gate open, and motioned me to stay put.

Ten minutes later a pair of older cats approached, both of them looking sharp enough to shave with. The older of the two was draped in a chestnut colored fedora and matching Burberrys, pressed grey slacks, a maroon short sleeved shirt, and a silver vest with a matching bow tie. He took me in, but gradually. The other cat was dressed in black from head to toe. He completed the look with black ditty-bop shades, and a black rolled bandana around his salt and pepper hair that hung to his shoulders. I looked understated in my faded Wranglers, dark green t-shirt and beat up hiking boots with broken laces knotted together. I'd dropped a long way from the stylish drape of my early years.

The cat in black put out a hand. "My name's Billy. That's Doc. I'm told you're looking for us. Who are you, and what do you want?"

"It isn't you I'm looking for directly. I was told you run this place, and I was told someone I'm looking for lives here. My name is Vincenzo Cassiel Michelangelo Il-Cazzo. Most just call me Vinnie. Or Il-Cazzo."

A brief look of recognition flashed in Doc's eyes and disappeared. Billy gave a brief nod. "It's too hot to talk here. Come set a spell on the porch, have some lemonade."

I followed them down a path. We climbed into a golf cart and Doc drove a half mile through a maze of trees.

Trailers and cabins shaded by the foliage peppered the land. We stopped at a large wood and stone house. Doc and Billy climbed the stairs to the porch and I followed.

"So, who are you looking for?" Doc poured three glasses of lemonade from a pitcher.

"A girl I knew years ago. Her name was Stephanie Ann Baker. That name has changed at least once. I have a picture." I proffered my only photo of Steph.

"Cute girl. Why do you think she's here?" Billy was curt.

"Her grandfather told me as much. I met him in Scott's Bluff. Some years back a trucker named Bull told me about this place. It sounded like the sort of place the Bakers might be hiding."

Billy rubbed his chin. "Well, you're honest anyway. Bull mentioned you a while back. You understand that we won't confirm or deny who lives here."

"I'm glad. If it means the Baker ladies are safe, I'm beyond pleased, sir."

Doc looked up from his cell phone. "You had legal troubles in Seattle. An arrest for assault. You have issues with violent behavior, boy?"

"No. I have issues with thugs attacking me and expecting to walk away without a response. The goon who hit me like as not couldn't find a fat man in a phone booth, but he immediately swung a fist because I was in the area. I wasn't even part of the protest."

"You were acquitted."

"I was. I agreed to let him go his way and I mine. I have bigger fish to fry. Don't get me wrong, I dislike the president and his scum. I have more important matters to deal with, though."

I looked toward the swimming pond. Even that far north and west, the heat of July was intense. In deference to the temperatures the attire of those swimming ranged from full swimsuits to birthday suits. Some of the shapes without drapes made my breath catch.

"Enough small talk. If the person you seek is here, what if she doesn't wish to see you?" Billy's voice could have sheared marble.

I leaned back in my chair. "Then I'm gone. All Steph has to do is tell me she's found someone else. This is a million to one shot I'm playing."

The men lit cigars and offered me one. I declined. Billy blew a plume of smoke. "It's late. We won't send you packing tonight. There's a room in the main house, and you may reside there, for tonight at least. We can talk more in the morning."

Doc led me to another large building that resembled a camp lodge. He took me to a room on the third floor. The mini-fridge was stocked with water and snacks. He told me to help myself.

Four hours later I was laying on the bed, reading chapter five of *Alcoholics Anonymous,* the big book of AA, when someone knocked a 1-3-2 pattern. I rose and opened the door. There she stood. Her hair was styled differently, her body muscular, her bust fuller, the face as beautiful and pure as my memories of her. Sweat lined her face as if she'd been running

Steph looked up at me, hands behind her back, a sad smile on her face. "Took you long enough to find me, Vinnie."

I stepped back and she entered. "It's been a rough and wild ride, doll. I thought you'd have found someone else."

"I said I'd wait."

"Ten years?"

"For you. I can't believe you're here. I can't...I mean how..."

"Have a seat, babe." I opened two bottles of water. "I've known you were here for three years. I had to take care of some stuff before I was ready to see you again."

"You're here." She stood and sat beside me on the bed. I wrapped an arm around her.

"I never forgot you. It's been a long journey, if you dig the riff, but I never forgot you."

We spent the rest of the night and the next morning talking. OK, to be honest, we did more than talk. It was sensational. She forgave me for not waiting. I promised she was my only one going forward.

The next year was spent at the community. I worked beside Steph completing chores, attending counseling, hiking and swimming. In the winter we had snowball fights with Caroline and the community children. I spent time with Heather, explaining the details of her being a widow, making amends for teaching her daughters to commit theft. I now saw my behavior as theft of goods and services.

The community had recovery meetings, and both Doc and Billy attended them. I began attending from my second day. Life came together, as it will. I was free from the wreckage of my past. Steph and I had a long future ahead of us.

Afterward:

So that's the story. It's two years later, and springtime. Steph and I are living on the back forty of McFarland Ranch. We spend our major holidays, and part of each winter in Washington. We got married last year in a quiet ceremony. The money from ranching, while not in the ballpark of a gambler's life, is more than enough.

I text daily with Destiny and Kenzie. I located them through the church we'd attended in Brooklyn. They're well, and plan to visit once Steph delivers her twins. That's right, I'm going to be the papa of twins. A boy named Otis and a girl named Becca.

Julie Dimitrion came to visit last week. She lives with her husband in South Dakota now. Ronnie is married. We text daily. I lost track of the Chicago crowd, but if they're reading this, I think of you often. I was perusing an online chess club last week and spotted a name I recognized. Morelli and I are playing a game on a chess app.

Gina and Nicky came to Washington, as did Tori and Fisher. We had a long, cathartic visit. Amends were made, healing occurred. We hear nothing from our parents or their friends. I can't speak for my sisters, but I've reached a place of acceptance with that situation.

I sat down to write this story for my future children. I never expected it to take so long. I'll have to end here. Three ewes are expecting, and Zeke needs my help. Life goes on, if you dig the riff.